Also by Burr

Transubstantiation

Rebirth: A Zombie Tale

The Book of Benjamin
By Darren Lamb

Copyright © 2014 by Darren Lamb All rights reserved. No part of this book may be reproduced, scanned, or distributed in any printed or electronic form without permission. First Edition: February 2014
Printed in the United States of America ISBN: 978-1-50275-832-3

For Rowan

Author's note

When I was a young man, I had a job as a projectionist at Cineplex Odeon Movie Theater. One theatre Cineplex owned was called The Center Theater and it was a landmark in the Salt Lake Valley. It was the classic old style theatre they don't make anymore. It had a huge balcony and the giant red curtain which would slowly open for each show. I remember being a boy going to the Center Theater to see the *Star Wars* trilogy and finding out Vader was Luke's father while sitting in the balcony. I saw Rocky beat Apollo Creed and win the title in *Rocky II* at the Center Theater. My first date was there, my first beer was there, and when the flooding of 1983 hit, a giant sandbag river ran right down State Street and in front of the Center Theater.

I loved that place.

The Center was an old building though and there was debate about tearing it down or restoring it and preserving it as a historical landmark. The public was strongly voicing for restoration and Cineplex was leaning towards fixing the building up. This was the time I was working for the company.

The movie *The Passion of the Christ* was coming out and was going to be shown at the Center Theater. In case you're not familiar with the film, it caused a lot of controversy and there were many protests at the places showing it. Cineplex in Salt Lake received dozens of bomb and fire threats, but they were easy to write off and the film was scheduled to play.

Another projectionist and I were supposed to go to the Center Theater to put the reels of film together and screen it for any print flaws. We arrived at the theatre to find it destroyed. Vandals had broken in and demolished the place. The giant, red felt curtain and the movie screen had been slashed to ribbons. The projectors had been smashed beyond repair and small fires had done so much damage to the building that it couldn't be repaired.

The Center Theater was torn down and a shoebox theater was built in its place.

All because a few people couldn't handle others looking at their religion a little differently than they do.

Years later the movie *Dogma* came out, and on the DVD Kevin Smith actually gives a warning about taking the film seriously. He asked people not to hurt each other over a film that has a poop monster in it.

While this book is in no way a mockery of religion, some people are hyper sensitive about the subject, and take offense easily. If this is you...put down the book and back away slowly. This is not for you.

However, if you're not afraid to look at things from a different perspective and possibly have a fun time doing it, then I hope you find enjoyment, inspiration, and laughs in *The Book of Benjamin*.

Enjoy.

ENO
KRYPTONITE CONDOMS, AND STRANGE MRI'S

"Before the beginning we were nothing, and because we were nothing, we were also everything.
The only thing creation created, is the illusion that we are separate from each other.
Why else would we cut our neighbor and expect not to bleed?"
-The Book of Benjamin
Inside sphenoid bone

    Whoever said the truth shall set you free must have been freebasing Play-doh. The truth has never made anyone's life substantially better, let alone set them free. At least that's been my experience. In fact, I can remember the exact moment when the truth changed my life forever for the worse; it was before I was even old enough to talk, when the doctors diagnosed me as a freak. However, the universe apparently felt I needed a more recent reminder in my life, and saw fit to give me another dose of harsh, honest truth. The signs were all there in front of me, but when it's something we don't want to know about, our psyche has a tendency to overlook a lot of the obvious. It started with her going out almost every night without me and coming home with the smell of other men on her. Then she started taking phone calls in the other room. I started to find sexy new lingerie in the laundry I never saw her wear. Hell, it had been forever since she let me see the naughty mints and she began to pull away, not so subtly whenever I would touch her. Like I said, the signs were all there in flashing neon, yet the thought of her having an affair never even entered my mind.

When you're a medical miracle like I am, people expect there to be things different about you that have absolutely nothing to do with your condition. They feel like you should be able to know things other people would never possibly know, or you can magically never be hurt, or maybe at least have some cool Yoda type of wisdom we are all looking for. That makes my being ordinary all the more difficult.

Why is it so hard to find a girlfriend who will only let my X-wing fighter into her Death Star trench? I never asked her for anything freaky, and who knows, maybe I should have. Knock on a few forbidden doors and see what opens up. She would spend so much time telling me all the things she wouldn't let me do to her that most of my thoughts were monopolized by those pleasures I was being denied. For example; when she told me she wouldn't do anal, I probably would never even have wanted to try it until she told me I couldn't do it. Next thing you know, every time I see her naked all I can think of is poopy-trim, and Dirty Sanchez'.

The way I found out about the cheating was like this, I decided to surprise her one afternoon by coming home early and bringing her flowers. Truth be told, I had left work because Damon at the comic shop told me my shipment had come in and I was excited to pick it up. I had found some guy on the internet who had one of the *Harry Potter* vibrating broomsticks that had been banned because it found a market in the sex toy industry. I have a respectable collection of banned toys like the SpongeBob Patrick Pez Dispenser that looks like Patrick has a big pink Pez penis when you crank back on his body. The Internet guy traded his broomstick for one of my "trembling" R2-D2 figurines. It was a hard trade and he was definitely coming out ahead in the deal, but I had two of the R2 figures, so what the hell. I had Internet guy ship the broomstick to the comic book store because I know Damon is always there during the day and can sign for packages.

I come home with my NIB Nimbus-2000 sex broom, and a dozen roses when I see a Ford Focus in our driveway. I rationalize to myself now that it wouldn't have been so bad seeing them naked together if the fucker hadn't been wearing my vintage Christopher Reeve Superman cape at the time. Now, every time I see that thing all I can think of is his dick wrapped in that Kryptonite green condom.

Whenever you're cheated on, you're forced to examine your sexual inadequacies under a microscope. Kind of like a version of *This is Your Life*, but with nudity. I've been with enough women to be able to claim a mild level of experience. Most of my conquests have been nurses or medical students wanting to see if there is anything else strange about me, like maybe my penis might be on backwards too. I'm skilled but not a master. I mean let's face it…the clitoris is hidden better than the Bat-cave. That being said, I will proudly tell you how I am a member of the mile high club… solo aviation division.

But now I'm single again.

I leave the house with the broomstick tucked under my arm, wishing I could just jump on it, and fly away. As I walked to the rear of my car, R2-D2's head spins to follow me.

At the bottom of every medical form I have ever seen, there is a blank spot with a few lines. The heading for this blank section reads; Additional Information.

The Additional Information, or ADD-INF as it is often printed, in this situation is as follows. I have a Mini Cooper that I painted to look like an X-wing fighter. On the back end behind the sunroof, is R2-D2's head that spins and beeps and switches the deflector shields to the front and all that cool, co-pilot stuff.

My license plate reads Red 5.

♥

Oh shit, I'm sorry. Here I am going on and on, whining like a little bitch any you have no idea who I am. My name's Benjamin. I'll be your narrator tonight. Ben, Benji, Benjamin, it's all good. Before you even make the attempt, I've heard every Benjamin Buttons joke there is, so don't even try. Truth is I don't really care what you call me because you don't really give a shit what my name is anyway. I'm just putting it out there so we can be all cozy and intimate. You'll probably forget my name anyway by the end of this chapter because I'm not one of those assholes who talk about themselves in the third person.

I'm Benjamin.

How you doing?

It's nice to meet you.

Now back to the story.

Since the day I was born people have told me I'm special. Now, I don't mean that smoke blowing crap we do to little kids when we tell them that they can all be astronauts and ballerinas and stuff. Nor do I mean like all the Lenny's out there, who eat paste and name their toes. No. When people, and I mean highly educated people like doctors and scientists talk about me they use words like; miracle, impossibility, and phenomenon. There has never been anything like me in recorded history.

Now if you can take a minute and visualize what that must be like to grow up with. The best minds on the planet study you and come up with no explanation. Every day, people are telling you how you're special and you want to believe it. You want to believe it so badly. You want to believe, but you don't. You want to believe, because we all want to think there is more to us than the world sees. You want to believe, because we all need to. But every night as I lie in the darkness, waiting for some epiphany, some insight, some revelation as to what I'm supposed to do with all of this uniqueness, I find nothing.

Pulmonary hemo-reversai
That's what they call it.
All it means is, for some unknown reason, my heart pumps backwards. Blood circles through my body in the opposite direction than it does in everyone else. As far as they can tell though, everything else on me is the same. I've had every conceivable test run upon me. I've had so many doctors shove fingers up my butt that, now, when I meet a new doctor I could probably tell you their ring size before I could tell you the color of their eyes.

Zocor, Omacor, Sectral, Levatol, Demadex, and a million other pills have been tested on me. Beta blockers, Nitrates, Thrombolytic agents, and Diuretics have taught me more about the human heart than I ever wanted to know.

Three graduate students have written Doctorate Thesis' on my condition. I have been interviewed and studied by some of the top doctors and biologists in the world. I was even on Conan as "The Backwards Man" once, but the problem is that aside from my dyslexic heart, there's nothing really all that special about me. It's like finding out Jesus could just make a pretty mean filet-o-fish sandwich, but that's about it.

Everybody wants there to be something else.
I want there to be something else.
But the truth is, there's just isn't.
Once upon a time, some moron in the press suggested that I might be the next step in human evolution. I don't believe this for an instant, and neither would you if you could watch me some mornings struggle with that whole...the underwear has three holes but I only have two legs conundrum. Suggesting I was this next step, or some higher form of humanity pissed a lot of people off. Christian groups called me an abomination against God, while this other cult type group looked to me as the next savior.

ADD-INF: The cult members called themselves the Metaphysics of Materialism. They sent this really hot chick, who wore a lot of latex to follow me around and to "receive my message"

No, I wasn't their savior.

Yes, I fucked her anyway.

Causation, Determinism, Existentialism, Utilitarianism, Metaphysics, Stoicism, I studied all of them hoping to find the answers, but all I really found is that I'm not the only one who feels like they are floating through life. It seems like everyone is waiting for their purpose, to start writing the next great American novel, to lose weight, for someone to ask them out. We wait, and then we're gone.

I tried Zen Buddhist meditation, Shamanistic soul retrievals, Vegan fight clubs, Chakra alignments, palm readings, tea readings, the Atkins diet, Kabala. Nothing worked.

Even with all of this knowledge and experience making me a pretty well rounded guy, even being the medical miracle of the century, even being truly one of a kind, my girlfriend still decided she needed something more.

♥

I stop at a 7-11 to pick up a Slurpee and a bag of Cheetos, but while I'm sitting in the parking lot in my car, the girl behind the counter begins looking at me like I'm a stalker, so I leave. I drive back to the comic shop because I really don't know where else to go.

Inside the door of the comic shop, a 6 foot tall statue of Green Lantern welcomes customers. The statue even has a little, green LED light in his power ring.

Damon sees me come through the door and asks me if I thought Leia was genuinely a hostage or if she wanted it?

ADD-INF on Damon. He's one of those comic

snobs who will only read 'mature' titles. If there's spandex or a cape anywhere to be seen, Damon will snub his nose at it. He's one of those guys who reads *Sandman* or *Preacher* and thinks this somehow makes him more sophisticated than those of us who read *Daredevil* or *X-men*.

He reaches into my bag and steals a Cheeto and then tells me not to touch anything with my orange fingers. He then sees the Super Big Slurpee and realizes it's pretty early in the day for that kind of drinking and asks me what's wrong. I tell him I'm not really comfortable talking to him about it and he pulls an Obi Wan action figure from his pocket and asks me to show him on the doll where I was touched.

Nothing is sacred with Damon.

I tell him to stop eating my Cheetos and he asks me if I finally caught my girlfriend cheating on me.

Green Lantern holds up his power ring, looking like he should be flipping me off.

When Damon follows up by asking if I caught her with Mike or Antonio, I try not to heave my cheesy poofs. I didn't know the guy in the day-glow green condom, but it wasn't Mike or Antonio. I ask Damon how long he has known about this.

He asks me if I want the red pill or the blue pill about this, and then decides to lay it on the line. Everyone knows about the cheating, he tells me as he pulls out a pack of Marlboros and offers me one. I don't smoke but, I take one anyway, then he tells me how six months ago, when I was out of town at the Kevin Smith signing, that he banged her too. He then tells me I should smell my R2-D2 vibrator when I get a chance.

Interestingly, I'm more upset about the R2 violation than I am about Damon sleeping with my girl.

I'm so numbed from the vision of the Superman cape pumping up and down, that Damon's confession doesn't even faze me.

Damon then informs me how he's going to help me out with this. I ask him if his idea of help will be fucking my sister while wiping his ass on my *Incredible Hulk* #181.

He takes a drag and then looks at my unlit cigarette. A Zippo with the words "Fuck Communism" materializes and soon the taste of burning menthol fills my mouth.

It's because of my backwards heart he says.

I wish an anvil would fall out of the sky and crush him like they do in cartoons, but it doesn't, so I offer him a Cheeto and decide to listen to what he has to say.

He tells me the problem is how I'm a nice guy. He blows smoke out of the side of his mouth and I see tiny orange cheese flavored flecks floating in it. I'm a nice guy and that's not what women are looking for, he reveals. He takes another Cheeto and wipes orange fingers on his Levis. He tells me how at any time, I can hear any woman in the world whine about how they just can't meet any nice guys, when the reality is they all know plenty of nice guys and shit all over them. What's worse, he tells me, is the ladies probably were never interested in these men simply because they *are* nice guys.

He spells it out how, since I have a backwards heart that my views on love are backwards.

He tells me how he's an asshole women know he's an asshole. He uses women like shake-and-bake bags, but they line up for it. He informs me how he's what women want. They want the black hat, not the white hat. They want someone who will objectify them, who will be abusive to them, cheat on them, and steal from them. My girlfriend did. He asks me to think about why his Friday nights are never lonely while I, more often than not, have to use the self-service pump in the gas station of love.

Damon tells me I always have the option of going gay. How it's not something to look down upon. That even Luke was gay.

Luke Skywalker was not gay and I tell him so.

All the Jedi were rump rangers, he claims. He sells his point by stating how it's obviously true, because the only thing they care about and pass down through the generations are their light sabers, which happen to be about twelve inches long and are shaped like a cock.

My Slurpee has melted into a sticky, blue goo and the menthol is giving me a headache. Damon invites me to hang out and take my mind off of it, but I'm not in the mood. I go to the back of the store and pick out some Japanese Anime because I'm too embarrassed to buy porn and then head home.

When I get there, she's gone, and she's taken all of her stuff with her.

She's really gone and I'm alone.

♥

David Hume believed the past isn't a strong enough resource to predict the future. Just because the sun came up yesterday doesn't necessarily mean it will come up today. I hope Hume is right. Maybe the next woman won't feel the need to "feel the need" with every other guy that comes along.

There is one thing I've found which helps quite a bit though. While I was out searching for the meaning of life I took one of those fire walking courses. A transcending pain to reach enlightenment type of thing. An overcoming fear to achieve nirvana experiment.

There was this martial arts guy there who was trying to teach us how to break a board with the side of our hand. Some of us went right through the board, most of us, myself included, could not.

You see, it's not that physically breaking the board is difficult; it's overcoming the obstacles in the mind that makes it hard. Our eyes can't see what's on the other side of the board, and since we naturally fear what we don't understand, the mind prevents the hand from passing through to the unknown side.

After watching us slam our hands into the inch of pine for about a half an hour, Mr. Miyagi decided we needed to try something new to channel our inner Bruce Lee.

He walked us over to a table and pulled out a deck of cards. He told us how the fear of hurting ourselves prevents us from fully committing to anything. It's why we don't ask for raises or ask people out who might be out of our league. We don't want to experience the pain.

He took a shirt pin and stuck it through the center of a card, the two of Diamonds, and laid the card on the table so the pin was sticking straight up into the air. He then showed us how we were going to slam our open palm down on the pin as hard as we could. If we were fully committed, the pin would bend. If we hesitated, even a little bit, it would stick into our hand. He demonstrated for us a few times and sure enough, the pin bent and he was fine. Then it was my turn.

The five of Clubs lie on the table with the pin sticking right through the center of a club, looking like a miniature version of the Washington Monument. Needless to say, I hesitated and the pin pushed so far into my palm that it made a little peak in the skin on the back of my hand. I never forgot how it felt. The pain was excruciating, but for one instant, everything else went away. That moment of pain was the happiest, clearest, and most focused I had ever been in my life.

I've modified the pin drill a little bit since then. If you ever feel depression kicking in give this a try. Get a deck of Uno cards and a box of shirt pins. Pick a card at random. If it's a five, put five pins in the card, if it's a three put three pins in and etc. I use the color of the card to determine the pattern I lay the pins in, but you can do it however you want. If you get a draw two, use two cards, and combine the pin total. Draw four uses four cards. I'll let you make up something for the wild cards. Just FYI, you can fit four hundred and thirty seven pins into a card if you take your time. Any more than that and the card begins to lose its integrity.

If you come into my house, all of my towels have this weird tie-dye pattern where they have soaked up the blood from my hand and there are broken shirt pins everywhere.

After a thorough inspection to make sure all of the cape fucker's things are gone from my home, I go into the bathroom and pull an Uno card.

Green seven.

If you feel the palm of my hand it's spongy yet rough from the scar tissue. My palm looks like it would if you had been resting it upon gravel while leaning on it.

As I slam my hand down, the things in my medicine cabinet rattle against the mirror. One of the pins hit's a bone and bends, driving the steel into the meat of my palm.

I slam my palm again and again until the card falls apart. Sometimes when I raise my hand, the card comes with it, making my hand look like one of those weird swim paddles they put on kids hands when teaching them how to swim.

I can't use chopsticks anymore.

When I lived in an apartment, I would do this until the neighbors would bang on the walls and floors. The drawer next to my sink, where most people would keep toothpaste and hair gel, is full of decks of Uno cards and boxes of shirt pins.

Once I was at a Toys-R-Us and bought about a dozen packs of Uno cards. The girl at the counter commented on them so I told her what I use them for. She laughed, thinking I was joking or flirting, and then she introduced herself. I gave her my name and when I stuck my hand out to shake hers, she saw the bandages. She called her manager and they asked me not to come back.

I sit on the toilet and use a Leatherman to pull the

pins from my palm.

For the first time since I found out she was cheating, I am happy.

♥

I don't connect with people very well. I think, somehow, I'm socially dysfunctional, and I really envy those people who seem to be able to talk to anybody. Bump into a stranger, start up a conversation, no problem. Not me.

There are very few places in the world where when you speak, people truly listen to you. One time I've found is when you're giving a eulogy.

Today's funeral is for a twenty something woman, who died in an automobile accident. It's sad too, because this girl was stacked. The MC of death asks if there is anybody who would like to say a few words. I would so I do.

Now I'm not some karmic douche bag who is going to speak ill of the dead. I always say something nice. I just tell a story that I wish had really happened.

I tell them how, this one night, I was in the fits of a heroin withdrawal and was panhandling outside a movie theatre, hoping I could score a fix, these three guys got pissed because I guess I asked for money one too many times and that was when one of them got all Jackie Chan on me and decided to beat me like I was a Hitler piñata at a Jewish bar mitzvah. The other two jumped in soon after, but I can't really remember much of what they did because I was all but unconscious by then.

I do remember how there were all these people just standing around. I guess it was the busy time in between films. They just stood there, waiting to get their popcorn, and jumbo soda and watched as these three guys almost killed me. Some of them even shot videos with their cell phones. You can see it on You-tube if you know where to look.

Everyone wanted to watch, but no one wanted to help.

It wasn't until one of the attackers pulled out a Zippo and tried to light me on fire that I actually thought I might die.

That was when (insert name of the dead girl with amazing tits here) showed up. She somehow got between me and my attackers, and sprawled her body on top of mine.

She took out her cell phone and took pictures of all three men.

She also asked the people standing around if they really wanted to live in a world where dozens of people could just stand around and do nothing as another human being was being beaten to death in front of them. The three guys took off and she then turned to help me.

I was going into cardiac arrest, so she started to give me CPR. Now if you've ever taken a CPR class, you know that one of the first steps is to ask a bystander to call 911. She did, but everyone just kept on watching the show.

Apparently, I didn't even warrant a phone call.

The paramedics later told me how dead chick put her cell phone on speaker, set it on the ground next to my head, and breathed life into me.

In between breaths, while giving me chest compressions, she talked to the dispatch officer, and got medical help to me.

All the while, twenty to thirty people stood by to watch.

I tell how as I laid on that cold concrete, with what would later be determined a punctured lung, crushed skull, and more broken bones than I like to think about, how grateful I was to be alive.

Thanks to her.

It makes people feel good and tells them something they didn't know about the deceased.

Sometimes, I'll tell how the recently departed came to visit me in the hospital and offered some prophetic wisdom that changed my life.

I have another story, where I was living under an overpass when the living-impaired person invites me into their home, buys be a change of clothes, and gets me a job.

I never say anything bad. I just try to make them feel a little better about their loss. Isn't that why we go to funerals anyway?

♥

I work for a tiny, local candy factory so I rarely ever have to wear cologne. The high fructose, corn syrup smell never really leaves me, no matter how many times I take a shower or wash my clothes. My boss is a sweet, old Italian man named Ferninni, who looks more like a fat Mario than a Gene Wilder.

Just to make sure we're on the same page here, yes, when I think of Willy Wonka I think of Gene Wilder. Not the Johnny Depp, Tim Burton piece of crap.

Don't even get me started on what a true Oompah-Loompah looks like.

I stare into the dryers and get lost in the colors. I'm supposed to look into the dryers quite frequently to make sure the beans don't start to melt, but experience has taught me that smell has a lot more to do with it than sight. I'm not complaining though. Staring into the dryers is probably the most Zen like thing I do in my life.

Mojito green, Pomegranate burgundy, and Grape purple swirl around in chaotic entropy, as my mind tries to keep up. As often happens in these moments, my mind turns to masturbation.

For me, if I'm happy, I hardly spank it at all. If I'm sad or stressed out, it happens more and more.

Lately I've been hitting it so hard, my shoulder probably looks like Quasimodo.

I remember thinking how I really needed a change

in my life, and let me tell you, if you're actually dumb enough to put something like that out into the universe, you had better be pretty damn specific as to exactly what you mean.

♥

How I met Naomi and became the next savior happened like this; with the spectrum of medical test I have taken over the years, as you can probably imagine, I'm in almost every medical information system that exists. About three months after I got rid of all the cape fucker's stuff, I get a call from a hospital in Salt Lake City, telling me how they have this patient who is suffering from a rare form of osteoporosis, and needs a bone marrow transfer, and… oh my stars and garters, I just happen to be a perfect candidate.

If you were to ask me anything about the human heart, I could probably give you a correct answer. That doesn't mean I know anything about bone marrow, or what makes a good donor, or even what the procedure entails. Before I can think about responding, the lady on the phone tells me the patient will more than likely, die if I don't give my marrow.

The invisible gun points at my temple, and I tell her I would be more than happy to help.

The Phone Lady tells me that The Church of Jesus Christ of Latter Day Saints will even buy me a round trip ticket and put me up while I'm in town. I ask her why the church is involved and Phone Lady tells me the patient is a Mormon Church member.

I don't know anything about Mormons, other than that whole multiple wife thing. I heard a joke once about Mormon underwear, but I didn't get it so it didn't stay in my head.

I ask if I can bring my comic books with me to read. Phone Lady tells me that would be fine.

About a half hour later, Phone Lady calls me back

and tells me I'm scheduled at a local hospital to have an MRI run. She tells me not to eat or drink anything for breakfast.

About an hour after that, a lady from a Travel agency calls, to inform me that I will be leaving for Salt Lake City this Friday.

The next morning, I show up to work late with a note from the hospital, and give it to Mr. Ferninni. He knows my medical situation, so my missing work to see doctors isn't exactly new. My boss is great. He knows we have a tedious job and he does everything he can to make it better. He has never given me a hard time when I've asked for time off, even though I'm sure he knows that I've faked a couple of doctor's appointments, just to get away from the Jelly Bean Machine, so I wasn't surprised when he gave me the time to go to Utah. I was a little surprised when he gave me a hug after I told him why I was going.

I am a Jelly Bean Buffer.

I have been for the past eight years.

Not just any jelly beans mind you. Gourmet jelly beans.

Basically, after the corn syrup shell is applied to a bean, I feed them into this huge dryer type thing that has felt cotton all along its inside walls. If you ever had a rock polisher as a kid, picture one of those, on a large scale. The beans tumble around, the corn syrup solidifies, and the beans come out all shiny. It's a completely mindless job, but I like it and it gives me time to think.

Cappuccino brown in one machine.

Raspberry maroon in another.

There is a kind of surreal, disassociating effect that happens when your world changes suddenly. I'm sure Psychologists have a fancy term for it, but if they do, I don't know what it is. As I watch the brown beans twirl around, and feel the warmth from the driers I realize I never asked Phone Lady the name of the patient who would be receiving my bone marrow. I don't know why the thought came to me. At the time I wasn't even sure if I would even meet the person who would be receiving my marrow.

It turns out that we would meet, and we would end up saving each other in more ways than you might imagine.

♥

I decide to pop in to tell Damon I will be out of town for a few days, and to buy some Graphic Novels for the plane ride and hospital stay. He doesn't ask me about my new found singleness, but I can feel his curiosity hovering in the air above us, like one of those fart clouds you used to see in *MAD* magazine with the little lightning bolts shooting out of it.

He warns me about the Mormons and compares them to Zombies, Vampires, and married people who won't stop until you have given up your identity and become one of them. In the same breath, he tells me to put down the *Daredevil* book I have chosen and read something with a little more substance, like something from Vertigo, *Hellblazer,* or *100 Bullets* for instance.

In the jelly bean world, Damon would be a buttered popcorn jelly bean. They are pretty to look at, have a unique taste, but really doesn't have any right being a jelly bean. Damon's an acquired taste.

I blow it off when he tells me, how maybe the doctors will discover something in my bones, like Wolverine's adamantium lined skeleton or Plastic Man's elasticity.

Green Lantern stares at me from the corner of the store.

As I go through my pockets, searching for my wallet, Damon sees my keychain and goes into his usual rant.

When I was a kid, I couldn't get enough of those old, stop motion, holiday specials they used to show around Christmas and Easter. The idea that the illusion of movement came from these photographs of dolls, which never really moved at all was enough to vapor lock my young mind. Rudolph was my absolute favorite. I often wondered if he had his heart on his nose and that's why it was red. I also bought into the whole 'just be yourself' message the program feeds us. The best character in Rudolph is Hermey the Elf. He's the little guy who wants to be a dentist and spends his whole life being ridiculed for it until he saves Christmas by fixing the tooth of the big snow monster.

My keychain is Hermey the Elf.

ADD INF: I used to want to be the guy who decides whose head gets to go on a Pez dispenser.

Damon points to my keys and asks me why I still have that thing. He tells me it sends the wrong message. He tells me it's no wonder I'm single. He asks me when the last time I was hit on by a guy was.

Damon's theory is that Hermey was a transsexual. That's why he was so conflicted. Even the name was a dead giveaway; Her-me. He once told me Hermey and the Charlie in the box were secret lovers and that's why they were banished to the land of misfit toys. Personally I always saw Hermey with the little polka doted elephant but that's just me.

ADD INF: I used to want to be the guy who punched the center hole in vinyl records.

Damon always tries to sell me a keychain that looks like the Death Star, because he says it would go perfectly with my X-wing car. He's probably right, but I'm not ready to let Hermey go yet.

♥

Security stops me at the airline gate because something sets off the metal detector. This pisses me off a little bit, because I'm intentionally traveling light so I won't have to deal with any of this post 9/11 crap. When they scan me with the wand it beeps as they pass it over the bandages on my hand. The Uno cards gave me a Draw Four this morning. The TSA officer makes me take off the bandage and shines a little pen light into my palm. Another TSA officer comes over and the two of them pull out three broken shirt pins that have embedded into my palm. I didn't even see them when I wrapped my hand, but it was enough to set off the metal detector. I make a mental note to buy more shirt pins when I get home.

Unfortunately, I never make it back.

♥

You would think that if God was going to pick a savior, he/she/it would pick someone better than a guy who has to masturbate to drawings of Power Girl from the *Justice Society*. Maybe someone who looks a little more like Brad Pitt than Elmo. Someone with an education, charisma, or power. More importantly, someone who actually knows a little bit about religion, so when doctors discover a supposed religious text hidden within the strands of my DNA, I just might be able to understand it a little bit.

I fly into Salt Lake City, not really knowing what to expect. When I step off the plane, there is a woman at the gate holding a sign with my name on it. Now, I'm not going to waste your time telling you how the earth moved when I saw her, or that she went into slow motion, and *Dream Weaver* began to play in the background because frankly, I would botch it up. But I can tell you something did happen, and I got all kinds of tingles in my hanger downs.

She tells me her name is Naomi, and when I stick out my hand, she ignores it, and gives me a hug instead. When she pulls away she notices the look on my face, she laughs. She informs me that I must be confused. Truth be told, I'm not confused, what I'm doing is hopping that my little light saber doesn't pop up, because I wore sweat pants so I would be comfortable on the plane.

As she walks me to baggage claim, she loops her

arm through mine and makes me feel more like a man than I have in quite some time. I'm telling you ladies, if you ever want to get underneath a man's skin, forget holding his hand or putting your arm around him. Simply place your hand on the inside of his elbow and he will feel like he should be wearing a cape.

As we stand around the baggage carousel waiting the bags from my flight to be vomited up, she tells me it's her son who will be receiving my bone marrow, and she hopes it wasn't to forward of her to meet me at the airport, but she felt she should do what she could to make my stay more enjoyable.

ADD INF: Her son's name is John. He is three years old and has a very rare form of osteoporosis that the doctors can't get their heads around. He was born with both arms broken and a skull fracture. His body ages faster than it should. He has mild cerebral palsy and a plethora of other ailments. He's been subjected to test after test since he stepped out of the womb with little to no progress. I haven't even met the kid yet and already feel like he's my long, lost brother.

I tell Naomi about my heart, because I want her to know I understand a little how her and John's life has been. I also want her to be informed of everything about my medical history the doctors might not pass along for confidentiality reasons, because she's the kid's mom and has a right to know.

My bag finally comes and I don't really know what to do next. I wasn't expecting someone to meet me here.

She asks if I have hotel reservations and when I say no, she offers to let me stay at her place. There's nothing sexual about it, although The Force is definitely strong with this one. She's just trying to be nice because I'm helping out her kid. I would feel a little funny staying in her home so I decline.

She asks if she can at least give me a ride to a hotel

and I accept. I tell her about one I *Mapquested* that's only about a mile from the hospital and she takes me there. I picked this hotel because I brought my skateboard and don't really want to hassle with renting a car.

Later on, in my hotel room I'm amazed to discover there is no porn available on the pay-per-view. When I call down to the desk to complain about it, the guy simply says "Welcome to Utah".

Now I know for most people, a night alone in a strange city is a recipe for adventure, but I'm just not that exciting.

Lying in the bed, staring up at the strange ceiling I think of the cheating bitch again and decide to rub one out. Yes, I still think of her when I go a few rounds with the bald headed champ. It takes a while, and by the time I'm done, my hearts pounding so hard I can almost see it behind my eyes.

I need to get in shape.

As I lie there, listening to my heart, and feeling my pulse throb in my head, I wonder if what I'm feeling is different from what everyone else feels. Does my dyslexic heart somehow alter my perception of the world around me? If my heart is truly so unique and rare, just what am I supposed to do with it?

I close my eyes and picture my old girlfriend in a Wonder Woman outfit, letting me tie her up with her magic lasso.

Ten minutes later I'm asleep.

♥

One of the things that *MapQuest* won't tell you, and in my infinite wisdom I wasn't able to figure out for myself, is that Salt Lake City is in the fucking mountains. Walking through the avenues to where the hospital is located is like climbing Everest. Everything is either all uphill or downhill depending on your direction. Mine happened to be up.

I pushed my skateboard up two blocks of vertical insanity before giving it up, because another thing *MapQuest* doesn't tell you is apparently there is no oxygen in Utah. I'm sucking so hard, but it feels like I'm breathing through a straw. I think the Mormons stopped here simply because they just couldn't go any further. I've got to get in shape.

I'm not even through the revolving door of the hospital yet before a security guard tells me I can't skateboard there, so I strap my board to my backpack full of comic books.

As I walk into Same Day Surgery, I see Naomi sitting with a small boy in the reception area. After giving me a brief hug, which I store for later mental examination she introduces me to her son, whom I'm here to save.

Osteoporosis is a disease that normally affects older women or women with eating disorders. The calcium of the bone weakens and causes the bones to be prone to fractures. Of course, I didn't learn any of this till later when the doctors told me about it so why I'm telling you about it now at this point of the story really doesn't make any sense, but I'm the narrator and it's my story so fuck off.

John is three but he only looks like he's maybe six months tops. He rides in the tiniest wheelchair I have ever seen. The oxygen tube up his nose looks just as natural as his M & M's hat. It's weird. It's like seeing a baby with a little higher cognitive functioning. He sticks out a little baby hand and says how he's pleased to meet me. I ask him if he likes comic books. He tells me that he's never actually read one but he's seen the *Spiderman* movies. I tell him we'll get along fine.

As we sit in the waiting room, a couple of guys in scrubs come out of an office, point at me, and then disappear again.

Naomi tells John about my backwards heart and I whisper into her ear that her name is "I moan" backwards.

She blushes but places a hand on my knee. I know she's probably only being nice because I'm helping her kid, but if the opportunity arises, I'm hitting that.

Finally, a group of people wearing green scrubs comes over to us, and I ask if the scrubs are the funny Utah underwear I read about on the Internet. I get a bunch of blank faces so I decide to shut up. A doctor asks me if I wouldn't mind coming with him alone.

Naomi gives the doctor a look, and without saying a word shows me just how many times she has faced off with doctors over the past three years trying to help her son. She knows something is wrong before being told. I say that since John is getting my marrow that maybe they should hear what he has to say too.

He takes us into a room filled with other people wearing scrubs, all looking at various x-ray films in lighted frames on the walls. He explains to me how my hospital back home sent them my MRI's, and informs me that an anomaly has been discovered. He tells us how neither he nor any of the other doctors have ever seen anything like it.

I assume he's talking about my heart, and tell him he should have been made aware of my condition and that's how they found I was a possible donor in the first place.

I'm no Quincy, but I figured they should have known about my heart before I got here.

John wheels his chair over by me and spins the wheel on my skateboard.

Naomi walks over and looks at the films.

The doctor tells me it's not my heart. That the MRI is showing unusual calcium deposits on the inside of my hip bone which was used for the sample scan because that's where they will be taking the marrow from.

I walk over to where Naomi is and look at the film for myself.

It's hard to make out what I'm seeing because the MRI makes everything look like you are seeing it through those night vision goggles the stalkers use, but one thing is instantly apparent. These calcium deposits, if that's what they are, have a definite structure. Almost like a weird font in another language.

The doctor points to a specific film and asks if it means anything to me.

In the center of the film, quite clear, are five letters which appear to be English, surrounded by hundreds of smaller characters which are too small to make out, but look like everything from Chinese to Latin along with a lot of others that I can't even recognize.

The letters are backwards, which for some reason doesn't surprise me.

NOMIS

♥

Before I left for Utah, I picked up a Bizarro action figure from Damon's shop planning to give it to John, who back, then I didn't even know of as John. Just something for a kid to play with or for me to play with if he didn't like it.

I have a lot of action figures around my place, but most of them I keep in their boxes in case I decide to retire early. I always open the Bizarro figures though. If you walk around my home, you will see an Alex Ross Bizarro on the television. Bizarro from the animated superman series sits on the back of my toilet. The Ed McGuiness Bizarro, my personal favorite, protects my laptop when I'm not home.

The first time I saw Bizarro I was probably around six or seven. My mom left me at the revolving comic rack at the neighborhood grocery store while she did her shopping. Even then the illustrated worlds held me tighter than television ever could. I was looking for a Superman issue I didn't already have and could possibly con my mother into buying for me when I saw him.

The cover showed all sorts of destruction. The Daily Planet globe was crushed. Jimmy Olsen was kneeling over the very dead looking Lois Lane. Fires burned, people screamed, and in the forefront of it all stood Superman, backlit, so you could see none of his features. The only two things you could see were his eyes burning with heat vision and the backwards 'S' shield on his chest.

I was hooked.

In Bizarro world everything is backwards. That's why Bizarro's a bad guy. In that first issue Bizarro welded together a drawbridge with his heat vision, not because he's evil, but because he thought the bridge was broken and was trying to fix it.

Sometimes, quite often in fact, I feel like I'm Bizarro which is why I open his action figures and play with them. I look around at this broken world we live in and wonder why everything is backwards.

People text message and e-mail each other a hundred times a day. We live in a world where I can online chat with someone half way around the world as if they are in the same room as me. Cell phones, pagers, tablets, Blackberries, people walking around with things plugged into their ears making them look like 7 of 9, only not sexy.

All these communication tools and yet people rarely ever speak to each other.

We ask people how they are doing without really expecting a reply. We chat for hours online with people we don't know while barely acknowledging the existence of the people that we live with.

If you want to shut a person down, you don't need kryptonite, evil monkeys, robot ninjas or secret lairs. If you want to make a person uncomfortable or if you want them to leave you alone…talk to them.

Really talk to them.

Tell them what you think about as you lie in bed at night. Tell them that you're afraid of being alone, but don't know how to be with someone else either. Ask them when was the last time someone just held them as they cried. Ask them when was the last time someone held them simple because they are a human being and human beings need to have that every once in a while. Offer to hug that person.

They'll leave you alone for a very long while.

This isn't Bizarro world.

At no time do I feel more like Bizarro than when it comes to love and relationships.

In Bizarro world, women like the nice guy, and try to hook up with him often. Not here. Here, the more abusive you are, the more dates you get. Treat a woman like shit, sleep with her friends, cum on her face, steal money from her, and maybe even smack her around every now and then, and she will be yours forever.

Now I know I'm soap boxing here, and you are probably wondering about those backwards words they found inside my hip bone, but again, I'm the narrator. You're not. Deal with it.

If you happen to be reading this and you are a female. These statements may seem a little offensive to you. If that's the case, I'm sorry. But it needs to be said.

Chances are, you at some point in your life, have lamented to your friends how you just can't seem to find one of the nice guys. I've heard women do it SEVERAL times, and you know what…you're full of shit. I guarantee you, at some point in your life, probably a lot more recently than you would care to admit, there was someone who would have done anything just to buy you a cup of coffee, and you weren't interested in him simply BECAUSE he was a nice guy.

Damon's words from the comic book shop still sting with their freshness.

So, fuck off and don't whine to me about it, because you can walk into any comic shop and fall over three of four nice guys who will worship you and who haven't seen a vagina since Spiderman first wore the black suit.

Now, what I'm saying is true, I wish more of you

hotties would come over to the Bizarro side, however, don't paint me as a saint. I know I'm doing this nice bone marrow donation for a complete stranger and all, but truth be told…since I first felt Naomi hug me in the airport, I've been trying to figure out a way that I can use this operation to get her into bed.

Even Bizarro has a penis.

♥

When the first word was discovered there were people who were saying it was an anomaly, but it wasn't until the full CAT scan got back that people started using the word; miracle. It wasn't until someone started interpreting the words that people started calling me a savior.

I told you before that I'm in no way shape or form a religious scholar. I remember one time, a friend took me to church and then got mad at me when I asked him if since Jesus was a carpenter, was there ever a time when he looked at the cross, and thought, 'I can probably build one better than this'?

My third day in Utah was spent mostly at the hospital. They took me into a board room where my MRI files were plastered all over the walls. The board room must have had thirty doctors in it. Now, with my past, I'm kind of used to this type of thing, however, when one of the doctors kissed my hand and then held it to his cheek, I knew something was up.

There were letters and symbols all throughout my whole skeletal system: English, Latin, Chinese, and Aramaic. The doctors told me they had discovered over seventy symbols in various human languages and over a thousand that they had never seen before. Looking over my files, I saw some symbols that almost looked like Kryptonian.

Nobody knew quite what to make of the "writings", which was a term I wasn't too comfortable with but that the doctors seemed to use when referring to the markings. For me, the term "writings", implies someone wrote these things. If there is writing, there must be a writer. The one thing everyone did agree on, was that the writings seemed to have a cognitive essence to them and they weren't spelling out meaningless gibberish or SPAM mail.

I know this is probably going to sound naïve and even a little stupid, but I really didn't care about any of this. I just wanted to give John my bone marrow and go home. The doctors told me they were reluctant to do the transfer because they would have to drill into my pelvis and might destroy a piece of the medical find of the century. One doctor even said that with all of the health issues John was already suffering from, the bone marrow transplant would really just be delaying the inevitable, and really wouldn't do anything to improve the quality of John's life. When Naomi heard this, she threw a glass of water in the doctor's face. I told them if they didn't do the transplant today, I was leaving and taking the medical miracle with me.

They did the transplant.

Afterwards, the problems really began, but before we get to that, let me tell you more about the meetings.

The day after the transplant, I was driven to Brigham Young University to meet with professors in the Linguistic, Theology, Biology and Philosophy departments. The Philosophy professor claimed he could find a full ethical and metaphysical practice within the writings. He said if he understood it correctly, the writings could prove Kant's Categorical Imperative wrong. He mentioned some things about Spinoza and Kierkegaard, but I really couldn't follow it that well.

The biology department wouldn't say what they found, but all of them were white and looked at me like I was something they couldn't comprehend. One of them kept looking at his hand like it would start talking to him. None of them would touch me when I offered to shake hands.

    The next day I met with the President of the Mormon Church and something called the Quorum of Twelve. They asked me if I wouldn't mind staying in Utah for a little while longer.

OWT
INFLATABLE DOUGHNUTS / PETER AND THE ROMAN

"216"
-The Book of Benjamin
In large font from inside the skull; these were the only set of solitary numbers found within the body.

The day after the transplant, Naomi drove John and me to the local comic shop because I had extinguished the stash of comics I brought with me. John and I sat in the back of her SUV or Mormon Assault Vehicle as she called it, both of us feeling ridiculous sitting on those little inflatable doughnuts because of the holes they drilled into our asses.

ADD INF: When you're a medical miracle, like myself, the whole medical process becomes mundane. A lot of people go through their whole life without ever having a major medical procedure, so when they do, it becomes a little earth shattering. The veterans don't care. They pick their own anesthetic with the same passion as they choose a video to stream. Go into any cancer ward and you can see what I mean. You'll see people going through chemotherapy, wearing their little yellow Lance Armstrong bracelets, and not caring or even noticing all the people in the room with them don't have any eyebrows.

The reason why I'm walking you through this is isn't so you think I'm a hard ass or I don't care. I just want you to understand the comfort I have long since found with my own mortality, which I think you will be able to understand without any great difficulty.

Now, picture that same disassociated passiveness in a three year old boy.

It will break your heart.

Are you with me on this? Because it's important.

That's why seeing John light up when we walked into the comic shop made this whole trip worth it. Not just the bone marrow transplant but everything else that happened because of it. The writings, the Mormons, the assassination attempts, the healings, being crucified...all of it was worth it because of that one moment.

John took my hand and guided me from comic to comic asking who the various heroes on the covers were and what they could do. I was looking around the shop for the Japanese section because I wanted to make sure I wouldn't have to explain anything embarrassing to John or Naomi, but I still wasn't used to what life in Utah was like yet, and hadn't realized that finding a picture of a boob in this state was harder than getting real drink.

John seemed to gravitate towards the X-Men, which didn't really surprise me because when you got right down to it, he was a mutant too. I picked out a couple of age appropriate X-Men books that highlighted the adventures of Wolverine, who John told me reminded him of myself. I asked him why as my ego inflated to frightening proportions at being compared to the toughest guy in the Marvel universe.

John said it was because Wolverine was short.

I told him I wanted my bone marrow back.

Naomi found a Bizarro Action Figure, and insisted on buying it for me. I couldn't bring myself to tell her I already had this one waiting for me back home, so I let her buy it.

Since John was still struggling with learning to read, I picked out a couple of Wolverine action figures for him, as well as the X-Men DVD package. Naomi protested when I offered to buy them for John, saying I had done enough already, but I explained to her how she was truly in no position to educate her son on the finer aspects of superheroing, and she knew it.

Back on our inflatable doughnuts, John and I argued over who had scored the coolest action figure as Naomi drove me back to my hotel. The two of us had to return to the hospital the next day for a follow up exam, and Naomi offered to pick me up in the morning, which I was very thankful for, because the thought of skateboarding uphill with a big hole in my pelvis was almost enough to make me cry.

Later, as I'm back in my hotel room thumbing through comics, and feeling a bit restless, I'm debating if my hip will tolerate trying to go for a walk through a nearby place called City Creek Canyon, when there is a knock at my door.

It's Naomi.

She's alone.

Before I can even invite her in I have a semi.

She asks me if we can talk. She doesn't *tell* me we need to talk. This might seem like the same thing to you and maybe I'm splitting hairs a little but after my last relationship this is a huge difference.

She sees the Bizarro figure she bought me on the night table, out of his box, ready to defend me as I sleep, and smiles. She sits on my bed, touches Bizarro's cape, and then begins to cry.

My first thought is John. Well… my second thought at least. I ask her if John's alright, she shakes her head and very quietly says 'no'.

I begin to ask what's happened when she emotionally vomits it all out.

She tells me how she doesn't understand what's going on or how any of this can be happening. How she tried to shrug off this whole ordeal with the writings in my bones, and the craziness with the doctors, until she was sure John was going to be alright, but now she doesn't think she can.

I ask her where John is now and she tells me that's how the problem started. She can't figure any of it out. She explains how John has to sleep in an oxygen tent, and usually by Eight O'clock his medications have knocked him out cold. But tonight, he has been up watching his X-Men DVDs and playing with his action figures until well past midnight.

She decided to let him stay up because so rarely his medication will allow him to do so. She decided to make cookies, you know, because she's a good mom and her son needed some comfort food because he had a rough day of surgery and has to go back to the hospital the next morning. She explains how one minute, he is sitting on the couch on his inflatable doughnut with his oxygen tubes in his nose watching the DVD, and the next she comes in with a plate of cookies, and the tubes are out, and he's standing by the coffee table having a battle with his two action figures. When she tried to put the tubes back in, he told her they were superfluous, and he wouldn't need them anymore.

Superfluous. His exact wording.

When she finally got him to sit down and eat some cookies, he asked her how Superman tucks his cape into his pants when he's Clark Kent? He asked how come the Hulk's pants never come off when he changes and how come they are always purple even when Bruce Banners might be blue or tan before the transformation. When he started to ask her about the comparisons between Xavier and Magnito to Martin Luther King Jr. and Malcolm X, she called for a baby sitter.

I didn't know what to say. While this all sounded strange, you have to remember I had only met John a couple days before all of this. I couldn't understand how unusual this behavior was for him, but I could clearly see Naomi was upset by it.

I sat next to her on the bed, held her hand, and listened.

When I took her hand, she stopped talking about John for a while and just touched my fingers, then my arm, then my face and chest. I thought she might kiss me, but she didn't.

"Bone words are what John had called them," she said.

She told me how before she came to see me, she had tried to change John's bandages. There was blood on the gauze, and little black flecks of dried blood on her son's smooth little bum, but nothing else.

No wound. Not even a scar.

When she asked her son about it, he said the bone words had healed him. Then he touched his mother's face, and told her the bone words would heal her too.

The bone words would heal us all.

♥

After Naomi left, I was more than a little sexually frustrated. I know, I probably just need some angry rebound sex, but that's not quite how I feel about Naomi. It's too early to tell but I think there might actually be something there.

Anyway, after she left, I called down to the concierge and asked him send up a deck of Uno cards and a box of shirt pins from the hotel gift shop. When he brought them to my room, I complained that all the movies on my television have the nudity and sex scenes edited out of them. He told me they were called "Clean Flix". Another Utah specialty. I had had enough of religion to last me for the rest of my life at this point, which is funny to think about now because it really hadn't even started yet. I was also tired of Utah, and wanted to go home.

The concierge asked me what I was going to do with the shirt pins. I asked him to bring me a quart of mayonnaise, a CPR Dummy, and a stopwatch. He stopped asking questions after that.

Twenty minutes later, the front desk called telling

me they had complaints of banging coming from my room.

The next morning in the car, John asked why my hands are always bandaged.

As we approached the hospital, we could see several news vans parked out front. Technicians were setting up satellite links. Television reporters were checking makeup.

NBC, ABC, FOX, CNN, and a few I didn't recognize which I'm guessing were the local stations.

Before we could enter the parking lot, Dr. Ormsby, the doctor who performed the bone marrow transplant, called me on my cell phone. He described the commotion at the hospital, and asked if we could meet him at a place called the Huntsman Cancer Institute, and to try to not let anyone from the media see me. Naomi said she knew where this Huntsman place was and we were off.

Low and behold, the Huntsman Institute is built on a mountain just like everything else in Salt Lake, and I was dreading the thought of pushing a skateboard up here if I had to stay much longer. It was nice of Naomi to drive me around while I had this inflatable doughnut attached to my ass, but I was actually craving a little alone time.

Naomi goes in through a side door, and then to the front desk to tell them we are here and to find out where we have to go.

John and I hang outside by the door because it still hurts like hell to walk, although John seems to be doing much better with it than I am. In fact he left his doughnut in the car, while I cling to mine like it's a life preserver. Sitting outside, basking in the morning sun, is a girl of maybe twenty-three sitting in a wheelchair. She smiles at me, and I notice her smooth bald head under a Superman baseball cap. She catches me staring and asks me if I have never seen a cancer patient before.

I fake it and tell her I was looking at her hat, which was what caught my attention before the baldness. We got to talking comics for a bit, and before I left, I took off the hat, rubbed her smooth head with my bandaged hand, and told her I hoped she would be ok.

Naomi came out with about a half a dozen security guards as well as Dr. Ormsby. He looked panicked, and told me he had been waiting by the front entrance with security to avoid any incidents. I asked him what he meant and that's when he told us about the media release.

Someone, not a hospital employee, I was assured, but how I would ever really know is beyond me, had told the media about me and my meetings with the Mormon presidency. I guess this doesn't happen very often, or it must have been an extremely slow news day because the media reported everything they knew about the writings within me, and had interviewed several of the professors and church authorities I had spoken with.

Overnight, I became a freak, a celebrity, and a savior.

The first word interpreted was the first one I saw. The backwards Simon.

I didn't know any of this back then, of course, but now I've been forced to become something of an expert on religion. Simon was someone who happened to be standing around when they were getting ready to crucify Jesus. Just some guy waiting to see the show. When Jesus became too exhausted to carry his own cross, the Roman guards pulled Simon out of the crowd, and made him help Jesus carry it to Mount Golgotha.

He was just some random person who happened to be picked out of a crowd. It could have been anybody, but it was him, and now he is forever linked to one of the most famous stories ever told.

Now, for me, Simon was this game you played with lights when you were a kid. But somehow because his name showed up in the writings, people have interpreted this to mean I am to be the bearer of Christ's salvation. I am to carry Christ's message.

Me.

ADD INF: Just to throw a little perspective on this, when I was eight I had to be taken to the emergency room because I tried to fuck my toy cement mixer, and got my penis stuck. Now *I'm* in charge of man's salvation.

I understand now how I really am the salvation for mankind because I've been told so by The Pope, The Dalai Lama, and even Oprah. But I'm getting ahead of myself.

Dr. Ormsby took us into an examination room under security escort. He examined the site on my hip where they had drilled and didn't find anything unusual. There were no infections and the wound seemed to be healing at a normal rate.

John, on the other hand, was an entirely different story.

His wound had completely healed. His bone density had also increased by 500 percent in less than twenty-four hours. Dr. Ormsby ordered some cat scans to confirm this, but he seemed confident that John's osteoporosis had all but disappeared.

♥

I feel like I should apologize to you, dear reader. If you heard about me and then thought to read this book hoping to learn more about why I am the way I am, you must be disappointed. Like I told you from the beginning though, I don't understand a whole lot about what's happened to me. Maybe that's why Jesus or Buddha or any of those guys didn't write their own stories. They let philosophers and poets and people who can use words more eloquent than 'fuck' tell the tales.

That being said, I feel like I should *really* apologize for this next part. You see, when I told you how I don't know anything about religion, I wasn't completely honest. I know the basics. I know how Jesus was crucified and then three days later became a George Ramero character. I know

Moses parted the Red Sea, but I couldn't really tell you why.

People ask me the big questions all the time, and it frustrates them when I tell them that I don't know. It frustrates them even more when they discover I'm telling the truth. I really am clueless.

I hope I've been able to explain things so you can understand the story so far, because if you're not keeping up now, this next part will definitely lose you.

Quantum Physics.

Anybody who tries to tell you they understand Quantum Physics is pulling your leg. It's easier to understand why Paris Hilton is famous than to understand this stuff. However, for this next part, we need to understand just a little bit.

What I want you to do is to picture a carbon atom. If you don't know what one looks like it's the symbol the superhero The Atom wears on his head. Now at the center, there is the nucleus. Those things flying around are protons or electrons or neutrons or some type of tron…shit, I just don't know, ok?

Anyway, if you were to enlarge that carbon atom to the size of a house, the nucleus would be about the size of a basketball and the various "trons" would fly around the outer perimeter. Traditional science looks at what the nucleus is made of, and how many protons there are surrounding it, and what happens if we add a proton here or subtract an electron there. I think that's called a chemical reaction.

Visualize the carbon atom the size of a house again. The basketball nucleus and six even smaller, maybe ping pong ball size, protons flying around in house size circumference around the nucleus. That's all there is, the rest is just empty space.

But what about all that empty space?

What happens in the space which constitutes more

than 99% of the atom's size?

This is what Quantum Physics asks.

So what does all of this have to do with me?

The day after John and I went to the Huntsman Center, Dr. Ormsby called, and asked me if I would be willing to come back to look at something with him. He wouldn't tell me what it was he wanted me to see, but I had to wait for him to medically release me to fly before I could go home, so I figured why not.

The next morning I took a cab alone, because I didn't think I could take another day of being with Naomi without vomiting out some pathetic declaration of my attraction for her, and I wasn't quite ready for that level of rejection yet.

When I got to the hospital, there weren't any press crews around. I didn't know it at the time, but this would be the last time I would go anywhere without the Paparazzi taking pictures, or some television reporter shoving a microphone in my face, or someone asking me to touch them to make them well, or having someone try to kill me.

But, I'm getting ahead of myself.

I paid the driver, and grabbed a Superman graphic novel I picked up from the comic store Naomi took me to, and started to head into the hospital. On a bench, I guess, would normally be for smokers to use, however, I'm not sure they allow smokers to live in Utah, sit's a woman who waves at me as I approach the door. She has long red hair, like the girl in that Pixar movie *Brave*, piercing green eyes, and a body that makes me look twice.

I wave back, and she points to the book I'm carrying, and gives me a thumbs up. I hold it up so she can see the cover, and she asks me if it's a good story or not. I tell her I don't know yet, and she smiles at me. I wave, and head into the hospital.

Once inside, I'm directed to an office on one of the upper floors, where Dr. Ormsby sits. Joining us are several new doctors who work here at the Cancer Institute. They all shake my hand, which hurts, because I've been playing a lot of Uno back at the hotel.

The new doctors explain to me a lot of things about Cancer I really don't understand. They show me all kinds of charts and X-rays. One even has a tumor sample in a Petri dish-type of thing. They tell me about chemotherapy, and walk me through how it usually works.

I'm waiting with trepidation for them to drop the hammer and tell me they've discovered I have some weird backwards type of cancer in me, with cartoon pictures instead of tumors, when through a door, in the back of the room, walks the redheaded girl from outside.

I tell everyone I really have no idea what's going on.

They tell me they feel the same way.

One of the doctors takes me over to an x-ray, stuck to one of those light boxes mounted on the wall. It shows a brain tumor about the size of a softball. He then shows me a film of a liver that's covered in these little white dots. He explains how the dots are cancer growths, and further points them out with a little laser pen. He tells me chemo hasn't worked and how there's nothing they can do for this patient, except for make them comfortable and wait for them to die.

He asks me if I wouldn't mind meeting this patient.

I ask him what any of this has to do with me.

Another doctor shares how, just two days ago, they had a similar case that has shown remarkable progress, and they don't have any explanation for it other than me.

Quantum Physics asks what's in the empty space that makes up everything.

There are places inside the human body where there is nothing but emptiness. These places exist within our bones. The doctors tell me when they drilled a hole into my pelvis to extract bone marrow; they released whatever was in the nothingness inside of me out into the world. That nothingness, somehow, went into John and now he's doing much better if not completely healed.

My Uno game has put tiny holes in the bones of my hand.

Two days ago, I touched a girl, and now her cancer has completely vanished.

That's when I realize I met the redheaded girl the first time I came here. She's the bald girl in the Superman hat I talked to. She's the cancer patient that has been cured.

I ask her what her name is.

She tells me it's Mary.

♥

OOOH! I know what you're thinking. The girl, whose cancer I cured is named Mary. Just like the girl Jesus pulled the demons out of. Coincidence? Creative liberty taken by the narrator? All the religious buffs who read this may have also noticed the reference to Naomi's son being named John seeing as how in the Bible, John was the one who foretold of the coming of Christ, and how Naomi's kid was kind of how word got out about me. Also…for those of you paying attention, it says somewhere in the Bible how 'a child shall lead them'. John's a child so all of this must be true, right?

What the fuck are you thinking? Of course it's all coincidence. I'm not the savior. The sooner you understand that, the easier this whole thing will be for you. If your life is so sad and broken you have to look to a guy, who once bought all seven seasons of *The Gilmore Girls* just because he thinks Lauren Graham has a wonderful ass, as your only hope for salvation you might want to crunch a little more tinfoil on your antenna because you are getting some heavy feedback.

This isn't a complex story I'm telling here, people. I'm not John Steinbeck. You can probably figure out everything I'm going to tell you, long before I actually tell you about it. Like how I mentioned all the stuff that's going to happen to me, like being crucified, and how the Mormons saved me, and stuff. Now, some writers call that foreshadowing. I call it not being able to tell a fucking story straight.

Or, like how I started this whole story telling you about how my girlfriend cheated on me with some other guy. Gee, do you think she might come back at some later point in the story? Or Damon's comic book store? Why did we need to mention that? Do you think the big climax at the end of the story, when we figure out what the words mean, and when I have the confrontation with my ex-girlfriend, but not before Naomi and I fall in love, and everyone has grown into better people because of this experience? Do you think all of that might happen inside Damon's store?

I'm not trying to give anything away here; like Bruce Willis is really a ghost or Rosebud is a sleigh. I just want be on the level with you. To let you know I'm not trying to trick you or spin some wild yarn. I'm just telling the story. You were the one who picked it up and began to read so take some responsibility.

Anyway, you've stuck with it this far, and I thank you for that. I'm sorry I use the word "fuck" so much. We've taken a pretty good chunk out of the story already so why not go the rest of the way with me? I hear there are cookies at the end.

Let us continue.

After Mary's recovery became a public matter things happened very fast. Once this snowball started rolling, it was almost impossible to stop. I was on talk shows, met with Presidents, had Nike name a shoe after me, and I came to the realization that sex with a plethora of strange women, who care absolutely nothing about you, is still pretty great.

However, there were a few things that happened right before the media frenzy hit, that I think is important to mention. I want you to see the whole picture.

After the Doctors told me about Mary's situation, and asked if I would be willing to look at patients with other diseases I kind of felt a little overwhelmed, and needed a little break from it all. Just time to digest and process this craziness, so, I decided to go to movie by myself. I don't even recall what movie it was, but it was there that I noticed how people were starting to react differently to me. I went to a matinee show, and while I was standing in the ticket line, the couple in front of me was having trouble deciding what to see. The guy suddenly turns to me, and asks me what film I'm seeing. I didn't make anything of it, just someone being friendly. I tell him, and they decide to buy tickets for the same show.

I like to get to my movies a little early so I can get a good seat, and catch the trailers. I get some popcorn and a Coke so big, I would probably need a dialysis machine if I were to ever to actually finish drinking the whole thing, and headed into the theatre. I'm the first one there, so I pick a good seat towards the back.

A few teenage girls come in and sit directly behind me. No biggie right? At least they're not in front of me. However, the next group of people to come in *did* sit right in front of me. There's like fifty rows in this theatre, and apparently we all have to sit right next to each other. Just as I'm thinking this, in walks the couple who I saw buying tickets earlier. Not only do they sit on the same row as me, they sit in the seat right next to me. Not even that courteous, in between chair people use for coats, or that homophobias use to prove they're not gay when seeing a film with their male friends. It keeps going on like this. About thirty people come in and we're all packed together like a scene form *Amistad*.

I don't know why it happened, but from that point on this was to be the norm for me everywhere I went. If I were to go into a coffee shop and sit down, within ten minutes, every table around me would be full. If I were at a urinal and another guy came in he would always go to the urinal right next to me.

Personal space became a thing of the past for me.

Complete strangers would tell me anything.

One day, I asked the barista behind the counter for a large decaf, and she told me when she was five she once tortured a cat.

Another time, while crossing a street, a man walking in the other direction confided in me that he was embezzling money from his job.   He hugged me before I crossed to the other side of the street.

Why this happened, I can't say. Did I ever take advantage of it and say…sleep with women who wouldn't have noticed me otherwise. Damn straight I did.

Look…There is probably something I should explain here. I've said it time and time again, but I really need you to understand. I'm not a savior. I'm not a miracle. I'm not even special.

I'm an anomaly.

That's it.

Let me ask you, though, if fame and notoriety, money and acceptance, love and purpose were suddenly dropped in your lap, what would you do with it?

Would you adopt a bunch of kids from impoverished countries or would you buy a Lamborghini?

Would you save the whales or pay someone with implants to wear a Catholic school girl outfit and pay a little attention to your own blow hole?

Yeah, right.

I guess it's just me then.

♥

Here comes the part of the book many of you were probably dreading. That being said, religion plays a central part of this story, so did you really think we would make it through the whole book without ever talking about God?

Now, before you cringe, or look around for the money plate, let me put you at ease. I'm not going to tell you anything about how cloning goes against God's will or how if you have a single impure thought in your life you will spend eternity burning in Hell or if you just send me 20 dollars and the number on your credit card, I will teach you the secret handshake to get past the velvet ropes in heaven. You've heard that stuff all of your life. It probably didn't have a big impact then and you definitely won't get any revelations from me.

One thing I *will* do, is try to explain why people kill each other, judge each other, and hate each other over their beliefs, in what is basically the equivalent of an imaginary friend. But before we get to that, I need you to go out and kill all the Jews for me because, let's just face it, they're evil fuckers.

Obviously I'm kidding here…BUT…if for one instant you read that and thought 'OK maybe I should' or 'That's the most offensive thing I've ever read' then just put down the book right now, get a shotgun, and take one for the team because you are part of the problem here. One thing I can tell you for certain, and let's not forget, I'm supposed to be the savior, not you, is that God never wants you to kill anybody in her name. Read that sentence again because it's probably the most important one in this whole book.

Ok…sorry…I got a little preachy there. It won't happen again.

ADD INF: Every once in a while, I get a little pissed about what happened to me. I'm sorry and I don't mean to take it out on you my dear, dear reader. It's just that, things were going really good with Naomi, and why someone thought putting a bullet through her head would make me…whatever. I don't think I'll ever understand it. Besides, you try typing with Stigmata wounds.

But now back to the whole God thing.

Now, I'm painting with a very broad brush, so give me a little leniency here, but there are basically two thoughts on God that separate all the religions. Ironically, it has nothing to do with what God wants or what God is, but rather where God exists.

It's pretty silly I know. It's like, if we had one of those giant maps they have in malls with a "God is here" dot, then all would be wicked spiffy in the world. But let's look at the sides of this silly argument, so maybe we can at least understand what we're fighting over.

One group believes that God is within us. The other believes that God exists outside of us? Understand? This is why people want to let the nukes fly, right? Just please, oh please, let me touch Carrie Keagan's boobs one time before we all kill ourselves, OK?

The Christians, Jews, Muslims, Atheist, and a few others believe God is a physical being separate from us who has a body, e-mail address, and a subscription to *MAXIM*. I also hear he's a Red Sox fan. He created us in his own image (which is really a scary thought when you analyze it).

Outside God, being a separate entity from ourselves, is thought to have powers that we don't have. Outside God is better than us and is something we should try to be like, although we will never achieve that goal on this plane. Outside God created us. All we can really hope to be is a friend on his Facebook page.

Just one thought on Outside God; Nietzsche said 'only man possesses such an ego to create a super being that cares so much about our existence that he will monitor our every action, every thought, every deed, and everything else we will ever do'.

I can't even remember what I had for lunch two days ago.

On the other side of the debate, we have the Buddhist, the Quantum Physicist, the Taoist, and basically all those weird earth muffin people, who believe God exists within us and everything else.

Before you get all pissy and scream at me that Quantum Physics is a science and science doesn't concern itself with God, grow up a little bit. Science has *always* been about God.

Einstein, when asked if he believed in God, said he believed in Spinoza's God. Spinoza was one of the biggest Inside God advocates out there. If you haven't ever heard of Spinoza you should check him out. He was around the time of Descartes, but unlike Descartes he didn't write for the masses. Descartes was terrified of being killed when he came out with his Cogeto-ergo-sum theory. To denounce God in writing meant death on most cases. Remember Copernicus? He was in a tower just down the street from Descartes. In a nutshell, Descartes' theory states that he is a thinking being and therefore he exists. You've heard of this before I'm sure. I think therefore I am (although Descartes never actually said this). However, Descartes then goes on to say that since he exists…God must exist as well. It was kind of like going from A to B to Q. Personally I wonder if he threw the whole God thing there just so people wouldn't crucify him.

Now Spinoza had his own theories that are different than Descartes, but Spinoza had the huevos to publish what he really felt.

Sorry to get all philosophical there. Did I sound smart? Savior like? Well someday I will tell you about an accident I once had, involving a Popeye the Sailor Man Pez dispenser that resulted in seven stitches and an em-bare-ass-ing scar. They never found his pipe.

So this side believes God exists within us. Kind of like the midichlorians that enable us to use The Force. God exists within our DNA or within that elusive thing we call a spirit.

So to sum up, Outside God people look upward.

Inside God people look inward.

Got it?

If you can imagine, when I showed up with these mysterious writings on the inside of my bones and with by backwards beating heart, both of these groups starting looking to me to figure out how my discovery fit within the parameters of their premises'.

Parameters of the premises. That's a lot of P's

The poopy Popsicle pedestal proved prestigiously proud people pork puppies periodically.

Ponder profusely.

♥

I walk onto the sound stage, shake Oprah's hand, and sit down on the famous couch to share my story with the world. The hullaballoo about my phenomenon has been out for a while now. I've done probably around twenty talk shows as well as various other news and entertainment programs. *E!* did a *True Hollywood Story* episode on me, even though I've never been to Hollywood, and *VH1* did a behind the music segment despite the face I'm not a musician. However, nobody's bigger than Oprah.

By this time, the scientist had figured out a few more things about what was happening inside my body, but every answer only led to new questions. John had almost grown to a normal size three-year-old over a three week period and his osteoporosis was all but a memory. Mary's cancer slipped into complete remission and cancer specialists from around the world had confirmed that by mixing Mary's blood with certain types of chemotherapy drugs would cause remission in other patients. Those patients' blood could then be used to treat others with similar results. By the end of the decade, many doctors and scientists were saying cancer would be a thing of the past, like polio.

But, that's not what Oprah wanted to talk to me about.

The part of the story that Oprah wanted to know happened like this…

One day, about a week after I met Mary, I was still in Salt Lake in my hotel room when the phone rang. I picked it up, said 'Hello', but no one was there. I hung up and never thought about it again, until I was sitting on the Oprah couch and they brought out this teenage boy whose parents had called me that night out of desperation. The boy's name is Thomas (I swear I'm not making this up). Thomas was born deaf and was not a candidate for cochlear implants or any other type of treatment. His parents called my hotel room, and held the phone up to Thomas' ear. I said 'Hello' into the receiver and within twenty minutes he was hearing his mother's voice for the first time.

Oprah set up an experiment to try the same thing on live television. She placed forty deaf people in the studio audience, and by the first commercial break they all could hear.

Blind people who "looked" at me could suddenly see.

The crippled who touched me could stand and walk.
The lonely found love.
The anguished discovered peace.
Bitchin.

One serendipitous event that led to some of the greatest discoveries about the writings on my bones came from what a few people deemed as an act of terrorism. Personally I think calling it 'terrorism' is a little grandiose, the reality of it didn't even equal up to a bar fight.

Stephen Keatings wasn't the first person I cured, but he was probably in the initial ten somewhere. Stephen was born blind and remained so for forty-three years of his life. Then one day, Stephen went out for a walk, and happened to pass LDS hospital as I was skateboarding down the street towards my hotel. Three blocks later, Stephen could see with better then 20/20 vision.

Having gone his entire existence without seeing and then rapidly possessing sight obviously came as a shock to Stephen. Imagine this for a minute. Picture going over four decades, imagining what the color green is. You've had friends and family patiently and impatiently try to explain it to you. You've touched the leaves and grass to understand what green feels like. You even know the depth of light rays needed to cause greenness. You know what green sounds like.

Earlier, I mentioned Hume's missing shade of blue theory and I was thinking of Stephen when I mentioned it. The empirical force of experiencing that green stimuli would probably be enough to melt your brain.

There Stephen is, buckled to his hands and knees on the sidewalk trying to understand what's happening to him. He pulls out his cell phone and calls his girlfriend, but not before seeing the letters on the small phone screen that make up the woman he loves name for the very first time, but having no knowledge of what those letters represent.

When Edison showed the first motion picture to the public, the film was of a locomotive approaching a station. People ran from the theatre because they thought the train was going to come out of the screen and run them over. These were people who had possessed the sense of sight all of their lives.

If Edison's train could affect the seeing in such a way, sympathize with what Stephen experienced when he saw the ambulance screeching up to him with full lights and sirens. Imagine within an hour of receiving the 'gift' of sight, being taken into a hospital emergency room. Seeing a different shade of green on all of the hospital scrubs. Seeing the red of blood.

It must have been like Siddhartha seeing the old, sick, and dead.

The hospital released him because there was 'nothing wrong'.

For the next two weeks, Stephen stayed in the apartment he shared with his girlfriend, Malory. Three things troubled Stephen most when it came to seeing. Glass and photographs were tough for Stephen, but Malory's plasma television was just too much to fathom.

While I'm sure I don't need to explain why the concepts of clear and various dimensions would be difficult for Stephen, I want you to take a second and imagine about that Plasma TV and what it would be like.

Stephen was not feeling blessed. Sure there were good parts, like finding out Malory was even more beautiful than he had imagined. Seeing the curve of her calf. Seeing her naked breast. Pretty cool, huh?

But then there were things like animation and reflection and pixels.

One night, Stephen and Malory are sitting on their couch, trying to get comfortable with the TV again, and they see this stunningly good looking guy on the news. This person had just cured a girl who had terminal cancer by simply touching her. The reporter said this man had also cured a small boy by giving his bone marrow. They said this man's hands were miracles and could heal anything. The plasma TV said, this guy was spending a lot of time at LDS hospital which was only a few short blocks from the couch where they now sat.

Steve and Malory came to the conclusion that I must have somehow touched Steve. They were wrong, but at this time, we didn't know people could just see me or hear my voice to be cured.

The next day, Stephen left his apartment for the first time since his miracle. He decided to go for a walk by the hospital. He also chose to take one of those frozen food knives Malory had in the kitchen drawer.

I'm sure you can see where this is going. Long story short, as I walked out of the hospital's main entrance, I saw a man standing against the yellow tape the police set up to control the media. He just stood there, looking at me, with his right hand extended towards me like he wanted to shake hands. I didn't want to be rude, so I took Stephens hand, and now there are two metal hooks where my right hand used to be.

Now, I'm a pirate, as well as a savior.

I'm not complaining though. Typing this is kind of a bitch, and I was a righty when it came to masturbation. There's nothing quite like deciding to rub one out, first thing in the morning while you're still half asleep, and scraping cold metal along your shaft.

The only time it truly bothered me though, was when they crucified me. Since I didn't have a hand, they decided to drive the spike between the bones of my forearm.

That kind of sucked.

Oprah brings Stephen out to tell his side of the story. The studio audience boos at him like they are on Jerry Springer or something and tries to make him out as the villain, but when I ask them not to, they stop. I hug Stephen and tell him I'm sorry for what he's gone through. Malory is there as well and she tells the world how Stephen is actually doing much better, but he still has a way to go before he feels normal again. She says the hardest part is getting Stephen to open his eyes throughout the day.

ADD INF: Oprah has several other of these "accidental curing victims", as she calls them, on to tell how sometimes being handicapped is better and how they were happier before. However, what we found out, through trial and error, was if these people encountered me in any way for a second time, all the trepidation went away and they were alright with their new lives. I set up a 1-800 number to speak to anyone who had suffered from something I had done. Once it was up, people with various handicaps could call, I would say hello, then place them on hold for a minute or two, then talk to them again and they would be just fine.

On the second half of the program, Oprah brought several people from the science community to explain some of the new discoveries that surrounded me. Several of these findings I learned about right there on Oprah's couch.

After Stephen cut off my hand, it was sent to a laboratory at the University of Utah Hospital. Several medical, linguistic and ethics experts from around the world flew in to run test. The biggest discovery, by far, was that the markings weren't just inside my bones. They covered the inside my veins as well. That led to more cat scans, which showed I had the symbols on all the inner linings of my body. One mathematician said the writing's on my large intestine alone were roughly equal to all the information currently held on the Internet. Another expert said with all the veins in my body, scientist figured that they had translated $0.026 \times 10\text{-}438^{th}$ power of the information stored in me.

ADD INF: I don't understand the difference between baking soda and baking powder.

Around the time the program was being taped, a physicist had created something he called "transparent titanium" from a formula found within one of my finger bones. He called the bone by name, but I don't remember what it was. It's the bone that a wedding ring would sit on if we wore them on the right hand.

Another was working on something he kept referring to as negative space. He explained his findings, and to be honest it all pretty much went over my head, but if I understood him right, he was developing something like a portable hole that had no limit on its capacity space. Remember in the Bugs Bunny cartoons when Daffy Duck would jump into Bugs' rabbit hole and then Bugs would pick up the black circle and place it in front of a truck or something like that? That's basically what the portable hole is.

Now once again dear reader I want to shed a little perspective on this situation. There, in front of the television world, in what was Oprah's biggest viewing to date, the greatest minds, the most pious religious leaders, political figures, and normal working class people were calling in saying how I could very well be the greatest thing to ever happen to our race while I'm sitting on the couch wondering if I can talk Oprah out of some of those chocolate covered gummy bears she had back in the Green Room.

♥

I should probably tell you about Michael Flemming. Poor Mike was one of the people who slipped through the historical cracks of this story, and I'm quite sure you've never heard any mention of him before this. I, myself, didn't even know about Michael until after I died. In the afterlife, your perception changes a bit after you cross over and you are able to see the big picture on a much greater scale. Just FYI, that's all I'm going to say about what happens in the great hereafter so quit asking. You'll all find out soon enough, so have a little patience for fuck's sake.

About six months before our chance encounter, Michael was injured quite badly in a construction accident. Mike worked as a roofer, and one morning he took a four story fall of the roof of an apartment complex to avoid someone swinging a boom. It was something right out of a Laurel and Hardy episode, aside from the multiple leg and pelvic fractures. Michael compressed his spinal column in the fall in such a way that he was almost always in considerable pain.

The insurance settlement was glacially slow in coming, and the financial burden became quite difficult for Michael to bear. With the impossibility of doing any type of physical labor, Mike's wife was forced to take a job, and the family took a huge cut in their financial income. Anyone who has ever been married will tell you, money problems can be the end to a lot of relationships. Michael tried to take a position as a data entry computer jockey, but he couldn't sit in a cubical for the extended hours because of the pain he constantly felt in his legs and back. One night, after a shift, Michael found he was unable to stand, let alone walk across the parking lot to the bus stop. The doctors had taken away his driver's license because his reaction time was shot, and besides, he was taking way too many pain medications to operate a motor vehicle.

Michael became somewhat blacklisted by the other construction companies and was looked upon as an insurance risk by potential employers. His union was great in helping, but his physical labor career was over.

Michael had to go to physical therapy for three hours daily, and he pushed himself to his limit in every way. You see, Mike is one of those men who believes in working for his keep. He was a proud man who had always been able to carry his own weight, plus a good part of the weight of those people around him. That's one reason he had such difficultly sitting on the sidelines of life watching everything else go by. Mike wanted to be a good husband and to support his wife, whom he truly loved with every fiber of his being. When she would complain about their financial troubles, Michael took it very personally, and was usually left quite hurt and feeling like a failure.

One of the few moments of relief Michael could find from his physical pain was swimming in one of the local gyms. It wasn't even a full size pool, just a two lane training pool, but the water took some of the pressure of his damaged body and Mike could walk the length of the pool and feel a small amount of the strength return to his legs and hips.

I'm going to shift gears in the story here for a little bit, so please be patient with me.

Do you remember the *Wonder Woman* series with Lynda Carter? I'm sure you do. For most guys my age it was either Lynda Carter, of Carrie Fisher who gave us our first chubby. I bring up the *Wonder Woman* series because they did something in the television series that was fairly common in the comic book world. When they had to cut to another scene, this little yellow rectangular box would show up on the screen with the word 'meanwhile' written inside of it. Remember it? Ok, picture that little yellow box right now, because I need to give you another viewpoint on this story for you to fully appreciate it.

Meanwhile...

By this time the media latched on to me and my abilities, and grabbed on like a pit bull. I seriously suspect, at any moment during that time period if you exposed yourself to television, the Internet or any other type of media, you would have seen my face somewhere. You couldn't get away from me. It was kind of like when Anna Nicole Smith died and that was all people could talk about for a month or two. The paparazzi were all over me.

ADD INF: As with all media hype, probably around eighty percent of what was being said and reported wasn't true. Naomi and John had all kinds of lies printed about them in the tabloids, which I'm not even going to dignify by repeating here. Nothing said about them in those repugnant magazines was true. I hope I've painted a clear enough picture about how genuinely good hearted Naomi is and John...well, John is my hero is so many ways.

The media, it seemed, was always giving me some new power I didn't possess. Some new discovery that the brains of Cal Tec or MIT discovered about the writings within me which I could never be able to understand even if the greatest minds of our nation tried to patiently explain it to me. I'm sure it was frustrating, and more than a letdown when people would build up these unbelievable expectations of me and then upon meeting me or seeing me on some talk show, discovering I'm just a normal person, with no greater understanding to the meaning of it all than they possess themselves.

The whole thing made me feel locked in an abyss of insecurity.

Book offers, made for TV movies, talk shows, twitter accounts, Facebook groups, pod casts, webisodes, political rallies, Skype debates, I just couldn't get away from it.

I did what most men do when they are faced with an overwhelming sense of responsibility, I hid. The times I had alone were few and far between, so I learned to cherish each and every one of them. One of the places where I found some solitude was at this 24 hour gym that had a tiny lap pool. I would try to sneak in there during the early morning hours and splash around for a while.

There is something deeply peaceful about floating in water. I'm not sure if it somehow takes us back to the time when we were in the womb, but I love how everything sounds when your head is under the surface. I will never be Aquaman or anything, but I got to the point where I could hammer out a mile or so almost every time I got in the pool.

One night, I showed up to get some laps in, and there was this other guy in the pool.

Three guesses who that was.

I didn't talk to Michael. I'm not sure why, because from what I understand, he's quite a nice person. It's just that sometimes men have no idea how to communicate with one another. Take the urinal protocol for instance. There is this inherent DNA gene code inside every man that tells him how to behave during this situation. If a person is at the urinal next to you, you may either begin talking as you approach your urinal, or wait until you are both done with your business, then begin chatting. Never and I do mean *never*, walk up next to someone, start peeing and then ask them what's up. It's very awkward and you will make the man next to you try to pinch it off so he can get away from you.

Just don't do it.

Thus sayeth The Lord.

Anyway, I began to swim my laps, and Michael walked his laps in the lane next to me. We probably passed each other a few dozen times and I never once thought anything about it until after I had died. What I didn't know was, how the pain Michael felt in his back and legs was gradually decreasing as the night went on.

Michael noticed though.

By the time he left the locker room, Michael was completely cured.

I have heard people say, if you don't have your health then you don't really have anything. But when you are drawing disability from numerous organizations who decide to investigate you because your doctor abruptly stops sending in reports, then being healthy can kind of suck.

In Michael's defense, he never tried to scam anybody. When he realized he was better, he stopped drawing disability and immediately tried to find work again. The problem occurred when Michael's doctor ran a new set of x-rays to monitor his recovery. There was no evidence the pervious injuries had ever been there. No scar tissue. No bone fusions. Nothing.

This was what the insurance lawyers pounced upon. Michael had absolutely no explanation for what happened to him, so the insurance companies and the federal government prosecuted Michael for fraud.

He was found guilty and sentenced to 15 years in prison. During his third year he was stabbed to death in the prison laundry room, because another inmate had mistaken Michael for someone who had "dissed" him earlier.

On the bright side, neither Michael's back nor legs ever bothered him again.

I'm really sorry about what happened Michael.

♥

On the first Sunday of the month, Naomi invites me to go to a Mormon church for something called Fast and Testimony meeting. It's a time where members of congregation get to address their fellow church goers and describe how the church has influenced them in positive ways. After about ten minutes in the audience I see the pattern.

One by one, the Mormons would walk to the pulpit and begin the mantra;

Hi my name is _____, and I know this church is true.

It kind of felt like being in an Alcoholics Anonymous meeting. Even the little kids, who couldn't have been more than five, knew what they were supposed to say up there. Go through the motions, tell everyone you believe, and you will end up in the Celestial Kingdom.

I don't know why, but this really bothered me.

♥

No doubt, there are some of you reading this, who are pretty disappointed with the lack of actual teachings I'm providing here. I hope you will understand, though, I really don't want this to be some type of self-help book and I *really* don't want it to become any type of dogmatic works to be followed without introspection. Better men than I have tried, and the world is still no better off.

Moses gave us a ten step program.

Buddha cut that down to eight.

Jesus even narrowed it down to one, but we still don't get it.

I feel it's important to tell you some of the things I didn't do and all the ways that you and I are exactly alike. Now, when I tell you there's nothing special about me, I mean it. This is not like when a girl, who is so skinny you can see what she's thinking, tells you she's fat.

Ask yourself this question: If you could drastically change a stranger's life for the better, simply by touching them, saying hello, or even looking in their general direction, wouldn't you do it? Can you imagine any reason why you wouldn't do it?

Of course not. You're good people.

Schopenhauer claimed, when you see another person suffering this transcendental existentialistic transformation occurs within us and we have the ability to see how we are all the same. We're all connected, and refusing to help another in a time of need is refusing to help ourselves.

This is what it's like for me. When I take AIDS from a man, or when I heal arthritis in a Labrador, it takes nothing from me. What makes it even easier, is these people go away and I never have to see them again. There is no vulnerability in it for me. As sad as it is for me to say, I make no connection with these people.

Naomi taught me about connecting to another person. All of my actions seem trivial and petty when compared to her.

Whenever I do something savior-ish I always feel weird. I don't like it when people act obligated to me. It makes me very uncomfortable. Naomi never once made me feel that way. When this whole thing first started, I thought she was hanging around because I helped her son, but that quickly went away.

Naomi was the only person who treated me like an ordinary guy throughout this whole fiasco. When I was with her I could just be me, and not the Alpha and Omega.

There was this one night I will always remember when I think of Naomi. I tried to sneak into the comic shop to see what was new and to pick up my hold when I walked into the lens of a paparazzi camera. It was a total accident and completely my fault, but it split my eye open and I had to have four stitches. Well, it came time to get my stitches out and I just didn't desire the mess of going to a public place again. Naomi rested my head in her lap, held a flashlight in her mouth, and took out the stitches, one by one, with a pair of sewing scissors. When she was done with the stitches, she just let me leave my head in her lap while she gently stroked my hair. I don't think I've ever felt more loved in my life.

It takes something I rarely possess to attempt to cross the abyss that lies between us all and open myself up. Now ladies, I know there are a butt load of creepy guys who look at you and see nothing more than a piece of ass. I understand you need to protect yourself and each other from these slimy men. But please…try not to be a total bitch when a guy happens to asks you out for a cup of coffee. Try to remember this person is extremely vulnerable. Be gentle. If you're not interested, tell him you're involved with someone else. If he doesn't take the hint, then he is a scumbag and deserves to be maced.

It's the vulnerability that makes it strong.

Let me put it this way, who's a greater superhero, Superman or Batman? Now Superman can move planets and perceive cellular structure, but when he's staring down the barrel of a gun, is there any bravery in his actions? Not really, because he knows nothing can hurt him. Before you go off and tell me that Superman had weaknesses too, remember who you're talking to. I know about the whole Kryptonite thing, but I don't think having an allergic reaction really constitutes as a weakness. The Superman analogy is important to my story, because I was never really in any danger either. When I went to Africa to cure the leprous I wasn't afraid because I knew I wouldn't catch leprosy. When there's nothing to fear, it's difficult to be afraid.

If I'm Superman, Naomi's Batman.

Everywhere I went, Naomi went with me. I remember how cute she looked in her chemical protective suit as we walked through the chemically saturated streets of Iraq. She brought me a cup of coffee once, while I stood over a mass grave in Kosovo. She hugged me when I was covered with blood after someone sent a child, strapped with explosives to kill me at a home for abused women.

These weren't dangerous places for me, but anything could have happened to Naomi. Yet there she stood.

I'm a pretty young guy, so I haven't really experienced many acts of love that aren't in some way sexual or erotic. But when it happened, when there was this person giving herself completely to me, and so many other strangers we encountered along the way, having that total vulnerability that I, myself, will never possess, moved me in ways I will never be able to express.

Naomi was the miracle, not me.

♥

The Jews believe they are God's chosen people.

Christians believe the only way to salvation is to accept Jesus as your savior.

The Mormons believe they have the one true gospel.

Actually, I think the Mormons were kind of on the right track when Joseph Smith supposedly, asked God which of the churches were true, and God said none of them were. This might be the truest interpretation of God's words I have ever heard of, or at least this line of thinking seems to be congruent with the teachings that have come out of the words. I'm not going to be one of those assholes who tell you what God thinks or says, because I'm sure you've determined by now I am nowhere near that wise or enlightened. But then, Old Joe Smith blows the whole theory by coming up with some new theology and claiming it's the one and only true church, according to God. No wonder they tarred and feathered him.

What is it about organized religion that feels the

need to rein supremacy over all the others? Even the so called Unitarian churches reject the eastern religions, the Wiccan and Norse beliefs, not to mention all the Scientology, or any other religion which isn't creator based.

Far be it from me to tell any of you whether your religion is the one true church or not. That's for you to decide, not me. However, there is a danger I have personally suffered greatly from that stems from this absolutist beliefs.

Let's ignore the hubris we mere humans make when we try to interpret who or what God is. If you're already making that mistake, then nothing I can write about here will change your mind.

However, I would like to suggest, and I need you to stay with me here, because it might get a little weird, that there may be individuals out there who practice your same religion, who might not be as emotionally balanced as all of you good people reading this.

Fanatical people.

People, who when faced with something that doesn't fit into their parameters of right and wrong, would rather destroy that thing than to possibly change their way of thinking.

People with rifles.

People with bombs.

People with box cutters and passenger jets.

Do you see where I'm going?

It's not the religions that are wrong, or even that they create these people, it's the beliefs embraced by these elitist thinking people that one is right and all the others are wrong which leads to violence.

What?!

How dare I suggest such a thing?

You're right.

It was a very pompous, arrogant thing for me to say. I should probably be punished for uttering such dribble.

Maybe someone should find me and beat me to the edge of consciousness. But wait, before you do that you should have one of those call-in-to-vote things they use on American Idol to let the general public decide my fate. Then, they could make be drag an I-beam a few miles through town, then mount said I-beam atop the highest bridge in the city, and shine a bunch of those lights that Batman uses for the Bat-signal on to it, then you could use a bolt gun to fire stainless steel threaded rods into my upper arms and shoulders, then leave me hanging in the spotlights until I die.

    That seems like a good idea.
    Oh wait…you guys already did that.

♥

    Before things got so out of control that I couldn't go anywhere, I decided it was time to take a much needed vacation. I had made a little bit of money from various appearances and interviews, so I wanted to do the dream vacation. I desired to do something monumentally epic. I think even then, something in the back of my mind was telling me how this was all going to end soon, and badly. I craved to participate in an event that would last with me for the rest of my life. Go somewhere and see things most people will never have the opportunity to see. Maybe even do something that could have a spiritual impact upon me. Cross something off my bucket list.

    This really only left one choice: The San Diego Comic Con.

    I suggested the idea to Naomi, and truth be told; I made it sound like I wanted to go because I thought it would be something John might like, rather than tell her it was true Geek Nirvana. I'm sure she saw through this ploy, but if she did she never let it show. She didn't even punch me when I said it was too bad John didn't need his wheelchair anymore, because if we shaved his head, he could make a pretty good Charles Xavier.

When I told my security detail about it, they told me there was no way I was going because they would not be able to protect me while I was amongst the crowds. I reminded them how very recently I had my hand cut off under their watch and they dropped the argument. I was still a free man living in America at this point after all. The courts had not yet classified me as Non-Human and Homeland Security wouldn't deem me a threat for a few months yet.

I did promise my security team I would wear a costume, which would hide my identity, and I've never felt more like a real super hero in my whole life. I found an amazingly authentic looking Spiderman costume and even was able to rig a prosthetic hand under the spandex so I wouldn't have to wear my hook. Naomi wanted to wear something that could go with my costume, so she wore a Spiderman costume as well, but hers was in the black version. I have to say, Naomi rocked the spandex with the best of them. Sometimes, I would find myself staring at her curves beneath the skin tight material, and was extremely glad I had the foresight to wear a baseball cup under my tights.

It was John's costume that was the big hit of the Con. He even won some money in the costume contest, but quite honestly his outfit made most people a little uncomfortable. When he found out I was going to be Spiderman, he quickly asked if he could be Dr. Octopus. I thought this was a little ambitious for a costume idea, but John is such a nice kid that he makes the impossible seem easy. I asked him if he would like some help making his costume, but he said no, and told me how there was something he wanted to try.

I've often thought about John and why he seemed to change more than anyone else I worked with. I don't know if because he was the first one to receive any of whatever was going with me, if he got a concentrated dose, or if somehow it was more…pure with John. I will never know. But the kid developed an intellect far beyond his years and could sometimes put people off when they talked to him.

Friday morning I knocked on Naomi and John's hotel room to see if they wanted to go to the lobby and snag some breakfast before the craziness started. The door is answered by a three-year-old Alfred Molina. John has somehow found a tiny trench coat, wig, and sunglasses. He looks amazing, and I'm so proud of him.

Then I see the arms.

Four metal arms that look like living snakes slither out of John's back. Each arm has these three pinchers on the end that look somewhat lethal. John tells me to hold out my hand and when I do, a cold metal pincher gently places a piece of *Hubba Bubba* into my palm.

I ask him how he's doing it and he tells me he just thinks what he wants and the arms do it. He then tells me he made them this way because that's how they were in the movie and he wanted to seem authentic. In his little mind, this is all the explanation that's required.

As we walk to the lobby for breakfast, I ask Naomi how she got all that metal through security at the airport. When she informs me John had already thought of that, and asked her to take him to the local *Home Depot* here last night, I see something in her face that is a perfect split of motherly pride and absolute terror.

Upon entering the lobby to our hotel, we see Damon and Mr. Ferninni (of course I brought them along, too) sitting at a table enjoying their breakfast. Damon is in full Jedi garb, and Mr. Ferninni is in, perhaps the most appropriate costume of all; Willy Wonka. As we approach the table, Damon sees John in his costume, and holds up his hand for a high five. To his credit, he doesn't completely recoil when a robotic arm lashes out and strikes his palm.

I can tell Mr. Ferninni is already going to be a big hit at the con just by the reception he's getting in the hotel lobby. He looks nothing like Johnny Depp or Gene Wilder, but exactly like the Willy Wonka most people picture in our mind's eye. He has a big Santa stomach, like all candy makers should, and he has a genuine appreciation for sweets that can't be faked. Not once during the con did anyone ask him who he was dressed as yet everyone knew he was the Wonka. He also scored a ton of points by being able to produce bags full of candies made in his factory. The egotistical part of me wonders if people would mob him if they knew I had probably made the majority of the candy he was passing out.

My security entourage insisted that I take a team with me, but fortunately they looked so much like the *Men in Black,* that people thought they were part of the fun. It's euphoric to gaze around the hotel lobby, because all of these nerds are here for the same reason we are. In this moment, there is nothing unusual about witnessing Slave Leia pouring coffee for Batman.

Walking through the hall to the convention floor feels like being pushed through the birthing canal before being reborn. Three feet inside the door, Damon and I stop and embrace like children on Christmas day. In case you don't know anything about Comic Con, one of the perks of going is the official Comic Con swag bag they give all attendees. The bag is easily big enough to bury a body in, and by this time next week, eBay will have hundreds of them listed for auction being bid on by people who couldn't be here. Some people use the bags as a status symbol, proving that they are the elite of the geeks, and at every single San Diego Comic Convention there is at least one person who has made their costumes from various swag bags. I asked John if he wanted me to carry his bag for him, but he said he was ok and used the robotic arms to heft the sack high enough it wouldn't drag on the floor.

An unusual bonding quality permeates these Conventions. Sure, it's tons of fun seeing the new toys that will soon be coming out, meeting your favorite artists and writers, and possibly even bumping into someone famous. But the real joy and pleasure of it is walking among the thousands of people who, in many ways are just like you. People who often wonder if it might actually be possible to put on a rubber suit and help people. Thousands who put serious thought into what they would do if bestowed with a power ring or if a Genie granted them one super power, which ability they would choose.

Steampunk, Anime, leather, spandex, latex, ridiculously fake to supremely real looking, costumes of every kind are everywhere. There are so many people I want to take my picture with.

At one point during the Con, this young boy gently tugs on my arm, he's maybe six wearing a Spiderman T-shirt. I assume he wants his picture taken with me because about a hundred other people have asked for photos with Spiderman already, although, far more have asked to have their photos taken with Naomi for obvious reasons. When I look around for an adult with a camera, I don't see one anywhere. In fact, there doesn't appear to be anybody with this kid. I squat down so I can get on eye level with the child and he tells me, in the saddest of whispers, that he is lost. It takes me a minute to realize what's going on, but when it hits me my heart swells up like the Grinch's did upon understanding the true meaning of Christmas. This little boy is afraid and in need of help. He came to me because he thinks I might actually be the real Spiderman. My superhero mojo kicks into high gear and I pick up the youth and leap onto the top of one of the merchants booths. After yelling for a few moments, somebody hands me a megaphone, and within seconds, everyone around is checking to see if they have all the members of their party with them. Soon, a panicked looking woman in a Deadpool T-shirt fights her way through the crowd towards me, and the boy lights up when he sees her. The mom thanks me and my new friend tells her that's what Spiderman is supposed to do. I take a picture with the boy and his mom and it's probably my favorite photo taken that day. Well, maybe the second favorite.

Later in the day, we are waiting in line to see the panel for *The Blue Beetle* movie, when Naomi squeezes my hand, and points to a man sitting on the floor across the hall from us. He is wearing jeans and a Superman T-shirt. Puzzled, I look at Naomi and shake my head, not realizing what I'm supposed to be noticing. She mouths something to me and I explain to her how I can't read her lips while she's wearing a black Spiderman mask and she tells me to look at his sign.

The exhausted looking man is holding a white poster board fastened to a long stick that is leaning on the wall behind him. Five words in thick black letters stand out.

"Will Cure Cancer for Comics"

The fellow geek is sitting cross legged on the floor, with his hands in his lap, so I didn't initially see the plastic pirates hook he has covering his right hand. Suddenly, I'm laughing my ass off, and am on my feet walking over to the guy.

I *have* to get my picture taken with him.

"That's the best costume I've seen yet," I tell him.

He tells me he has actually gotten a little bit of flak for wearing it and apparently not everyone is seeing the humor in it. I want so badly to take off my mask and reveal who I am, but I was told very explicitly not to show my face.

For me, this is exactly what Comic Con is about. I have a real love hate relationship with Cosplay. I think it's one of the most enjoyable things in the world, but you need to put a little effort into it. You can't just wrap yourself up in aluminum foil and expect to pull off The Silver Surfer. It's no secret, there's a definite sexual aspect to seeing all these gorgeous women dressed scantily as some of my favorite characters, but the ones who really get me going are the ones who are unique and original. I mean, sure Slave Leia is hot, but I've seen about twenty of them since my last trip to the bathroom.

Naomi tells me to scoot together with my doppelganger for a picture. We both hold an end of his cancer sign and he thrusts his plastic hook towards the camera. The man offers to shake my hand and doesn't seem too thrown off when I offer him my left.

The line for *The Blue Beetle* panel starts moving, so I head back to the group to grab my stuff. Picking up the ginormous bag, I think to ask John again if he wants me to carry his, but when I look around, I don't see him. When I finally do, I kind of wish I didn't.

Four metal arms slither around my mimic in a grotesque cocoon. John must have designed the arms to lengthen somehow, because each arm has to be at least twenty feet long. Two of the metal pinchers methodically shred the 'Will Cure Cancer for Comics' sign, while the other pair snaps violently around the man's head.

John begins to say he doesn't find the situation funny and people should be showing me more respect than he has been seeing lately. John throws a lot of words like blasphemy, heresy, and sacrilege into the man's face. The mechanical arms squeeze tighter after every syllable John utters, and my mind tries to ignore the loud crack that comes from beneath the cacophony of metal.

"John, let him go!" Naomi tells John in a voice only mothers possess, and for the briefest instant, I see in John the three year old boy he should be. But then it's gone. Others are pushing away from us, because their afraid and unsure of what Dr. Octopus might do next (he is a bad guy after all). Voices cry out for security, while others scream at John to release his hostage.

John wears a face of uncertainty, and I wonder if he has somehow lost control of the tentacles, but then they slowly begin to unwind and retract into his back. One of the man's arms looks like it now has three additional joints in it and bends in all kinds of ways that God never intended. The metal arms droop at John's side and his head lowers in a pouting motion.

If it's true that I have some type of power, I'm positive John has more of it.

"What the hell is wrong with you?" Doppelganger asks as he slumps to the floor cradling his fragmented arm.

Mr. Ferninni grabs a hold of the man's arm and begins to put traction on it. His size is enough the keep the man pinned down and make him stop thrashing. John hasn't stopped looking at his shoes since he decided to let go.

"It's ok John, I'm sure you didn't mean to hurt the man," Naomi says, as she squats down beside him. The spandex stretches across her ass in a way most distracting to the situation.

I look around to see if security is anywhere to be seen. My bodyguards just stand there in their *Reservoir Dogs* outfits and do absolutely nothing.

"What are you doing?" I ask them.

"We should really be going now sir," one of them says.

"I'm not going anywhere. We need to get this man some help, and besides, I'm a huge *Blue Beetle* fan so I really don't want to miss this panel."

This is the point where the Con turns to shit.

"I'm going to kick that kid's ass," a man wearing a Spock costume says from behind my *Reservoir Dogs*. It's an empty threat and everyone knows it. Everyone that is, except Damon.

There is a whoosh as Damon's blue light saber springs to life. With all the fury of Obi-Wan when Qui-Gon fell, Damon starts pummeling the Spock with his replica saber.

"Treckies are pussies you asshole!" Damon says, not slowing down in the least with his attack.

Two or three times, Spock raises his arm in a defensive posture, but many of the blows bounce off his head, and one pointed latex ear falls to the ground before me.

Mr. Ferninni stands up, more in effort to avoid getting struck by Damon than anything else.

"Damon, stop that!" Naomi says in the exact same tone she just scolded John with.

The plastic tubing that holds the blue 'laser' cracks and splinters. The saber makes a strange humming noise, like if Lucas had used an 8 bit synthesizer to create his effects. None of this slows Damon down though. Several people are standing around with their cell phones out, videotaping this. Before we leave the building, this is going to be all over You-tube.

At some point, my security detail decides all this might look bad for us, and gets Damon under control. Comic Con is a place where you get to dress up and be your favorite character for a day, and as I look at the ground, I see a mess that used to be a man in a pretty damn good Spock costume, that now looks nothing like the Vulcan ever should. His bowl haircut wig is tilted at an impossible angle and the one missing ear is on the floor by my feet. Suddenly, I can't breathe through the spandex mask, and the sight of John picking lint balls out of the carpet with his mechanical pinchers becomes too much.

I take the mask off without thinking and gulp a few deep breaths. Spock is holding a hand to the side of his head trying to find out where his missing ear went. When I kneel down beside him to pick up his fake, rubber prop, he flinches for the briefest moment, and my heart breaks all over again. I tenderly pull his hand away from the wound only to see some scratches but nothing that appears too serious. I pick up the pointed ear and gently place it back on, but my prosthetic hand won't bend in the way that I need it to, and there's no way to take it off without removing my whole Spiderman Suit.

ADD INF: The thing I miss most about my real hand is playing the Uno game.

My security detail seems far more interested in trying to block people from filming this than with helping me, or anyone else, for that matter. I think I need to get rid of them because I don't want to live my life this way. I know they are trying to protect my public image, but I fear their inaction to help this man might be far more damaging to my image than anything Damon or John have done.

Then I completely hate myself for turning into the guy who worries about his image.

A black, gloved hand gently rests on my shoulder, and I know without looking that it's Naomi. I tell the man everything's going to be ok, and I want to say at the sound of my voice he seems to calm down, but I think it's just his body going into shock.

"You shouldn't have threatened a little kid." Damon shouts.

John's gaze meets mine for the briefest of moments, but I can see the fear and sorrow in them. I give him a little head bob to try to let him know I understand on some strange level, and that this is all going to be alright.

A couple of paramedics show up in their latex gloves and their tackle box first aid kits. They ask me to step back, so I do, and I'm reluctant in my movements.

"It's you." Spock says.

The paramedics are wiping the blood from his ear, and then start checking his body for other wounds.

"Where are you bleeding from?" one of them asks.

"I think it's my ear."

"Ok. Are you bleeding from anywhere else?"

"I'm not sure," Spock says.

The paramedics continue to wipe his head and then

begin to check his neck and shoulders.

"I'm not seeing a wound anywhere," one of them says.

His ear is perfectly fine. Blood smears along his cheek and matted in his hair, but the ear is attached and looking perfectly fine. Even the fake Spock ear is resting neatly in place. In a later interview, Spock would claim the hole where he had previously had his ear pierced had closed and healed, but I don't know if that's true or not.

"What did you do to me?" He asks.

Naomi picks up the broken lightsaber and repressed the urge to smack the shit out of Damon with it. She gives him the mom look, and I really hope on some level she doesn't blame me for this mess. I pick up John and we decide to get out of there while we still can. As we're walking down the hall, John gives a little wave to the Spock with a metal pincher.

Back at the hotel, Naomi boots up her computer, and sure enough, we are all over the internet. I haven't even had the opportunity to mentally process what has happened since we left the Con, but somehow, other people have had enough time to edit videos and post replies.

I'm really starting to not like my life.

ADD INF: I never did get to see *The Blue Beetle* movie.

♥

I discovered this really interesting phenomenon during this adventure I want to share with you. I met a lot of religious leaders along the way, and they all seemed to have one thing in common…they were all surprisingly laid back.

When I met the Dalai Lama, I had to go through a sort of preparation training on the etiquette requirements of meeting such a religious leader. These Buddhist emissaries' told me all kinds of things, like how I was never supposed to sit so that I was elevated higher than His Holiness, when and how often I was supposed to bow and all kinds of other crap that had me so flustered I'm amazed I just didn't shit myself on the spot.

Before you think I'm picking on the Buddhist, I had to go through the same type of ordeal when I met the Pope and when I met President Gordon B Hinckley. Ironically, I also had to go through something far more extensive and ridiculous when I met Oprah and Larry King.

But the strange thing was, when I actually met these religious icons, all the hullabaloo went right out the window. They didn't give a rat's ass about all the ceremony crap. None of them.

When I talked with the Dalai Lama, he was easily the kindest person I've ever met. We conversed about the meaning and the implications of the writings within me, sure, but for the most part we just hung out. We talked about comic books and he told me in China Batman was called Peng-fo Hop, which translates into 'flying rat man'. I told him about a series called *Bulletproof Monk* by Gotham Chopra, and promised to send him a copy.

His Holiness even rode my skateboard.

When I had lunch with the Pope, I was told it's customary to bring a gift. I brought him a bone that came from a finger of my severed hand. I was worried he might find the gift offensive, or even be repulsed, but he really seemed to like it and assured me he would share any findings his Roman scientist discovered.

If you can imagine this, there I am in the Vatican, drinking this amazingly good Italian coffee with the Pope, and he asks me what I think of Jesus Christ. Talk about a hot seat. What do you say to the Pope when he asks you something like that? I stumble around the question for a bit, and then for some reason I thought of my Superman cape rising up and down as some unknown stranger fucks my girlfriend in my own home.

I've asked myself a lot since discovering the infidelity, if I would have wanted to know about the cheating sooner. If I could handle her just telling me how I wasn't enough for her, and the answer I always come to is, yes, I would have wanted to know. Sure, it would have hurt, but not as much as the alternative.

So I decide to tell the Pope what I really think.

I tell him how I have actually been reading a lot of the Bible since they discovered my anomaly, and about how I've had the opportunity to speak to a Cornucopia of people from various faiths about their beliefs and religious practices.

I tell the Pope I really admire Christ, and how it seems Jesus would be a pretty great guy to have a Slurpee with. I say how it would be a blast to take the savior to the next Comic-Con. I explain how I believe Christ was one of the great teachers in human history, and how I wish more people would embrace his teachings.

The Pope nods at me and pours me another cup of delicious coffee.

Then I say I'm not so sure about all the miracle stuff so many people seem to focus on. I tell him I believe Jesus should be more than a George Ramero prop. The Pope didn't know about the *Dead* series, so I promised I would send him a copy, and I did. I asked him if it really mattered if Jesus walked on water or not, or if he really pulled demons out of people? I questioned how come people don't focus on the trials he went through in the garden with Satan or on the things he said at Gethsemane?

I tell the Pope how I really like how Jesus taught in parables, and make the comparison to how Stan Lee told so many different *Spiderman* stories to convey that with great power comes great responsibility.

I tell him I'm not sure it even matters whether Jesus was God's son or not, or if he really came back from the dead or not, but how the teachings were what truly mattered.

Then I wonder if they still behead people in Rome.

But the Pope was fine with everything I said. He told me he heard I was a comic book fan and proceeded to show me all the relationships between Superman and Jesus Christ. About how Jor-El was really God and how Kal-El was Christ. It was fascinating. When I got back home I looked up the *Superman Returns* teaser trailer online and you can really see the comparison there. It's plain as day and blatantly right in front of you.

Check it out is you get a chance.

Later, I had a meeting with a Rabbi and told him about the Superman/Christ comparison, mostly as a way to make conversation, but he jumped all over it. He told me Superman wasn't a Christ figure, but rather a Moses figure. His crystal rocket ship was like the basket Moses' mother had sent him down the river in. Superman was here to show us how to become better people. To lead us on an exodus beyond our current ethical capability. It surprised me by how passionate he was by the Superman parable, but then he told me all the best stories make us want to grow and be better. That's all religion is and will ever be.

It was refreshing, because I had been raised to think if you take religion lightly, people will probably kill you for it.

Maybe I was actually right about that last part.

♥

One thing that really sucked about my life, once things got rolling, was how I had several different people booking public appearances, interviews, and speeches for me. These engagements always make me feel inadequate, because I've never really been a charismatic person. I once read in this psychology magazine, that in a list of fears, public speaking ranked number one. The number two fear was death. The next time you go to a funeral, remember the person giving the eulogy would rather be the one in the casket.

      Often times, I would show up to these events with little or no preparation for what was about to happen. I was never given the opportunity to screen questions. I didn't have people writing me bullet points on little flash cards or giving me information on prompters. Everything you ever saw me do, or say, came completely cold, and was truly authentic. In all of this, that's the one thing I can claim with absolute certainty. If you doubt me, go watch my interview with Stephen Hawking again. I thought it would be hysterical to answer all of his questions on a Speak and Spell. The nation didn't find it funny though, and if I had any type of advisors or people guiding me, I'm sure it never would have happened.

      One talk, in particular, got thrust upon me at the University of Oregon. I was a guest speaker for the Theology and Philosophy department. Students could come hear me speak and get some extra credits for the courses they were enrolled in, if they wrote a paper on my talk. This always cracked me up because I never went to college and now I'm supposed to be an educator. God truly does work in mysterious ways.

      On the stage of the theatre, is a single metal folding chair where I'm ushered to, and a very nice lady helps me make sure that my microphone is attached and functioning properly. I was later informed they had to move me to a larger venue at the last minute, because student turnout was much higher than expected. The microphone lady hands me a bottle of water and asks me if I need anything else. I blow into my microphone to ensure it's working then I'm ready to go.

      A voice from the crowd asks me if I will turn the bottle of water into wine and the tone of the engagement is set. I tell him that if I could, then this would be a lot more fun for everyone present.

      "I'm afraid I don't have anything prepared for

things like this. Besides, I really don't want to waste your time telling you a bunch of crap you don't want to hear anyway. I've found the best way to do this is to just open up a dialogue and try to honestly answer your questions to the best of my ability. That being said, please understand many of the things I'm experiencing in my life lately, I do not have a good explanation for. Is 'I don't know' an acceptable answer for everyone here to the things I honestly do not know and can't answer truthfully?"

There is some scattered applause and then two lines quickly form in the aisles. The house lights are on so I can see the faces in the auditorium. This always makes me feel a little more comfortable. Also, the fact most of these kids are around my age helps a lot too.

"The Bible tells us to beware of false prophets. Are people accusing you of being one, and if so what do you say to those people?" a man in a Raiders hat asks.

"That's a pretty good question. I would have to say I'm the furthest thing from a prophet there is. I actually didn't even know I was going to be speaking here today until my people told me about it. I don't have visions or anything like that. There are no voices in my head telling me what to do. But more importantly than any of that, I'm not trying to lead anybody anywhere. I don't have a message or catch phrase, so if that's why you came here today, I'm really sorry, but it's the truth."

A man who looks like he might be on the faculty asks a question from the other isle.

"You once said it's possible to learn as much from comic books as it is from the classical spiritual texts. Do you honestly believe these fictional stories compare to historical fact?"

"Wow. That's a pretty loaded question," I say.

"First off, even I wouldn't be dumb enough to compare someone's religious beliefs to something as trivial as a comic book. If I'm remembering the incident you're referring to, I believe I was talking about people who have a difficult time understanding religious dogma and doctrines. The human race has been arguing about the interpretations of these books for eons. I think it's safe to say more people have been killed in the name of religion than any other thing in existence. I believe some people, especially those of the younger generations, are getting tired of all the anger and confusion.

"What I said was, people often have a difficult time knowing what's the right or wrong thing to do in any given situation. The youth of today aren't taught any moral codes or ethics like they once were. If you learned it's better to be nice to someone than to be a bully… that it's good to try to help each other even when it's difficult or might make you unpopular, and that knowledge came from Stan Lee as opposed to Socrates? Well, I'm just glad you learned it somewhere.

"I'm not knocking religion at all, however, when you ask a child (or most geeks for that matter) who their heroes are, they will tell you Superman before Buddha. Think about Comic-Con or Halloween…These are opportunities for people to dress up and pretend to be whoever they wish to be. Sadly, nobody dresses as Jesus or Muhammad. I don't think it's because they don't want to either. I think it's because they're afraid of the ridicule and misjudgment they might get from others. Nobody wants to hear, after you've spent hours making a costume of your favorite hero, that you're somehow being blasphemous by actually putting the costume on.

"I mean, think about this for a little while. Would it really be a bad thing if we could *really* worship spiritual leaders? What if your son or daughter told you they wanted to be Buddha when they grew up? What if next Halloween, some kid comes to your door dressed as Moses, dragging all his beany-babies along for makeshift Jews? Would you be offended? And if you are, does that say more about you or the child on your porch asking for candy?"

The microphone is passed and I'm happy to see people are starting to line up to ask questions. Otherwise, I would look enormously stupid up here because I have absolutely nothing prepared to talk about. I mean I have some pre bottled bullshit I've been trained to spout to reporters and stuff, but it always sounds fabricated inside of my head. I'm sure it sounds phony to the majority of the listeners as well.

"Does your heart really beat backwards?" a pretty little co-ed asks.

"I don't know if 'beating backwards' is the right way to put it, but yes, the blood in my body flows in the opposite direction than other people."

"Do they know why this happens?"

"Because I'm Australian. Things always flow the other way down under." There are some courtesy laughs and I decide comedy will never really be my thing.

"Honestly, the best reason that anybody has come up with is, that I'm just a freak of nature. I've had some of the best doctors in the world examine me and none of them have been able to give a reasonable diagnosis."

"Do you think you experience or see the world differently because of your condition?" she asks.

"I don't really know. If I did perceive or experience things differently, I would have no way of knowing because this is the way I've been my entire life. It's like that old philosophy problem: how do I know that what I see as green is what you see as green? Maybe you see it as pink, but because we've both been taught that when we see that particular color it is called 'green', we think we all see it as the same thing, but who really knows?"

There are some questions about how the doctors discovered the words inside of me and how my life has changed since the discovery and I'm happy because I like the meaty questions. It means people are mentally engaged in this topic, and if they are then someone much smarter than I might just figure it all out.

"Some people say your existence directly contradicts the *Book of Genesis* and in particularly creation theory. What are your thoughts on this?"

"I've never really understood why we hold the *Genesis* as the end all be all of God's entire plan. I mean by chapter three, God's hopes go to shit, and his plan falls apart. I actually really like the *Book of Genesis,* but I think we have a tendency to focus on the incorrect things. Like for me, where it says God created man in his own image, people have used this to argue our superiority over every other thing on the planet, and also to balk at almost every relevant scientific discovery to speak of. For me, (and it's really important you understand this is all just my opinion, and let us be honest here, who the fuck am I?) when God's plan fails in chapter three, this is the example of him making us in his own image. None of us actually know what it is we really want and I'm sure if we had the power to create a universe on some level, we would screw it up to. That's what I think it means about us being made in his or her image."

"So you're insinuating that God isn't perfect?" Another student follows up with.

"I don't remember ever reading anywhere in the Bible where it says God *is* perfect. I could very well be wrong on that, but I think the whole perfection title is something we slapped on God. Not the other way around."

A question is asked about John and whether I condone his actions which can only be the result of the You-tube video of us at Comic-Con.

"I love John. He's become a dear friend to me and we hang out quite often. One thing people need to keep in mind is that John is three. Three-year-olds sometimes do things that might not be fully thought out and are impulsive. He's a good kid. His hearts in the right place and that's all I'm going to say about that."

The mediator hands the microphone to a girl behind him, and there is a long pause as she searches for words.

"It's ok," I tell her. "I know what you really want to ask me. Go ahead. Ask me your question. Everyone in this room had been dying for someone to ask it."

She looks at her shoes for a little while and then speaks very quietly.

"Are you a fake?" She asks.

There's a rustling in the crowd and one of the officiators rushes to take the microphone from her.

"Wait. Wait," I say holding up my hands. "Don't rush her off. That's a perfectly acceptable question. In fact, I dare say it's *the* question. Anything goes here people. Nothing is off limits, ok?" The officiator reluctantly hands the microphone back to the lady.

"What's your name?" I ask.

"Valerie"

"Well, Valerie, since you had the balls to ask the authentic question, you get to sit up here with me, ok?"

She walks to the stage and someone produces another metal chair for her to sit in. There is thunderous applause in the auditorium and the energy levels increase tenfold.

She offers her hand for me to shake and doesn't seem put off when I offer her my left.

ADD INF: A lot of people are strangely offended by this. I don't really understand why, but it's even worse when old habits kick in, and I instinctively offer up my right.

"How are you doing today?" I say

"I'm fine," she says, but I can tell she's nervous.

"Valarie just asked the question I ask myself at least a hundred times a day. I really wish I had a good answer for this question, more for myself than any of you, if we're being brutally honest here. When the doctors first told my mom that my heart pumped backwards and how I was a genetic anomaly I was a little afraid, but after a while I kind of thought it was cool. Like maybe I was a superhero or something. If it were a super power though, it would be the lamest one out there. It would be like being bitten by a radioactive potato bug, kind of neat, but ultimately pretty useless.

"The greatest power that my heart seemed to give me was the ability to sleep with girls who were stupid enough to think there was something special about me. When the words were discovered, they meant nothing to me. I think it's important we all understand that. I never had the moment when I thought 'this means something'. It never happened. It still hasn't to this day.

"I. Didn't. See. Anything. Special.

"Every time I hear of people who've been somehow affected by me, the very first thing that enters my mind is doubt. It has to be some strange type of coincidence. It's happenstance, that's all. How could it not be?"

I see Naomi standing by one of the auditorium walls and I smile.

"Since all of this happened, I have seen people who are so sad and lost, looking for something to believe in, and desperately hoping it might be me, or hating me because I, in some way threaten something they already have found that hope in. I wish I could be something inspirational for people, I really do, but on the flip side of that I-Ching coin, if I happen to be that for anyone out there, thank you, but you should probably keep looking for something more substantial.

"So am I a fake? Maybe Valarie can help us find that out? Would you help me do that Valarie?"

There's applause and Valarie says she will help.

"What I would like to do, is see if we might be able to help someone here today. Is there anyone here who has some type of handicap? It would be great if this person is someone who most of you know, or have seen around campus, so you know they're not a plant by me, and more importantly, so that you might be able to talk to them and ask them about the experience once I'm gone. Is there anyone here who fits that description?'

There is some finger pointing, and a little applause. A woman of maybe twenty stands up from about the fifth row. I can see that she has to use crutches to walk and I would guess she has some type of cerebral palsy, but I can't be sure. She makes her way to the stage and the applause grows much louder. It's easy to see that she is known by most of the students here and that she's loved by the majority of them. That should make this easier.

The same man who brought out a chair for Valarie manifests another one for the woman walking to the stage, and before I know it, I'm the creamy delicious center of a co-ed sandwich. The right leg of our new addition looks to be a few inches shorter than her left, and it's twisted at the knee quite badly. She has a smile on her face though, as she climbs on the stage. She raises one crutch over her head for the audience in an act of triumph, and I like this woman instantly. Her smile is one of the most disarming things I've seen. People only get smiles like that after years of practice.

"Hi. I'm Ben" I say and when my hand touches hers, I swear her crooked knee straightens just a little bit.

"I'm Anna," she says, and when I ask her how she ended up this way, she tells me she slipped on a banana. Anna banana. Now I love this girl. She tells us how she does, in fact, have cerebral palsy and like all people who have this disease, she was born this way. I ask if she happens to know any of the people here and there are tons of cheers and applause. When I ask if we have ever met, she tells us she had never even heard of me before, but her roommate told her about the event and she needed the extra credit.

I ask the audience if some of them will tell us how they know Anna, and the microphone is passed around. One girl says she's been a friend of Anna's since high school and also gives me a half joking warning that if I do anything to hurt Anna, she will hunt me down and make me regret it. I confirm that Anna has had this condition the entire time the girl has known her. A football player tells how Anna interviewed him for the college newspaper two years ago, and he had to meet her in the journalism department because of Anna's difficulty in walking across campus, and how she had the crutches back then. One thing that's crystal clear, without my even having to ask it, is that Anna is living a pretty full life and a lot of people here care about her.

"What I would like to try to do is see if instead of directly healing Anna by touching her, if I can touch someone else who happened to be touching her. I would like to see if whatever is happening can pass through another person like an electrical current."

Naomi looks at me questioningly, because I've never tried anything like this let alone in a very public forum.

"What I'm hoping is, that the person in the middle might feel something, and then be able to share with us what the experience was like. In fact, if you're all willing, what if we make a human chain with everyone here in the audience? Would you like to take part in an experiment with me to see if we can't possibly do something for Anna here?"

The applause and cheers are almost deafening, and Naomi starts checking out where the exits are in case we need to make a fast escape.

ADD INF: I have absolutely no idea what I'm doing.

"Please take a moment and introduce yourselves to the people around you, because I'm going to be asking you to hold hands. Also, I think it's odd how we as a species, will sit in a seat next to someone for an hour or two and not say hello to each other. Who knows? Maybe the stranger next to you might become important in your lives somehow." I ask the front row to stand up and form a line up onto the stage towards Anna, and then I take Valarie with me, and head toward the back of the auditorium. The audience links hands with those next to them reaching across the isles when they have to and the people on the ends either reach in front of them or behind them and soon everyone is connected. Anna sits on the stage not quite knowing how to feel about all of this, and I really hope I don't let her down.

Valarie is on one end of the chain, with Anna on the other end. All I have to do is reach out and take Valarie's hand to connect us all.

I ask the audience to take a few moments to close their eyes and visualize on Anna being cured from her Cerebral Palsy, to desire for Anna living a long, healthy, and happy life. I explain how when I say the word 'go' I will take Valarie's hand completing the chain and we all will be connected. I ask the audience to watch Anna in that moment, and to pay attention to what they are experiencing.

The auditorium becomes pin dropping quiet as people think their happy thoughts about Anna. Naomi takes this moment to mouth the words 'what are you doing?' to me. I make a V with my good hand, point it to my eyes, and then to my chest, telling her to keep her eyes on me. On the stage I see the slightest twitch in Anna's right leg.

"Go!" I yell, and Valarie reaches out her hand towards me. When I don't take it she looks at me, and I put my hands in my pockets, shake my head, and point to the stage. Anna very slowly stands up. It's like watching one of those stress balls return to its natural state after being squished. The leg that was once so bent and misshapen seems to grow muscles it had previously been denied. There's a moment where it appears she's experiencing a little dizziness or nausea or something, but it passes quickly. There are tears streaming down her face, and as I look around the auditorium, there are more than a few tears on the faces of the people here. Anna is going to be just fine and everybody here knows it.

Valarie looks at me and her confusion is almost palatable. I lean in close and kiss her on the cheek.

"You asked the question, so you get to know the truth. I don't think any of this is me, Valarie. I think it's you" I say and wave my hand across the audience. Naomi takes my hand and we quietly exit the back of the auditorium, leaving the students with their newly healed friend.

ADD INF: Anna was completely cured. Everyone in the auditorium got straight A's that semester and went on to live long and happy lives.

♥

After taking off my shoes and arguing with a TSA agent about the amount of shampoo I'm allowed in my carry-on bag, I board a flight for New York, so I can be on Letterman. The Letterman people bought me a first class ticket, which for some reason makes me feel uncomfortable flying like that. I'm not a high maintenance person, and I often feel stupid when the flight attendant offers me something and I have absolutely no idea what I'm supposed to do with it. Like those little hot towels, what am I supposed to do with this? Rub one out?

I shuffle down the aisle to row 4, and sitting in the window seat of my row, in the very seat next to mine, is no other than Darla Crane.

I know I've been name dropping a lot in this book, and I understand it makes me sound like a schmuk (a new word a learned from my Jewish friends). I'm not doing it to brag or make me seem cool. I've just had the opportunity to meet some famous people, and if I say Brad Pitt, you know who that is as opposed to me telling you about Tom the guy from Tech-Support who I helped quit smoking. However, when it comes to Darla Crane, her name is truly worth dropping.

Now I'm sure that most of you out there have no idea who Darla is, because life is full of all kinds of cruelty. But for those of you who do, the name alone is enough for a semi.

Some people might label Darla as a porn star, and yes, she has done a few of those movies, but her true fame lies in the bondage and S&M arena. Darla is *the* bondage and force fantasy model. Furthermore, she is the type of woman men wish God would make a little more often. She has this long, red hair that goes on forever, these pale, blue eyes that look amazing behind a ball gag. But her claim to fame are the naughty mints. My God, if I could only be a Sweater Sherpa on the mounds of Ms. Crane. Huge breast that put all others to shame. Now stay with me because I'm not talking about those fake and ridiculously massive silicone pouches of Daphne Rosen, just perfect and pure, as God intended them to be.

Darla looks up and clearly recognizes me because I've been in the media a lot lately. She blushes a little and I can see she is dreading spending the next eight hours sitting next to the religious nut who is probably going to tell her how her life is a waste and she can expect eternal damnation. However, at some point after takeoff, we both will be receiving those little bags of about five peanuts so maybe it might all be worth it.

I sit down next to her, trying to hide the raging wood that I've developed, and try to repress all of the fantasies I've had involving her and a Velcro wall.

We sit there awkwardly during takeoff, pretending

we don't know who the other is when I realize I could be missing a once in a lifetime opportunity here, and possibly a mile high experience by simply being shy.

I introduce myself, and when I tell her I'm a big fan, she seems genuinely surprised. When I confess that I used to be a member of her website, the walls come down, and we have a great conversation. She tells me how she read about me in the papers and saw an interview I did on MTV.

She asks me about the bandages on my hand, and I try to explain my Uno card game. When she suggests that I must like it rough, I almost cum right there.

ADD INF: Darla is wearing a low cut shirt that shows cleavage you could probably park a bicycle in.

She asks me if I think what she does for a living is wrong.

Porn, and the sex market is a multi-billion dollar a year industry. If you can run an internet search on something, chances are you will find some type of porn linked to it. Clowns, anime, Pez dispensers, marshmallow Peeps, boy, girl, young, old, light, dark, fetish, hardcore. It's all there. If it exists, somebody, somewhere is getting off on it. You would think someone would build a big amusement park, with branches on each coast, based on our sexual desires and inadequacies. Some place with a fun house that has a hall of mirrors, which leads to a giant clitoris, and a gift shop selling dildos with more veins than Iggy Pop's forearm. A place where everyone could fuck a Scarlett Johansson or a George Clooney or an Elmo. A place where they sell hats with handlebars instead of mouse ears.

Other countries have places like this, and they're not declaring war on everybody. Amsterdam has a very low hate crime rate of occurrence. London has the Goth clubs. Bangkok has…well everything. But hatred seems pretty low in these places. While, here in America, people are so wound up and pissed off that you have to wear body armor to church. All of this is happening every day and Darla asks me if what she is doing is wrong.

You know, I think if they could label loneliness as an actual disease, they would find the death rate to be higher than Cancer and Heart conditions combined.

I tell her more people should be thankful for women like her. I tell her she should be wearing a cape, but then remember that she already did that in some superhero sex video.

I ask her if she knows about my healing power of touch. Of course, everyone knows about this by now so she says yes. I ask what she thinks would happen if we could somehow combine the power of her breasts with the power in my hands. She tells me that there's only one way to find out.

ADD INF: I'm not allowed to fly Delta airlines ever again.

ADD INF: It was totally worth it.

♥

I realize at some point with my new found savior status, I've really neglected my previous life. I really didn't want to be one of those people who let a little bit of fame go to their heads and forget about who they used to be, so I pull some strings, and have Damon and Mr. Ferninni flown out for a weekend in Barcelona, where a group of scientist are testing a theory that has something to do with string theory, which I probably wouldn't be able to understand even if there wasn't a language barrier between us.

There is a theory, that by studying the writings which are contained within the double helix of my DNA, scientists might be able to show how far we currently are in our evolutionary growth. It has something to do with mapping the human genome code. If we are merely at a momentary pause in our evolutionary process, then what could this mean for the mapping process? Could this further our mapping abilities or shut them down all together?

I have no idea what half of that stuff even means.

All I know, is I get to hang out in Spain with some of my closest friends.

When I see my boss, he tells me that people have been coming to the candy factory in droves trying to get some of the jelly beans that I, myself, have buffed. He also tells me he has now made a special type of gumball that has writings on the inside shell, kind of like a fortune gumball. He brings me a bag of the new product and I give one to Naomi and John.

Naomi's says something about keeping your feet dry and John's is too difficult to read. Mr. Ferninni tells me it's a pretty big problem with the design, but that doesn't stop people from buying them by the case.

Damon informs me that he gets a lot of lookiloos in his comic shop asking about me, but very few of them actually buy anything.

We tour the Sargada Familia and the Picasso museum and later in the evening we all dine on some really great paella. It's so wonderful to be with them again, and to let them get to know Naomi better. My ex really did a number on me when she cheated, and I wasn't really sure how I was going to pick myself up after the cape fucker, but now I seem to have turned a corner and I'm developing something special with Naomi that I never had with my ex.

After a while it's painfully obvious Damon is more than a little miffed with me. At first I sum it up to schatenfreud, but then I try to put myself in his place. Not even a year ago, I was still bumming money off him to buy Slurpee's.

As we walk through the streets, I get him to hang back with me a little bit, and I try to explain. I tell him it's like when Han Solo picked up the light saber in *Empire* to cut open the Taun-Taun. Yeah, it was cool, but everyone knew Han was no Jedi.

I tell him it's just like how Barry Allen was struck by lightning and became The Flash or how Kyle Rayner was blindly chosen to wield the Green Lantern Power ring.

I tell him it could have happened to anybody and that if I hadn't flown out to Utah for this bone marrow thing, nobody would have even known about it, and I might still have a hand instead of stainless steel hooks.

He tells me things are cool, and he even brought me some new graphic novels to check out.

But, I'm not so sure.

♥

It's about this time in our tale that it becomes necessary to talk about Wendell McNikol. Now, Wendell's not really a bad guy although I'm sure some of you might paint him to be the villain of this story, but it's just not the case. Wendell is a religious fanatic. Of which religion I'm not going to say because, let's face it, they all have more than one, and besides, pointing a finger at his religion really isn't the point of this book, and wouldn't change the outcome anyway.

However, to be able to understand Wendell, we need to understand a little bit about the human condition. So, let me sprinkle some existential fairy dust here. The two most difficult things for the human mind to grasp are the concepts of infinity and nothingness. Think about this and you'll see what I mean. Put aside all of your thoughts about what happens to us when we die for a second, you can come back to them later if you choose.

Try to wrap your imagination around the concept that when we die, that's it for us. No afterlife. No reincarnation. No Heaven. No Hell.

We just cease to be.

Pretty scary huh? A-boogha-boogha.

Nobody wants to believe that. Even the people who do believe this don't want to. So we look for things to ease our mind. Things like the promise of a thousand virgins or judgment day or eternal salvation or being reborn as someone else. Anything has got to be better than the alternative, right?

So, if you were to find something as powerful as a religious belief to take away the fear of nothingness, you would probably take it. Now, imagine finding it, investing a few years of your life following that philosophy, and suddenly someone shows up with evidence that might prove your theory wrong. What would you do?

Well, for Wendell, this meant following me to places where I would be appearing publicly and staging protests. It meant sending hate mail. It meant setting up blogs and web sites all claiming I was an abomination, but more importantly, wrong. It meant sitting outside my hotel rooms with a cell phone scanner.

Some other things it meant for Wendell, was losing a wife of thirty three years because of his obsession with me. It meant restraining orders and jail time on more than one occasion. It meant losing a government job and pension. Eventually it led to him lying in the back of his pickup truck on one of those foam mats campers use to sleep on, looking through a scope at my chest, while his finger slowly applied pressure to a trigger.

It meant putting a 30.06 round into my body.

♥

Probably one of the safest things about superheroes and possibly the most appealing is the big logo they all seem to have on their chest telling everyone who they are. The uniform is important. Even in the comics where they don't wear the spandex, the heroes and often the villains, have their standard thing they always wear which sets them apart from the normal people. John Constantine has his tan trench coat. The Minutemen have their reservoir dogs' black suit and ties. Jonah Hex has his facial scars. Even by not donning bright spandex, they still end up making a fashion statement.

That's important. When your house is on fire and about to collapse on you, then you suddenly see the big red and yellow 'S' and you know everything is going to be ok. I think that might be why pictures of Jesus all look the same. You see the beard and the hair and you know who he is, just like seeing Constantine with his trench and cigs. Buddha is the same way, the little fat dude sitting on the ground.

ADD INF: The little fat dude really isn't the Buddha, I don't think a lot of people realize that.

I wish I had a symbol.

♥

If you ever debate theology for longer than ten minutes, you come across the presence of evil argument. Basically it goes like this: If God is purely a righteous entity, then how come evil exists? The two main arguments are that: (1) God is not a purely righteous entity and the evil that exists in the world is just an extension of the evil that exists in God. Or (2) God is not all powerful and therefore unable to prevent the existence of evil.

I am here to tell you that evil exists in the world. And I'm not talking about Wendell or the others who have tried to kill me...they were just people who became a little confused or lost, and who among us hasn't been there at least once in our life. No, I am talking about tangible, palatable, evil that will make you wonder why Noah ever built the ark in the first place.

I'm talking about Lawyers.

My father once told me to avoid any litigious situation like it was the plague. It was the best advice he ever gave me. I had some people around me who were wise enough to get me some protective legal counsel when things started to get out of control. Lawyers who protected my image...which I can't even type without getting a bad taste in my mouth, and lawyers who tried to protect me when some newspaper would misquote me or when someone was looking to extort money from me.

ADD INF: The savior gig pays shit in case you were planning anything.

I always looked upon lawyers as a necessary evil, but it wasn't until they started suing me for allowing evil to exist, that I came to realize just what a wretched hive of scum and villainy they are.

Only a lawyer will tear off your dick, anally rape you with it, then give you a Dirty Sanchez the whole time saying 'quit hitting yourself, quit hitting yourself'.

Let me explain, just in case some of you haven't seen the video.

While I was in Japan visiting some Zen monks, there was a horrible earthquake which wiped out a large area of the country. As if that weren't bad enough, the quake caused a massive tsunami which did damage on a scale that was previously unimaginable. It was easily one of the most horrific things in human history, and by far the worst thing I have ever seen and for those who were affected, 'sorry' is just woefully inadequate.

Before the quake hit, a Japanese television crew had accompanied me to A Zen monastery to see in the monks could create a mental vibration that would match the vibration my body naturally produced. The hope being, if they could match it, they might be able to channel some of the healing abilities I seemed to possess. It was an experiment that was never completed.

When the quake hit, chaos ensued, which I'm sure I don't need to explain. Luckily for me and the monks, the monastery was pretty high in the Nagano Mountains and somewhat isolated, so almost all of the destruction missed us.

But we could feel it.

Once we were outside, the television cameras

captured actual footage of the tectonic plates shifting beneath us. It was terrifying to be there, and honestly, if Naomi wasn't with me, I'm sure I would have suffered from some post traumatic breakdown.

This was when the video you probably saw happened.

I had never been in an earthquake before, and truth being told I get a little motion sickness. I can't stand roller coasters. Nor can I read in a moving car without getting nauseous.

As you probably remember from grade school, when earthquakes happen they don't happen all at once. There are these fragmented tremors that follow called aftershocks. Usually the aftershocks are smaller than the initial quake, at least I think so, but I'm not a geologist.

I'm utterly freaked out and literally shaken a bit at this point so…I threw up. That's ALL that happened. I threw up.

However, that one moment of nausea that just happened to be caught on tape was the source of more litigation than anything since the holocaust.

ADD-INF: Unless you're an experienced drunk, most people, when they violently vomit will drop to their hands and knees.

I dropped to the ground and began to whistle beef. I was doing the techno-color yawn. I was so sick, I swear I was trying to turn myself inside out in some way. However, by some strange random happenstance of fate, in the same instant I placed my hand upon the ground to steady myself, the tremors stopped.

Let's be very clear about this here. I had nothing to do with the earthquake and I surely didn't have anything to do with it stopping. Not a thing.

As I'm sure you know, we live in an age where viral images spread throughout the world very quickly thanks to Facebook, You-tube and all the others. The news footage of my throwing up is one of the most watched videos in our history. Every frame of it has been broken down and analyzed from film students, conspiracy nuts, and anyone else with a few free minutes to kill at a computer. Like some strange Rorschach test, people seem to see whatever they want in that video. The only thing I can think of when I see it is that's an awful lot of soba noodles coming out of me.

The thing that makes me really sad about the video, is how it came to overshadow the real tragedy the quake and tsunami caused. Nobody seemed to be paying attention to the actual devastation. It was like how when Janet Jackson flashed her naughty mint during the Super Bowl and people overlooked how it was one of the best Super Bowl games in history. It's almost like the hype of the media machine produced some kind of Jedi mind trick that made us question if these really were the droids we were looking for.

♥

When the first law suit came in, I completely ignored it. My legal team (yes, I had one I'm embarrassed to say) told me I had nothing to worry about. When the suits reached the triple digits, we knew we had a problem.

The law suits all basically stated, since I had "stopped" the earthquake with my super-cool-touch-of-planetary-stabilization-powers, then I was therefore responsible for not stopping the main quake that had caused so much carnage in the first place. It didn't matter I was over one hundred miles away from the quakes center when it happened, or that I had no prior evidence the quake was coming.

I was the messiah after all.

Wrongful deaths, property damage, emotional suffering, negligent miracle performance. You name it…I was sued for it.

I know I shouldn't take any of this personally.

When tragedy hits us we all look for something to blame. But these attacks really hurt my feel bads. I mean I didn't sue any of the people who ripped my body to shreds like it was a giant string cheese after I was crucified. Why were these people suing me?

♥

The first lawsuit I lost didn't come from anyone who was actually hurt in the quake, but rather from a big business mogul. One of the major oil companies sued me because the tsunami interrupted their shipping and drilling schedules for a few days, hence causing them a kazillion dollars in profit. The verdict ordered me to pay 278 million dollars, of which I had about $3.75. I honestly could do nothing but laugh when I was ordered to pay. Apparently if a Judge says you are supposed to pay a fine, money will just magically appear. It doesn't matter that most people will never make $278 million in their lifetime. It didn't matter my current job only pays me around thirteen dollars an hour and I've been forced to cut my hours to almost nothing because of all the savior crap everyone asks me to do. Someone needed someone to blame and I happened to fit the bill.

What I didn't really understand at the time, was that this big oil suit would establish something called precedence. This opened up the floodgates, and soon other rulings began to come in against me.

A stock broking company sued me because the market happened to dip particularly bad one day, and with my super awareness, I should have warned people the flux was going to occur. I was found guilty for failing to warn people about something I had no way of knowing would happen and is something of a regular occurrence.

Of course, I had no way of paying these outrageous fees the courts were ordering me to pay. Jelly bean buffers really don't make much money. To make matters worse, a few years before this craziness manifested into my life, some guy tried to sell one of his kidneys on EBay which the government found to be illegal. This set the precedence that prevented my making any money off of the words within my bones, or whatever healing powers I might actually possess. Truth be told, I wouldn't have accepted money anyway. Not out of any ethical guidelines, mind you, I could never accept money, because there is a very large part of me that really feels like this is all a strange coincidence and that I have absolutely no powers at all.

   When I had no way of paying, the courts did the only thing they felt they could do. They imprisoned me.

EERHT

TONGLEN MEDITATION IN THE GARDEN OF GETHSEMANE

> "You should reach the limits of virtue before you cross the thresholds of death."
> -The Book of Benjamin
> Inside left brachial artery

The world continued to revolve while I was incarcerated. Most events happened on the outside and I didn't really have much to do with any of them, but it's important to note them all for this record to be accurate and complete.

A pharmaceutical lab in Belgium somehow got a sample of my DNA. This really isn't surprising, and it probably wasn't very difficult for them to acquire, because people from all over the globe were examining parts of me or running thousands of tests I knew nothing about.

Think of Henrietta Lacks and the HELA cells, it's the same type of thing.

I was somewhat ok with all of this, because I've had various medical professionals running tests on my body all my life. The thing I found somewhat creepy was that quite a bit of the samples collected went 'missing'. When my hand was cut off, the middle bone of the index finger was stolen and worn around the neck of man who truly believed I am the second coming of Jesus. He still wears it to this day.

Others wore samples of my blood in vials around their necks, or kept napkins I might have wiped my mouth with, in plastic bags. I don't understand the attraction for doing something like this, although if Jessica Biel ever let me sleep with her, I probably would never wash my junk again.

One of those things I honestly believe to be coincidence, but others might believe to be something more was that everyone who carried some piece of my DNA with them led very long and happy lives. Their marriages were successful, they were financially stable, they had no health problems, and all of them gave significantly to their community in some way or another.

This laboratory in Belgium was called The Proximus Project, and they had the idea that if their scientists could decipher the words, and interpret their meanings before anyone else did, then maybe this information would give them an advantage in the corporate world. Possibly they could patent something that came from me, or if there were any predictions that might be used to invest in the right stocks, or if some new pharmaceutical product could be made from my samples, they wanted to be the ones to discover it.

The Proximus Project decided the best way to achieve their goals was to clone me.

Since there are no laws regarding the rights of clones in Belgium, they could make an infinite number of me and then hundreds of scientists could simultaneously dissect and analyze me, therefore rapidly speeding up the discovery process.

Since there is no way to clone a fully grown adult, about a year after the project started, there were all these little me's being born to surrogate mothers. Almost every one of these infants were slaughtered and dissected shortly after their births.

Experiments were run on everything you could imagine; stem cells, mitochondria, bone marrow, DNA fragmentation, epithelium tissue, and everything else you can find in an Anatomy textbook glossary.

ADD INF: Not one clone made from my cells possessed the writings, nor did any of them have a backwards heart.

So if it makes you feel any better, you didn't just kill me once. You murdered me exactly 113,798 times.

♥

Something else which happened while I was in prison was that John really started to become the person who I'm sure you all see in your mind when you think of him. Because of John's efforts, I was only in jail for months instead on the massive amount of years I was originally sentenced to.

The amount of people who came forward to protest when I was sentenced, completely floored me. I have never had people (most of whom were strangers) stand up for me in the way you people did. It's almost enough to make up for that whole crucifixion thing, but not quite. I joke, but it's something I take seriously. Almost everyone I met came to me with open arms and a healthy sense of curiosity. It was a very small percentage that were evil and mean.

John began talking to the media about my case and his voice snowballed into hundreds of thousands, which were impossible to ignore. Most everybody saw the conviction for exactly what it was; an attempt by corporate America to screw ordinary citizens out of even more money. The oil companies faced their lowest public opinion ratings yet. It was even lower than the BP oil spill or the Exxon Valdez incidents. John, with Naomi's help I'm sure, began staging protest at all the big oil companies and on Wall Street. So many people showed up at the Wall Street protest that the National Guard had to be called in, and New York City fell under a state of marshal law for the first time in history.

Big oil tried to fight back at the gas pumps, but even lowering the cost of gas to less than two dollars a gallon in some places didn't seem to be helping them with their cause at all.

For one of the first times in history, people stopped driving and quit buying from the companies who sued me for losses. When the president passed a bill, giving large corporation's tax breaks and bail out money to ease the burden, people went ape shit. So, while I was learning how to make toilet bowl alcohol and Christmas tree shivs, John was rallying a planet to get me out of the big house. In those days, he was the person he had hoped to be. He was having a huge positive impact on the planet and people were joining him.

The first thing he did for my release was to set up a Facebook page, which had a link so that every time someone would 'like' my page, congress would get an email asking them to set me free. Gmail actually asked John to take down the page because it kept crashing their systems. People could post on the wall, but so many people were posting, it was almost impossible to actually read anything. The posts would just scroll across the wall like movie credits. However, this spawned several other groups who had similar effects. My Twitter account had over a million followers, even though I have never sent a tweet in my life. There were websites selling t-shirts to pay for lawyer fees, Boston had a Run for Freedom 5K that circled around the commons, PayPal had an account set up in my name, but I was executed before I ever got to see how much people donated to it. Australia, honest to God, set up a kangaroo race with monkey jockeys. Someone sent me a video of it and it has to be one of the funniest things I've ever seen in my lifetime. It also raised a quarter of a million dollars.

Then, there were the groups of people who had supposedly been helped by me. There were so many of these claims, that there was no possible way I could have worked with each one individually. If some of these were people who had encountered me by pure happenstance, I can't say. Many of these individuals made the argument that the money I had saved the government in health care and insurance money far outweighed the amount corporations were claiming to have lost by my failure to stop an 8.5 earthquake.

There is something to be said about those who reach out to you when you're struggling with something. I received so many letters and cards and care packages and blessings while I was in prison that the mail center just had to start distributing the candy and snacks I received to the other inmates. This made me incredibly popular on the inside. You would be surprised the amount of protection you can buy for a *Butterfinger*.

Somewhere in this timeframe, John started to preach about me. Like all things it started slow and nobody paid much attention to it at first. Talk shows and news programs would have him on because my incarceration was the new buzz item the media couldn't let go of no matter how much I might have wanted them to. I understand why the media and people interviewing John would ask him such deep questions, hearing a three year old philosophize about anything can be interesting, but with John it was almost hypnotizing. He developed this way of stringing words together that made people feel completely at ease with him. The charisma and logic he could produce was staggering. He would be invited to these debates all over the world and it was completely different than the ones you usually see, where the speakers just attack one another and try to make each other look bad.

John had the way of genuinely hearing everybody, and making them feel like they were exactly right in everything they were saying. He just could also make them feel open to incorporating his theories into theirs as well. He made people feel like they were talking to him about the same thing no matter what the subject topic.

It should be stated that I never once told him anything to say. He came up with his beliefs completely on his own. That being said, I really can't say I disagree with anything he preached. I just doubt I had anything to do with it.

This was probably around the time Wendell McNikol started to pay attention. Remember Wendell, that guy a few pages back, sitting in the bed of his truck with a high powered rifle?

There seems to be something ingrained into our human nature that when we see something we don't fully understand and are maybe even a little afraid of, we want to destroy that thing. This is especially true for people who suggest the world has the potential of becoming a better place. Gandhi, King, Lincoln, Copernicus just to name a few. Take a look through history at the people who have pioneered for change and the betterment of mankind, almost all have been killed. What does this say about us as a species? Why do we kill the very ones who are trying to lift us up?

Wendell had this reaction to John.

We will come back to Wendell, but please remember he is hiding offstage, waiting to make his entrance.

John was booked as a guest on the *David Letterman* show, because he was becoming something of a celebrity in his own way. Naomi and John made the trip to New York while I was actually doing a stint in solitary confinement, but more about that later, I didn't even know the Letterman incident happened until I was released.

John walked onto the studio set wearing a Spiderman T-shirt and a pair of neon green Chuck Taylors. When he sat in the chair next to Dave, he became the youngest person ever to appear on the show alone.

"How come that man doesn't have any hair?" Were the first words out of John's mouth as he pointed to Paul Shaffer and his band. There is a lot of laughter from the audience, and from that moment on John had everyone eating out of his hands.

David asks John about the bone marrow transplant and if there's any lingering health issues John has had to deal with.

"I feel better than I have in my entire life, Dave, but since I'm only three, that's probably not saying much. I haven't really racked up tons of life experiences, yet." I can imagine Naomi sitting back in the green room worried about John and what might happen to him on the show, as well as being worried about me and what might happen to me in jail.

"What's that?" John asks, pointing to the cameras. Dave explains it to him and tells him the one with the red light on top is the one he should be looking at. John starts playing a game with the camera men where he would look directly into a camera until the red light would go on then he would look at another camera making them chase him for his facial shots.

"So, do you like Spiderman?" Dave asks.

"I like the character, but he's not really scientifically accurate." The audience chuckles, and Dave encouraged John to explain.

"Well for one thing, if he really had spider powers, his webs would probably come out of his bum instead of his wrists." This is one thing that I actually *had* told John over and X-box game late one night. The one piece of information my prophet gets right had to do with things coming out of a fictional characters ass.

"Can my mom see me right now?"

"Well, I guess she can if she's watching from the green room."

"Hi Mom!" John stands on his chair and looks for the camera with the red light on and then waves his hand so hard it looks like it might just fly of the end of his arm and hurt someone. "Why is it called a green room?"

"Well, that's where the people wait before they

come out here." Dave says.

"But, it's not green."

"No, I suppose it's not."

"Then you shouldn't call it a green room?"

"What do you think we should call it?" Dave asks. John thinks about it for a second or two and then spots the microphones hanging from the ceiling.

"What's that?" He asks.

After his segment, but before the stupid pet tricks bit, one of those Kardashian girls who no one really understands why she's famous, came out as a guest of the show. John slid over to the next chair down from David's desk as the media leach came out from behind the blue curtain. It was impossible not to notice the florescent pink cast she had on one leg or the crutches she limped out on. The cast was, of course, the first thing Dave asked about, and she said she had fallen down some stairs exiting a club and had broken both the bones in her lower leg. She whined that she had actually considered not doing *The Late Show*, because the break had just happened two days ago, and it still hurt quite a bit to walk on it.

John continues to look at the microphones above him and then looks at the pink cast like he's just noticing it for the first time. With a touch that looks as causal and as quick as someone touching an oven burner to see if it's still hot, John touches the Kardashian.

She turns to John, and starts to say hello, but stops before any words escape her lips. John is back to playing the game with the camera lights, and the pause is almost palatable before Dave asks the young lady if she's ok.

"What did you just do to me?" She asks John.

"I fixed your leg," he says, and then points to a camera and tells the Kardashian she should be looking at the one with the red light on top.

"You fixed her leg?" Dave asks.

"Yeah. It should be better now. When do the

animals come out and do their tricks?" John says nonchalantly. The show goes to a commercial and a paramedic who works for the show rushes out and starts looking at the pink cast.

"Get it off of me. I want this off of me right now, please." The diva says, as the paramedic warns her against this and the show's producers look like they want to kill him on the spot. The camera's never stop rolling. Soon, a dremel is produced and the cast is off. The paramedic examines her foot and says it looks fine. He admits that he has no way of knowing without an x-ray, but everything seems to be ok.

The Kardashian rubs her calf and shin and then timidly stands up. She takes a few gentle steps and looks like someone who is trying to be quiet by walking tippy toes, and then she begins to cry. Doctors would later find out the leg had been completely healed. There wasn't even any scar tissue from the break on the bones.

"How did you do that?" Dave asks, once everyone is back in their chairs.

"I can do it because I believed in Ben," he says in the exact same tone he used when I had asked him why he made his Dr. Octopus arms so detailed. Like he was a little surprised at how dumb we all are.

"Did you know they call it a green room even though it's not really green?"

♥

Arrhythmia, pulse, throb, tachycardia, ventricular fibrillation, holter monitoring, cardiac catheterization, beta-blockers, quinidine, procainamide, murmurs, blood thinners, tetralogy of fallot, mitral valve prolapse, congenital (this word has the word 'genital' in it, snicker), pericarditis, atherosclerosis, edema, ablation, echocardiogram, diastolic pressure, aneurysm, flutter, infarction, pericardium, angioplasty, hibernating myocardium, annulus, ejection fraction, aortic insufficiency, intracardiac tumoratria, ventricles, endocarditis, atrial flutter, myxoma, atrioventricular node, bicuspid valves, holter monitors, bradycardia, cardiomyopathy, mitra valve disease, occlusion, palpitations, septum tears.

    Then there's me.
    Your heart beats BOOM.
    Mine beats MOOB.

♥

    Naomi came to visit often, and one of the most humiliating things I've ever experienced in my life was talking to her through the Plexiglas, while wearing handcuffs, and an orange jumpsuit. John refused to come see me, because according to him, only bad people were supposed to be in prison and if he came to see me, it would somehow be admitting it was ok I was incarcerated. I didn't mind though, between him and Damon, I think I received every comic book printed during that period.
    It was quite funny watching these very scary and dangerous criminals coming to my cell asking to read the new *X-men* or *Wonder Woman* (I honestly don't want to know what they did with the *Wonder Woman* comics, but they never seemed to make it back to my cell). I didn't really have many problems with the other inmates. They quickly found out I was getting all kinds of swag sent to me and I was willing to share. Cons love their sweets. I was well protected, especially if I happened to cure a kidney stone or take away some awful memory that haunted an inmate throughout their life.
    I never talked about Naomi to the other inmates, no matter how much I missed her.
    Before prison, there was this day Naomi and I were in Sudan trying to prevent the genocide in Darfur. I was feeling very overwhelmed, and entirely out of my element. It had all just become too much to deal with. There are all these things I'm supposed to be able to do and I have no

fucking idea how it works.

What if I did something wrong?

What if I could do more but I don't know it?

There was so much I wanted to do, so many children dying of malnutrition and violence, but it was a bigger problem than I could fix. I would make one child healthy and two others would die waiting in line to see me. Mothers who had no reason to hope for anything, were looking at me with belief and pleading in their eyes, as the Janjaweed soldiers, who weren't much older than the kids I was trying to help, pointed their rifles at us and waved their blood stained machetes.

I lost hope. If I was what the universe had chosen to save the world, than we were royally fucked, because I just flat out am not strong enough to carry all that hopelessness. I was pissed off at the entire situation I never asked to be a part of. As we were walking back to our campsite, I saw men pulling out boxes of Hefty trash bags, because the supply of body bags had long since run out. Kids who had never felt an orgasm, let alone love, were being buried in coffins with yellow twist ties.

"I don't want to do this anymore," I had said. Naomi thought I was talking about something that had to do with the camp we were in. Maybe I didn't want to sleep in a tent anymore or maybe I didn't want to drink the water that remained cloudy no matter how many times you filtered it.

"You don't want to do what anymore?" She had asked.

That was the first time in my life the words 'emotional breakdown' seemed to make sense. It was way too powerful and painful for me to verbalize. I had barely made it through the day and knew I didn't have it in me to relive it through conversation. Thankfully, Naomi didn't push. She just let me sit with my head in her lap and stroked my hair, telling me it would be ok. I'm fairly certain they teach women how to do this in that special meeting they all had to go to in junior high when their bodies began to change. Men have no idea how to pull this off. Damon would have called me a little bitch and told me to cowboy up.

Naomi knew exactly what I needed and gave it willingly. How many times in a person's life does something like that happen?

After we sat on the bed crying and holding each other in the hot desert heat, she did the only thing she could do to get me going again; she geeked out on me.

"A wise man once said that with great power comes great responsibility."

"I'm trying to take responsibility but…"

"Try? There is no try. Only doooo," she interrupted. I thought she had the worst Yoda impression in the history of man, but knew better than to say so. Besides, it would have just been me dodging the conversation. I tried to kiss her, but she pushed me away and continued.

"Listen, you were the one who took the red pill on this one. You could have just walked away when the doctors first discovered whatever the hell is going on inside of you. You didn't even have to go that far. You could have said 'no' when they asked you to help my son. For whatever reason, the power ring chose you. You are the one who exploded in front of the gamma bomb, you are the one bitten by the spider, you are the one who was shot here from another dying planet, and no matter how many times you fly around the earth backwards, that shit isn't going to change."

It's almost impossible to argue against the wisdom of Stan Lee and George Lucas (before he went crazy that is. I mean, Jesus, did you see *The Clone Wars*?) I truly loved the fact I had a woman in my life who knew enough about the world I lived in to throw this argument at me. The cape fucker with the green condom fetish never could have done it.

"I bet Gwen Stacy never had to put up with this crap," she had said.

Naomi can always make me smile, even in the abyss of prison.

The guard of the visiting room is named C.O. Despain. Despain hates my guts because he thinks I have an influence over the other prisoners. It's not true; it's just that mutual respect goes a very long way in this place. Despain also hates me, because one night he showed up to shift with one of the worst case of food poisoning I've ever seen. He spent most of the night in the monitor room hugging a plastic garbage can, but we could still hear him whistling beef down in the cell blocks. The barest minimum of his job required him to walk the hall of the block four times per shift, and the first time he tried, I honestly thought he was going to pass out. The second time he tried he took the plastic garbage can with him. As he walked passed my cell, I reached my hand through the bars and offered it to him palm up.

"Touch my hand," I said. It's very much against policy for a guard to do this. But I'm about as threatening looking as cotton ball and the other inmates on the block were watching Despain, probably in hopes that he would die.

"I'm not touching you," he said, and I could smell the vomit from his breath and the bucket.

"C.O. Despain, by my calculations, you've only been here three hours. Your shift isn't even half way over yet. Do you really want to spend the next five hours with your head in that bucket?"

"I'm still not touching you."

"I'm not asking you to hold hands or go steady or anything. Just touch it, like you're giving me five." I turned my hand palm down so he would be less worried about my possibly grabbing him. Some of the other inmates were starting to taunt him, and I could see a lot of hands holding mirrors sticking out of their cells hoping to see something happen.

Despain set the bucket down in the center of the block then took three somewhat shaky steps towards my cell. With one hand on his baton, he slapped the back of my hand much harder than he had to. Our contact was probably less than a quarter second, but that was all it took. The food poisoning was gone, and most of the color had returned to his face by the time he made it back to the monitor room. What I didn't know at the time, was Despain was also in the peak of a herpes outbreak that night and I cured him of venereal disease, too. I don't know if he somehow thought I was aware of his STD or why he would care if I did, but Despain's hate for me became almost palatable that night. You could almost see it seeping off of him in the way comic artists draw those black, wavy lines when they want to convey something stinks.

I'm polite to Despain. In fact, I'm polite to all the guards. However, since that day Despain always gives me a wide birth whenever I'm around. Maybe he thinks if I touch him again, I could bring his herpes back or something worse, like leprosy. Either that, or I was just the first genuine freak he had even encountered and he didn't know the protocol for how to behave.

He warns Naomi and me not to touch the glass, and that our conversation is being monitored and recorded. I thank him and as I'm pulling up my chair, I see Naomi give him a tiny wave. To my genuine surprise, Despain waves back and the corners of his mouth raise ever so slightly. It's hard not to smile when a pretty woman smiles and waves at you.

It's impossible not to feel humiliated wearing the shackles and orange jumpsuit. However I think Naomi knows on some instinctive level, that if she wants to be a part of my life, she had probably better get used to seeing me do stupid things. I pick up the phone and try not to think about why it might be sticky.

"How are you holding up?" She asks. For the most part I can handle it when things go wrong for me. I've had a lot of practice in that area. Today though, I feel like King of the Grumpy Asses, and I'm fully ready to throw myself one hell of a pity party. I know there are people on the outside working to get me out of this hell hole, but it all seemed so far off and the time in here passes so damn slowly. There is no peace in here whatsoever, I mean, I have a lot of people who would probably protect me because I'm their hookup for comic books and chocolate bars, but I'm 135 pounds of scrawny, whose sex appeal might start turning heads in here soon. I really don't want my teeth knocked out or for my anus to look like Dumbledore's sleeve. Knowing my luck, anally raping me will probably give you Jedi powers and a Green Lantern ring.

I tell Naomi I've been thinking of ways I might be able to financially hurt some of the companies who sued me. I figure if I'm going to do the time, then I sure as shit might as well commit the crime. Up until now, I've been trying to use my powers for good, and even though I've screwed up a time or two, I think I've been successful. If this is how the world is going to repay me for my gift, then maybe it was time to get all Magneto on the planet. Maybe it's time to rule instead of being led.

Why the hell not? It's not like the leaders of the world were doing a bang up job of saving us from each other. I've lost count of how many countries the United States is currently at war with. If I were in charge, maybe I could stop all the senseless fighting, and punish those who profit over war and the death of soldiers too young to legally buy a beer. Maybe it's time for us, as a planet, to stop fighting over the stupid things that are written in archaic books that are obsolete. So far, the words inside of me have yet to be used to hurt or oppress anyone (besides me that is), let's use the words as law and get everyone on the same page for the first time in history.

Not a single person has once asked me what I want to do with my new savior status. Maybe it's time to karmically bitch slap the world and lay down some fucking guidelines.

Naomi listens patiently, nodding here and there, and letting me get it out of my system then she asks me to place my head against the glass. Whenever I've done this in the past, she kisses the other side of the glass, and then we quickly separate before the guards can start yelling. I take a deep breath and lean my head against the Plexiglas, wondering if I will ever be able to actually feel the softness and warmth of Naomi's lips again.

There is a very loud slam as Naomi punches the Plexiglas as hard as she can, bouncing the plastic window off my forehead. As I rub the now forming goose egg, I can see an almost perfect print of her knuckles where she tried to hit me on the glass. She quickly holds her palms up to Despain, who just laughs and tells us he didn't see anything.

"What the hell was that for?" I ask.

"For stinking up the place with whiny bitch smell!" she yells.

Another inmate, a few booths down from us, looks at me then quickly looks away but not before I see the laughter trying to burst free from his body.

"Are you done?" Naomi asks.

"Yes. Sorry."

"Good. Because the one thing they've yet to find within your body is a bar code. You are not a product to be sold, you are not something to be owned, and you would look really stupid in a Magneto helmet."

That was a little harsh, but probably true.

"I'm getting really sick of hearing how you didn't

ask for any of this and how you're a victim in this whole thing. Do you know how many people would kill to be in your position? People who are dying for something, *anything* to happen in their lives? People whose existence seems so boring and trivial that they feel if they were to just disappear, no one would even notice? It's a lot higher number than you seem to remember and that's really sad, because it's not too long ago you were one of those people. Do you remember the time when some stupid girl, who was too dumb to know what she had, cheated on you and you thought it was the absolute worst thing that could happen to you?"

    I tried to say something, but the look she shot me through the Plexiglas made me think the better of it.

    "I remember sitting on my couch, rocking John as he lay slowly dying in my arms. I prayed and I prayed for something to help him. I was pissed off at how unfair the situation was, but I never lost hope or faith that he would somehow get better, that somehow my life would get better. Then you showed up.

    "We've never really talked about it, but I'm sure you probably said some very similar prayers before you came to Salt Lake. You wanted to be special and to be able to help people if you could. You wanted to matter. Which is beyond stupid, because you already were special, and you were already helping people? I'm not just talking about your backwards beating heart, I really doubt that had anything to do with you reaching out to a complete stranger and deciding to help us.

    "The problem with prayer, is that most people don't really understand how it works or what they really want out of life. If you pray to God to make you strong, he's not going to explode a Gamma bomb on you, or grant you mutant powers, although that's pretty damn close to what happened with you. What God is going to do if you pray for strength, is put you in situations and give you opportunities to *be* strong.

"While you and Damon were reading your comic books, dreaming about how great it would be to have powers, and to be a hero to someone, God was paying attention. You have been blessed so much because God actually listened to you and gave you what you wished for. It might not be exactly how you envisioned it, and it might be more than you can handle at times but tough shit. That's how God chose to bestow all of this on you. Now, I can understand why you're a little bit pissed off right now. What happened to you is *screwed*, but I'm not going to sit here and listen to you whine about how tough you have it when you actually have the power to do something about it. Stop being the guy who's drowning in a wading pool and STAND THE FUCK UP!"

I sit there feeling about at tall as *The Atom*. The absolute worst thing about when a woman yells at you, is most of the time they're right. I know our time is almost up and I don't want us to end our visit like this.

"What would you have me do?" I ask.

"Just ask yourself one question. Truly ask it and think on it for a while. Ask yourself if this is really the best you can do. If this *is* your best then that's great, but if it's not, and I think we both know it's not, then you need to ask yourself what your best would be like. What would happen if you really cut lose with your gift?"

Despain walks over and when Naomi waves to him, the smile is back on her face and I wonder how I ever got to be so lucky. That feeling lasted until I got about half way back to my cell. The feeling lasted up until an inmate shattered a light bulb filled with gasoline in my face and another one threw a lit match.

♥

It took me four days to regain consciousness. I had an intubation tube in to help me breathe, because my airway kept trying to swell shut. A doctor explained to me how I had inflicted some damage to myself trying to put myself out. I had run in to a wall and fallen down a flight of stairs, but much of the damage happened when I tried to put out the flames with my metal prosthetic hand. I had ruptured my right eye and lost my right ear.

The first time I saw my raw face, I thought I could probably pull off a pretty good *Deadpool* costume at Comic Con if I ever made it back.

I read a lot while I was in the infirmary; there really wasn't much else to do. There's only so much *SpongeBob* a person can watch before it starts to do damage. One book I read had quite an impact on me, which I will explain in a little bit. It was called *Comfortable with Uncertainty* by Pema Chodron. I didn't know what it was about, and truth be told, I picked it up from the prison library cart because it was a fairly small book, and I wasn't sure how bad my head would hurt from trying to read with only one eye.

The book is about a Buddhist meditation technique called Tonglen. The theory is fairly simple, just as our lungs convert oxygen to carbon dioxide, with Tonglen meditation, a person takes in the pain and suffering of whomever you're doing the meditation for, then converts it inside our body and exhales love, peace, and all kinds of warm fuzzies. It sounded good, but I really wasn't in the best mindset for it right then.

There wasn't a lot of pain, because in third degree burns the nerve endings are destroyed so they don't feel anything anymore. The radial burns hurt though, and it still hurt my throat and nose to breathe. Although that's not exactly true, my nose didn't hurt because I didn't have one anymore. The sinus cavity however, was quite painful as the air would pass through it.

Naomi wanted to see me, but I wouldn't allow it. I didn't want anyone to see me like this. I knew my self-imposed isolation couldn't last though, and one day a couple of guards snuck into the infirmary and snapped a few photos of my destroyed face, then sold them to the tabloids. This was how all my friends' first saw just how bad I was injured.

At one point the guards basically carried me through the block so the other prisoners could see I was still alive. There were rumors of prisoners rioting because of what had happened to me, but I believe this had more to do with their candy supply being cut off than it did with any type of loyalty to me. One of the Correction Officers told me that the two men who burned me had been torn apart in the exercise yard the day after my attack. When I asked him to explain, he said that they had *literally* been torn to pieces. He told me that it took them quite some time to die, and the amount of enjoyment the guard seemed to take from this chilling fact gave me the heebee geebees.

The prison understandably received a ton of flak from my supporters. Once the pictures went public, there were organized protests outside the front gates, and every news crew in the nation was asking to either interview me or someone from the prison staff. The prison was looking quite incompetent in the media, and a lot of the prison staff was staring to take it personally. I was told that once I was well enough to be discharged from the infirmary, I would be doing 40 days of solitary confinement.

I think the warden was hoping that if he could keep me quiet and out of the media for a little while, all of this might settle down, and he could go back to a somewhat normal work day. I also think a lot of this decision was made with the thought of my protection in mind. The rumors of riots were constant, and there were more than a few incidents in the yard that led me to have some roommates in the infirmary here and there.

The tube finally came out of my throat, and I was led to a room no bigger than a walk in closet to begin my stretch in solitary confinement.

I understood immediately why prisoners refer to

solitary as 'the hole'.

I've never felt so alone.

♥

I really wish I could have seen my friends during this time. From what I understand, everyone really stepped up and tried to help me. I believe that the people who show up when you're struggling will tell you who your friends really are better than anything. Their efforts to protect me and get me released are not forgotten.

♥

I knew I would be going into solitary confinement as soon as I was released from the hospital, so I did my best to mentally prepare for it. I would be lying if I said that there wasn't a small part of me that was actually looking forward to spending some quiet time alone, to mentally catch up with the Tilt-A-Whirl that had become my life. That feeling got me through about the first fifteen minutes.

Then I figured it was time to get started.

While I was lying in the hospital, trying to remember how to breathe on my own I thought about the things Naomi had said. I thought about them long and hard. The way I see it, I can either throw myself a ginormous pity party and continue to bitch and moan about how interesting my existence has become, or I could embrace it. I had been doing so much bitching lately, that people could probably see my vagina, and it was time to let that shit go.

I remember reading somewhere about the double slit experiment in quantum physics, the one that prove that an atoms behavior will change based upon how the observer expects it to react. I thought about the book I read on Tonglen meditation and wondered just how far I could take it. Could I still have an impact upon the world while being isolated in a prison cell? I had forty days with nothing else to do to find out.

I sat down in the middle of the tile room, and like Siddhartha, I made a commitment not to stand up again until I had caused an impact upon the world. If I was to spend forty days alone, it was going to mean something when it was over. I was a little worried, because I've really never tried to meditate before, and had no idea what I was doing, other than the instructions in the small book, but I also had been skateboarding with the Dalai Lama and how many people can say that. I had shaken hands and been blessed by pretty much every religious leader in the world, and I knew there were thousands of people on the outside who were wishing for my safety. If anyone should be able to do this, it should be me.

Why the fuck *not* me?

The concrete floor was cold, and I had the feeling that no matter how long I sat there it would still be cold when I stood up. There were no windows or televisions or internet or comic books or porn or smartphones or anything else to distract me. There was just a small slot in the door where the guards could check in on me and pass me my tray of food.

I thought about maybe rubbing one out just to clear my head and have one last shebang before getting busy, but the mood inside the room really didn't lend itself to sexual fantasies.

The book suggested having a mantra to focus on during the times when the mind would wander from the breath. I spent about an hour trying to think of a mantra that meant something to me and that would be worthy for what I was trying to do here.

Nothing came.

Then suddenly everything came. I was an ubergeek; I lived in the world of superheroes and science fiction. I had tons of mantras to choose from. Stick with what you already know when you can't find your way.

"In brightest day," I began in a whisper.

"In blackest night, no evil shall escape my sight. Let those who worship evil's might, beware my power; Green

Lantern's light."

Nothing happened, but when have you ever achieved something that really mattered on the very first try? I focused on my breath.

Pain in. Love out.

Over and over I did this. My mind wandered a lot more than I would care to admit, there is this Bugs Bunny cartoon where he's giving CPR to Elmer Fudd. Bugs grabs Elmer's feet and keeps saying, 'Out with the bad air. In with the good'. This image probably ran through my head for at least the time it would take to watch *the Lord of the Rings* trilogy; I'm talking the extended version, where the ending of the last movie lasted for most of 2003. I think some people missed Christmas that year because they were waiting for Peter Jackson to wrap things up.

I threw some Derrida at the Green Lantern Oath and deconstructed every word in my mind until I transformed it into my own personal maxim. The one line that kept screaming in my mind was 'beware my power'. Maybe the world has a reason to be afraid of me. The planet should beware my power, because I hadn't even really tried to use it yet and I was still changing the world.

Beware my power. Pain in. Love out.

ADD INF: I became very warm while doing this meditation. Sweat dripped down my back, but not my head, because the sweat glands there were now gone.

I realized that if I sold my power, I would never have to work again and could give Naomi and John the kind of life they deserved to live. I could have so much money, that the cape fucker would cry herself to sleep every single night because she was too stupid to stick by me. I could make Batman and Iron Man feel impoverished. I could have a butler, but not some old dude like Alfred or Jarvis, but someone like Jennifer Lawrence or Carrie Keagan who believed that the sun rose and set in my pants.

Maybe Sinestro and Magneto are right; the one with

the power should be the one who rules, and I am the one with the fucking power that the world should beware. I could be a God on this planet.

Heads of state would ask my permission before making decisions, because my finger would be hovering over something much more deadly than their missiles and biologicals. My face should be on T-shirts and why the *fuck* hasn't someone made an action figure out of me yet? That is just unacceptable.

Guys like Damon and me won't have to feel afraid to go to high school anymore. I would be what everyone on earth wanted to be. I would be the one that little kids write about when teachers ask them what they want to do when they grow up. It should be my face pressed into coins and printed onto bills. It should be me that the people pray to.

Then I remember another maxim from Green Lantern; Power corrupts. Absolute power corrupts absolutely

"But is that really the best you can do?" Naomi's voice asks from inside my head. For some reason that I can't explain, I reach out with my left hand and touch the cold cement of the floor around me. I take a few slow, deep breaths and let it go.

Beware my power. Pain in. Love out.

The heat returns and I try to become engulfed in it. I try to let it burn away all the fear and doubts I have inside of me. That stupid voice that's lived inside my head for as long as I can remember and the one that I've somehow convinced myself is me. I hate that voice. There are so many things that I didn't do simply because I was too afraid to even try. So many women I never asked out because I wasn't muscular or handsome enough. The voice that keeps telling me that all of this is simple coincidence, because there's no way that something this meaningful could revolve around me. Who am I to be a catalyst for something better than what we've been doing? Telling me that the only reason Naomi is with me is because I've helped her son.

I touch the floor again and an inferno inside my bones burns these fears away.

"Flame on," I say, and I swear the temperature in the room rises noticeably.

Just breathe. That's all there is to do in here. Breathe in oxygen, breathe out carbon dioxide. Breathe in death, breathe out life. Every breath changes the world.

I have absolutely no idea how long I've been in the hole. I'm sure it's been at least a few days, maybe a little more than a week, but it doesn't really matter. There are no windows to the outside, and the guards turn the lights on and off in strange, nonsystematic rhythms. When I'm not sitting on the toilet, eating or sleeping, I'm sitting on the floor, breathing in and breathing out.

The concrete floor is warm to the touch.

Thoughts of sex are probably the thing that distracts me the most. I think about how the number of women I've slept with had quadrupled since going to Utah. I playback every sensuous moment in my mind over and over again, women are another thing I could have more of if I put my mind to it. I have been with porn stars, 'A' list celebrities, supermodels and damn near every one I've set my mind to. What if I tried a little harder? Maybe it's time for a little payback. How many women in the world shit all over the nice guy, simply because they know he will take it? How many other guys did the cape fucker sleep with that I don't know about? Maybe I should look her up and try to emotionally abuse her for a bit

And not just the cape fucker either. Every woman who has looked down her nose at someone like me. Every single one of them who has let a guy buy them drinks all night long, let the man pay for all the dinners and tickets even though she has no intention of ever sleeping with him. They should all bow down to me and suck me off in the process. The philosopher Immanuel Kant said never to use someone as an end instead of a means. Fuck that and fuck them. I say, use them until they can't be used anymore. Fuck them all until the mere sight of a nice guy makes them cringe in fear, respect and desire.

But what about Naomi?

In no way have I been anything that resembles faithful to her. She never asks me about it, but I can see it in her eyes that she knows. She's probably the only woman in the world that I honestly want to be a better man for. She makes me a better man simply by being at my side. She doesn't try to fix me or make me her project. The only thing she's ever asked from me is the attempt to do better, to be more than I think I am. The best part is, that she makes me believe I can do it.

I breathe in, and I smell her skin in my nonexistent nose.

I breathe out and the water inside my toilet bowl begins to steam.

"Beware my power," I say

My left hand is closed so tightly that it almost looks like marble. I can feel my backwards pulse in my fingers, so like a lotus blossom rising out of the muck, I slowly open my hand. The crescent moons of my fingertips, form little red smiley faces in my palm. Again I touch the earth beneath me, and this time, it does begin to tremble at my touch. It's nothing like what happened in Japan, but the reinforced concrete walls groan, and a light stream of dust tries to fall onto my head.

Firefighters call it a flashover.

It's when the temperature inside a room becomes so high that *everything* inside the room burns. The force of the blast inside my cell blows out the non-load bearing walls, and several pieces of rock tumble into my cell from the floors above me.

Nothing touches me.

The flames lick my body like a thousand playful lovers incinerating my clothes and charring the floor around me. The alarms of the prison go off, and I can hear the confusion in the halls, as the guards and inmates try to figure out what has happened. I feel better than I ever have in my entire life. I can see the strings of energy that connect us to each other and to every living thing on the planet. I'm positive that I can pluck and strum these strings, and make music that would put Jimi Hendricks to shame. There are five colored strings of light coming from the fingertips of my left hand that extend beyond my vision. I take the prosthetic claw off my right stump, and a thick beam that almost looks like a white laser extends from the scar tissue. Beams come from my eyes and my nose and my mouth. I'm afraid to look at my pee and bum hole, because I'm pretty sure things are coming out of them too.

  The white laser, shooting from my right stump begins to flicker and my broken cell starts to look like a rave with a strobe light and glow sticks dancing to the beat of my pounding pulse. The light is so bright, that when it pauses, the flames of the room look like darkness in comparison. Like shining a flashlight into a prism, the white beam splits and fragments into colors I swear I never imagined could exist before. Inside all the beams coming from me are these little, black specks that look like scattered coffee grounds and I know that if they would stop moving so quickly, I would be able to see that they are words hidden within the light rays. Words in every language known to man, and probably more than a few that are not known telling us what it all means and literally lighting the way for us to follow. The only way this could be cooler, would be if there was a giant bat shining in the end of the beam.

  There is no pain, but the smell of burning hair fills my cell, and my body becomes as smooth as a cue ball.

  The light begins to coagulate at the end of my arm,

and the colors swirl into each other making a kaleidoscope of colors that put the Laser Pink Floyd show Naomi and I took John to a few months back look like a lame screensaver. Life lines and love lines of light stretching out into infinity, loops and swirls and arches and wrinkles in a cacophony of colors. The light dances around my face as well, causing me to blink. That's when I realize that I have eyelids again.

Take that Green Lantern.

The lights flicker and pause, allowing the flames to engulf my body like they are forging me into something alchemic. The guards are outside my cell trying to figure out how to get in, but aren't having much luck and I can "see" the prison fire brigade laying hose and trying to get the sprinkler system to engage.

"Naomi, come get me," I whisper into the firestorm, and I'm positive that she hears it and will come.

Someone with a Halligan bar is finally able to pry to door open, and the pressure in the room drives everyone back into the hall. Liquid orange rolls over the fragmented concrete of the solitary hallway. I can hear the prisoners from the other cells, screaming to be let out, but I won't allow the flames to reach them. They are safe.

I slowly stand up and walk towards the door to my cell. Before leaving the room, I look back, and there is an almost perfect heart shape on the floor where my legs and ass had been sitting. The heart is entirely undamaged and untouched by the carnage eating the rest of the cell. I walk into the hall way, and see the guards standing at the far end. Some are trying to point hoses into my cell, others are pointing guns at me, *and all* look like they want to run. I softly wave at them with my new 'hand' and tell them not to be afraid.

One last act of Tonglen and I should be done.

I close my eyes, thinking how wonderful such a simple thing like this is to be able to do. I touch my face and can feel my nose and ear where they are supposed to be. Other than being hairless, my face is fine again.

I take a long, deep breath in pulling the flames and light into my lungs. All the pain that the entire world is feeling in this moment goes into my body and is incinerated there. I hold the breath inside of my chest for a moment and stare at the heart shape that's left on the floor. From my perspective, the heart is upside down. My heart. I get it now.

I breathe out, and for the first moment in the history of mankind, even though it only lasted for a few seconds, the world was at peace. People across the planet felt a momentary reprieve from the fears and pain that comes from daily life. The blanket of my power wrapped them in a cocoon of protection and love.

"I'm going home now," I said to the guards.

Then I was gone.

ROUF
THE HAND

"You are not who you think you are."
-The Book of Benjamin
Inside patella

Why is it so easy for us to hate each other? This is a question I have asked quite a bit, and to anyone and everyone who I think would make an honest attempt to answer. Some people have used Darwinism as a justification, claiming the survival of the fittest often depends on violence and aggression, so I decided to read the *Decent of Man* to see if I could understand it further. People who site Darwin as a reason to be selfish or violent or greedy or detached, should really read this book, and learn what they are talking about. He mentions the survival of the fittest two times in the entire text. He mentions love and cooperation ninety three times.

♥

John touches my smooth head and laughs. I'm not exactly sure why, but to him it's the funniest thing in the world. I was hoping I might look cool like Michael Jordan or Vin Diesel, but John's laughter doesn't do much to encourage the thought. I don't think the hair is coming back, and I somewhat worry that if John doesn't stop rubbing my head, my scalp is going to become translucent.

The PlayStation controller feels good in my hands, both my hands. I hadn't realized how much I missed playing video games until John suggested we play some *Little Big Planet*. We sit on the couch playing, and I feel normal for the first time in months.

Naomi's much more interested in my new hand than my new face. I gave her a back rub last night (yes, that's what I'm calling it so shut up about it), and as I let my hand hover above her skin, the tiny peach like hairs of her back would reach out to my palm and sway like blades of grass in the wind. The hand is solid to the touch and I can hold things in it, but light seems to pass through it. If I hold my hand up to a candle or light fixture, I can see the light shining through the strange flesh. One night, we even tried it in the night sky, and you could see little stars through whatever material the skin is made of. The plasma like substance seems to be trying to imitate skin and flesh tones.

Naomi wants a medical team to examine me and especially my hand, but the last time doctors looked at me my life got real confusing very quickly, so for right now I just want to play video games with my friend and cuddle with the best thing with boobs that's ever happened to me.

John's whooping me good at LBP and I try not to call him on the modifications he's made to his controller and to the gaming platform. I would switch over to *Mortal Kombat* but Naomi doesn't like him playing that game because she thinks it's too violent. Thank God at least one of us has some sort of moral compass.

Damon and Mr. Ferninni are coming over tonight for a barbeque, and I'm going to try to set Damon up with Mary, the cancer patient in the Superman hat who was the first person I healed after John. Finding a cute woman, who can appreciate a graphic novel is just way to rare an opportunity to let pass.

We are supposed to be celebrating my 'release' from prison, but I'm just happy to be spending time with the people I love (I know you're probably waiting to hear about how the police and the media handled my escape, and I will tell you about it, I promise, just let me have this moment, ok?).

Naomi invited some of the doctors who have worked on John and myself in the past, and I know this is her attempt to have them check me out and examine me without my knowing it, and I know that she's only doing it because she loves me and is worried about what might be going on, so it's easy to let it slide, and it's actually fun to see some of these medical professionals with a red *Solo* cup of beer in one hand and a burger in the other.

After the party ends and I'm doing the dishes, I think to myself that Damon and Mary might have hit it off.

It's a truly wonderful night and I'm very happy. Too bad things turned to shit.

♥

As much as I wanted to hide and try to fall off the grid, the world wasn't having it. Rumors ranged from the somewhat believable to the completely absurd all over the place about what had happened at the jail, some claimed I had killed several guards in an escape, some said I had perished in a fire, while others said my militant backers had used stolen construction equipment to break me out. The most believable report was that a boiler in the prison basement exploded beneath my solitary confinement cell, and I had just walked out of the ruble into the night, while the DOC staff was dealing with the fires and evacuation of prisoners to other cell blocks.

I decided it was time to make a public appearance, so my friends and I sat down and discussed the options of how to do this and do it right. John thought I should simply set up a podium and hold a press conference, but that felt a little too State-of-the-Union and more than a little pompous. Naomi wanted me to go on a news program and be interviewed, but when it came to picking a station they all seemed equally inept, phony, and political. Plus there was the fact I was a currently a fugitive from the law, there was a very good chance authorities would be at the studio to pick me up before I could get the chance to talk to anyone. Some of the studios we talked to declined us for this very reason; others would only meet with us in some secret location. I wanted to send a strong message I was not the bad guy, so that meant no hiding.

This really only left us with one choice.

The Daily Show staff was willing to deal with any backlash that might come from having me on their program. They even offered to provide a security detail that ensured I wouldn't be taken into custody while I was in their studio or on their property. However, this proved to be unnecessary, because once word got out I was going on the show, several organizations showed up to protest my arrest and to keep the police at bay. It was quite comical to see actually, groups from MADD and DAR were standing side by side with Hells Angels and PFLAG members. It was touching to see, especially when Naomi told me it was because I had pulled all these people together and given them something to believe in. I was the common denominator for the world now.

There were police forces in full riot gear present, but none of them wanted to start lobbing tear gas grenades into a peaceful group, standing outside the studio of one of the most popular cable programs in the nation.

I had done tons of interviews and met hundreds of celebrities, but this time it felt different. Before, I had always gone into these things with a mild disbelief, never feeling like I should take it seriously. I would try to be chagrin and light hearted because, frankly, I didn't believe my own hype. This time though, I felt driven and like I was actually taking charge of my life.

Host, Jon Stewart, actually opted to scratch the monolog and other segments to devote the entire episode to my interview. The only other time the show had done this was when President Obama had been on it. It was an honor and I was humbled.

There was something none of us had thought of, which started the interview on a strange note. Jon introduced me, and as I walked out to the chair, the studio lights threw prisms and sparkles from my hand in every direction. I knew light would pass through it, but I had never thought of what it might look like under dozens of stage lights. I didn't even notice the phenomena until I extended my hand for Jon to shake.

He hesitated for the smallest of moments then took my hand in his.

"That's the weirdest thing I've ever seen," he said as we sat town.

"Thanks for having me here," I said

"I had some questions I wanted to start out with, but after shaking your hand I have to ask; how do you masturbate? Are you a righty or a lefty?" There's laughter in the studio and then Jon asks if he could get a camera to focus in and get some close up shots of my hand. To me, the hand looks normal most of the time, sometimes I might catch a reflection coming through it, but I can feel and touch things with it so sometimes I forget that it's not really a hand. I can see on the monitors though, how the cameras are having difficulty focusing on it. It's like if you try to take a video of a television screen or computer monitor, there's some feedback and the picture distorts a little.

"But it's solid," Jon says. "I can feel it when I shake your hand. Can I touch it again?"

"Sure." I hold out my hand, and Jon gently pokes my palm with his index finger while making a little squeaking sound. He asks me to hold a pen and I give it a twirl between my fingers. He even lets my crumple one of those strange blue pieces of paper he always has on his desk.

"Since we announced that you were going to be on the show, we've received thousands of e-mail and tweets suggesting questions people want to see answered. The staff and I have gone through as many of those as we can, but most of them boil down to two questions. Are you the messiah and if you are…um…what do you want?" Jon says.

So many people ask this question. So many of us want something to make sense of the world we live in and give them some type of guidance. It breaks my heart that many of these people are so longing for this comfort that they will even see it in me.

"I'm not the messiah any more than this is a news show," I say.

"So, you're not the reincarnation of Jesus?"

"No, I'm not. I'm not the second coming or anything even remotely like that."

"Are you sure? I'm Jewish, so you can tell me anything," he says, and I'm so thankful for his humor and personality, which are so comforting and disarming.

"I promise you, I am way too big of an idiot to be placed in that category. If people could spend any amount of time with me in the natural world, they would quickly give up this idea of my being anything else."

"So, how do you explain all of this?"

The red light on top of the camera shines and I think about John's appearance on Letterman.

"Jon, ever since that bone marrow drill popped a hole in my pelvis, and these writings were discovered, I've been asking myself and anyone who I thought might provide an answer that very question. I'm sorry, I know it's not very exciting or good television, but the truth is I just don't know. Nobody else seems to know, either. There's a lot of theories flying around out there, but that's all they are; theories."

"Do you have a theory on this?" he asks.

"I have a possible idea, but as the great profit Kevin Smith tells us, ideas can be changed, but changing a belief...that's hard."

"So, what's your idea?"

"Before I answer that, I want to ask you something; do you know why I came on your show? It's because your program was the only one that had the balls to hear what I have to say."

There is a roar of applause from the studio audience and I can hear the crowds from outside the studios screaming as well. Someone has set up monitors on the outside walls and people are watching the interview from the street. Jon quiets us down and I continue.

"We asked everybody for an interview. No one would touch us. For the people at home who can't see what's going on, in and around the studio, there are armed guards here to protect me from being taken into custody and wrongfully imprisoned again. There are thousands of people here who are putting themselves between men in riot gear who have guns and myself, just so I can come on this program and speak. I thank you all for that. If this happens to turn ugly with the authorities, please don't harm anyone. I'm speaking to people on both sides of the protest here. Don't hurt anyone. This isn't worth that."

"That would be good," Jon says. "If anything happens to the studio they take it out of my pay." There is more laughter and then he continues. "So, what kind of explanation can you give for the events we've all seen on the Internet and the stories we're hearing about?"

"I'm so glad you asked, and I wish I had a better answer, but the truth is I just don't know. I have some thoughts I'm willing to share, but please understand that I could very much be wrong in my thinking."

"Yes. Please share," Jon says.

"I want you to think about the scenario I'm going to present here. Really think about it before simply dismissing it. I believe there's truly nothing special about me and I'm not saying this like when a skinny girl says she's fat just because she's fishing for compliments. Yes, I have this backwards beating heart, however, I don't think it's related to the teachings scientists are finding within me. I just think it was because of my heart condition that the teachings were discovered at this point in our history."

"What do you mean? And who's your HMO?"

"What if the words are in everyone? Maybe not in everyone at this very moment, but what if there is a lot more of us than people are currently thinking are out there with these writings? What if I just happen to be the first person they were discovered in? That basically means that all I am is the piece of toast Alexander Fleming discovered penicillin on. Maybe there are more people who can do the things I can than we think. We all saw John cure that awful Kardashian's leg on the Letterman show. I think we're going to see an increase in this very soon. Maybe this is simply part of the next step in human evolution."

Jon holds up a finger and then turns towards a camera.

"Republican's, the views expressed on this program are in no way the opinions of *The Daily Show* of *Comedy Central*." There's more laughter in the studio and then he continues. "So, you're saying you're an evolutionist as opposed to a creationist?"

"Well, X-men is a way better read than the Book of Genesis."

Jon again gives the disclaimer about opinions expressed on this show.

"It's funny though, our understanding of the Bible has evolved with us over time. We think of certain things much differently now than we once did. I think people's interpretation of the Bible is like Lucas constantly changing the Star Wars films. If Han didn't shoot first, we can't just edit things around, add some computer generated footage, and suddenly change that. We can't change the stories just to make it work for us. People in the comic book industry do this all the time and it makes fans furious. When DC launched their new 52, it meant we lost Wally West, Donna Troy, and then Barbara Gordon was suddenly out of the wheelchair. The geeks know what I'm talking about here and they were pissed."

Jon nods, clearly not wanting to reveal his level of geekdom.

"If there was one message you wanted to get out to the people watching this program tonight, what would it be, and if it's a brand name, please be sure it's one of the ones that advertises with us?" Jon asks

"First, buy your candy from Mr. Ferninni's shop. There's a really good chance that if you buy jelly beans from him, I had a part in making them. Second, buy your Comics from *The Backing Board Comics*. My friend Damon will treat you right. Third, be nice to each other. If you ever feel the urge to hurt another person, either with violence or words, because of something I've done or said, please don't do it. Finally, donate bone marrow, it will change your life."

The interview continues and finally Jon thanks me for coming on his show instead of Colbert's

Naomi and John meet me in the green room, and I'm so thankful the police haven't raided the studio yet. I wasn't exactly sure what I was expecting to happen when we left the building. I was positive there would be police who would try to take me back into custody, and all I knew for sure was come hell or high water, I would not be going with them tonight.

Naomi's eyes meet mine and there's genuine happiness in them that I don't think I will ever truly understand.

"What are you doing here?" I ask, and she looks at me with confusion. "I mean why are you here with me? You know this might go down badly and probably isn't going to end well. It might even be dangerous. So why are you sticking by me? Why are you so good to me, Naomi?"

She blushed ever so slightly and hugs me like she means it.

"Do you know how I knew you were a good person that day we met at the airport? It wasn't because you were coming to help John, although that was definitely a mark in your favor. There were a few things you did that day on a subconscious level that stood out in my mind. I've seen you do them a thousand different times since then and you've probably never even once thought of them."

"What kind of things?" I ask feeling very self-conscious.

"A woman knows how to spot a certain type of man. Hell, we know how to spot fifty different types of men, and we can usually put you into one of these categories before you've even opened your mouth to talk to us. It's the little things men do when they think no one is watching, that really matter. I think it was either Schopenhauer or Batman who said; our truest nature is who we are when we're alone."

She sees that I'm not understanding and so, as with most things, she dumbs it down for me.

"As we were walking through the airport, we had to go through a door to get to baggage claim. It's a little thing, but you opened the door for me, and then looked behind you to see if there was anyone you needed to hold the door for before letting it go. I see you do this every single time you go through a door. I don't think you're even aware you're doing it, and that's my point. You do it because that's the kind of person you happen to be. While we were at bag claim, there was an old woman waiting for her suitcase. When it came around you lifted it off the belt for her and helped her stand it up on its wheels so she could go. There were maybe forty people standing around watching and you were the only one who did anything."

I honestly remember none of this

"I follow you because you're a good man, Benjamin. Come here for a second. I want to show you something."

We walk to the studio doors and I see the rows of police with their plastic shields and tear gas canisters and batons and guns. Then there is the other side. People from every walk of life who showed up to support me, and if not me, then to support the idea that people shouldn't be imprisoned for something they have no control over, or simply because Corporate America happened to lose some money. It's really amazing to see, and I'm so not worthy of this type of support.

    Naomi points, and then I see it. Walking down the street, in between these groups of people who are probably going to clash with each other any second, are these two teenage girls carrying FREE HUGS signs. As I watch, a policeman breaks his ranks, lowers his shield for a moment, and hugs one of these girls. Several people cheer and the officer even stops to shake a few hands of the protestors before falling back in line.

    I look into the eyes of the police officers, men and women, rookies and veterans, and I can see that none of them want to be here. None of them believe in what happened to me. They are here in hopes that no one will get hurt and that they can keep the crowds safe.

    "Those two girls have been walking up and down the line since before your interview started. I bet, between the two of them, they've hugged over a thousand people." Naomi says.

    "That's pretty amazing," I say.

    "They are here because they want to be the type of people you tell them they can be. People are actually *listening* to the things you're saying, Ben. I don't think you really get that."

♥

    The first time I saw comic books as more than simply meaningless entertainment was in 1976, when I walked into the neighborhood 7-11 to buy a Slurpee. There it was, bigger than life, in the magazine rack. There weren't comic book stores or things like that back then, so most of my early comics were bought at grocery stores or at that local 7-11. The best part of that day was that, what happened was completely unexpected. Today, there are so many websites and preview magazines, that by the time a comic actually comes out on the shelf, people already know everything that happens in it, and have debated the plot points in chat groups. If you don't believe this, think about whatever blockbuster movie is coming out into theaters this next summer. What do you already know about the movie? Chances are, you probably know more than you even realize. There was a time when the world wasn't like that though, and things could still surprise you.

Sitting in the magazine stand was the first oversized size comic I had ever seen, and the thought that comics could ever be bigger than the standard single issue had never even entered my young mind. However, that wasn't the only thing I couldn't wrap my head around: This comic theoretically should not exist. It was like a vacuum in space or a *Twilight* movie that was actually decent. Looking at the cover, I felt the earth move in a way I had never felt it move before. It was like all the universal truths that I had grown up with were now somehow proven wrong.

There on the front cover, were two things that were never supposed to be seen together; Superman VS the Amazing Spiderman.

Just in case that last sentence didn't quite blow your mind like it did back when I first saw it, let me explain to you why this was such a phenomenal event, and was an even bigger shock to my young mind, than when Vader told Luke he was his father.

Until that moment, there were basically two separate planes of existence in the comic book universe, Marvel and DC. Fans loved to argue over who would win in a race between *The Flash* and *Quicksilver* (who is basically Marvel's version of *The Flash*), or *Iron Man* and *Batman* (who is basically DC's version of *Iron Man*). These were always fun debates to get into, because there was never any way to prove an argument and we were always left to wonder, what if?

But now…here were the two biggest characters from the two greatest companies, together in one book. This changed everything. I felt like Copernicus discovering the earth wasn't the center of the universe. All of this, for only two dollars, and worth every penny ten times over.

Our nation was celebrating its bicentennial, and I remember buying this masterpiece of work by Neil Adams and John Romita Sr. with quarters that had the bicentennial stamp. The VHS home movie system was introduced and Apple Computers were formed by a couple of crazy guys working out of a garage that same year.

May you live in interesting times.

When I look around and see all the conflict in the world, I often think of that comic I read until the pages basically disintegrated in my hands. It's the best example that comes to my mind when I visualize cooperation (which sounds an awful lot like corporation don't you think?). What would happen if everyone stopped competing with each other and started working together? What if we pooled our resources and shared ideas?

I know this is crazy talk, but is it really?

Stan Lee and Carmine Infantino, respectively the heads of Marvel and DC at the time, put aside their companies' competitiveness for the simple reason that they hoped to have a bestseller on their hands. By combining their two greatest heroes in one package, they were reaching out to each other's fans, and attempting to attract new ones, by publishing a book starring the two characters that *everyone*, fans and non-fans alike, had heard of.

What if more companies did this with each other? For example, what if all our cell phones used the same type of charger? What if I didn't need to by a *PlayStation, X-box* and a *Wii* just so I could play *Little Big Planet, Halo, and Mario*? What if bologna was square like our bread?

I don't think these ideas are completely unreasonable, and these are just the first three that came off the top of my head. Imagine what people with actual creative genius could do together. Maybe we wouldn't have to hear our waitress ask us if *Pepsi* would be ok, every time we ordered a *Coke*. Maybe our cell phone bills wouldn't be hundreds of dollars, and we wouldn't have these confusing plans that even the people who work for the cell phone companies can't understand.

Maybe we could all have healthcare and medications.

Maybe, we wouldn't have to make weapons to defend ourselves from our competitors.

Don't get me wrong here. I think competition is a wonderful thing and it can push people to greater levels than they might not achieve without it. However, it's when competition becomes damaging to the loser that it becomes bad. We can watch the Super Bowl and we don't actually worry about the wellbeing of the losing teams. We know that they will be well paid for the entertainment value the game provided.

I know I'm sounding like Pollyanna here, but I really believe we could do more as a species if we spent more time working together, than trying to prove each other wrong. Worrying less about having more than our neighbors and killing each other over money. Crazy notion, right?

♥

The video of John curing the woman on *The Late Show* went viral almost immediately. However, there were still a lot of people who kept going back to the video of him at Comic Con. I should specify the San Diego Comic Con or SDCC, because there are a lot of cities who run conventions, but the SDCC is the mother of all Cons, and the one most people think of when you mention Comic Con. When we tried to get tickets for the next year, SDCC sent us a letter asking us not to come back. They stated security issues and technical difficulties, but it was obvious they didn't want to deal with all the drama again.

John set up a website teaching people how to make his Dr. Octopus arms and soon they were popping up at conventions all over the country. One person took the idea and shrank it down, per John's website instructions, and made a Medusa wig where all the snakes would move and have a life of their own. It was a really cool costume, but I don't even want to think about how much that wig must have weighed. The costume arms found their way into the construction trade, because they could be used to move and hold heavy equipment.

One fire department, out of Cleveland combined the arms with the Jaws of Life tools and claimed that they had cut emergency vehicle extraction to practically nothing. They posted a video of a lone firefighter (a woman which I thought made it all the more awesome) tearing apart an SUV like it was made of papier-mâché.

Surgeons were using the arms in surgery. The military were using them for mine removal and bomb disarmament. Housewives were using them to do dishes.

Of course, there were a few people who had tried to use the arms for less than noble purposes. However, John had set something up in the web posted design that prevented the arms for being used for evil. When I asked him how he had done, this he just gave me the look that asks why I'm so dumb, and what life could possibly mean for him, since he was only three and already smarter than the supposed savior of the world. He then told me that the arms won't do anything bad because he won't let them do anything bad.

That sounds simple enough.

I think John did all of this as a way to apologize for what happened at Comic Con. The media really raked him over the coals for his outburst, and I was asked about it almost every time I was interviewed. Even after he was on Letterman, a lot of people still chose to focus on the Comic Con video.

This really sucked, because everyone makes mistakes and if we're not going to let go something a three-year-old does during a fit of emotion at arguably the most exciting event on the planet, then what chance do I have when I screw things up?

I think I was privileged, because I got to spend a lot of time with John and got to see how he was still a kid underneath all that had happened to him. He still got excited when I would bring him a candy bar from the grocery store, or when Naomi and I would dance with him to the *Yo Yo Gabba* theme song.

Those moments helped keep me grounded, and enabled me to take things very lightly. That was John's true superpower. Although for some reason, he insisted on keeping the inflatable doughnut they made us sit on after our bone marrow procedure. I couldn't lose mine fast enough. I never quite understood that.

♥

ADD INF: I'm afraid. I feel very much alone, which might sounds strange because there are people around and with me all the time, but none of them know what it's like. Things are happening within my body I don't understand. So far, I've done a pretty good job of bull-shitting my way through the questions and interviews, but I can't lie to myself. John looks to me for hope, Naomi looks to me for hope, millions of complete strangers are looking to me for hope, and I'm completely hopeless.

When I'm alone at night, I just stare at the ceiling and try to replay inside my mind exactly what happened to me while I was in solitary confinement. I look at this…thing at the end of my arm. It responds to my thoughts. The 'fingers' flex and bend how I want them to, but I don't ever think of it as my hand. I'm afraid when I touch Naomi. I'm afraid to ruffle John's hair. If you knew how many times when I'm 'curing' someone that I simply put on a show and hope something happens, you would be utterly disgusted,

I don't even know what melanoma is, how am I supposed to understand how to cure it?

There's no one I can talk to about this. Naomi tries her best to listen, but my grasp on the English language prohibits me from explaining. She tells me to believe, but believe in what? What is this great and powerful thing I'm supposed to believe in?

I talk to people about faith, yet I have none myself.

I have the power of the gods, yet I still can't let go the pain of losing someone who cheated on me, was abusive to me almost every day, and who probably hasn't had a single thought of me since she left. God, when I say it like it sounds so pathetic.

It's ok that we talk like this, isn't it dear reader? Now that I'm dead, I want you to know the truth, warts and all.

♥

John decided to start a blog, along with a Facebook and Twitter account. There's some law prohibiting minors from doing this, but by the time anyone got around to trying to enforce it, he had so many followers, the social networks were afraid of the backlash they might endure if they ever tried to shut him down.

One day, he asks me if I would be willing to try an experiment with him. Someone had sent John a book in the mail on Reiki. You would be amazed at the types of things people sent to him. However, he actually read and responded to the letters he received. In the book, there is this Reiki Master who had taken a Xerox copy of his hand and sent copies of it to people around the world. The book claimed the energy work could be done simply by placing the copy of the Reiki Masters hand on the patient's body.

John thought if we took a copy of my hand that maybe the same thing could work.

We went to the local Kinkos, and I placed my hand on the glass counter, and closed the lid over it as best as I could. As the glowing green light scanned my hand, I tried to think happy thoughts, and hoped that whatever we was doing might be of help to people and bring happiness to whoever saw the photo.

I'm sure you've seen toner cartridges in black and white copiers and know how copy machines work. The black ink is transferred to the paper and you get these charcoal looking images.

My copy came out in color. On a black and white copy machine, that only uses black carbon toner, the copy of my hand came out in color.

In the picture, you can clearly see the stump of my forearm sticking in from the side of the image. There's nothing that looks like a hand anywhere though. When I was a kid, I went to a local fair where they had a spin art station set up. This was what the image looked like. Colors swirled into each other, almost like a Pollock painting, like the image would have texture if you were able to touch it.

John held up the copy, and the man behind the counter decided to come over and check the machine.

"That's impossible," he said when he examined the copy.

"We get that a lot," John said.

We made a dozen copies, of which the only constant was the dark silhouette of my amputated arm. Each image was radically different in the color scheme and size of the swirls, but the swirls were always there, and always going in the same direction. John asked if I thought if we were to go across the equator, if I believed the colors would swirl the opposite direction. Odd as it might sound, I actually thought they might.

The clerk asked if I would sign one of the copies, I

ended up signing five, and as we were leaving the store, he posted one of the copies on the wall behind the register

We tried to take some digital pictures once we got back home, but the results weren't as spectacular as the ones from the copy machine. I guess some things just can't be captured in pixels.

John scanned the photos and had them uploaded to his Facebook page in no time. People were so taken by the images, that they were copied and shared more than any other set of images in history. One woman posted on John's wall, asking him if he could send her one in the mail. This set off such a chain from threads of people asking for copies of the image, that John came up with an idea; if people would donate five dollars to any charity of their choice, completely on the honor system, I would take a copy of my hand while saying that person's name, I would then sign the image to them with the magic hand and send it off to them.

I was skeptical about the honor system and told John we had no way to monitor if people were truly giving the money to charities, but he told me we should have faith in people, that people usually want to do the right thing, but just need to know how.

It's kind of hard to argue with a three year old when he talks with more wisdom than you possess.

Soon, the stories started being posted on John's wall how the images were, in fact having some type of healing effect on people. One man claimed he had taken his image to a tattoo artist and had his photocopy permanently inked onto his hand. He claimed he had a golden retriever that had developed a pulmonary infection, and was going to be put down if the dog didn't soon respond to the treatments. The man sat on the floor petting the dog all night with his tattooed hand. The next day, he took the dog to the vet, and the infection was gone. He sent us a picture of the dog and of his tattoo. John thought this was a sign that he and

Naomi should get a dog. It was a nice try, but Naomi wasn't having it. Even after John placed the photograph of the dog on the fridge, Naomi still put her foot down to the idea of getting a dog. She was right, of course, we had begun to travel quite a lot, and a dog would be left at home alone way more than it should ever be.

After I was gone, they found a beautiful golden retriever puppy, which John named Hairy Allen because John liked The Flash, Barry Allen. Hairy Allen lived a long and happy life.

Stories were soon being posted from all over the world claiming similar results.

By far the strangest story about my hand happened when the action figure of me was built. I was on the *Ellen* show, and made the comment that a spiritual journey and life was a lot like an action figure. Some people will buy a new figure and keep it in its packaging out of fear the figure will lose resale value if it's opened. They use cool acronyms like NIB, new in box, or MOC, mint on card. I said, life wasn't something that should just be purchased and then stored on a shelf. What good is it to own a Bible if you never read it? Ellen gave everyone in the audience a Superman action figure that day. Naturally, someone who saw the program came up with the idea to make an action figure based upon me.

The figure was pretty poorly made and looked like it had been put together from scrap parts. I think the head came from an old Charles Xavier figure, because the face looked a lot more like Patrick Stewart than it did like me. It had the bald head though, so I guess that's all that mattered. A few years ago, there was an Aquaman figure that had a clear plastic "water" hand and the figure of me had this same type of clear plastic hand.

Daniel Thomas, a boy of six, who loved his action figures and played with them pretty hard. All of his figures were scuffed up or missing limbs. The accessories the figures came with had long since vanished. His Captain America figure no longer had its shield and a Wolverine figure was missing the claws from one hand, all the wear and tear that shows how a toy is loved and played with regularly.

Danny's father had seen one of my figures on Amazon and decided to buy it for his son as a kind of joke. The figure hadn't yet become a collector's item and could be picked for around fifteen dollars. To his father's surprise, Danny loved the figure. One of his teachers at school had shown a video of me curing some people in a Veterans Hospital, so Danny knew who I was and what I could do.

One day, while playing with his figures, Danny gets it in his head to recreate what he saw in the video, so he laid his Captain America figure on a tissue for a makeshift hospital bed and then touched the clear plastic hand on my figure to Caps head. The scuffs in the plastic became smooth and the faded, scratched paint became vibrant and fresh, and stranger yet… when Danny lifted the tissue, there was a brand new Captain America shield.

When his mother came into the room and saw Danny playing with the new action figure, she asked him where he had gotten it. When Danny explained what he had done, his mother told him that lying was bad. When Danny *showed* her with his Wolverine figure, she called his father to come home from work and get the figure of me out of their house. When Danny's father got home and saw what was happening, he did what any concerned loving parent would do in a similar situation: he made a video and posted it online.

Other people with the figure tried this with similar success, but my action figure's hand would only fix other action figures. When the hand touched a Barbie or a Batman figure, it would be restored to mint condition, but if the hand were to touch a Tonka truck or an Easy Bake

Oven, nothing would happen.

When I first heard of this, I thought it was the most preposterous thing I had ever heard, but then Damon got a hold of one of my figures and showed me one night while we got quite drunk on mudslides in his comic shop. Damon had a slew of old Mego superhero dolls from the 70's that he was now selling in mint condition on EBay for a small fortune. As we got drunker and drunker, we wondered why there wasn't a line of savior action figures, like the Jesus League. There could be a Gandhi figure that would get skinny when he got mad, because he wouldn't eat like a reverse Hulk, or a Jesus figure that when the battery died, you could just put him in the sun for three days, then the battery would recharge and he would come back to life. There were others we came up with, but they got lost somewhere between the buzz and the hangover.

There was a new Green Lantern Standee in the shops window with his green LED power ring, shining brightly into the darkness. When I asked Damon if I could possibly have the old one, he told me that it *was* the old one. He had used my action figure to fix it.

If felt good to hang out in that comic shop with my friend and just be silly. Of all the things I miss about my prior life, those moments would probably top the list.

♥

John's website took off like wildfire. His Podcasts would often crash server sites and he was raising quite a bit of money for various charities. John never asked for donations, but people who would write to him asking for help or asking him for my help would include all kinds of things, often times large sums of money. I don't know if they thought the cash would somehow move them to the top of our request list, or maybe they were just looking for something they could contribute, but we always sent these donations back to the sender.

People were starting to book John for speaking

engagements, and Naomi was amazing about helping John get where ever he could, but sometimes she just had to say no. John once protested and claimed he was more than capable of traveling by himself and got incredibly miffed when we explained the laws regarding minors. That didn't stop several groups from setting up video conferences with him. and the first time I saw a stadium full of people waiting to hear this little kid speak, it freaked me out a bit.

It was around this time that John started preaching "the message"; if people would just put faith in me, they could do anything. To prove this point, John started performing miracles at an astronomical rate. He would never do anything during his pod casts or video-conferences because he felt it was too easy for people to believe it's a trick or somehow staged if they're not there to experience it in person.

One of the major cruise lines held an interfaith cruise throughout the Caribbean and invited John to come speak. Since the cruise line offered to comp John's guardians if it would enable him to be present, Naomi and I decided maybe some time in the Caribbean might not be the worst thing in the world. We didn't tell anyone I would be on the ship, because this was John's thunder and I didn't want to take anything away from him.

The cruise was great fun and we had some amazing people at our dinner table. There was a couple from Uganda who were working with the Invisible Soldier movement that I could have listened to all day long. Another man at our table told us about how he came home from work one day to find his wife in bed with another man (I instantly connected with him). He decided in that moment he could either kill the two of them, then probably himself, or he could try to let go of it and start living his life again. He found some Buddhist meditations that helped calm him down, and now he spends his life trying to learn as much as he can about his mind and releasing anger.

  I met up with him on the deck one night and told him my story about the cape fucker and the day-glow condom. Why do people so badly harm those they claim to care about the most? I hate the fact I still think about her and ask myself why? I know it's dysfunctional on so many levels, but things changed so quickly for me so soon after the betrayal, that a lot of me hasn't had the time to properly process the whole thing. It does get better though, and talking to this man who has seemingly transcended the experience, gives me hope that I will be able to do it too.

  The cruise was a supremely fun experience, seeing all these people from different faiths hanging out on the sun deck together, playing shuffleboard, and listening to each other share their views. I wish more people could do that in the normal world. Why do we get so afraid or angry when someone thinks differently than we do? Is it because it shines a light on all of the things that we honestly have no way of absolutely knowing about, so we're required to take them on faith?

  I heard an Imam speak, who taught me more about the Muslim faith than I had ever previously known. Everyone immediately asked Naomi if she were Mormon when they found out she was from Utah, it was fun to listen to, because I had those same questions and misconceptions about Utah not too long ago. There were these two completely insane guys who spent their time smuggling abducted children out of places with no statutory rape laws and where human trafficking runs rampant. These two had obviously been friends for a very long time, because they threw the banter and insults at each other in the way only the dearest of us would ever try to get away with. The very best part about them…one was a Catholic priest and the other a Buddhist monk. They quipped how they were looking for a Jewish friend so that everything they did would then sound like the beginning of a joke. A Jew, a Catholic and a Buddhist walk into a bar…

There was a fine line we had to walk with John on certain things; he hated it when people treated him like a kid, yet he still very much wanted to do all the little kid things. Whenever a waitress or checkout clerk would see him and talk to him like an infant, he would become furious. Fortunately, he seemed to understand this really wasn't meant as cruelty or malice of people, so he could shrug it off. However, Naomi and I had to listen to him rant about such encounters afterwards. He still loved to run and play with kids his age, but whenever they would eventually tell him he was weird because he didn't talk like the other kids, and could do things the other kids couldn't, he would become sad and withdrawn. I worried about the isolation he must be living in. The cruise staff had no idea how to handle this. John yelled at our dinner hostess on our first night, because she asked him if he wanted to sit in a booster chair or a high chair. After that, the hostess treated John just like she would any other adult at her table. The problem, was John didn't really like to eat adult food. While we were all eating crab legs, he just wanted some Mac and Cheese. I was able to catch our hostess away from our table and explain it to her, and from that moment on, there was always kids selections printed on an adult menu. I have no idea how she did it, I'm guessing the ship had these menu's somewhere, but we seemed to be the only table that got them.

When it came time for John to give his presentation, Naomi and I found a place backstage, and tried to help with the last minute preparations. I asked him if he really wanted to wear a Spiderman t-shirt, cargo shorts, and flip flops to address the crowd. He told me these people were here on vacation and maybe I needed to get the stick out of my ass.

I was worried my speaking engagements were becoming like a road-side evangelical faith healing workshop. I really tried to steer clear of that image, but it seemed to be the part people were most interested in.

Everybody wanted to be part of the miracle and had to see it for themselves. Since John had done a lot of his engagements on video-conferencing or podcasts, he was able to avoid it. However, since he had been on Letterman, whenever people got the chance, they asked him to do something and I had no reason to think tonight would be any different.

We didn't know it at the time, but Wendell was on our ship, and in the audience. He had started to take an interest in John over the past few months that was bordering on the creepy. He had never tried to contact John, or do anything to set off red flags, so he was covered in the blanket of anonymity. It wasn't until later, when he let the bullets fly from the back of his truck that we even knew who he was.

John was introduced and there was a thunderous applause. Spirits were very high on board, and we were all primed to have a good time and possibly discover some new things about life, and our place in it, also most of us were hammered drunk. Some people in the audience held up signs of admiration, and one woman even flashed John. It was very awkward, but then John lightened the mood by telling the woman it was much appreciated but his penis was about half the size of a Vienna sausage, and she could probably find something a little better and bigger from some of the other men onboard.

"Would you mind if I maybe try something a little bit different today? It seems that whenever I give talks like this, people focus so much on what miracle I may or may not do that they really don't pay attention to anything I'm saying. It's not the miracle that's the important part, it's the message. It's the message that allows us, and I do mean *us*, to achieve the miracle. I'm hoping, if we can just get it out of the way, we might be able to focus on what's really important. So let me ask you all right off the bat, what would you like me to do?"

This made me cringe, because I would never in a million years open myself up to a question like that, let alone in front of a crowd this size. I looked at Naomi and I could tell she was thinking the same thing. We were somewhere in the middle of the Atlantic Ocean. No security detail could sneak us out a back door so we could quietly slip away if things went wrong.

"Can you get me a new Ducati?" One man shouts, and there is laughter from the crowd.

"Dude, you're on a cruise ship. Where would you ride it? Besides since you can afford to take this trip, I'm fairly certain you're doing ok financially. What I usually ask the audience for is something that can be easily verified as not fake or some kind of hoax. Something I could in no way have staged or have any prior influence over. Because of that, I really can't suggest anything, because then it becomes my idea and becomes biased.

"Something I was thinking might be fun though, what if we could do something for someone and then never let them know about it? Like a surprise. What if we could make a person's life significantly better without their ever knowing of our involvement? The reason I'm suggesting this, is that I've earned a certain amount of fame by helping people; I mean after all, we're all here on this boat and in this auditorium to hear me," John claimed.

I cringed a little bit when John said this, because there wasn't supposed to be a headline speaker on the cruise, and I'm sure some of the other speakers might not be happy at the suggestion they were merely John's warm up act.

"It's been suggested I might in some way be profiting from this, which is somewhat ridiculous, I'm three and not old enough to really understand money or greed. The thought is ludicrous when you think about it, but it's really infuriating when people make these accusations about Ben. Ben lives a very simple life, and is the kind of guy who would give you the shirt of his back if he thought it would help you. His character was like this long before the words were discovered. He's the kind of guy who will really listen to you when you speak, the kind of guy you can call a friend. Even if he does totally suck at X-box."

There is wave of applause and Naomi gently touches my back with her fingernails in the way only a woman can.

John asked us all to join hands and breathe with him.

ADD INF: We ended up curing an entire youth cancer ward in Chicago. It took a while for us to get the results, because people's cell phones didn't exactly have internet access in the middle of the Atlantic Ocean. However, as the ship got closer to shore, reports from passengers soon started to spread that we had been successful. No one, besides those present on the ship, ever found out about our involvement or success until I wrote about it here.

Someone in the audience asked about the afterlife and what John thought it would be like, and if any of the world's religions were right in their interpretations.

"Maybe we should be focusing more on the things we can actually do while we are here, than worry about some possible reward we might or might not get after we die," John said as a way of dodging the question.

This is where the thoughts inside Wendell's head became dark.

Six years before taking the cruise, Wendell had a near death experience.

Wendell had a job as a cubicle jockey, doing computer support for a major credit card company. His days were filled with looking at monitor screens and the grayish felt walls of his cubicle. He liked his job and believed he genuinely helped the company run more efficiently. However, Wendell found himself getting quite soft around his midsection and was starting to develop the type of ass his co-workers termed the 'secretary spread'. To combat his expanding girth, Wendell decided to buy a mountain bike that he would ride the sixteen miles to and from his work each day. Soon the love handles were gone and his calves were like granite. He no longer felt stupid walking into work with his biker shorts and helmet. He was feeling better than he had in years and people were starting to compliment him on his weight loss.

Then, one day on his ride into a work, a stray dog ran out into the street nipping at his leg and the spinning wheels. In a moment of pure instinct, Wendell swerved to avoid running over the dog and into the path of a bus. After the impact, Wendell's heart stopped beating for a minute forty three seconds while the fire department used inflatable air bags to lift the bus off of him. He coded three more times on the way to the hospital and his doctors told him he shouldn't have survived, and the fact he had was something of a miracle.

Wendell had the full 'near death experience' in the back of the ambulance. He saw the tunnel of white light and heard the voices telling him it wasn't his time to go yet. Lying in the ICU, eating through a tube, and shitting into a bedpan, Wendell decided since he had survived, maybe there was something he still had to do with his life. He made a promise to himself his life would have meaning and he would do whatever he could not to waste it.

A friend brought him an inspirational book called *Chicken Soup for the Survivors Soul,* which was filled with all kinds of heartwarming stories about people who had overcome amazing setbacks. There was a story in the book that changed Wendell's life almost as much as the bus had. It was the story of Doubting Thomas and the Pharisees.

The story goes that when Thomas went out to teach the gospel, he went to a city where a great Pharisees heard of him and demanded an audience. The Pharisees told

Thomas that if his faith in Jesus was so great, he should go forth and build a great city in the Pharisees' name. Massive amounts of gold and treasures were given to Thomas who quickly went out and gave it all away to the poor and the desolate. When the Pharisees asked to see his city, Thomas said that he had created a wondrous city for the Pharisees…in heaven.

    Wendell decided he would spend the rest of his life building his kingdom in heaven. He had done a lot of good and helped many people, but his motives were always more about securing his own place in the afterlife than any altruistic gestures.

    He heard about the cruise and had seen some of the things John and I had done, and Wendell was very interested in hearing what we had to say and possibly learning if he himself could perform the miracles that we claimed everyone has the power within them to do. When he heard John say that worrying about the afterlife is basically a waste of our time, Wendell naturally took offence.

EVIF
LOBSTER TRAPS

"We think too small. Like a frog at the bottom of a well who believes the sky to only be as big as the top of the well. If we climb from the well, we can see how large it truly is."
-The Book of Benjamin
Inside the nucleus of a white blood cell

In 2011, DC Comics in an attempt to boost comic sales and to make things easier for newer readers decided to do a reboot on their entire universe and the majority of their characters and titles. They ended up cancelling numerous titles while starting over with number one issues on all characters, so we could start reading a brand new Batman #1 and experience the story again from the beginning. Reboots happen fairly common and comic geeks are more than familiar with them. Especially in comic films, there had been a Hulk reboot, the X-men and Spiderman franchises were rebooted, and there had been about a dozen different actors who had played Batman by this point, so changing things up and starting over wasn't exactly a new concept.

However, there had never been anything done on this type of scale before, and even the most veteran of comic book readers faced some confusion and frustration at the universe they now found their heroes in. Barry Allen once again took the mantle of The Flash, but Wally West, his kid sidekick who had worn the costume for the previous twenty years, was now lost in some existential writing loophole. Popular titles such as Power Girl and Zatanna got cancelled, while titles such as Grifter and Stormwatch (which quickly vanished because nobody cared about them) were added to the roster.

Some very major changes took place in the reboot,

which displeased fans across the globe. Alec Holland was no longer the Swamp Thing, Barbara Gordon was not the wheelchair bound Oracle and was once again Batgirl, Sinestro had taken over as the Green Lantern of Earth, Poison Ivy became a good guy, and Aquaman was now a major player in the universe. If you don't know anything about comics, I hope you can sense the magnitude these changes meant to readers. Continuity was a thing of the past. Those epic moments that defined certain comics, such as The Joker beating Robin to death with a crow bar, or Superman being killed by Doomsday had suddenly never happened.

Many characters such as The Question, The Martian Manhunter, The Atom, and Dr. Fate were now just gone with no explanation. Others, such as Supergirl and the Teen Titans had their histories completely rewritten

However, in the middle of all this chaos, one thing caused more upset than anything else. Would you like to know the thing that seemed to upset people the most? The change that made national news? It was Superman's underwear. Those little red bum huggers with the yellow belt he had worn for seventy years were now gone. In the new universe, Superman had a solid blue bodysuit and a red belt that looked more like something Batman should be wearing than Superman.

The underwear was gone and people were extremely pissed off about it.

It gave me something to think about as the bolts went through my arms into the I-beam. It provided me with something to contemplate as I struggled to breathe under the weight of my own body and as I waited to die.

I did have one hell of a view though.

I was crucified on top of the Golden Gate Bridge. There was a lot of debate as to where it would happen, but the city of San Francisco paid a lot of money, and the famous bridge made sense from a security aspect. All authorities had to do was seal off the bridge, and then people couldn't be close enough to interfere, yet still near enough to see all the action.

I mentioned earlier how some people across the bay tried to shoot me with a .22 caliber rifle. They were far enough away that the bullets had lost most of their velocity by the time they reached me, but they still stung like a bitch.

The water looked so peaceful under the night sky. If only they would have gotten the spotlights out of my face, I might have been able to enjoy it a little more. I remember seeing there was something going on at Candlestick Park. Maybe it was a Niners game, but I wouldn't know.

Delirium set in at some point, because I could swear there were a few moments when a beautiful woman with long, red hair wearing a very sexy, blue dress was standing on the bridge underneath where I hung. I tried to speak to her, but she never said anything. She did, however, pull a stuffed penguin out of a purse and leave it at the bottom on the I-beam I was bolted to.

That's when I knew I was crazy. That's when I knew I was going to die.

To numb my fear, I did what I always do in times of stress and sorrow, I thought about comic books.

I thought about Superman's underwear.

What was it about the missing red underwear that seemed to set people off?

I thought about how upset I got whenever I saw them doing something in movies or on the page that didn't fit with their character. Like when *Galactus* was a cloud or when *The Punisher* was carrying around a fire hydrant. Geeks have a loyalty to this stuff that borders on the obsessive. Apparently, religion fans don't like it when changes are made to their heroes either.

A lot of people throughout time have had ideas about what the next spiritual revolution might be.

Unfortunately, I didn't fit into anybody's preconceived notions of what that step might be like. Maybe it was because I *didn't* fit into any of these paradigms that so many people actually did believe in me. Maybe that's hubris talking. The only two people who I'm sure believed in me were Naomi and John.

Why were people so angry? Why was it so easy for them to kill me?

Maybe they were just killing the idea I represented.

Maybe they were just killing the guy who had taken away Superman's underwear.

♥

After I left prison, I decided I should lay low for a little while, and I was really interested in learning more about this Tonglen meditation, so I found this little Tibetan monastery in Nova Scotia that was run by Pema Chodron, the woman who wrote the book I had read in prison. I thought the quiet might do me some good and all my friends seemed to agree that I could benefit by learning to have some focus in my life.

I wrote a letter to the Rinpoche explaining my situation and basically asking for sanctuary, because the authorities were probably going to make a move to put back behind bars soon. Three days later, I received a call from the monastery telling me they knew me and was aware of my situation. They told me everyone was welcome there, regardless of their situation, and that they would make arrangements for my stay.

You've got to love the Buddhists.

Nova Scotia is gorgeous, and the Gampo Abbey Monastery had to be nestled inside one of the most beautiful mountainsides I had ever seen. A ten minute walk took me to the shore where I could watch the cold waves of the Atlantic crash into the cliffs and count the lighthouses as they shone like stars down the shoreline.

Thankfully, my new celebrity status meant little to

the people there, and I was treated just like everyone else. Sure, I would get the occasional question, and people always took an interest whenever they saw my hand, but for the most part, I just sat on a meditation cushion, called a zafu, and went inside my mind.

I began to practice Tonglen in earnest. Soon, I was able to control the heat I generated, but it was always hottest during the mediation sessions. It was funny watching people try to open windows in the meditation halls that had been painted shut for years. One cold morning a person brought in a cup of tea and sat it on the floor next to me while I tried to breathe in the suffering of mankind and breathe out loving kindness. When the session ended, the cup was steaming, and he enjoyed the hot beverage as we put the zafu cushions away.

Before I left, Naomi bought me the newest model IPhone, that could do almost anything. It allowed us to Skype and I was able to see her face and hear her voice every day. The phone also had Siri on it, which proved to be a lot of fun, because I would ask it questions about the meaning of life and which superhero would win in a fight against each other. More often than not, Siri could give me some type of answer, no matter how ridiculous my question had been. It's an amazing piece of technology.

The food in Nova Scotia took a little getting used to, especially the water, so my first few days there were spent mostly in the bathroom. During one meditation session, I could feel my stomach gearing up for a particularly violent episode. The gas pressure built up to the point of physical pain and I was faced with the choice of leaving the session during meditation, which was kind of a no no, or toughing it out. I chose to stay, because my ego didn't want the people there to think I was half-assing my practice.

The situation kept getting worse, until the meditation inside my mind had stopped and all attention was focused on the gas pain. I looked around the tranquil hall and it was truly a postcard moment. The sun was just rising and you could see steam rising from the dew drops outside the windows. There were maybe fifty of us, all sitting statue still, and the silence was almost tangible. That was when I broke. I had tried to reposition myself on the zafu to alleviate some of the pain I was in, when it came out like a stripper jumping out of a giant birthday cake. The fart sounded like Godzilla's scream in the silence, and I swear I felt the ground beneath me shake a little bit. There was about a second of silence while all of our minds said 'well that just happened' and then the Siri on my IPhone spoke up.

"I'm sorry, Ben, I did not understand that last request," it said in its robotic voice.

That was all it took to break the composure of the room. Everyone lost it, and soon we were all having giggle attacks. The laughter would start to die down and then someone would snort, and the whole thing would start right back up again. It was an awesome way for us to connect to the human experience. Not a single person made fun of me, but I did notice that the guy with the tea never left his cup next to me again.

♥

ADD INF: Yes, I tried to masturbate with the new hand.

♥

Unfortunately, when I first got to the Abbey, I was developing something of an ego. In my defense, I think it would have been a little hard not to. Part of me was starting to believe my own hype. I mean, I had actually skateboarded with The Dalai Lama, had coffee with The Pope, helped thousands of people with some really traumatic things, and let me think…oh yes…I created a hand out of pure thought. I was pretty freaking awesome. My jailbreak was a major issue in the upcoming presidential election, so many people were booking appearances with me, I could probably rival Stan Lee, and millions seemed to be hanging on my every word. Not to mention the fact that Naomi sometimes let me touch her boobs.

I was the shit.

This feeling lasted all of about two seconds upon meeting Pema Chodron. Pema's superpower is being able to completely nuke a person's ego in the most direct and compassionate ways. She's like a surgeon with a laser carving out all the garbage a person stores inside their mind. There are few things in life more humbling than having your ass kicked by a somewhat elderly Buddhist nun. Pema flat out doesn't give a hairy rat's ass about what you've done in the past. The only thing that matters to her is what you're doing right now. This moment is all that matters, and if you're not using it properly, Pema will let you know about it. There was this one time when I helped change a flat tire on one of the trucks the monastery uses for various tasks. Nobody asked me to do it, I just happened to walk by the truck, saw the flat, and decided to change it. I wanted to carry my weight and do my share of the work. The tire kicked my scrawny butt. It took forever for me to get the lug nuts loose and the jack was probably made sometime around when they were putting sound into motion pictures. But I did it. I changed the tire by my lonesome.

When I was done, I put the jack behind the seat where I found it, and casually tossed the tire iron into the back of the truck. Pema saw this and asked me why I was so sloppy in putting the tire iron away. She said I had done a beautiful job, right up until I thoughtlessly threw the tire iron. She said it was sad and like watching a good movie with a crappy ending.

I know, I'm probably painting Pema to be somewhat of a bitch, and I really want you to get that's not the case at all. She is a beautiful woman, and her kindness is stronger than Jonn Jonzz. She has a smile and a laugh that makes a person want to hang out with her. She is wise beyond her years and has forgotten more about spirituality than I will ever know.

  She teases me about never going anywhere without my cell phone and calls it my lifeline to the outside world. She mocks me by saying it's hard to ship out to sea when you're still tethered to the dock. The teasing is very fun, but I can tell she's also being completely serious about my attachments and unwillingness to let go and take the ride.

  She tells me that this moment is the most important thing in existence, because it's the only thing we ever truly have control over. The only choice we will ever really make in our entire lives is what we are going to do in this moment.

♥

  The United States petitioned to have me returned, but the Canadian government chose not to extradite me. They claimed it was because they refused to send police into a religious temple to arrest me, but I think the real reason had to do with the hundreds of thousands of letters and emails and petitions asking for me to be allowed to stay. The world wasn't aware of how exactly I had gotten out of prison, but the United States government knew. The security footage had been watched hundreds of times by Homeland Security agents. My lawyers were sending me letters stating the Department of Defense was now looking at me as a possibly threat to human safety.

  I would find this funny because I can't even make a grilled cheese sandwich without doing some type of bodily damage to myself, so the thought of my being organized enough to be a threat to the American public seemed preposterous. But then, Naomi reminded me how the thought of America invading Iraq because they might have had something to do with the 9/11 attacks once seemed silly too. That we could drop a nuclear bomb on a civilian city, wait a good three days to think about what we had done, and then do it all again to another city still seems impossible.

    People were telling me I should be afraid of my country. Citizens of my own country were warning me I should be frightened of my government and not come home again. When things start getting really serious, my natural defense mechanism is to throw humor at the problem, and try to get others to lighten up about the situation. However, with this instance it didn't seem to be working at all. Then, Damon told me what was happening at home. Naomi would joke about it all and deny to me it had happened, but Damon told me some of the harassment she went through by local law enforcement while I was in prison. Some of the things he told me made me wonder if I actually *could* be some type of weapon. I asked John about it, but he wouldn't tell me anything. He just sat there staring at his shoes trying not to cry. That upset me more than anything he could have said.

    He was afraid for his mom and I was the reason.

♥

    With a lot of help from the people at the Abbey, my Tonglen meditation skills began to improve. Before, whenever I would heal someone, I would just touch them and sort of hope for the best. As I've mentioned prior, there were even a lot of times when the healing would happen without my even trying. When I was locked up in solitary confinement, it was the first time I had ever tried to focus it. Before coming here, my attempts felt like my mind was trying to shine a light on whatever I was trying to fix. I tried to explain what this was like to Pema one morning and she seemed to understand perfectly.

    "All a laser is, Ben, is light that's focused," she told me.

    Tonglen meditation was helping me turn my power from the Batsignal into Superman's heat vision.

As I sat on the cushion, breathing in and breathing out, I started to be able to control how the heat came out of me. When it first started, it just radiated from me like I was a sun, soon I could focus it into different parts of my body, or sometimes into an outside object, however, doing so was always risky because I could start fires in almost no time at all if I wasn't careful.

The heat was always present, though, no matter how hard I tried to suppress it, I never could. I remembered something from my high school science about thermodynamics and how energy can never be created or destroyed, only redirected. The heat always had to be redirected into something. One engineer who was on retreat at the Abbey thought he could design a type of collector/transformer that could somehow harness the energy and convert it into power. He asked my permission to run some test and I thought; why not?

One day though, I had what I guess could be called a "breakthrough". I had been focusing for weeks on how to best help people with my power. I really wanted to do the right thing, but had no idea exactly what that might be. The heat was building inside me, but I was managing to keep it in check. Then it was as if an outside voice were speaking from inside my head. It was as if thought was coming from someplace outside of my consciousness. Like the thought might not even be my own.

"What if there's nothing to 'fix'? What if there's no one to 'help'?"

Assuming there is something to fix is assuming something is broken. In trying to help someone, there is the implication they need to be helped. What if this isn't the case? What if there is nothing wrong with anything or anyone in the world, and everything is just perfect as it currently is? What if there's nothing for me to do, no one to save, nothing to make better, or to try to control? What if all I'm supposed to do is just accept things as they are and let them be?

I told Naomi this during a Skype conversation, and she told me she finally thought I might be on the right track. I mentioned this theory to Pema, and for the first time ever, she didn't look at me like she couldn't believe that out of a billion sperm, I had been the fastest.

How could I possibly think that the universe, something that has been in existence for billions of years, has something that needs to be fixed by me? What kind of an arrogant prick have I been by trying to fix things that would probably be just fine without me? Don't get me wrong, I think I've actually been doing some good lately, but if the words had never been found within me, hell if I had never even existed, the universe wouldn't even notice.

I think from now on, I will only change things people ask me to change, and not place my own judgment on what needs to be done.

♥

While I was in Nova Scotia getting my Buddha on, the outside world kept spinning. John continued his speaking tour, which had now taken on a different aspect where the media would bombard him with questions as to my whereabouts. Protesters from both sides of the argument would show up wherever he spoke, and Naomi told me there were always federal agents present. She told me how, whenever she drove anywhere, there were always black SUV's with tinted windows following her. I checked in with Damon and he told me similar stories, but Damon seemed to thrive on this and would constantly try to play jokes on the agents sitting outside the comic shop and his home.

I felt awful my friends were in this situation, but I didn't know what I could do to help end it.

♥

My newfound peace and tranquility lasted about a week before I went bat-shit, rage crazy. This was when

John Peterson went missing. The call came through on one of the few phones at the Abbey asking for me. My ego was so close to just blowing off the call and not taking it, but when I heard the caller say they were with the Salem Massachusetts Police Department, and they were investigating the disappearance of a young boy, well you can't really ignore that now, can you? The officer on the phone told me her name was Belkin and why she thought I might be able to help her. I was on an airplane by the end of the day.

When I stepped off the plane at Logan airport, there were a dozen homeland security officers waiting to take me into custody. One officer clamped a handcuff to my left wrist and then paused unsure of how to proceed. He touched my hand and could feel it was solid, but whenever he tried to put the cuff on it, the metal loop would just slip off the end of my wrist where the stump had originally been. This seemed to piss him off and he claimed I was resisting arrest, so I was thrown to the ground, while half a dozen agents went through the same process of trying to place me in handcuffs.

ADD INF: It hurt. A lot.

I took a deep breath in and by the time I let it out, I had generated so much heat the agents were literally jumping off of me. Several pulled their guns but couldn't quite muster the justification to shoot me there on the floor of concourse C.

"I'm fully cooperating and I don't wish to see anybody hurt, especially me. Can we please put the guns down now?" I said.

Officer Belkin stepped forward with the Governor of Massachusetts, as well as camera crews from every Boston station. When she told the Homeland security agents (not to mention all the people at home watching this unfold on the live television news broadcast) how I had returned to America to help aid in the investigation of a missing child, half of them looked like they weren't sure exactly how to handle the situation. The other half still looked like they wanted to shoot me.

I was so afraid, I'm amazed I didn't pee and/or pass out. I wanted to be strong, but when they slipped the plastic riot cuffs above my elbows and cinched them tight, I actually wondered if it was all going to end right then and there.

None of the Homeland Security agents seemed to be interested in, or even listening to anything Officer Belkin was saying. One or two of them even looked as if they might shoot her if she interfered. She protested, and the Governor made some rather pathetic attempts to establish power. People in the airport were starting to gather and soon the cell phones were out taking pictures and video.

A hood was placed over my head, and soon I was in the back of a vehicle speeding away. I could hear Belkin screaming in protest and I wondered if I would ever see Naomi again. No rights were read to me. I wasn't offered a lawyer or a phone call. I wasn't even told what I was being charged with.

I soon found myself inside a room that wasn't exactly a prison cell. There were no bars or windows, but I had the feeling if I was to try to open the door, it would be locked and something bad would probably happen to me. The air was stale and I thought that I might actually be underground somewhere. Maybe they had put me inside some type of bomb shelter. One thing was absolutely clear though; I wasn't going anywhere.   Even though I was learning how to control things, I really believed what had happened at the prison had been a one-time thing.

They left me alone for hours inside that room. Alone, except for the only other two objects inside with me; a metal folding chair I sat on and a stainless steel table that looked like something for autopsies. The heat inside the room was turned up to full blast and I knew this was an interrogation technique designed to make prisoners tired and more willing to cooperate. This made me smile.

I figured I was going to be there for a while, but I was getting really tired of the waiting game. Maybe I could do something to speed the process along a bit. I sat down on the center of the table and tried to go inside like I had learned at the Abbey. The Tonglen flowed into my lungs with each breath, and soon the table beneath me was warm to the touch. Well…might as well give this a shot. I took a deep breath in.

"In brightest day."

I remembered how it felt laying my head in Naomi's lap as she took the stitches from my eye after I banged my grape into a paparazzi camera. The half-smile on her face as she told me I needed to take better care of myself, because she might not always be there to patch me up. The way her fingers would stroke the palm of my hand before she interlaced them with my own.

I exhale and the temperature easily rises by ten degrees.

"Please stop that," a voice through a hidden speaker somewhere inside the room says. I breathe in.

"In blackest night."

I remember watching the colors swirl inside the jelly bean buffer of Mr. Ferninni's shop. Sometimes it was like catching a rainbow inside a black hole. The coffee jelly beans were my favorite, because the smell they put off was almost strong enough to give a person a caffeine buzz. I remember him hugging me when I told him I was going to Utah to donate bone marrow. I remember my first day on the job when I would screw up batch after batch of jelly beans, because I would either take them out of the buffer too soon or too late. Mr. Ferninni never once lost his patience or got upset. I think about his Willy Wonka costume and how happy it made me when he came with us to Comic Con. He was…is…like a father to me in so many ways.

I exhale fire into an already burning oven.

The door to the room opens, and half a dozen agents come in, all of them armed with tazers. I guess they have decided not to kill me just yet after all.

"No evil shall escape my sight."

I suck the pain and suffering around me into my lungs and cremate them in the flames of my love.

John believed in me back when I was just a geek with a skateboard and a broken heart. I never had to prove myself to him, because his mind is more trusting than mine will ever be. I love that kid. When I hear him laugh while we're watching *Adventure Time* or my old *Superfriends* DVDs, it makes me wonder what would happen if I were to ever have a child of my own. I know I can never take the place of John's father, but I hope he and Naomi will at least give me the chance to try.

I hold the air in my lungs for a few seconds before releasing it into the interrogation cell.

The Homeland security agents are having a hard time breathing, because the air inside the room is almost scalding their throats, but they never lose composure or take their weapons off sight of me.

"Sir, if you do not stop what you're doing we *will* taze you," the voice from the speaker says. I sweep my gaze around the room, making sure to meet the eyes of every agent present.

"Let those who worship evil's might."

I breathe in and one of the light bulbs above me explodes.

When we were young, Damon and I used to play this weird version of hide-and-seek. During the summer, when school was out, and kids could stay up a little bit later at night, the kids in our neighborhood would have these massive games of hide-and-seek, with around twenty kids jumping fences and climbing trees. It was basically our own version of spin the bottle. The boys would always try to hide with a girl, and then make out with her like mad until they were found, or it was time for someone else to be 'it'.

Both Damon and I were way too shy to try anything like that. He told me about this one time, where he ended up hiding with Donna Springer who was one of the early developers in the neighborhood, and how she had let him touch her boob. He got this distant stare in his eyes when he told me about it, and all I could do was wonder what type of magical experience that must have been like.

Most of the time though, Damon and I would hide pretty close together, and usually in a place where we could see 'kings' and watch where the others were hiding. This usually meant we were up a tree or inside a bush. Nobody ever looked for us inside the bushes, probably because the other kids were smart enough to know how dumb of a hiding spot that would be. Although now, when I think of it, maybe they thought Damon and I were experimenting with our own sexual confusion, and they were just avoiding dealing with that subject like the plague.

For some reason I can't quite explain, Damon and I carried the game into the daylight hours, and started hiding from the cars that would drive through the neighborhood. We would be walking home from school or something, and whenever a car would start coming down the street towards us, we jumped into the nearest bush and hid. The fact that Damon wore this bright, orange Aquaman jacket didn't seem to matter, and we continuingly amazed ourselves, with our Ninja like skill. Our parents would ask us why we were always so scraped up all the time, but seemed to sum it up to our childish stupidity rather than anything seriously dangerous.

I always feel safe with Damon. He's a true friend, and one of the few people who have continually been there for me. I can't even hate him for sleeping with the cape fucker. She positively radiated sexuality, and I don't think anyone could fight against that for long.

I breathe out, and two of the men with Tazers raise their arms to shield their faces.

I sweep the room with my gaze, making sure to meet the stare of every person there.

"Beware my power."

As I begin to inhale, they let the Tazers fly. More than twenty barbs penetrate my flesh in various places. For the tiniest of moments, I think maybe that's all that's going to happen, and then the volts or amps or whatever the hell Tazers use to make your head feel like a lightsaber, hits me. I flop around a time or two before falling off the table onto the side of my face, chipping a tooth on the tile floor.

The electricity stops, and I'm in awe of how quiet and still everything is. The moment lasts less than a heartbeat, but inside that perfect sliver of time, I'm back at the Abbey sitting on the meditation cushion in the cold air of Nova Scotia. I'm inside Damon's comic book shop, feeling the crisp pages of a new comic book beneath the fingertips of my old right hand. My lower lip tickles in the exact same way as when Naomi sometimes turns her head away from mine minutely, before returning her lips and kissing me hard. I raise my hand to try to grab the table edge, and my hand looks like one of the pulse reactors on Tony Stark's Iron Man suit.

That's the moment when the current hits me again.

The vitreous humor in my eyes seems to boil and it feels like my eyelashes are fishhooks dragging across my corneas. The charge stops and my vision has changed. I can see everything. The textures surrounding me are so clear, I can almost feel them just by looking. I can see things behind me, above me, within me, and within the others. This must be what Daredevil's radar sense is like, but it's more than that. There is a clarity to it that has nothing to do with perception. It's about understanding. I'm outside my ego and seeing things as they really are, and not how I think they should be, or how I want them to be. I can see what the others are thinking and feeling.

This must be how God sees things.

I'm seeing through the eyes of God.

They hit me with another charge and I begin to pee. I don't really remember anything else after that.

When I come to, I'm inside another room that has a cot sticking out from one of the walls. I'm wearing light blue coveralls and an adult diaper. I have no idea how long I've been out, but I have at least three days growth on my cheeks and chin. I'm not in handcuffs and my right forearm ends in an all too familiar stump.

With my left hand, I touch the cold tile walls, and am relieved to find they are not padded.

There's a camera in the corner of the room, and I wave my arms in front of it for a while, but it's a few hours before the door unlocks and the men with Tazers come inside. The only relief is the navy blue uniform in the sea of black worn by officer Belkin. She smiles at me and there's a friendliness there that can't be faked. I'm sure she's a tough cop, but I would bet she's one of the nice ones who haven't become bitter from spending years on the job.

"Can we talk?" she asks, and sits down on the edge of the bed with me.

The men with the Tazers never take their eyes off of me, and I would really like to avoid being shot with those barbs again. I rub the stump with my left hand and let my bootie covered feet dangle from the edge of the cot.

I ask about the missing child, wondering if it's too late to try and help, but Belkin assures me there's still a chance.

♥

In a Pigs Eye restaurant is rumored to have the best breakfast in Massachusetts, and based upon their French toast I would have to agree. It's thick and not the least bit runny, which is wonderful, because I can't stand runny French toast. The famous red roof is inviting and there is coffee on the table before we even get menus. I love this place.

Officer Belkin is one of those people who uses so much cream and sugar in their coffee, that I often wonder why they don't just order creamer. Agent Coulson, the homeland security agent who is now permanently attached to my side, takes his coffee black, but sticks his pinky into the air when he drinks, which would be fun to tease him about if I felt he possessed a sense of humor. I gave Agent Coulson shit about dying in *The Avengers* movie, but he didn't get the reference, and the third time I made the joke, he actually punched me in the head.

Belkin and Coulson have been butting heads, and egos, ever since they met, but they seem genuine in trying to find this child, and hate anything that seems like we're wasting time, like breakfast, but my team needs to know the details if we are going to help.

John Peterson, age 3, was taken from a park, a quarter mile from the restaurant we are currently eating in. Some moron thought he was Naomi's John and took him hoping to either extort some money from us, which is funny because as I told you the savior gig pays shit, or to make some type of statement. John Peterson's mother has raised John by herself, and his father has never been in the picture. She's a teacher at a junior high school and has no money whatsoever.

There were Amber Alerts and tons of media attention, because of the connection to me. People throughout the world offered money to help pay whatever ransom might be asked, and John Peterson's face was all over the Internet within hours of his abduction. There has been no word from whoever has taken him. No demands. No statements.

He's been gone five days.

The authorities have asked for our help, thinking that whoever took John might be an employee or associate of mine. I have no employees and all my associates are here with me except for Mr. Ferninni, who had to stay home and keep the candy factory running. The police have pretty much exhausted their options and have yet to discover anything. They are hoping maybe I can pick something up using my powers, that might provide some new evidence, and give them a fresh lead.

This is another time in my life since the words were discovered within me that I feel I have absolutely no idea what's happening in my life. The thought of this little boy possibly being hurt because some Dr. Sivana wannabe has a grudge against me, breaks my heart. However, I've never tried to do anything like this, and I don't have a lot of faith I'm going to be of any assistance at all.

Damon is strangely attentive and channels his inner Batman. He asks questions I wouldn't think of, examines maps, and types a lot of notes into his IPad. I hear things have been going well for him and Mary, and I'm guessing he's hoping this newest escapade won't keep him away from her for very long. However, it seems more than just that. Police don't ask guys like us for help in solving cases. We never get opportunities to be the hero and save the day. Damon probably knows this is going to be the only time in his life anything like this will ever happen and he's not about to let it slip by.

Naomi was very conflicted about bringing John into this, but when he heard this boy had been taken because of some twisted case of mistaken identity… he feels responsible and isn't going to sit on the sidelines for this one. He's already saturated the Internet with You Tube videos, Facebook groups, Twitter feeds, and every other social media out there asking for information. He's even offered to perform a miracle of choice to whomever provides information that will lead to the safe return of

John Peterson.

    I think John's intellect freaks Agent Coulson out a little bit. He seems to get unnerved and even hostile when he's around John for any time period longer than a minute or two.

    Or maybe he just thinks we're wasting everyone's time.

    After breakfast, Belkin takes us to the park where John Peterson was last seen, and there is something ominous about looking at the empty playground where terrible events have happened. There are fliers stapled to almost every tree in the neighborhood with John Peterson's picture and the police hotline's number on them.

    Thankfully, no media are around, and I'm not exactly sure how local law enforcement pulled that off.

    My eyes meet Officer Belkin's, and she gives me a small nod letting me know it's ok to look around. I walk to the center of the playground and sit down on the shredded rubber padding. I take a few breaths, say the Green Lantern oath, and the hand is back at the end of my arm glowing brightly. The fact they once burned witches in this city doesn't escape me.

    Damon sits on a swing and begins punching GPS coordinates into his IPad. John walks around the playground, touching things, trying to find a connection. Naomi reassures Belkin and Coulson we know what we're doing, even though we don't.

    I touch the ground and my hand sinks into the rubber. I try to 'feel' something, anything that might give us a direction to start.

    "Come on Goose, talk to me" I say to myself, and I can see my breath in the cold Salem air.

    I remember how Pema Chodron told me we're all connected in ways we often can't see. How many steps the cup of coffee I just drank, with my French toast, had to take before it ended up in my stomach. How we so often think we are individual waves, instead of part of the ocean. How we see ourselves as Marvel fans or DC fans, instead of seeing ourselves as comic book geeks. Republicans or Democrats, rather than just idiots.

He must have been frightened. Fear is a powerful emotion. Maybe it lingers because of its weight. I try to find the fear John must have felt at the moment he knew he was in danger. I reach out with The Force trying to touch the fear, and my hand trembles under the strain of my concentration.

I feel like a complete idiot and that's the only thing I *do* feel. I've got nothing.

Television and movies have taught me the first few hours are crucial in missing person cases, especially when it involves a child. We are days into the investigation and my being delayed by Homeland Security didn't help matters. I have the feeling I'm here more as a media band aid instead of an actual part of the investigation. I'm sickened this boy might be dead because of some fascination with me, and poor John is beside himself with grief. He's working harder than any of us and the strain is starting to show. Naomi tries to get him to take it easy, to maybe try and catch a nap here and there, but John won't have any of it. He's exhausted, frustrated, and feels helpless, just like the rest of us.

Damon keeps sneaking off for hours at a time, and when we ask him about it, he will only tell us he's checking on a theory and it's not worth wasting everyone's time with it.

Officer Belkin tries to hide her frustration at being my babysitter and does a way better job of it than Agent Coulson does. I wonder if they both pissed off someone to be stuck with us. I'm sure they must dread going to their supervisors, telling them how we're making absolutely no progress, and that this had all been a ginormous waste of time.

I'm shown hours of security camera footage, photographs of hundreds of people I do not know, I'm asked over and over if there's any connection between myself and John Peterson or his family, my financial records are gone over with a fine tooth comb, I give DNA samples, and there's still the question as to whether I will be taken into custody or set free after this is all over. Belkin assures me my assistance will be considered, especially if we're successful, but Coulson's hand is never far from his gun, and he never leaves my side.

♥

John Peterson's body was found submerged inside a lobster trap off the Newport coast of Salem, exactly four days after our arrival. It was Damon who made the discovery, on a completely random hunch, that happenstance threw at him. Although, I think Damon might have been better off if he hadn't been the one to solve the case.

When we found out we were coming to Salem, Mary somehow got it in her head that Damon had to bring her back an actual lobster trap, because she thought she could convert it into a type of fashionable end table like she saw in a magazine, or maybe even a type of vault where Damon could store his valuable comics in. Damon had been doing his research and wanted to find a real trap, and not the fake ones they sell in the souvenir shops.

This was how Damon found John Peterson.

Lobster traps have these special buoys that the lobstermen paint in specific ways so they can identify their traps and not cross into each other's territories. Damon had been racking his brain trying to think of some clever way to paint his buoy that would represent Mary. Some way he could turn the buoy into a romantic gesture, so whenever she looked at it she would think of Damon and their relationship. Damon would walk the shores looking at the various lobster trap buoys trying to get some type of inspiration or ideas on how to paint Mary's buoy.

This is an incredibly stupid way to find a body, but it's how it happened.

Damon had taken his morning coffee down to the beach to spend a little quiet time looking at the buoys and clearing his head before we began another hopeless day looking for a boy, whose chances were long since passed, but no one wanted to admit yet. As Damon sat there drinking his coffee, and looking at the floating markers, he noticed something strange, that he later told me he struggled with even mentioning to anybody because it seemed so silly.

There seemed to be three separate lobstermen working that part of the coastline, because there were three different colored buoys out floating in the waters. There were red ones, blue ones, and yellow ones. Damon thought this was cool because it was the Superman colors bobbing in the cold Massachusetts Sea. Mary loves Superman, so Damon decided to take a few pictures of the buoys to send to her tonight after we got back to the hotel.

That's when he saw the one buoy that didn't belong amongst the others. It was out of place, because it looked exactly like the one Damon had sitting in his hotel room, waiting to be shipped to Mary.

This buoy was an unpainted white Styrofoam.

Damon thought for sure he must be seeing it wrong, but his camera has an amazing zoom lens on it. When he zoomed in on that white Styrofoam, he instantly knew what was going to be inside the trap. When he told Officer Belkin about it, she initially seemed to feel this wasn't something to waste their time over, but Damon's passion about it eventually won her over and she made the call. The local Leo's (Law Enforcement Officers, I'm picking up on the lingo, pretty cool huh?) wanted me to go on the boat to retrieve the trap, because that's basically what I was there for, but Damon asked if he could be the one to go instead.

If I had known how it was going to affect him, I would never have let him go.

Agent Coulson, Naomi, our John, and I stood along the shore watching as the men on the boat retrieved the trap. For myself, I knew John Peterson was going to be inside the lobster trap when I saw how hard the two officers had to pull on the rope to bring it to the surface.

Later that night I went to Damon's hotel room to check on him, but he wasn't there. Coulson agreed to let me go search for Damon, but insisted on coming along. Now that the body had been found, it was logical I might try to escape, and possibly flee the country again, so there was no way he was going to leave me alone. As we started to get into Coulson's car, I spotted Damon across the street, sitting in the parking lot of a 7-11, drinking a Slurpee. Some things are the same wherever you go. We walked across the street, and in a rare change of character, Agent Coulson hung back as I sat down next to my friend. I had to smile when I saw an extra Slurpee and a bag of puffed Cheetos waiting for me.

"Hey man," I say, resisting the urge to ask him how he is doing. I know how he's doing; shitty.

We sit there in the darkness, watching the traffic go by, and try to ignore the fact there's an armed man fifteen feet away from us watching our every move.

"Do you remember when we used to do this?" he asks and smiles. "You would bring me Slurpees and we would sit outside the comic book store arguing if lightsabers were supposed to be phallic symbols or not."

"I do."

"I still think they were. Darth Vader just wanted to give everyone a smack down with his giant red laser herpes penis."

"It's not a penis. Lucas was trying to show how the more technology advances the more it reverts back to our own primitive nature," I say and the argument begins.

"Come on! That whole series is nothing *but* cock."

I pick up the Slurpee and take a swig. If he wants to go the rounds, then bring it on.

"First off…You said 'butt cock,'" I say, and even Agent Coulson cracks a smile. We laugh, and for the first time since I can't even remember when, I feel normal.

"You know, there are times when I wish you had never gone to do the bone marrow transplant. I know that's a terrible thing to say, and you know I think the world of John and Naomi. But when they pulled that kid out of the water, it just all became so wrong."

"I know," I say.

"No. You don't know. Don't get me wrong, it's been fun being the Robin to your Batman, seeing all these places I never would have, had it not been for you, meeting Mary (she has piercings, you know?), hell, even feeling like I'm part of something…I think I would give it all up if I could take back seeing that piece of floating Styrofoam. Do you think you could do that for me? Can you throw some Jedi mind trick at me and make me forget about today?"

I take another drag off my Slurpee and look at the pavement a moment before opening the Cheetos bag.

"Do you want to talk about it?" I ask.

"His legs were broken. Did you know that?"

I didn't.

"It looked like someone took a sledgehammer to them. They weren't just broken, they were pulverized. I'm sure they're going to have to cut the trap off of him to get his body out of there. There's going to be no way to pull him out from the way he was jammed inside. He had two fingers sticking out of the cage and wrapped around one of the small metal bars, like he was holding on to it. Does that mean he was alive? Do you know that, Ben? Can you tell me if he was alive when he went into that trap and into the water?"

Of course I can't. I didn't know any of this. In fact,

my stupid mind never even thought about the size of a lobster trap in relation to that of a small boy. Sometimes, hell, *most* of the time, I can be a fucking idiot. Damon reaches into the bag for a Cheeto and as he pulls his hand out, little flecks of orange dust fall to the charcoal grey asphalt. If I look hard enough, I can almost see a picture, as if the orange particles are some type of Rorschach test.

Damon holds something tight in his hand, and when I ask him what it is, he shows me a tiny silver cross on a chain.

"His mom gave it to me," he says. "She said it was for bringing her child back home to her." Damon throws the cross across the parking lot and Agent Coulson gives him a dirty look.

"Hey, fuck you, Coulson! You can't intimidate me. I'm not the one of the watch-lists. You guys can tap my phones and break into my comic shop all you want, but you don't scare me, and do you know why? Because you're just the Star Trek guy in the fucking red shirt beaming down to the planet's surface. You're cannon fodder. You piece of shit. You couldn't even survive through the first Avengers movie and now you want to give me your Steven Seagal looks?" Damon stands up and takes a step towards Agent Coulson, and I put a hand on his shoulder before he can get himself killed. I hold up a palm to Coulson and his shoulders slump, reminding me of the way a little kid will pout when he doesn't get his way. I wonder if John Peterson ever did that.

"Damon, calm down man," I say, and instantly regret it.

"Don't tell me to calm down!" He snaps at me, and shrugs my hand off his shoulder. Agent Coulson's right hand moves to the inside of his jacket. I shake my head and he nods an acknowledgement, but his hand doesn't come out of beneath his armpit. Some part of Damon's self-preservation instinct kicks in and he turns away from

Coulson.

"You know what? Fuck this. I think I need to stop watching the Ben show and get off this ride for a while. I'm out of here. Peace." He walks away, holding up a peace sign that loses one of its fingers after a few steps. He pauses long enough to pick up the silver crucifix and then he's gone.

XIS

PEPTO BISMAL WITH A WISKEY CHASER

> "Behavior is the purist indicator of the truth.
> Trust only movement."
> -The Book of Benjamin
> Inside right tibia

I was never more frustrated with John and his new found intellect than during those next few days. It's hard enough arguing with a four year old, (He had a birthday, God help us), but a highly intelligent, passionate, and reasonable four year old is almost impossible. We were all living with the shock over what had happened to John Peterson. Someone had died because of me, and in our naiveté, we thought we could make sure it would never happen again.

We were very wrong.

I tried to call Damon, but he wouldn't answer. A Facebook post showed him back at the comic book store, so I knew he at least made it home safely. We stayed in Salem for the funeral, and then a few days more to help with any follow up investigation. It was the least we could do while I waited to see what Agent Coulson and the Department of Homeland Security was going to do with me. It was over a pizza back, at the hotel, when John first brought up the idea of tracking down the killer. Naomi didn't want to hear any talk like this, but John can make a pretty good argument when he wants to.

"Why can't we do this?" John asked, as I took my second slice of pepperoni.

"Because we're not cops, John. It's their job to find and prosecute him, not ours."

"You mean, those same police that wrongfully imprisoned you, and are probably going to do so again as soon as this is over?"

I tried to think of a way to explain this, but John wouldn't give me any time to process my thoughts.

"What about the Magneto argument?" John quipped.

Naomi's eyes met mine for the briefest of moments, and I could tell she was thinking about our conversation in the prison, when I had said frighteningly similar things. She got up and walked to the window to stare out into the streets, as she had started doing so often as of late.

"What do you mean John?" I ask, pretending the same thought hadn't been occupying my nights since Damon found the body.

"We can do things the police can't and/or wont. We can make sure this never happens again, because the thought of dealing with us would just be too frightening. Magneto was right and you know it."

"Yes, but this isn't a comic book, this is real life, John." I countered.

"Then why the hell do we spend so much time reading and discussing comic books? Comics *are* our lives, because they are more real to us and make more sense than the fucked up reality of the world we live in. Why do you think comics are so popular? It's because they make sense to everybody on a primal level, because we all want to be able to help out and make a difference in some way. People would rather be Batman, than the President. They would rather save the girl tied to the train tracks, than go to work at Wal-Mart. 'With great power comes great responsibility.' We have that great power. Don't we have a responsibility to use it? I know you want to do this. If you weren't that type of person, then we never would have met in the first place, and I would probably be dead by now."

The truly shitty part about this is, he's right. Ever

since I read my first comic book, I've wanted to find a scenario in my life where I could save the innocent by punishing the guilty. I've wanted to be the hero. I've wanted to matter.

"Ben," he says taking my hand. "He died because of me. I can't live with that."

"I'm going to go for a walk," I say and Coulson gets up, and follows me out the door.

During the time I was sitting on my ass in the park trying to get some psychic hoobajoo vibe on where John Peterson might be, the God Vision *did* show me one thing very clearly; it showed me exactly who killed John Peterson and where I would find him. I've known, but I've kept the information to myself. I tried to convince myself the reason I kept it a secret was because I wasn't absolutely sure, I mean was I really going to accuse a person based on some strange sense of cognition I've recently acquired? The real reason I didn't say anything is for all the reasons John just told me. Magneto *was* right. If the abductor wanted to kill a kid because of me, then I was going to make him suffer for it.

I need to get rid of Coulson.

Newton said, that for every action there is an equal and opposite reaction. I've lost count of how many people I've healed, and for the first time ever, I wonder if the door can swing the other way? If I flip some I-Ching coin inside me, could I give somebody cancer instead of taking it away? Could I place a tumor inside the cerebellum of an already sick mind? I've cured people by phone, text message, e-mail, and almost everything besides carrier pigeon. Could I kill somebody the same way? There's something cold in my stomach that thinks I probably can. However, I have to be sure.

I take a deep breath and there is a rumble from Coulson's torso. His stride slows ever so slightly, and his left palm comes to rest on his stomach.

"Are you ok? You're looking a little pale," I ask, and take another breath. The rumble is much louder this time, and Coulson lets out a tiny belch. His walk now has a definite pucker factor to it and I'm starting to feel a little sick myself. I remind myself Coulson's not a bad man. In his mind, he's the good guy of this story, and I have no doubt he's an exceptional field agent, otherwise he wouldn't have been assigned to me.

I take another breath, and there's a wet sound that freezes Coulson in his tracks, and a thick sheen of sweat appears on his face.

"I need a bathroom," he says to no one particular.

"I bet there's one at that gas station we just passed," I say, and gently take a hold of his arm, which he doesn't shrug off or protest when I guide him towards the door. Inside, I ask the attendant where the bathroom is, while giving him my best 'these are not the droids you're looking for' mental push hoping he will focus so much on Coulson and the wet noises erupting from him that he won't even notice me.

When we get to the bathroom door, Coulson hesitates not sure what to do with me, so I give another push, and whatever force of will that was holding his sphincter closed gives way and he bolts through the door.

"Can I get you some water?" I ask, over the splashing noises.

"…Pepto…" He manages to get out through a few moans of pain. I find the Pepto and leave two bottles by the door, and then I'm off to find out if I have it in me to kill a man.

♥

The gun is heavy in my hand, and not at all like I think it should feel. It's cold and crude, not like a lightsaber or a power ring. I've never held a gun, let alone fired one, and now that it's in my hands, the reality of the situation weighs heavy on me. It takes me twenty minutes to figure out how the bullets go in, and then another fifteen to find out where the safety is. It's a miracle I don't shoot myself trying to figure it out. For some reason, my new hand won't hold the gun which made working it considerably harder. By now, an APB will be out and every law enforcement agency in Massachusetts will be looking for me.

I don't have much time.

Fortunately, I didn't think this would take long. The God Vision had already shown me all I needed to know. I knew where to look.

ADD INF: I'm deliberately avoiding using this fuck's name, because he doesn't deserve to be remembered for what he did.

I took a taxi to Boston, and thought about doing something stupid, like giving the cabbie an extra C-note to forget he saw me like they do in the movies, but then I figured that would be the easiest way to ensure he noticed and remembered everything about me. Instead, I just tried to be as average and plain as I possibly could. I would hide in plain sight, until I was finished, or I was caught, whichever came first.

I won't lie to you, the comic geek in me was loving this. I felt like The Punisher or Wolverine. It was a dark fantasy, but the part of my head, where Naomi's voice lives, made my head feel guilty. As I sat in the back of the cab, I listened to my heartbeat, and thought about the blood flowing through my veins, passing over whatever words had been inscribed on those inner recesses, flowing over instructions and wisdom like the wind passing through a Tibetan prayer flag.

Was *this* all the words had to teach me and the world?

I wonder if Naomi knows I'm gone yet. I'm sure she will know exactly where I'm going and what I'm planning to do. I wonder if Agent Coulson ever went back to the hotel after he came out of the bathroom, or if he just started to work the radios, and search for me.

I put my hand inside the pocket of my hoodie, practice taking the safety off the gun, and getting used to how it feels in my hand. I took this literature class once, and the teacher (a beautiful, full blonde whose name I can't recall for the life of me), explained how a gun holds a certain structure for a narrative. Whenever an audience sees a gun, there's a slight anxiety because they know at some point during the story, the gun is going to go off. It's the not knowing when, or who it will be pointed at when it's fired that fills us with trepidation. Now that I've introduced a gun into this story, am I bound to fire it? Will the bullet find its proper mark, regardless of my actions? Have I put something in motion that can't be undone now? There's the tiniest of clicks as I flick the safety on and off. I imagine the little red dot on the side of the gun, showing it's ready to fire becoming visible as I flick the switch up then disappearing again as I flip it back down.

Red.

Black.

Red, again.

The gun seems trivial somehow, this guy deserves more than a bullet. Damon told me I didn't know what it was like to see the boy being pulled out of the lobster trap, but that wasn't exactly true. I can see and feel what the boy went through during those last moments of his life. The gun seems like a somewhat impotent weapon to use against such a monster. I wish I had something greater, like a nuke.

I wish I was back at the candy factory right now, watching the colors swirl and feeling the warmth coming off the jelly bean buffers. I need the peace I find there in a way I never have, before or since.

Gunmetal steel is one of the few colors jelly beans don't come in.

The cab drops me off outside the Boston Commons and I sit on the grass, watching tourists take the duck boats around the pond, as I try to work up my courage for what comes next. The Band-Aid theory seems to be the best in this scenario, just rip it off fast and be done with it. I find the bar that's older than most of the western states and go inside.

I grab a table right by the door and immediately find him sitting at the bar, drinking something that comes in those little tiny glasses. I'm so tempted to just walk over and do it right now, but there are a lot of people in this place, and I would like to possibly pull this off without going to the electric chair. Fortunately, it doesn't take very long for him to head into the men's room, and I figure the universe isn't going to provide me with an opportunity better than this.

As I walk past the bar, I grab a stack of about five cardboard coasters, and go into the bathroom.

He's at the urinal, so his back is to me, and I do a quick scan of the bathroom to ensure we're alone, before I jam the coasters underneath the door preventing anyone else from interrupting our get together. I try to think of something witty and bad-ass to say, but nothing comes. I just stand there looking at him, which is something men tend to get creeped out by inside bathrooms.

"Is there a problem?" he says, but doesn't face me. Words continue to escape me and I feel the need to pee very strongly.

"Look, if you're a fag, you had better be out of here before I turn around," he says, and there is the familiar sound of a zipper going up before he turns to face me.

The look on his face almost makes everything worth it. It's beyond obvious he knows who I am, and I think he has a pretty good idea of why I'm here. When I pull the gun and point it at his face, he's positive. There is the loudest click I've ever heard in my life, as I flip the safety, and stare down the gun sights into his face, and I wonder what he will look like after the bullet has done its work.

The manual for the handgun said it has a trigger pull weight of eight pounds, and it already feels like I must have at least twice that resting upon it as I begin to squeeze. He tries to say something, but I have tunnel vision so bad right now, I can't hear much of anything.

We stand like that for an eternity before I learn something about myself: I do not have the morale flexibility within me to take another person's life. When his elbow connects with the bridge of my nose, I learn something else about me: I am not Batman nor am I Daredevil. I have not spent years developing my martial art skills. I am one hundred forty pounds of nothing that is so out of shape even my scrawny frame had a beer gut. Christ, would it kill me to do a sit up every once in a while. If I live through this, I make a promise I will at least play the Wii instead of the X-box a few times a week.

The next few moments go particularly bad for me. To say he kicked my ass would be like saying *The Phantom Menace* was just a bad movie. He punched me with so many rights that at one point, I was actually hoping for a left just to get a little variety. My tongue dances around the places where my teeth used to be, and my eyes were swelled to the point I couldn't see anymore.

When I finally regain consciousness, the gun and my wallet are gone. There's something in my mouth, and when I gently pull it out, it's a bloody cardboard coaster. I suppose I should be grateful it's the only one I find shoved into an orifice. I don't think I've been out for too long though, because I'm sure people come here on a fairly regular basis, and I can still hear music coming from the bar area.

I manage to get to the sink and splash some water on my face. This is harder than you might think it would be, having only one hand. The cold water feels good on my face, but the reflection in the mirror above it isn't that handsome.

What the hell am I going to tell Naomi?

What am I going to tell Agent Coulson?

I make myself as presentable as possible and walk into the bar. Amazingly, he's still there, sitting where I first saw him having another drink.

"Do you want a drink? I'm buying," he says, and pulls out my wallet from his coat pocket. As he does he makes sure I get a really good look at the gun as well.

"Actually, yes, I could really use a drink," I say, and the bartender hands me a tan colored liquid that's exactly the same shade at the butterscotch flavored jelly beans, but I really doubt it's anywhere near as good. It tastes like carpet and gasoline, with a sprinkle of dirt thrown in for flavor, and the holes in my gums where my teeth used to be scream as the alcohol passes over them. I force myself to swish it around a bit before I swallow it. I set the tiny glass down on the bar and the bartender fills it again.

"Make sure to tip him well," I say and start to walk away.

"I'm not going to see you again, am I?" The killer asks. I wish I could say I refused to answer because it was cool, or because I was tough, but the truth is, I just didn't have anything to say.

Outside, the streetlights hurt my eyes, and when I spit into the gutter, it comes out red, and doesn't taste like butterscotch jelly beans. That's when I see John. How the hell he got away without Naomi noticing is beyond me, but I'm sure she must be freaking out right now. I have no idea how he followed me from Salem to Boston. Not to mention, it's really creepy seeing a little kid leaning against the wall of a darkened alley when you have a two drink buzz coming on.

"Did you do it?" He asks.

"John, what the hell are you doing out here? You can't make your mother worry like this."

"Did…you…do…it?" He asks, and then

unbelievably takes a step towards me like he's going to hit me or something. Even more unbelievable, is that I take a step back.

"No John. I didn't do it."

"Why not?"

"Because, it turns out Magneto was wrong. Or at least I have more Xavier in me than Magneto. I don't have it in me to kill someone, no matter how totally evil they might be."

"Of course you don't. You're a good person Ben. That's why I'm here," he says.

"I don't understand."

"He's got to pay for what he did, Ben," he growls, and the air around me drops a few degrees.

"Then you do it." I start to look for a cab, and I'm not even across the bar's parking lot before I hear the screams. I was hoping John would just follow me back to the hotel, and we could tell Agent Coulson who the suspect was, and be done with all of this, but it didn't happen that way.

I once read in a psychology book that if you could somehow show an adults nightmare to a child, the child probably wouldn't be able to understand it or know why it's frightening. However, if you could show a child's nightmare to an adult, the adult would go insane from fear. We all tell our kids about the boogeyman, but we never tell them what it looks like. We just let the dark parts of their young minds run wild and create horrors that defy all logic and physics.

I think about going back in to retrieve him, but before I can move, the bar implodes.

At least he could have gotten my wallet back first.

♥

There's a history in comics of the sidekick taking over the mantle of a hero after the hero falls. Bucky became Captain America, Wally West became The Flash (that was until DC did their stupid universe reboot in 2011), and Dick Grayson became The Batman. It even works on the bad guy side of the equation. Captain Boomerang's son started wearing the stupid boomerang scarf after his father died, and Taila constantly tried to take the mantle from her father, Ra's Al Ghul.

If I'm the hero of this story, and I really hope by now you've realized I'm not, I'm just the narrator, and it's really easy for us to make the narrator into the hero, because that's what we do to the voice inside our head. It's there with us constantly and it never fails to offer information, so there's no way it could possibly be evil or wrong or anything like that, is there? But if I *am* the hero, then John would probably be my sidekick.

I can't let him continue to go on like he has been. Lately, he's been getting more and more fanatical, and I'm not just talking about the implosion the other night. His web lectures are beginning to become political, and he seems to have less and less tolerance for those who see things differently from him.

One night, we got into a heated argument, because I miss the little, yellow oval that Batman used to have on his chest uniform. Neil Adams and Norm Breyfogle used to do some really cool things with that oval in the panels of their work. Often times, Batman would be in the shadows hiding, behind some unsuspecting thug, and the only thing that could be seen would be the yellow oval and the two white eyes of his mask. I loved that.

John quickly pointed out Batman shouldn't have the oval because, it made him a target for gunfire, and because it made it more difficult for him to hide. Now, you can't really fault John here. He's only four, and doesn't remember the time when superheroes had style and flair. Now everything has to be practical. The Punisher seldom wears his white boots and gloves anymore. The Riddler never wears the green spandex suit anymore. Characters like Aquaman and The Phantom are now looked upon as silly, while Deadpool and Deathstroke are acceptable even though their costumes look just as ridiculous.

Kids today. They got no respect for tradition.

He probably thinks Darth Maul is better than Darth Vader. I won't even mention the argument we got into about who shot first, Han or Greedo (it was Han BTW). Also he keeps trying to convince me how SpongeBob has a subliminal socialist message, but that's neither here nor there, so back to the Batman oval.

John had been riding me pretty hard about my lack of video game skills while playing *Lollipop Chainsaw,* so I thought it might be fun to tease him back a bit.

"Oh, well, if we're going to throw logic into this, let's look at some of the other impracticalities in comic books. How do the Hulk's pants stay on?"

"Hulk's pants stay on because Banner wears special stretchy shorts that Reed Richards made for him. That's why they're always purple," he retorts.

"Really? Stretchy underwear is plausible but the yellow chest oval is too much?"

His lips tighten, which is his obvious tell that I'm getting to him, so I decide to do what any good friend does when they find out they are annoying you: I bugged him further.

"Why does Daredevil's mask have eyeholes?" I ask.

"Daredevil has eye holes in his mask to further protect his identity. If people were to see a mask without eye holes, they might make the connection that he's blind and figure out he's really Matt Murdock. The eyeholes make people believe he can see."

This is actually a better answer than I was expecting. He really is a sharp kid and it's a lot of fun seeing his mind work when he's being creative.

"How come some Jedi fade away when they die, while others have to be burned?" I ask.

"Oh, so now we can just bounce around genres to make our point? Stick with comic books"

I hate it when he's smarter than me.

"Fair enough. How does Wonder Woman find her invisible jet?"

"Wonder Woman's jet isn't actually invisible. That's a misconception. All the invisibility aspect means, is that it cannot be seen by radar. We have stealth bombers and drones that can do this, so I don't think her invisible plane is really far reaching. Along with that, we also have quite sophisticated lie detectors and truth serums our government uses for interrogation. Maybe Paradise Island was just a little ahead of the times, or Dr. William Marston had the foresight to see where technology was going."

We play our game in silence for a few moments before I can think of another example.

"Well what about…" I begin, but John pauses the game, sets down the controller, and turns to face me.

"Look, I know you're just trying to get a rise out of me, but I'm really not thinking this is funny. This isn't something that should be joked about and you know it. Just as many people live by the moral teachings of Stan Lee and Jack Kirby, as do those who live by the teachings of Jesus or The Buddha. It could be argued that comic book heroes inspire and empower more people today than the Bible or the Koran. Hell, maybe we should start leaving graphic novels in hotel rooms, we might reach more people. The only difference between comic books and religion is, that people don't kill each other because someone thinks the X-Men are better than the Justice League. At least not yet."

I reach over to start the game again, but John stops me.

"'No Ben. You have to get this because someday very soon, people are going to be telling your story, and you might just get a say in how that story is written. What message do you want to leave for future generations? What do you want to say right now about the discoveries the words will reveal after they do an autopsy on your body? Because, you know that's going to happen, right? Scientist, governments, and every other agency you can think of are going to be studying your body, cell by cell, to see what can be learned."

The X-box goes into sleep mode and I set the controller down on the table.

"John...why did you do that back at the bar?" I ask.

He takes a look around to room making sure his mother and Agent Coulson aren't anywhere around, then begins to stall. John has a huge tell when he has something to hide. He will rub the tip of his left, middle finger against his pant leg and look to his left. He does it every time, and it's all too familiar when I see him do it now. He tenses a little bit like he's going to argue the point, but then his bottom lip begins to quiver and the tears start to fly.

I hate it when people cry. I mean, who doesn't right? But I never know how to handle the situation. With girls, you have to be really careful, because nothing will piss a woman off more than if you're holding her while she's crying and you pop a chubby. And how fair is that? I mean, if you're going to rub your body up against mine and let me hold you while you're vulnerable, I'm probably going to go for it. If that bothers you, go cry on someone else's shoulder, and get them all sexually frustrated.

With guys it's a little different.

When a guy cries to another guy, there are basically two schools of approach in handling the situation:

1- Ignore the fact he is crying and try to solve his problem with logic and reason, or...

B- Call him a fag and tease him mercilessly for crying like a girl in front of you.

But when it's a kid crying, man, I have no clue. I think of all those WWJD bracelets and wonder how Jesus would handle the situation. I decide to try the compassionate route.

"Tell me about it." I say, and then sit back because God gave us two ears and one mouth so we can listen twice as much as we talk. It takes him a few minutes to formulate his thoughts into words, but it eventually comes out.

"Sometimes…I have a hard time controlling my emotions," he begins.

"I know I'm not like other kids. I get that, I really do. Something unexplainable has happened to me, I will probably never understand. I'm thankful for it and I really want to be a good person. But in many ways, I'm just like any other child. When I get angry and upset, I feel like I don't have the emotional maturity to deal with it. It's like there are no options to calm things back down again once it starts. I think what happened, was like a controlled temper tantrum, if that makes any sense. I knew somebody had to do something, but I didn't know what that was, or who it should be. When you took off, I knew you were feeling the same way that I was, but I also knew you are smarter than I am, so maybe you had a better plan or something."

"I just had to see how it played out," he continued

"I thought, 'Ben will know what to do'. He will make it right and maybe provide some type of understanding to this chaos. So I followed you. I didn't know what to expect, but when I saw you walk out, trying to hold your nose on your face, I knew it hadn't gone that well. All I had to do was look in your eyes and I knew you didn't have any better understanding of this than the rest of us."

I nod slowly and look at my lap.

"Please, get that I'm not judging you for this. I think this entire situation doesn't make sense, no matter how you look at it. But you were my last hope on this, Ben, and when you came out of that bar, I knew that there was just nothing that could be done to make this right. Nothing was going to bring that poor boy back and give him the life that he deserved to live. It's not fair and I just couldn't take it."

He starts to cry a little bit harder and I get a glimpse of the old John, the kid I first met at the hospital who asked me about skateboarding and cartoons, the kid who shouldn't be dealing with any of this, and whose biggest problems in life should be the crust not being cut off of his PB&J. I see that child and realize he's a lot closer to the surface than any of us have realized.

"I was so mad," he says, and I put my hand on his shoulder.

"It's ok," I say.

"It's not ok? If Coulson finds out what happened, I will probably end up in jail or something."

"Nobody's going to put you in jail," I say.

"Why not? They put you there."

I don't have an answer for that, so we sit in silence for a while.

"Do you hate me?" He finally asks.

"What? Why would you even ask that? No, I do not hate you. I could never hate you, buddy."

"I just seem to be making a lot of people angry or upset with me lately."

"Are you talking about this kidnapping, murdering piece of shit? Because that had nothing to do with you, John, that was just a very sick person who thought he could get some free money, and when he realized he couldn't, he panicked and did something stupid. That was not your fault. You get that right?" I ask.

He nods his head in a reflex motion, but I can see some part of him will probably always blame himself for the loss. Of all the things I seem to be able to heal, I wish I could take this pain away from this oh-so-small boy, more than anything else. He starts to cry, and presses his head into my chest. As I hold him, I can feel his body shake beneath the power of his sobs.

My dad used to tell me how men don't cry and he

would often make me stop before I could even begin. I hated him for that. He would say things like, 'Quit crying before I give you something to cry about.' He told me this at my mother's funeral, and I remember packing all that pain and loss down inside of me, and 'being a man' for the service, but later that night after everything had ended, and my father had drunk himself to sleep, I went back to the cemetery, and just leaned against my mother's tombstone and cried until the sky began to lighten. I know I'm not John's father and I never will be, but I'm what he's got right now, so I make the decision to just let him cry.

"There's going to be others," he manages between the sobs.

"What do you mean?"

"People don't like us, Ben. They say they do, and I think on some level they appreciate our help, but they are afraid of us because we're different from them and they can feel it. At some point, that fear is going to make them do something irrational, and when that time comes, it's not going to end well for us."

This is one of the few things John does that really creeps me out. When he talks like this, when he prophesies, he gets this glaze in his eyes that makes him look way older than he is, and his voice takes on a kind of robotic quality, monotone cadence, and not really speaking *to* anybody. He just speaks, and I hate almost everything he says.

♥

It's difficult to walk in the strait jacket, but Agent Coulson holds onto my arm and supports me so I don't fall as I'm escorted through the secured doors into the cold auditorium. Deja vu kicks in as I see the single chair facing a row of tables. My slippers slide easily across the linoleum floor and Agent Coulson asks me if I'm feeling steady as he sits me on the lonely chair. I ask him if a cup of coffee would be out of the question, but he just smiles and puts the keys to my jacket into the pocket of his scrubs.

The man sitting at the center of the long table tells me his name, even though I already know who he is, and know that he knows I know who he is. He opens the thick file in front of him with my name on it, and the hearing that will determine if I spend the rest of my existence in a place like Guantanamo Bay, or possibly have a somewhat normal life, begins.

The people at the table talk about me like I'm not here, but I really don't mind. I've been advised to keep my mouth shut and answer all questions as briefly and as directly as possible. They talk a lot about the fire at the prison and my escape, about the possible risk I might be to myself and others, about my God complex and persecution phobias.

Naomi sits at one end of the table and she looks so pretty with her white jacket over a conservative dress. It shows just enough calf to be intriguing. She speaks eloquently about the people I've helped and the good I've done. She makes the case that I don't possess the ability to be malicious, and therefore couldn't possibly be a threat to the outside world. She says since she's spent more time with me than anyone else during this past year, that her opinion is the one people should be listening to.

The Secretary of Defense warns how I'm a threat to national security, and need to be imprisoned until further information on my abilities can be gathered. The President reminds him I'm an American citizen. Words like; Patriot Act and Constitutional Rights are thrown back and forth like some strange verbal badminton game.

Agent Coulson tells how I stole a bottle of Visine from Naomi's purse during one of our sessions, and put it into his Diet Coke to make him sick, and that was how I was able to escape his watch. I don't protest, because I know my powers make people nervous, and this explanation seems to put the people on the other side of the table at ease.

It makes more sense than the truth.

At one point they want to examine my hand, so Coulson has to undo one of the arms of the strait jacket. I scoot the chair up to the table and lay my arm across it, giving everyone there the best possible view. The light dances across my hand, making it sparkle. They ask me to flex my fingers and test the range of motion in my wrist. Naomi touches the tip of each finger with her pen and asks if I can feel it, then she gently drags the pen across my palm, and watches as my fingers twitch. The people on the other side of the table nod and ask if I plan on hurting myself again. I tell them I didn't plan on hurting myself in the first place, and some of them write things on their clipboards. I'm tempted to do something, to show them exactly what I can do with the hand, but both Naomi and Coulson warned me if I try anything like that, I would probably go away for a very, very long time, so I just sit there and let them have their look.

They ask me some more questions, and then Agent Coulson secures my arm again, and I'm left alone while they debate my future. I think about doing the Tonglen meditation, but worry I might set my clothes on fire, so I just sit. While I wait, I try to figure out why in *The Dark Knight Rises*, when Bane stole all of Batman's weapons and was driving around Gotham in camouflage painted Batmobiles, nobody said 'Hey, that's Batman shooting at us."

After what feels like forever, they finally come back in and sit at the table.

The President and the Secretary of Defense tell me I will be free go, but I will be required to have an agent from Homeland Security with me at all times. They tell me it's both for my protection, and for the protection of those I love.

Naomi also assures everyone there that she has my

best interest in mind, and she will also be keeping me out of trouble on the outside.

The strait jacket is taken off, I'm escorted through the security gates, and once again I'm a free man...sort of.

I feel the warm sun on my face and breathe the fresh air. It's so great to have all of this behind me, and the relief I feel is astronomical.

Now it's time to *really* go to work.

NEVES
GEEK LOGIC

"May all beings, without exception, be free from the pain and suffering that occurs in sentient life and find true happiness."
-The Book of Benjamin
Inside L-5 vertebra

I want to share a part of the story which is somewhat painful for me to express. It's painful, because it makes me appear weak, and there is nothing more fragile in the universe than the male ego. Also, I should point out how this part isn't going to make any sense. That's because this part is dysfunctional, and dysfunction seldom is logical. So before you start criticizing me, please know I understand where you're coming from. This part of me is very much broken, and I'm still struggling with it to this day.

Please be gentle with me on this.

Sometimes, the cape fucker's voice is still the one inside my head. More often than I would care to admit, she is the ruler I use to measure myself with. She is the mirror I use to view my reflection.

I still hear her telling me I'm useless, and how I need to get some therapy. Her favorite thing to do was to say the most awful, cruel things, and then follow it up with 'but I love you', like those words could somehow put the genie of destruction back in the bottle.

"You know, the only really bad thing I have in my life right now is you, but I love you."

"I'm quite sure a turkey baster would be a better parenting option than you would be, but I love you."

"Your dick bends at a weird angle, but I love you."

I hear this shit in my head whenever I attempt to do something good in my life. When I try to cure someone, I hear her telling me I'm nothing, and am I far too insignificant to ever make a difference, and then I have this terrible moment where I'm sure the healing, or whatever it is I'm trying won't work, and people will see me through her eyes.

But she loved me…yeah, right.

Sadly, I convinced myself her abuse was what real and true love was supposed to be, so now, when I see actual love, I don't know how to respond to it.

Bruce Lee once said, freedom only occurs within the boundaries we place around ourselves.

Jean Paul Sartre said, we are cursed with freedom, because we are always free to do anything we wish, but we are usually too afraid to act without restraint, or we are too pre-programed to behave in ways that already imprison us.

I guess the first step in emotional freedom, is seeing the bars we use to construct our cages. If I have bars that keep me caged, then she is the foundation those bars are placed into.

I want to be free.

I want to have Buddhist-like enlightenment, where I can let go of all this negative energy that uses me like a wet-nap.

I want to have the perspective to observe the situation as it truly is.

Now, I know some of you are thinking I should just replace the cape fucker's voice with Naomi's, and you would be correct. However, knowing you should do something, and being able to actually do it, are often two very different things. I should be able to rationalize how the world loved me enough to give me a place in its history. Even the fact that people crucified me could still be taken as a sign of love, if you look at it from the right angle. Love and hate are just opposites of the same coin, and sometimes it's impossible to tell which side will come up in the toss.

I really thought about not including this confession

in the narrative, but once I start editing things out, where does that stop? If there's something to be taken from this, it's that you should deal with all your emotional baggage right now, because sadly, it follows you into the afterlife.

♥

During my visits with various spiritual leaders, I asked a lot of questions, which basically boil down to the same thing; how do we find happiness? Did any of these historic figures and religious icons have the ability to make men happy? The answer has always been no. Jesus apparently had the power to bring the dead back to life, but he couldn't *make* you laugh at a joke if you didn't find it to be funny.

The Buddha, Moses, Muhammad, none of them could *make* you be happy. Even in the American constitution it says we have the right to the *pursuit* of happiness, and not the right *to* happiness. Right there is the problem. To pursue something is to chase something outside of ourselves. As if happiness is something that we need to find or capture or purchase. By pursuing, we look outside ourselves. Happiness always is, and has always been on the inside. When we pursue it, it's like when we are looking for our car keys, only to find that they are already in our hand.

Happiness is our own burden to acquire, but it's probably the only thing in the world where the more you acquire, the more others will also have. However, so many of us are struggling without it and our pursuits are in vain.

While I was in Japan, I learned a new word: Karoshi. It literally means death from overwork. I'm not making this up. So many people in Japan have died from the stress of overwork that there is now an official term for it. Japan has claimed the title of the unhappiest nation on the planet. The priority inside that country is on maximizing productivity and being successful. Happiness isn't seen as something to be valued, and as a result, people are working themselves to death for a goal they will never reach.

Japan isn't alone in this. America leads the world in antidepressants, and in places like Sudan, happiness is almost unheard of.

Why is the world like this?

Psychologist claim all the human condition is, is an attempt to ensure pleasure, and avoid pain. If this is true, then why are we so unhappy?

There are places like Bhutan and Denmark, which choose to make happiness an intricate part of their government's infrastructure. Why doesn't every country do that?

I once read this book by Richard Bach called *Illusions,* where he makes the claim that the only commandment God ever gave us is to be happy. This struck a chord in me, and I've done what I could to live my life by this theory, even before the words were discovered. Damon didn't open a comic book store because he thought it would make him millions. He did it because that is what he loves. You should see him on Wednesdays, new comic book day. This is the busiest day of the week for him, by far, because he has to bag and shelve all the new arrivals, not to mention ensuring his hold customers get all the items they've signed up for. If you ever want to see a person freak out, watch a geek who missed getting a first issue because it wasn't in his or her hold, and now the issue is sold out. However, when you see him early Wednesday morning, stuffing backing boards into polymer bags, while techno music blasts from his computer speakers, and he's got about three pots of coffee in his system…he is truly happy. Those are the very best moments of his life, when he imagines what his customers will experience when the big reveal is given over a splash page of the new *Justice League,* or when some new variant of an action figure comes across his desk. He lights up with pure joy that's infectious to be around.

Do what you love.

There will always be people who tell you it's a waste of time, and that you should do something meaningful with your life. Do you know what they call those people? Unhappy.

One of my favorite musicians is Lindsey Stirling. If you've never heard of her, you should check out some of her stuff. I promise you won't be disappointed. Lindsey is a techno/hip-hop violinist.

I'll let that sink in for a minute.

To say she's talented, is the king of all understatements, but everyone just expected her to play classical music because that's what violinists do, and how there wasn't a market for the type of music she wanted to play. It's impossible to be a musical lead on a violin. You might be able to play back up on a few songs, but nobody can center a musical career around a violin, especially in the techno or hip-hop world. These are the voices Lindsey hears every day.

When you look at Lindsey, it's very easy to see why people might be hesitant. She is a nice Mormon girl, who went to BYU, and has that girl next door quality. It's easy to imagine her in her Sunday best, playing hymns quietly on her violin, to accompany the piano in Sunday services. She looks like the typical good girl, school band chick.

Then you see Lindsey play.

Lindsey is like a God with a violin. If you want to see what true power is, watch her play. The notes come so crisp and so quickly, that I'm sure more than a few sneak by without perception. Her bow moves back and forth so damn fast, I'm amazed the violin doesn't burst into flame. Who knows, maybe she has special ones made out of Nomex and Asbestos. It wouldn't surprise me. What's even more amazing, is that she does all of this phenomenal playing, while bouncing all over the stage like a ferret on a coke high. I burned more calories watching one of her concerts through osmosis than I ever did during a session on the treadmill.

Lindsey *loves* to play, and it shows in every fiber of her being. Her infectious smile pulls you along with her through every melody. Seeing her play is like reconnecting with a long lost friend whom you've never met.

I think it's her happiness that is the key to her success. I know it's her happiness that makes me want to watch and listen to her.

Like Damon and Lindsey, I love it when I get to see people doing what they absolutely love.

There is no path to happiness. Happiness *is* the path.

Sure, there are times when life uses us like when The Hulk used Loki as his anger management doll in *The Avengers*. However, if we can find the things in life which truly make us happy, and hold onto them when the world spins mad, then we will have a center.

Having a happy center will make everything in the world ok.

It's like Mr. Ferninni's jelly beans. His beans are phenomenal. Even his black licorice jelly beans (which are usually everyone's least favorite) are amazing, because he uses real pieces of licorice for the center, and not licorice flavored goo.

Jelly beans are a tricky candy to make, which is why you don't see a lot of people making homemade jelly beans. If they don't have that special jelly center, then they are just a sugar shell, which can't hold its shape, and breaks apart under the slightest pressure. When there's no foundation for the shell to attach to, then the bean will have no form. In fact, without the jelly center, the candy shell would just blend together into a big pile of sticky nothing, that would be difficult to eat, and make a mess out of everything.

Watching Mr. Ferninni make jelly beans is just like watching Lindsey Stirling play the violin or watching

Damon bag comic books.

If I could ask one thing of you…if I had a message to share, it would be this; be happy, just because.

♥

Naomi holds my hand, and John runs a few steps ahead of us, as we make our way through the park. The leaves are beginning to fall and crunch softly beneath our footsteps. Naomi tells me how she likes this time of year, seeing the leaves change color, and feeling the cool touch of the approaching winters kiss. It reminds her of change. Naomi is one of the people who embrace change. Who looks forward to the surprise of the unknown.

I find change to be somewhat frightening.

John seems to be enjoying the fall as well. He kicks the leaves into the air and then tries to catch as many as possible before they return to earth. Sometimes, he will just stare in awe at a leaf he has caught, studying the vein patterns, as if they tell him secrets the rest of us will never know. In the summer, he would sometimes do the same thing with a blade of grass, marveling at the way it would fade from vivid green at the tip to the brilliant white of the root.

I remember one day, he asked how plants could eat if they didn't have mouths.

Not five minutes before asking this question, he had beat me three consecutive times at chess. John was like that sometimes, in a sort of *Rain Man* quality, where he could explain quantum mechanics, but not zip up his pants (by the way, he was very pissed off when he found out *Rain Man* wasn't a comic book character).

It was refreshing to see him still have the curiosity of a child. In so many ways, I feel I stole that from him.

Naomi's hand in mine gives me strength, like Popeye's spinach, or Hourman's serum. I feel invincible with her at my side, like I'm Superman and she's the yellow sun. Her thumb dances along the edge of my index finger as we walk and my skin never dulls to the sensation. Sometimes when we are sitting on the couch, watching television, she will softly touch my palm with the pads of her fingers or her fingernails. They say music calms the savage beast, but I disagree. I think it's the soft touch of a woman that makes everything right in the world.

    John tears out onto the playground, and I marvel at how accepting children are of each other. Within minutes, he is climbing ropes, and going down slides with the other kids like they are longtime friends, who would jump on a grenade for each other. I can attend to a party full of strangers and go the entire night without talking to anybody.

    If I look hard enough, I can see my breath, but I really have to be focusing to notice it.

    Naomi rests her head on my shoulder, and if an asteroid fell out of the sky and ended the world right now, I would die a truly happy man. A lightsaber swoosh noise goes off in my pocket and Naomi smiles at me as I pull out my cell phone. There are only a very select few who have this number, and they all have special ring tones. Damon's is the lightsaber.

    "How come Peter Parker can sew a totally bitching looking costume in his bedroom in like, twenty minutes, but when I spend months making a costume for Comic Con, it looks like shit?" I say into the phone.

    "Because Parker's a super genius and you're a bit of a mor-tard," he says, and I miss him all the more.

    "Hey is Naomi there with you?" he says.

    "Yes. She says you should remember you're just a part of my entourage, so you probably shouldn't give my so much shit all the time," I say.

    "Whatever turd-burglar. Put me on speaker phone. I actually want to talk to the both of you."

    "He wants to talk to both of us," I shrug, and push the speaker button on my phone.

"Hello Damon. How are things back east?" Naomi says. I'm so glad she's nice to my friends. I shouldn't be surprised by this, she's genuinely a nice person, and cares about everyone.

"Hey there, sexy lady. Are you done hanging out with that loser medical cluster fuck and ready to trade up to a real man?"

"You know...I just might be. Can you still hook me up with free comic books?" Naomi says.

"All you can handle, baby. I will even throw in the occasional action figure here and there."

I look over at the playground and see John still having a great time.

"Oh God, you make me swoon. How can I resist an offer like that?" My lady says.

"Are you two done? I'm sitting right here," I bitch.

"Stop whining, Ben." Naomi says, and punches me in the balls. Two seconds after my best friend calls, my girlfriend transforms into an eleven year old boy. How the hell did that happen? Girls can be so immature sometimes. I often wonder why I put up with it, but then I remember how Naomi looked when she wore a Zatanna costume for me and it all comes back to me.

"What's up dingle berry? What did you want to talk to us about? You crashed my Mini Cooper didn't you? Holy Shit you crashed Red 5!" I say.

"I didn't crash your stupid car, bodaggit. Now shut up, and listen to me for a second. I need to talk to you guys about Mary."

In all the years I've known Damon, he has never called me to talk about a girl. Of course, there had previously never been a girl to talk about, but this is definitely a new aspect to our friendship.

"Tell me you didn't screw things up," I say.

"No. Not at all. Things have been going really great for us. In fact, I've been thinking about turning in my amateur status and going pro."

Naomi looks at me, and the glow in her eyes radiates down to her mouth, and she smiles so big that I actually think her head might split around the back, and the top of her head will fall off onto the back of the park bench.

"Also, there's the fact that until recently she was pretty sure she was going to die, and now she is basking in the new possibility of life. I need to strike now, before it sinks in for her that she has options now." Damon says.

"Dude…Are you sure? This seems a little fast." I say, and almost laugh to myself. Everything that has gone on in the past year has happened so fast I can barely follow it. If I thought there was a possibility of her saying 'yes', I would ask Naomi the same thing right now.

There is a part of me that's a little jealous and afraid, because it has just been Damon and I for so long, but I know that's not really the case anymore, for either of us, and I couldn't think of a better girl for him than Mary. It's been awesome getting to know her since we first met outside the Huntsman Cancer Institute, what seems like forever ago.

In many ways Mary, was how I found out about the words, and the strange abilities that seem to be tied to them somehow. With a gentle touch of her smooth hairless head, the world changed in ways I could never have imagined. She was the first one to thank me for 'curing' her, and I will never forget the strange sensations that brought. There's always something that happens to a man when a beautiful woman shows gratitude. I like it when I seem to do the right thing, because that rarely happens to me, and I was in a very broken place when I met Mary.

The pain of my previous girlfriend cheating on me was still incredibly raw, and I was throwing a full blown pity party for myself whenever I was alone. I was going through Uno cards and shirt pins faster than I could buy them, and there was a real possibility I was going to have a breakdown of some kind.

I still often think about the difference in how Mary looked in the first few times we met. From her pale, small, withering body with no hair, wearing a Superman hat, sitting in a wheelchair outside a hospital trying to take in some sunshine and fresh air to the robust, beautiful woman with the long, red hair flowing in ringlets, who hugged me hard in the doctor's office as miraculous things were being explained to me.

In so many ways, Mary represents all that is good in me.

Damon walks us through how he is planning on asking the big question, and it sounds like a lot of fun. Every year in Metropolis, Illinois, they hold a giant Superman celebration people from all over the world come to. Damon is planning on taking Mary there, and proposing under the giant Superman statue that welcomes people into the city. He says Comic Con would probably be a better place, but since we've been banned from there, Metropolis will have to do.

There's a dance club there, called the Fortress of Solitude Damon, says we can book for an after party and I'm suddenly very excited to take part in this. Superman has been a huge influence on our lives, so it seems appropriate somehow that he's involved in this.

Then Damon throws out his second surprise of the day.

"I'm sorry buddy, but you are just far too geeky, and lame to have for a best man, so I'm going to have to ask someone cooler to step in for that role, but there is something I want you to do," he says.

"Wait, you're serious? I don't get to be your best man? What the fuck, man?" I say. Naomi punches me in the arm for cursing, but I'm genuinely hurt by this. Who else could he possibly ask to take that role? He doesn't have brothers or anything like that. He's not close with his father. I'm his best friend and this is what best friends are supposed to do for each other. How could he not ask me this?

"I have something else I want you to do for us, Ben. Something even more important to me than the best man thing. I want you to perform the ceremony."

This takes a second or two to sink in, and Naomi understands it a few moments before I do. She places her hand on my shoulder and I can see tears forming in her eyes.

"You want me to perform the ceremony? Can I even do that? I'm not a priest or anything." Both Naomi and Damon find this funny for some reason and begin to laugh. Damon tells me how the law is actually quite liberal in regards to this, and I could probably just appoint myself a priest in whatever religion we want to call the teachings that come from the words. They both assure me this is a doable thing.

Of course I say yes. I've never felt such an honor in my whole entire life. Just in case though, that night I register to be a minister for some online church to make everything legal and official.

♥

The ping and rattle of the MRI machine has actually become relaxing to me. I wonder if I have somehow regressed to when I was a baby, and the only way my mother could get me to sleep, was to put me in my car seat, and then set the seat on top of the dryer while it ran. She told me once, how the vacuum cleaner had the same effect on me. More often than not, I fall asleep when they're doing the scans, but sometimes I twitch in my sleep, and it screws up the readings. Today though, they are running scans on my left foot, and the position I have to stay in isn't really conducive to sleep.

The left cuboid bone is what the doctors are trying to read on today, but they are scanning the metatarsals as well, just in case. Last week, I tested a special MRI machine that is so sensitive it's supposed to be able to read the insides of my veins and arteries. If it works, it will mean at least another three years of going in for scans so they can cover all the areas where the words are written.

How it usually works, is that I come in for the doctors to scan a particular part of my body, then a team of biologists, engineers, and scientists study and interpret the findings. So far, they have only been able to decipher a small portion of my body, mostly in those places where the cavities are large, like the inside of my backwards heart, or the lining of my stomach. It's been suggested to me though, that they have enough raw data and scans to be studying my body for decades or even centuries after I die. One biologist thinks there might even be writings within the mitochondria of my cells and possibly along the inside of my DNA rods. Of course this is just hypothesis and the possibility to test such a theory won't exist for many years, so I actually have millions of my cells that have been cryogenically frozen for future study.

Many of the Brainiac's want to know, why the words only appear on the inside of my tissue linings and not on the outside as well. Sometimes, they ask me, thinking that since it's my body, I must therefore know something about what's going on with it. That's usually when I tell them about how one day, at the jelly bean factory I forgot to bring a can opener for my lunch and tried to open a can of tuna fish with a flashlight. This doesn't even crack the top ten things of stupid things I've done. They usually stop asking questions after that.

Sometimes, I get lucky, and get to look at the scans. It's quite beautiful in a strange sort of way, watching how letters and symbols swim in and out of the grey and green images. Sometimes, they are so perfectly clear, it's impossible to believe they exist naturally, and not something the crew from *The Incredible Journey* did inside of me with a wood burner. Once after a scan of one of my vertebrae, the operator pulled me into the viewing room to show me something he spotted during the procedure. There, along the inside wall of the Vertebral Foramen (not that I have any idea what that is, but it's what the operator called it) was the word "Believe". It was crystal clear in the scan, and it looked like if a blind man could touch that part of my backbone, he or she would be able to read it too. It was amazing and awe inspiring to see. The MRI technician was able to capture the image and sent the file to me at home. When I showed it to Naomi, she wept. That year, we used the picture for our Christmas Cards, and for some of the promotional items on my speaking tours.

Now the image hangs in the Smithsonian.

♥

The hood of Red 5 is still a little warm, but not so hot it curbs Naomi's desire to cuddle. She points out the constellations and then makes up these outrageous stories about them and how they got their names.

"That one there that looks like a smiley face on a stroke victim, that's called Casanovaopia. He was the god of canned cheese. His cheeses were the envy of all the other gods and they would often fight wars, and make prank phone calls in attempts to steal his cheese. To stop the gods from warring, Casanovaopia was able to slice his cheese into so many pieces, that everyone was able to enjoy a piece. We celebrate Casanovaopia every time we ask 'who cut the cheese?'," she explains.

We talk about the things we would like to do in the future. Places we would like to see and events we desire to participate in. Her aspirations are quite a bit higher than mine. She wants to see famous pieces of art, and the beauty of the pyramids, and Niagara Falls while I just want to meet Denny O'Neil before he dies, and maybe tour Skywalker ranch.

She rests her head on my chest, and I run my fingers

through her hair, as we gaze into the abyss of space and stars.

I ask her to tell me about John's birth, and after a few moments of silence, she begins the story.

"As far as the delivery, things went very fast. John was so small, only 3.1 pounds so he came out with little difficulty. We knew something was wrong with him from the ultrasounds and examinations, so it was very touch and go with him at first. He was placed in an incubator to help his tiny lungs develop and I think that may have been the hardest part for me. I felt so alone at the hospital, and I just wanted to hold my baby, but couldn't."

"Why did you feel alone?" I ask.

"I told you how the father had bailed the moment the first ultrasound showed that there was something wrong, and that John would more than likely be born with a handicap of some kind. It's strange, you know, he never even said goodbye to me? He told me loved me and he wanted to get married, plus there was the whole social pressure from being a knocked up, single and young Mormon girl living in Utah."

I don't fully understand this, but I've been in Utah enough to get the gist of it. I think being a single, pregnant woman would be incredibly difficult to bear anywhere in the world.

"My parents were upset when he left, because they believed I really couldn't do this on my own, and since having an abortion was out of the question, the responsibility would fall to them."

"Did you think about abortion?" I ask.

I hate myself for asking the question the moment it leaves my lips. I feel very insensitive for asking it, but she doesn't seem to be hurt by the inquiry. I guess with everything we've been through lately, why wouldn't we just be honest with each other, even about the bad stuff?

"Of course I thought about it. Every woman who

has ever found herself in an unplanned pregnancy has had the thought enter her mind at some point. It's a very frightening experience for a lot of reasons. For me, there was this huge amount of doubt I wouldn't be able to do it on any level, that my body was flawed in some way and the baby wouldn't survive or be born with something terribly wrong, and this was before we actually knew something *was* wrong with John. I was worried about the father and if I could count on him being there to raise a family with me. I worried if I was somehow cutting my life short and giving up on certain opportunities, like travel or education. But more than anything I worried about what type of mother I might be. What if I was horrible at it?"

"That's ridiculous," I say.

"Thank you for that, but the fear is always there. I constantly worry about John and his safety and happiness. I worry I might inadvertently do something to destroy his psyche or emotionally traumatize him in some way. That I might get sick or die and leave him abandoned in the world."

The hood of the car has cooled now, and Naomi snuggles into me a little bit. I give her a squeeze and kiss her head.

"How often do you feel this way?" I ask, trying to imagine what it would be like to be a parent.

She sighs and gives me a squeeze to let me know she loves me even if I am a big idiot.

"I think it all the time. This is the voice inside my head. It's the last thing I think about as I fall asleep and the first thing I think about upon awakening. I think about it when I strap him into his car seat or when I have to help him get something down from the high cupboards."

"Well, for what it's worth, I think you're a great mom," I say.

She gives my hand a squeeze, and I kiss the top of her head again.

"Do you want to hear something funny?" She asks.

"I always want to hear something funny."

"Before all this happened, before John…changed, he had this Dr. Seuss book he just *loved*. He would carry that book around with him everywhere he went, and I had to read it to him at least a half dozen times a day. The book was just hammered. It had teeth marks on the cover, there were tears on a lot of the pages, that had been re-taped to hold them together, but my favorite thing about that book was how John had written his name inside the front cover in big red Crayon."

I smile at the thought of a young John with Crayons.

"About three nights ago, I go into his room to check on him after making my middle-of-the-night-bathroom-run and he had this book curled up in his bed with him."

I try to recall if I've ever seen the book, but I can't remember.

"That's pretty cute," I say.

"Sometimes, I will see him carrying that book around with him as he makes his way around the house. I think there are still so many ways he is just a little boy. I know he tries to act like a grown up, like refusing to let me help him take a bath, or when there are other adults around, but when we are alone in the house, more often than not, I will find him in front of the TV watching Cartoon Network and eating Ritz Bits."

"It's so easy to forget he's only four when we are playing Chess," I say.

"You don't think I'm a bad mother for letting him get involved with all of this craziness, do you?" She asks.

"Of course not."

"Because, and please don't take this wrong, even though I'm thrilled he seems to be healed from his physical ailments, sometimes I feel maybe, whatever happened to him stole his childhood in some strange way. Maybe, he was better off before. Does that make sense?"

I've had the same thought about a million times since this all happened and I tell her so. The truth is, I've had this thought about everything and everyone I've met since I first took my skateboard into the hospital to give up my bone marrow. If I were being honest with myself, I would admit it even went back a little further than that.

It was when she cheated on me.

Sometimes, I wonder if I've just created everything that's happened since the infidelity inside my mind, as a way to deal with the pain of the betrayal.

"I guess we don't always get to pick the things that happen to us," she says.

I laugh, and am so thankful Naomi came into my life. Craziness be damned.

"No, we don't and for the record, I think it's because you worry about being a good mother that makes you a good mother."

"I'm not sure I understand."

"In comic books and movies, the best bad guys are the ones who think that they are the good guys; Sinestro, Magneto, Darth Vader. They all think they are actually making the world a better place. I think the same thing can be said about parents, it's the really bad parents who think they are the best parents. The ones who think they have everything under control and their child is perfectly happy and content in the world. Those are the kids who shoot up high schools and leave their parents to wonder why. It's the parents who lose sleep worrying about how their kid is doing that make the difference. The ones who worry about not being a good enough provider, or putting their child into the wrong school, or feeling bad because they gave their kid swimming lessons at eight instead of six. Those are the ones who make children feel loved. The fact you're concerned about being a good parent means that you're a good parent. The shitty ones just don't care."

"That's an interesting theory," she says.

"I'm an interesting kind of guy. Hey, if I ask you something, will you give me a totally honest answer and not a supportive girlfriend one?"

"I think I can manage that."

"Am I doing the right thing? I mean with all of this. I feel like a caveman who has been given an IPad. I have no idea what I'm supposed to be doing, or if we've even discovered everything I can do yet. What the hell am I supposed to be doing with all of...this?"

She takes her time, and really thinks about it, and my mind automatically assumes she's going to tell me all the things I'm doing wrong or should be doing better but she just needs to find the right words so she doesn't crush me like an insect under the weight of her disappointment.

"I think you are doing the best you can with an amazing situation. There is just no precedent on something like this, and we still don't know how it's all going to play out. I think you're doing exceptionally well with it all. Never once have you tried to gain anything for yourself since this happened. Everything you've done, you've done for others. How can that possibly be a bad thing?"

"I love you very much, you know?" I say.

"I love you back."

"None of this would matter if you weren't here with me."

"I know. I'm kind of awesome like that," she says, and we lay back to watch the earth spin.

♥

A lot of people criticized me because I never had any apostles. The reason I didn't, is because I'm not the fucking messiah, but people seem to have a difficult time grasping this concept, so let me try to explain if differently. I never understood what exactly it is an apostle does. I mean, aren't they basically an entourage? I hated that show. Seeing these people leach, and sticking their nose so far up another person's ass, they could probably remove a polyp by blowing their nose, why would anyone do that to themselves, and why would anyone want people around them like that? I just don't understand it.

It was like when we went to Comic Con, and saw Adam West and Lou Ferigno charging money to sign autographs or to take a picture with them. It's like it cheapens their celebrity somehow. I tried to just take a picture of Adam West as he sat behind the table at his Con booth, and there were more security on me than when Damon freaked out on the kid with the lightsaber.

"No photographs of Mr. West!" This huge security guard told me, and even tried to take my camera from me. No Pictures? What the hell is he there for? We paid a butt load of money to get our tickets, not to mention the hassles with booking hotels, standing in line for hours on end, and dealing with being packed into rooms so tightly, that if someone were to pass out or faint, nobody would be able to tell, because they wouldn't be able to fall down. They give everyone these ginormous swag bags you could probably bury a body in, and then expect people to be able to move around once they're on the convention floor.

No photographs of Mr. West.

Fuck you, Mr. West. You were the dumbest Batman ever, with your blue silk cape and beer gut. It's impossible to take you seriously in anything you do. You're a has-been who is living off the Batman franchise *in spite* of the massive setbacks you brought to the character.

Batuzi dancing, mother fucker, charging me seventy bucks to take a picture with my own camera. The bastard had more security around him than Obama. His entourage was pushing geeks around like it was high school all over again.

I have the belief that if someone were to give a shit about me enough to want me to sign something, or to care enough to have their picture taken with me, then I should be honored. Not inconvenienced, and I sure as shit wouldn't rape the situation for money, and sell myself like the cheapest kind of whore.

And why the hell did it take so long for us to get the series on DVD?

I bet Lee Majors never pulls this kind of shit.

Sorry, I went off there for a bit. I'm back now.

ADD INF: Ferigno was also charging sixty bucks to take a photo, but I'm not going to comment on that because the man still looks like he could break me in half just by looking at me.

ADD INF: I'm sorry Mr. West. I just wanted a picture of you, because you're the Batman of my youth.

♥

It was Mary who suggested I look outside the box to find some answers. In the DC Comics universe, there is a place called Star Labs, where all the superheroes go to figure out science stuff. Sadly, there's not a place like this in the real world. S.H.I.E.L.D. isn't exactly a part of my HMO.

Several scientists and experts in the medical field had been running tests, with little to no results, and it was getting very frustrating. I was becoming very impatient with the MRI's and being stuck with needles all the time, and it was starting to show in my attitude.

Then one day, Mary calls me. She and Damon had seen some television show, called Paranormal Investigations. It's one of these shows where they supposedly do scientific experiments on ghosts, physic abilities, and other paranormal phenomena, and she suggested I should call them and maybe even go onto their show.

Honestly, since a child had been killed because of me and my media exposure, I was a little reluctant to go back out into the public eye again.

Of course, I made the call, and they said they were

willing to work with me as long as I agreed not to attempt to manipulate the data in any way, so they could run truly honest tests. I agreed, if they promised to do the same on their end.

Now...my ego here insists I give some sort of justification for the interview and how the subsequent television episode turned out. I'm not a very charismatic person, and my social awkwardness knows no bounds. I make inappropriate jokes when I'm nervous and I'm far too stupid to ignore the elephant that is hiding in most rooms. However, I have always done my best to be completely honest with what happened to me since the words were discovered. I see no point in making my side of the story sound good, or to make me into some type of hero. I truly hope you've seen this by now. Unfortunately, the truth is sometimes very boring.

When the interview started, it became apparent to all, it was not going to go as well as everyone had hoped.

Walter Chavez, the host of Paranormal Investigations, sat me down in a director's chair on the studio set and we began our conversation, which would later be edited into the episode, which was finally aired.

As I walked onto the set after being introduced, Walter offered me his hand, and I shook it. If I had to pick a point in time during the interview when things started to go badly, it was here. As his hand wrapped around mine, the color came out of his face, and he made an expression that showed his obvious discomfort.

"Are you alright?" I asked and placed my hand on his shoulder, which Walter slapped away, with clearly more force than he intended. Walter, being a professional, quickly realized his staff had questioning and shocked looks on their faces, and immediately tried to cover up the incident.

"I'm sorry," he said to the stage crew. "I just had a little bit of vertigo right there when we shook hands." He found his way to the director's chair and someone quickly gave him a bottle of water. The makeup girl came over and applied some quick touch ups to Walter, and the shows Director called for the next take to begin rolling.

After some attempted witty banter between the two of us, Walter began to ask the questions I had been asked a billion times recently, which had been documented almost as many times.

"How did I first become aware of my 'powers'?"

"How has my life changed since the incident?"

This was really boring, and shit people already knew about, and Walter should have understood this. Then he did get to some interesting questions that no one had ever asked me before.

"What does it feel like to heal someone?"

The question completely floored me. It was such an obvious inquiry, but I hadn't expressed what it's like before to anyone, because no one had ever asked me, not even Naomi. I think about it for a moment, and the television crew gets nervous because dead air is the worst thing that can happen, but Walter had the experience to see this question just might produce a gem, so he gave me the space to figure it out, and I want to thank him for that.

"I've heard it said, the orgasm is the most powerful experience we can have. I don't really know, maybe death is a little more jarring, but no one has been able to tell us what that is like yet. I would imagine, being born must be pretty amazing as well. Unfortunately very few of us remember what that was like, and even those people who claim they do, I have to question the validity of their experience. I mean, are they really remembering what it was like, to go from one world into another or is it just some mental projection of what they imagine the experience should be like?"

I know I was rambling a little bit, but I figured they could cut out what they didn't want in editing, and I truly wanted to answer this particular question.

"The first few times it happened, I wasn't even aware of it. Perhaps it's entirely a subconscious thing, and asking how I do it is like asking your eyeball how it sees. It just does. However, the eye can't see itself, yet it performs its function without trying to manifest a sense of self, or sense of purpose, in what it does. It simply sees."

"There were all the accidental healings, and the other strange things that happened, but the first time I actually…tried…the first time I did it with intent, I was at a hospital with various doctors, running test, and experiments on me, trying to make sense of this mess. I had a moment, after drinking a fuck-ton of barium for some radiation screening procedure, and they had to wait for it to pass through my system before they could start screening. I walked to the cafeteria in my little hospital gown, hoping to buy some licorice or gummies to get the awful metallic taste out of my mouth."

I take a moment trying to recall the moment in my mind. The studio lights are glaring in my eyes and the red light on top of the camera, flashing, tells me to hurry it up.

"This man approaches me. He's a hospital employee, and no, I will not tell his name or the hospital this happened at. He had heard about me and some of the test they were running because, he was to be one of the people organizing the data from my tests. This man introduces himself to me, and then asks me straight up if I'm a fraud or running some scam, trying to become famous or something. He was the first of many to ask me this question. You see, he had a daughter in the hospital, suffering from leukemia, and things weren't looking good for her. None of the treatments she had been receiving were working and she was going die. Her father knew enough about the disease to lose hope, and he had no options left. He asked me, if I would try to help his daughter. How could I possibly say no to something like that?"

"I told him I had never done anything like this before, and I still didn't think it was even possible. No one doubted my abilities more than I did, and I didn't want to let him down, but he was desperate and insistent. So this guy sneaks me up to the cancer ward, into his daughter's room. There she was, maybe five, I never got her exact age, wearing the same type of stupid gown I was wearing and she looks *bad*. How this kid was still alive, I will never know. She had clumps of her hair missing, several of her teeth had fallen out, her eyes were so yellow they looked like corn, and she had tubes sticking in and coming out of every possible part of her body. It was heartbreaking."

I can see that Walter was expecting a simple and short answer, but he also realizes he's getting something new, which hasn't been said on any other show, so he lets me run with it.

"The dad introduces me as his friend Ben, and this little girl, who had already faced more trials than you and I probably ever will, looks into my eyes and smiles at me. Then she stuck out her hand for me to shake. 'It's a pleasure to meet you, Ben,' she said. Something I've never told anybody was that, when our hands touched, I saw a little bit of color come back into her face, and her grip tightened ever so slightly around my fingers. I think the curing happened then, but I didn't know for sure, and I felt like the father needed something more."

"So I gave it a try."

"I put my hand on her forehead, and I asked God, or the Universe, or whatever to take the sickness out of her. I tried to imagine my hand being a vacuum that could just suck the sickness out of her. I tried to imagine I was Darth Vader and was force choking the cancer to death. Most of all, I just wished with all my being for her to be better. Until that moment in my life, I had never been so connected or intimate with another person. I didn't even know it was possible. It was like, in that moment, I could see how she and I were the same, and I don't mean that we had similarities...I mean *the same*. I understood just how big everything is, how big I am, while at the same time being infinitesimally small. If I could have stayed in that moment for ever, I would have in a heartbeat."

Offset, Naomi gives me a smile, and I think there might be tears in her eyes.

"Was the girl cured?" Walter asks.

"Yes. She was cured. But it's so much more than that. For example, a couple of months ago, it was my birthday. I don't think my birthday is public record, but I'm sure someone could find it out if they really wanted. The point is, I get a lot of mail, and people send me a bunch of interesting things and requests, however, birthday gifts aren't something I really receive. This year, I get a package from the little girl. She *knew* when my birthday was."

"Yes, but like you said, she could have researched it and found out the date. That's really not uncommon," Walter interjects.

"This is very true, but I don't think it's the case. You see, she also sent me a package. She sent me this graphic novel, from this series I had heard about, but never read. It sounded interesting and I always meant to check it out, but there were always other things to read."

"I never told her I'm into comics or any other personal information about me. However, she knew I was, furthermore, she knew I would really like this particular series. It's easily one of my favorites and I probably never would have given it the chance if she hadn't sent it to me. It's not the type of story that would interest a five year old girl, and it's one of those Indi titles people outside of the comic book world would never know of. But she knew. She knew and she sent it to me for my birthday."

Walter ponders this for a moment, and then reshuffles his question cards, before moving on. There are a few meaningless questions before he lands on another important one.

"Why do you think this happened to you?"

I laugh and Walter looks like he's worried, like he's maybe offended me or something, but I reassure him and try to answer the question.

"It's a really boring answer but... I don't know. There's a huge part of me that thinks this is all some huge misunderstanding. There's an even larger part of me that *wants* this all to be a huge misunderstanding."

"What do you mean by that?" Walter asks.

"Well, a lot of people are thinking, and claiming I'm something I'm just not. It's actually very stressful. People have said I am the next stage of human evolution, that I might be the second coming of Christ, how I might possess some answer that will make everything we do on this tiny planet make some type of sense. This is kind of frightening from my perspective."

I take a breath and decide to go for total honesty.

"If you knew the man I was before any of this happened (and I would like to point out I am still very much that same guy), nobody would look to me for any type of answer or guidance. I have virtually no college education, I work in a candy making factory, I have girlfriends who cheat on me, I struggle to pay my bills, I can't eat an apple without getting all kinds of farty, and I can't download an app without asking at least three people for help."

"All these people come to me, looking for help, and it's just heartbreaking. They are dealing with things no one should ever have to deal with in life. They are lost and afraid and need some type of reassurance that everything is going to be alright, and maybe even a little bit of help here and there. If you can just be compassionate and put yourself in their place for a moment, imagine being so desperate that *I'm* your best option. Imagine feeling so lost in the world that when something strange happens, like what happened to me, you latch on to it and make it actually mean something in your life. I'm flattered when it happens and I do my absolute best to not let anyone down, but damn…it's a lot of pressure. Part of me misses the time, when the most stressful part of my life, was the delays in the *X-men* comic being published."

"Are you saying you're burdened by people?" Walter asks.

"No. Not at all. I've met some truly amazing people through all of this, and many of them have become dear, close friends, and those who I didn't become close with, I still have that connection I explained earlier. This connection has been, by far, the greatest and best thing that has ever happened to me. However, there is this fear of impotency, this doubt I'm not going to be able to do it, that this is all some sick joke, that I'm not good enough. That's just soul crushing and very difficult to live with."

"Are you a fraud?" Walter asks.

"I was actually hoping you could tell me. I would love for *any* of this to be explained. I could care less where the information came from. If we can discover something here, that will either prove or disprove me, than I think I owe it to those who care enough about me to follow all of this. I also think I owe it to myself and to those closest to me."

A lot happened, that ended up on the editing room floor, simply because it didn't make for good television, and didn't really provide any information, but I will list it here for the sake of being complete. Also, because of the one interesting thing that *did* happen no one, including me, ever noticed

There was the Ouija board test...

The show's producers had me wear these pressure sensitive gloves that could detect and display the amount of pressure each of my fingers were placing on the little triangle thingy. If I moved the planchette at all, the gloves would detect it, and prove it was me and not some paranormal experience causing the effect. Walter asked me over twenty questions while my fingers gently rested on the plastic.

Nothing happened. Well, that's not exactly true. At some point, I sneezed, and the gloves sent a signal to the monitor. However, this occurred in between questions and only proved the gloves were working properly.

Then Walter suggested that we repeat the experiment using only my "magic hand". They had me flex the fingers of my right hand against the triangle, and the glove over my magic hand could detect the pressure just fine. The questions were repeated and the results were the same.

Nothing happened.

After the Ouija board failure, they pulled a select few members from the studio audience to assist with the next experiment. Three people were given a series of flash cards with various shapes printed on one side. They would hold up the card so they could see the shape, but I could not. Then, using my psychic ability, I was supposed to tell the person the shape printed on the card. Since I possess no psychic abilities, and have never once claimed to do so, this experiment ended in failure as well.

It was during this test that the one interesting thing happened, no one has noticed, even now, after everything that happened.

Wendell was one of the people who ran the flash card experiment with me.

Of course, at this point, Wendell hadn't shot me yet, however, with all the research people have done on me since the crucifixion, the video compilations, the books, and the so called teachers of my way…all of it. I'm amazed no one has yet to notice this brief connection we shared that day.

Walter's team placed me in a room with EMF

readers, ultraviolet/inferred cameras, and EVP recording equipment. By this time, I'm feeling bad, because I can see the program is going nowhere, and I'm looking like a major idiot. I thought that maybe if I did some Tonglen meditation, I could raise the temperature in the room or something.

Nothing happened.

Even after the doctors came in and gave me my medication, the temperature in the room remained the same.

We broke filming to head to Cal-Tec for the next series of experiments. They have a small hadron collider there, nothing like the massive ones at CERN is Switzerland, but large enough for what we were going to try. The scientists there were going to pass various particles through my body, in particularly my hand, to see the affect it would have. Something like the double slit experiment, but with my body being the foil barrier.

I was assured everything was perfectly safe, but when you see the size of these hadron colliders, it's more than a little frightening to stand in front of one.

The team at Cal-Tec set up a very basic version of the experiment, where only a few different types of protons were fired at my body. Later, when the experiment was repeated by the CERN team in Switzerland, they fired everything they could think of at me, including antimatter. The results were the same and repeated several hundreds of times. My body deflected the particles and waves just like any physical matter should, even the really nasty radioactive stuff they didn't tell me they were using as part of the test. Things seemed normal, and I was beginning to think this would be another failed attempt to learn anything.

Then they put my hand in the collider.

Now…if you've made it this far in the story, you know I'm not a scientist, and I'm also a few fries short of a happy meal, so I can tell you what happened, but I can't explain how or why.

The particles and waves that they passed through my hand changed.

Some picked up electrons, others dropped neutrons. Some atoms they passed through me changed their physical composition all together. One element went into my hand and another came out the other side. They fired so many things through my hand that I actually fell asleep during some parts of the test.

One aspect seemed to excite and baffle the scientist was when they started testing the quantum theory ramifications of this particle change. They found, if I thought about a specific element, like gold or platinum for example, whatever element I was thinking of would be the element the atoms changed into. It didn't matter what was fired in, as long as I was thinking of one element, that would be what came out the other end.

I asked them not to tell my government how they could fire simply hydrogen atoms into my hand and get yellow cake uranium or plutonium. I have enough trouble with them now as it is.

There was debate this experiment proved what the alchemist had been trying to prove for centuries. My hand could literally turn lead into gold. Try having that thought run through your head as you masturbate.

Much later on, the there was talk of running the experiment again, but with the attempt to achieve *true* alchemy. Could a bad person be transformed into a good person? More on that later.

There was something the team tried to explain to me about the quantum I really don't understand, but will include here for those people smarter than myself: the fact I don't know the atomic structure of the atoms, or how electron conversion works, or basically any other science type stuff is proof the quantum theory works. Like in the double slit, experiment the results are dependent upon the desires of the observer. The light acts as either a particle or a wave depending on if it is being observed, and what the desired outcome of the observer is.

Basically, the reason I could think about argon, and have argon be produced, even though I have absolutely no freaking idea what argon is or what it's used for, means that the powers of the universe are so in touch with us, that we have the ability to literally change physical matter into our desires.

We make our universe by the thoughts we have. Not just in some new age, kumbaya, power of positive thinking way...but on a scientifically proven, physical way. When this was published, my marketing worth went through the roof.

The paranormal show sold DVD copies of the episode and transcripts from the data the experiments produced. It was the first time, ever, a scientific journal had reached the top of the New York Times bestseller list. It was at the top for a year and a half. I received a 2% kickback from the sales, and it was enough to set Naomi and John up for life.

I remembered there was one of my finger bones that remained intact from when my hand was cut off, and I wondered what might happen if we were to position it so that the particles from the collider might pass through the hollow part of the bone, where the words were. I mentioned it in a joking matter, and then was immediately left alone for about six hours, while various CERN physicists ran mathematical equations.

When they came back they patiently explained to me how the matter which was coming out of the other end of the particle collisions was greater than the matter going into the collisions at a geometric rate. Somehow I was creating energy and matter where there shouldn't be any.

They told me, that based upon the math, the output from firing particles through the marrow of my bones would be like focusing light into a laser beam. It was way too dangerous to attempt. I thought it sounded pretty cool. I was thinking light sabers and phaser guns

They were thinking black holes and supernovas.

♥

In the middle of one of the best dreams I've had in a very long time (let's just say it involved Jessica Biel, a lot of latex, and a Sit & Spin), I'm woken up by the sound of arguing coming from downstairs. I try to go back to sleep, hoping maybe Carla Gugino might show up with a Jenga game and her Silk Specter costume, but the noise is just too distracting.

I can smell coffee, so at least I won't have to kill anyone.

My fuzzy, Domo slippers keep my feet warm as I put on my robe, and go to see what all the commotion is at the ungodly hour of 8:00 AM. Going down the stairs, I pass Naomi on her way up. Seeing her in her yoga pants and tank top almost makes me forget about latex Jessica Biel. Almost.

"What's going on?" I ask.

"There's just no having a rational discussion with either of them. Men are stupid," she says, and walks past me mumbling a few things I believe to be curse words. Downstairs, in the kitchen, I find John and Agent Coulson sitting at the breakfast bar in a very heated discussion. I swear it looks like Agent Coulson would punch John out if he were just a little bit larger, and a tad older. John looks like he's trying to use his brain to explode Agent Coulson's head. I give them both a wide birth as I go to the cupboard and pour me a mug of Joe.

"You're an idiot. I can't believe they let you carry a gun," John says, and this is how my morning begins.

"Yes, I carry a gun, you Ewok looking bastard. I would shoot you with it, but the bullets are bigger than you are, and worth more too," Coulson says. The bags and redness in both of their eyes, and the two used coffee filters in the trash bin, suggest they've been doing this for most of the night, if not all of it.

"Let's get a fresh perspective on this, instead of just throwing barbs all morning. What do you think, Ben?" John asks me, and suddenly they are both staring at me. The kitchen has now become a field of land minds and hornets' nests. My defenses go up, and I really think about just going back upstairs to Naomi, and the warm bed, but then I remember how Agent Coulson really *does* have a gun, so I decide to do what I can to calm the situation down.

"What's the topic of discussion?" I ask, and sit down at the table.

"Star Wars, in particular, how does the Death Star move?"

For the record, I would like it known, that I really did have the thought this might just be the dumbest thing to argue about in the known universe. I really did. However, the geek in me immediately took over, and I was elbow deep in the conversation before my coffee was tepid.

I had honestly, never even thought about it before, but once I had, it seems like a pretty important part of the plot. I was always more concerned with why the Death Star simply didn't blow up that other planet which was blocking the Rebel base, as Luke was trying to corn hole it with a photon torpedo.

"Let me hear the arguments," I say. There are sighs, and groans because they've both been over this already, but I remind them if they want my input I need to be fair and nonjudgmental. Agent Coulson decides to go first.

"I believe the Death Star moves by propulsion, just like all the other ships in the franchise." This makes sense to me, and is pretty much where I stand on the subject, but John just couldn't see it that way.

"Then where are the jets? All the ships, from the

giant ones the Empire used, to the tiny X-wings, to the Millennium Falcon have thrusters on the back to move them through space. If the Death Star moves by propulsion, then where are the engines?" John counters.

"T.I.E. fighters don't have jets," I say.

"That's right!" Coulson says, leaping on a new nugget to prove his theory, he hadn't previously considered. "And the T.I.E. fighters are also a part of the Empires fleet, so maybe they have discovered some new fuel source, or something, that enables their fleet to run without jets."

"Speaking of that, how come we never see anyone stopping for fuel or anything? I mean Luke goes to Dagobah and back in his X-wing, and never once mentions fueling up. How big of a fuel tank could that thing possibly have?" I ask.

"Maybe it's a hybrid," Coulson says.

"Hybrid? Look, if you're not going to take this seriously, then I'm going to bed," John says. We table the fuel discussion for another time and return to the Death Star. Upstairs Naomi stomps around, and I'm guessing she's not to happy I've got myself involved with this.

"How do you think it moves, John? Please don't tell me you think it's The Force," I say.

"The Death Star is *way* too massive to move by jet propulsion. It's the size of a small moon for God's sake."

"But in space, size doesn't matter, because there's no weight. Jet propulsion could work on the Death Star just as easily as it could an X-wing, because there's no air resistance," Coulson interrupts.

Again…for the record, a large part of me hates myself for getting involved in this discussion. I wish I could tell you this was the only time something like this had ever happened to me, but that would be a gigantic, Death Star sized lie. Damon and I get into discussions like this about once a week.

"Ignoring the fact that your natural response is to go with the 'size doesn't matter' argument, let's be realistic. Size *does* matter, and it's just too big to push it around to where they want it to be."

"Until your balls drop and you have more than a Vienna sausage between your legs, I wouldn't be making with the dick jokes if I were you," Coulson quirks back, but there is a hint of a smile, so I worry a little less about him using the gun.

"So, if there are no jets, how exactly does it move?" I ask John.

"It moves just like all the other planets in the universe, gravity and spin."

I pour a refresher on my coffee, trying to absorb what John is saying, but I'm not quite able to see it.

"If that's the case, and I can see how that could be a basic premise for its movement in general, but how does it move into the specific positions it needs to be in to fire? How does it change trajectory when it has to acquire a new target? If your theory were right, then the Death Star would simply be floating around on some orbit, waiting for planets to come into alignment with its death-ray. That's neither effective, nor logical."

This discussion went on for a lot longer than it should have, or than you could even imagine. Geeks are very passionate about their Star Wars. The discussion reminded me of a story a Zen monk told me during my time in Japan; a Zen master is walking down the road, when he came upon two monks having an argument over the movement of a flag. One monk said it was the wind that moved, the other said it was the flag that moved. The Zen master frowned and told the monks it was the *mind* that moved. I told the story and neither combatants could understand the point I was trying to make,

"The death star doesn't move, your mind moves," I said. I don't remember much after that, but I woke up with a goose egg on my head, and my underwear pulled up to my nipples.

♥

The human heart beats an average of 72 times per minute. The beat volume at rest in the standing position averages between 60 and 80 ml of blood in most adults. Thus, at a resting heart rate of 80 beats per minute, the resting cardiac output will vary between 4.8 and 6.4 L per min. However, the cardiac output of Olympic medal winners in cross country skiing increased 8 times above resting cardiac output to approximately 40 liters for one minute of maximal work, with an accompanied stroke volume of 210 ml per beat.

The average adult body contains about 5 L of blood, so this means all of our blood is pumped through our hearts about once every minute.

Your heart beats about 100,000 times in one day and about 35 million times in a year. During an average lifetime, the human heart will beat more than 2.5 billion times.

It pumps an average of 1.3 gallons of blood per minute, 1,900 gallons per day, and 693,500 gallons per year.

It is one of the few organs that can grow in size depending upon the amount of exercise you do. An athlete's heart will be significantly larger than a sedentary person.
The Greeks believed, the heart was the seat of the spirit, the Chinese associated it with the center for happiness, and the Egyptians thought the emotions and intellect arose from the heart.

Men are at a greater risk of cardiovascular disease than women.

Every day, the heart creates enough energy to drive a truck 20 miles. In a lifetime, that is equivalent to driving to the moon and back.

The heart pumps blood to almost all of the body's 75 trillion cells. Only the corneas receive no blood supply

The heart begins beating at four weeks after conception and does not stop until death.

Plato theorized that reasoning originated with the brain, but that passions originated in the "fiery" heart.

The term "heartfelt" originated from Aristotle's philosophy that the heart collected sensory input from the peripheral organs through the blood vessels. It was from those perceptions that thought and emotions arose.

My heart has gotten me in to more trouble than anything else in the world.

THGIE

MALE BONDING AND THE LAST SUPPER

> "Once can be happenstance.
> Twice could be coincidence.
> Three times is habit."
> -The Book of Benjamin
> Inside aorta, written in binary code & Aramaic

Cardboard Green Lantern gives me the stink eye as I drink my half & half blue raspberry/Dr. Pepper Slurpee. Maybe it's because Damon has placed a Deadpool baseball hat on top of his head, and Green Lantern understands you really shouldn't mix franchises, even if the same actor played both characters. The green LED light is starting to dim, and I wonder if it can be replaced, or if when it burns out will cardboard Green Lantern have to go. There's a metaphor for life somewhere in there, but right now I'm too busy fighting off a brain freeze to see it clearly.

I don't understand how Damon eats the jalapeno crunchy Cheetos. He probably goes through a whole large bag per day at the comic book store. I can't imagine how Mary kisses him when he comes home at night. I'm a Puffed Cheetos guy, myself. In some parallel universe, I'm sure this makes Damon and I mortal enemies.

I love walking around this comic book shop. Seeing all the new things that come in week after week, new adventures familiar characters go through, recycled stories with some new twist, in a hopeless attempt to make it seem original and fresh, the truly bold and brazen ideas that are hoping to find a market, and the controversial updates to classic characters, which never fail to make the hard core fans fight for hours in chat rooms.

Wednesdays are the best days to be here, because that's New Comic Book Day, and we get to see the passionate and addicted fans rushing in to pick up their holds. Damon masterfully takes care of his regulars and it's a pretty thankless job.

ADD INF: Damon never once tried to use my "celebrity" to cash in, in any shape or form. He never told people he was the messiah's best friend and never used this fact for any type of personal gain. I never told him how much I respect him for that.

He hands me the latest issue of *The Incredible Hulk* to thumb through as he puts this week's shipment into plastic bags with backing boards. He asks me what I think of the new story line, already knowing what I'll say about it. Hulk is a touchy subject for us, because we both love the character so much, and we often hate what the writers do with him. Every decade or so, Marvel gets the idea that Bruce Banner and The Hulk should just be the same character without making the transformation. I call this 'Smart Hulk' because that's really all it is. The power of the monster with the brain of the scientist. This is what's happening now in the series and both Damon and I hate it. If you take away the danger of having the out of control rage we all can identify with on some level, then the character suddenly becomes hollow and pointless. Why the writers shoot themselves in the foot like this, I will never know.

A customer in the store recognizes me and asks me to sign a copy of a *Wolverine* comic for some reason.

Naomi made me promise I would find out how the wedding plans are going, but I feel awkward talking to Damon about that kind of stuff. Guys just don't communicate in this way for some reason, when we get together we talk about the things that matter to us, it's like

Damon and I can talk about comics for days on end, but emotions and stuff? Never in a million years.

"So, how are things going?" Which is probably about as close as I'm going to get to broaching the wedding subject, unless he brings it up in some way. Luckily, we have both talked about going to the Superman festival, someday, for most of our lives, and this provides us with a type of geek lubricant to talk about the wedding and all the details that need to happen with it.

"Um...ya...I'm supposed to ask you something bro," Damon says.

"What's up?"

"Well, Mary has this idea that maybe everyone in the ceremony could wear Superman capes, in keeping with the theme of the wedding and all."

"That would definitely be original," I say.

"I thought so too, but I wasn't exactly sure how you would feel about it."

I take a Puffed Cheeto and place it in his Jalapeno bag.

"Why would I have a problem with it?" I ask, genuinely not knowing where he's going with this.

"I just know you've had some negative association with Superman capes," he says, and pulls out another stack of comics to bag and board.

"Wow. I actually haven't thought about it in a little while," I say, and am pleased by the truth of this statement, "I must be getting over it."

"What ever happened to that cape?" Damon asks.

I put Hulk down on the counter and try to recall exactly what *did* happen to the cape.

"I don't think I ever got it back. I left a whole bunch of stuff there and I'm assuming that was included. It kind of sucks now that I think about it," I say and put another puffed Cheeto in his jalapeno bag.

"That truly does. How much did you pay for that

thing?" Damon asks.

"Oh, Jesus, I paid a little over eight hundred bucks for it, but that was before Christopher Reeve died. I can't even imagine what it would be worth today."

"Oh shit! That's right. I forgot he signed it," Damon says in a tone of true disappointment and tragedy.

"Yes, he did. It was truly one of the coolest things I've ever owned."

There are a few moments of awkward silence before Damon works up the nerve to ask the embarrassing question.

"Let me get this straight…some strange guy was *really* wearing it while he was fucking your girlfriend?"

"Yep."

"Wow. That's truly harsh buddy. I'm so sorry."

I go to the shipment box and snag the new issue of *The Walking Dead* and take another hit off my Slurpee.

"I think if her vagina had a password, it would be 'password'," I say.

"Listen, about that…I'm really sorry, Ben. It was a really shitty thing for me to do, and I never really apologized for it."

I don't know exactly how I'm supposed to respond here. It's not ok that it happened and he's right, it *was* a shitty thing to do, but it's in the past, and my life is better now, and we both know it.

"It happened. What are we going to do? It's alright," I say.

"No. It's not alright. If something like that were to happen to me…if some guy put his dick inside Mary…I honestly think it would break me. I would probably disappear into some fantasy world, too. You would never do that to me and I feel like shit for doing it to you."

"It was kind of an asshole move," I say flicking a Cheeto in his general direction.

"It really was. I wish I could take it back. She's the

only woman in the world who I'm ashamed to say that I fucked."

I don't like seeing my friend beat himself up, so I try to lighten the mood a bit.

"Yes, but even so, it was probably like that joke about the worst blowjob you've ever had," I say.

"I don't think I've heard that one," Damon says.

"Did I tell you about the worst blowjob I ever had?"

"No."

"It was fucking great."

I open another box from this week's shipment and set it down next to Damon. He hands me some bags and backing boards as he laughs, and I help him get things ready for the Wednesday rush. After a few moments of silence, Damon's curiosity about the situation springs to life, and he starts grilling me like only a best friend can.

"How did you not know she was cheating on you before you caught her in the act?"

I thought about that so much right after it happened. I knew. I just didn't want to know. I once saw this movie about quantum physics that claimed, when Columbus' ships approached the shores of the new world, it was impossible for the natives to see the ships, because they didn't have the concept of what a ship was. Ships like that didn't exist in their world yet, so their minds couldn't conceive it. The body cannot live without the mind, so the eyes couldn't see the ships, even though they were right in front of them.

When I first heard this idea, I scoffed at the notion. If this were true, then how does the human race come up with new ideas? Didn't someone have to envision the ships in their minds eye before they built it? However, now I think back on all the denial and bull shit feel-goods I fed myself during that period, maybe the boat theory makes some sense.

All the times she would run into the bathroom

immediately after receiving a text message, or the late night work meetings that seemed to happen more and more frequently. The biggest red flag I should have picked up on, though, was her constant accusations that I was cheating on her. It was almost funny if it wasn't so ridiculous. I would head to the comic store on Wednesday to pick up my hold and hang with Damon. I would send her text messages while I was here, and come home with a big stack of comic books, and a Slurpee hangover, but somehow I was supposed to have hooked up with some imaginary person while I was gone. She started going through my cell phone and computer. If a female happened to comment on something I did on Facebook, then that meant we were sleeping together. I was actually so dumb I found it to be flattering, in a way. I thought if she was worried about other women wanting me, then maybe other women actually *did* want me, you know, because all women want a 140 pound, pigeon chested, action figure collecting boy-man.

The thought that she was simply transferring her own guilt onto me never once entered my mind.

I explain this to Damon, and like a true friend he doesn't tell me how sad it really is.

A guy in sweatpants and a T-shirt that reads 'Joss Whedon is my Serenity' picks up the latest *Arkham Asylum* action figure, and I make a mental note to snag one of those for myself before I leave. I had probably better grab one for John as well so we don't fight over them.

"Hey, Damon, how come you never asked if I were a fraud?" I ask once we have the store to ourselves again.

He opens another box and puts the new action figures on display behind the counter then he turns on the X-box, signaling the prep work is now over, and we get to relax for a bit.

"Well, I was kind of there when the whole thing unfolded. I remember you coming in here, standing in almost the exact same place you are right now, telling me about the defiled Superman cape. I drove you to the airport, then you went to Utah. It all happened so fast after that, and you weren't exactly in a mental state to think up something like this. Also, and I'm not trying to be rude here or anything, but you're not smart enough to think all of the details that went into this. It's just way to complex, and there have been so many people involved in studying what exactly is going with you. It's too big. You don't think like that. Besides, you didn't really *need* to lie about something like this."

"What do you mean?" I say, as I grab a controller, setting my Slurpee and Cheetos in the place, offering the best economy of motion, so I can eat and play at the same time.

"As Batman would say; 'we need to look at who benefits'. You already had this crazy thing with your heart going on, so you were already an anomaly and unique. You had a pretty good life, it was simple, but it was good none the less. You've got a steady job, enough spare money for comic books, and friends who love you. Other than the shitty, abusive bitch in the bedroom situation, you had a very good life."

"I did, didn't I?" I say, and smile at the thought of much simpler times.

"Besides, Naomi and John, what exactly have you gotten out of all this? Let's see, you've lost a hand, been sued for billions, been wrongfully imprisoned, had your face and hair burned off. and that's just the highlight reel. Not exactly winning scenarios."

"Not really," I say.

"Besides, I have the greatest reason in the world to believe in you... Mary," He grabs his controller and we start to play. I know this might sound strange to some people, but Damon and I actually have our deepest conversations while playing video games.

"You and I...we're too young to die. We don't even think it's a possibility, and somewhere, we feel like we can survive anything the universe throws at us. Mary became really intimate with her mortality before I ever even met her. She's told me stories about the chemo, and the sickness it brought on, and all the other awful things she had to deal with. She told me about this one day, she was sitting in the hospital chemo ward with a tube pumping poison into her chest. She had a bucket next to her, half full of her own vomit, which she was probably going to fill before her session was over. She realized she was never going to see another birthday, and she wasn't even old enough to legally buy a beer."

I pick up my Slurpee cup, and hold it high.

"To Mary," I say, and Damon clinks his paper cup to mine. We play through a level in silence, but I can feel Damon is processing something inside. I let him run with it, knowing he will get to it when he's ready.

"Have you been reading the new Superman story arc going on right now?" He asks.

"The one about the clear kryptonite?"

"Yes. Remember the hype that came out about this before it ran, about how it was going to change everything we knew about Superman, and the crazy amount of my customers who were preordering copies?"

"I remember. We couldn't wait for it to get going," I say.

"Mary heard about it, of course, and now this story arc has become something of a big deal in our lives."

"How so?" I ask, not exactly sure where he's going with this.

"If you remember, this was back before you went to Utah, and before your story took off. Mary was sitting in that, all too familiar puffy recliner in the chemo clinic with her stack of comics to read while she fights off the urge to throw up every five minutes, and she sees the ads for the clear kryptonite story line. All the ads said it was the biggest crossover event of the year, running through all Superman titles, and would take us into the next year. Mary told me what it was like for her to look at that ad, and make the decision not to start reading it, because she knew she wouldn't be alive to finish it."

I pause for a moment, trying to understand what that must have been like, but then my video car begins to swerve off the road as Damon's car zips past me.

"I've tried many times, since she told me this story, to put myself into her shoes, but I just can't do it. It's too big for me to wrap myself around. She told me about seeing movie previews for the summer blockbusters and wondering if she would live to see them. Now, some of those movies are coming out on DVD, and she's still here. You had something to do with that, Ben."

A customer comes in, and Damon pauses the game, while he gets a hold from behind the counter.

"Mary loves it when I run my fingers through her hair. Those red curls really do something for me. She hated being bald," He says when we're alone again.

"I remember her wearing this Superman hat when I first met her. If she hadn't been wearing that hat, we might not have even spoken to each other."

"She still has that hat, although she had to let it out a couple of tabs when her hair grew back in. You're right though, that hat just might have saved her life. Superman saves people he doesn't even know about. Now, every Wednesday night after I close up the shop, I bring home the latest *Superman* or *Action Comics* issue, and we will lie in bed reading it together. It's a reminder we are alive, and don't own this moment, but we get to choose how we spend it. After reading the comic, I will usually run my fingers through her long, curly red hair and kiss every inch of her tumor free head. My life is a billion times better with Mary in it. She made it better in ways I didn't even have the understanding to know it was flawed."

It's so strange to hear Damon talk like this. He's usually so guarded with his emotions, and we normally just talk about superficial 'guy' stuff.

'I never asked you if you were a fraud because I've never had to," he says, and we go back to playing the game. After a few moments, he tells me that even though I have a magic hand, he still has the bigger dick, and all the ladies know it.

Later that night, I'm lying in bed reading about Superman and clear kryptonite, and I imagine Damon and Mary reading this same issue at this same time. It makes me wonder about how many other people might be reading this very comic at this very moment.

Naomi stirs in her sleep, and I run my fingers through her hair. She stirs a little bit and I kiss her head.

"Did you finish your comic?" She says, still half asleep.

"Yes."

"Did Spiderman save everybody?"

"Superman, babe, and yes, he did, but it's not looking good for him next issue."

"Oh no. That's too bad," she says, and traces her fingers along my stomach.

"I know. It's scary."

"Thank you for bringing action figures home for John. He loved them."

I set Superman down on the night stand and wrap my arms around Naomi to keep her warm.

"It was no problem. There's a pretty cool Lego X-box game coming out in a few weeks I'm probably going to need help beating, so the action figures are a way to suck up," I say.

"I love you, you know?" She says.

"I do. I love you right back."

"Wanna fool around?"

I turn off the lights and pull the sheets over our heads.

"Up, up, and away."

♥

I've got five vats going at once, and the sweet steam that comes off each one is arguably my favorite part of the job. I need to pay attention, though, because I'm making Root Beer jelly beans and Coffee jelly beans, which both have a deep brown color that would be really easy to mistake for one another, if it weren't for the strong smell each one produces. One day, I tried doing this with Cinnamon flavor next to Cranberry, and after losing my attention span for a moment, I had destroyed two full batches, and about eight hours of work, because I mixed them together.

Creamsicle orange, Lemon Meringue yellow, and a new flavor called Alien Poop, that's a bright green with flecks of brown, spin next to the two vats of Coffee and Root Beer I'm diligently trying not to mix up.

There's an elementary school taking a tour of the factory today, so I'm hurrying to get these vats done before any distractions arrive. Mr. Ferninni usually likes to bring these tours by the vats and explain how there's actually a person who buffs the jelly beans to a shiny, hard finish. Sometimes, I let the children place their hands inside the tumblers so they can feel the soft felt spinning around. This, often times, will turn their hands whatever color the last batch I had in the buffer was. One little girl touched the soft felt, but when her hand came away bright Cherry red, she screamed like an extra in one of the *Texas Chainsaw* movies. I make sure never to do red colored beans when the kids are coming in.

Mr. Ferninni looks excited as he comes over to see me. Last week, he perfected the procedure used to print words on the inside of gumballs, and now they can be read much easier, even though, when you tear open the gumball to read whatever is inside, it pretty much destroys whatever words were written there. Still, now people can make out various letters and sometimes even a word. Mr. Ferninni sells over 200,000 of those gumballs per month.

He comes over and drops something round into my latex covered hand.

"What's this?" I ask. It looks like some type of jawbreaker. It's hard and white, but instead of having the rainbow covered flecks, this one has letters and symbols.

"It's *your* jawbreaker," he says. and a large grin covers his face. He then goes on to explain to me how it's not an ordinary jawbreaker. Most jawbreakers change colors as you suck through the various levels of sugar, which is why if you were to slice one in half, it would look like rainbow layers of sediment inside a tiny planet. Rather than changing colors, this one will change letters and symbols.

"If you look at the letters on each sugar level as you eat the jawbreaker, it will spell out a special message. That one in your hand reads B E - H A P P Y, with a smiley face symbol at the end," he says, and I laugh.

"That's actually pretty cool. Do you think people will actually keep taking the candy out of their mouths to check the letters though?" He holds up his index finger and then pulls a piece of paper from the inside of his suit jacket. It's an order printout from the factory's website, 25,000 jawbreakers from one order alone. I'm still floored over this new development in our candy world, when he pulls out another piece of folded paper from his suit jacket.

"This is what I really wanted to talk to you about though," he says.

The paper is a notarized Will & Testament, leaving the candy factory to me. Before I can say anything, he holds up his index finger again.

"I've been making a fuck-ton of money off of you, Ben, the gumballs, now the jawbreakers, not to mention how my business more than quadrupled since this thing happened to you. You haven't taken a cent, no matter how hard I try. I also can see how you might need a place to someday hide or disappear into if things get too hectic. Think of this like your own personal Bat Cave…but with candy."

A bunch of children and a few adults come through the doors on the factory floor, and Mr. Ferninni waves his hand in a gesture that says 'well that's finished, now it's time to get back to work'. He turns to leave, but I place my hand on his shoulder, and he turns back towards me. I have absolutely no words, so I just hug him. He hugs me back. It's the first time this has ever happened.

"I love you kid," he says.
"I love you too, sir."

♥

It was somewhere around this time Wendell began to struggle with his inner demons. In hindsight, I really wish I had had the opportunity to just sit down with Wendell, have a beer, and maybe even play some X-box. Maybe, just maybe, he could have learned to become OK with my existence, and see how I didn't have anything to do with his belief system, his religion, or his classical representation of Adler's inferiority complex.

The Book of Revelation warns us about all the false prophets who will come into the world before the Second Coming. It's no great stretch of the imagination to see how Wendell viewed me as one of these frauds. I would like it pointed out here, that the *Book of Revelation* never actually says false prophets are bad. The problem is they might somehow distract people from listening to what Jesus had to say, so they might miss out on all the benefits from having Jesus as a savior.

Wendell was a good person who just got a little bit confused.

He felt that those people who hadn't heard the

message of Christ were truly doomed to an afterlife of eternal pain and suffering. Wendell's compassion for his fellow man took issues with this. In the deepest regions of his non-backwards flowing heart, he just wanted to see people being happy and to try to help that happen wherever he could.

After coming home from the cruise, he began talking to his wife about how disturbed he was by people's reaction to John. His better half really didn't see the problem with it, because she felt people are smart enough to decide things for themselves, and she believed when push came to shove, most people will make the right choice.

For the most part, Wendell believed this too, but he also believed humans are flawed creatures and stumble quite a lot along their spiritual journeys. If Wendell could somehow clear some of the obstacles from humanities' path, this would be a worthy endeavor for any human being. Kind of a Bodhisattva attitude backed up by the NRA.

When the thought to kill me first entered Wendell's head, he pushed it away and found it revolting. When Wendell was a young boy, he went on a Boy Scout weekend camp with the other boys in his neighborhood. One of the other youths had snuck a pump action BB gun along for the trip, and once they were alone in the woods, the scouts proceeded to shoot everything on the mountainside.

It was the first time Wendell had ever shot anything that resembles a real gun, because his mother had an aversion to them, so they were never allowed into his home. He liked how it felt in his hands. How the pressure inside the air rifle would increase every time he pumped the handle. Looking down the sights and putting the gun stock into his shoulder felt completely natural to Wendell, and he was surprised at the simplicity of it all. He missed on his first few shots, because he was afraid there might be a loud noise, like on television, or that the rifle might kick and hurt him, and then he would risk embarrassment among his fellow Scouts. When neither of these things happened, Wendell found he could hit almost anything he put his mind to. Once, he was even so bold as to put a pellet into a *Sprite* can that his Scout Master had set on a rock by the campfire while he opened a bag of marshmallows.

As dusk began to set onto that first day at camp, Wendell and two other boys took the air rifle into the woods for a little more shooting before their Scout Master made them stay in camp for the remainder of the night.

This was when Wendell first encountered death.

As the sun was beginning to set, a large owl began its night by sitting on a fairly low hanging branch, hooting, and watching the boys with a mild interest. One of the other boys, Shane Harrison, whose owned the pellet gun, and happened to be the Scout Masters son, raised the rifle and pointed it at the owl.

In that moment, Wendell knew he had the power to say something, do something to stop what was going to happen, but he didn't. He sat there in silence, and for the rest of his life tried to convince himself there just wasn't time to act, or nothing he could have done would have made the least bit of difference.

Deep down inside, though, he knew this wasn't true.

When the owl fell to earth, one wing flapped violently. and it made this awful hiccupping sound as it rolled around on the ground.

"Shit, it didn't die," Shane had said, and began pumping the handle of the rifle furiously. Wendell watched as Shane put no less than thirty pellets into the owl, and felt something die inside of himself every time the animal refused to do so. The damn hiccupping sound wouldn't stop, even though the bird lie face down on the earth. The wing had stopped flapping, but there was still this random twitch inside its body. The wing would rise ever so slowly, like the owl was trying to get away on will power alone.

It took forever and the damn bird refused to die.

Shane's arm got tired from pumping air pressure into the gun over and over, so another boy took it and the shooting continued.

"God, please just kill it already," Wendell had begged, but as the tiny ball bearings continued to fly, the owl continued to twitch and moan. Finally, unable to take it anymore, Wendell ran over to the bird and stomped it beneath the hiking boots his mother had called 'waffle stompers'. He could feel, and hear, the tiny, hollow bones crunch under the souls of his boot. He could see how the owl's body was a little more deformed every time he raised his foot.

The crunching sound was much worse than the hiccups.

Finally, the noises stopped, and the owl looked nothing like the magnificent animal it had once been, but just a pile of broken and bent feathers. There was blood and meat on Wendell's boot that would leave a stain for the rest of the boots life. The three boys stood there, looking at their handiwork, as the feeling of death encased them in sorrow. Wendell was breathing hard and he could see little puffs of white as he exhaled into the cold air.

"We probably shouldn't tell anyone about this," Shane said, and that's when Wendell hit him. Blood ran from Shane's nose like a hydrant. It was the first time Wendell had ever struck another person in anger, and he didn't like how it felt. He made a vow do never hit anyone else, as long as he lived, and he kept that vow until he punched me.

Shane began to cry, and after Wendell threw the pellet gun as far down the mountain as he possibly could, he began to cry himself. Shane didn't try to fight back, because the experience left all three boys drowning in a puddle of guilt and remorse. None of them tried to find the rifle. When they got back to camp, they put some ice on Shane's nose, telling his father he fell and hit his face on a rock.

The boys would remain in the same Scout Troop for the next five years, and would never speak of the owl, or the thrown punch again, but their friendship would always remain strained because of it.

That owl sat heavily on Wendell's mind when the thoughts of shooting me first began to surface. It seemed like he had tried everything in his power to slow my popularity and to turn people from the hype I had become. He had at least five various websites going, as well as focus groups on the various social media sites, all condemning me and my work.

The problem with religious protesting is, that the Westboro Baptist Church has made anyone with a sign look like some type of fanatic with a cause and that's exactly how a lot of people came to see Wendell. People in his church began to distance themselves from him. When he would reach out to other ministers for support and guidance, his calls were never returned. He then started to get banned from things like the Cruise lines and other speaking engagements. His money became tied up in slandering me and the few restraining orders people were beginning to place on him. His wife was becoming increasingly irritated by his obsession.

However, Wendell looked at all of this like the trials of Job. He knew that God would take care of him and somehow provide a way in showing people the truth. Wendell never lost his faith, which shows just how different the two of us are. Wendell never lost his faith. I never had any to lose.

After the shooting and incarceration, a prison psychiatrist diagnosed Wendell to be a paranoid schizophrenic. He underwent years of harsh and invasive treatments that never really seemed to help him.

Thorazine, Hadrol, Prolixin, Seraquel, Cognitive Behavioral Therapy, Tardive Dyskinesia, and Electro Shock Therapy.

None of these helped Wendell in any way whatsoever. In fact, he had many adverse reactions to some of the medications, and during these times, all rational thought left Wendell's mental ability. He was desperate to get his life back, but was becoming more and more aware how things were never going to be the same for him.

One day, in passing, he asked his psychiatrist about how they used to treat mental disorders in the past. The doctor told him about several different techniques, but the one that stuck in Wendell's mind was Trepanning.

Trepanning is the technique of drilling holes in the skull to expose the dura-matter, however, it also was used as a way to remove evil spirits and inner demons.

They found Wendell's body in a janitor's closet, where he had used a rolled up bottle cap and a hardbound book from the prison library, to attempt to perform the procedure on himself. Wendell had over 27 cuts and scrapes on his head before he was finally able to penetrate his skull.

Wendell never found peace.

His last words were 'I'm sorry'.

♥

When movies like *Jaws* and *Piranha* come out, people didn't go to them for plot points or for the acting skills. They went to see people get eaten. Some horror franchises like *Saw* and *Hostel* even came up with a term for it…torture porn. It's the part of us that makes us look at a traffic accident as we drive by, hoping we might see something gruesome. We hope we will see something graphic or interesting we will be able to tell people about later. One of the ugliest parts of our human nature is the moment when we drive by the accident and realize there's nothing to see. We have the tiniest moment of disappointment we will never admit exists within ourselves, and we are ashamed for feeling. We tell ourselves we're glad nobody seems to be hurt and shove our disappointment down somewhere where we can pretend it doesn't exist.

I'm not sure why we do this. I honestly can't say why it happens. Maybe it's because when we see things like, that we are reminded just how fragile our existence is, and how thankful we are to still be alive. Maybe it's because a part of us likes to see others suffer. I don't know. If you've got a theory, shout it out, I would love to hear it.

There was a movie out a while ago called, *The Passion of the Christ*. I don't want to give away the ending if you haven't seen it, but they crucify the guy at the end. Spoiler Alert. It was the ultimate torture porn flick. I'm sure there were a lot of people who went to see it for religious reasons, and as a way to connect to their faith, however, I also think a lot of people went to see it because they knew some guy was going to be nailed to a piece of wood towards the end.

If Mel Gibson does it in the name of religion, it becomes classy. If Eli Roth does it in the name of cinema, it's torture porn.

The point I'm trying to make, here, is that I know some of you out there are reading this book because you know how it ends and want to get the gory details. I'm not saying everyone…there are a lot of you who are reading this in hopes of understanding what the words mean, or maybe something I said or did resonated with you, and you want to expand on that. If this is you, I want to truly thank you. You are the one who made this journey worth it. However, if you are here for the torture porn, I just want you to take a moment and admit to yourself that's why you're here. If you've read a hundred and some odd pages,

I hope you can see me as an actual human being by now, and not some imaginary person who didn't feel things, and who wished things had turned out differently.

There's not much story left to tell.

So, let's get to it.

♥

The beginning of the end happened at a restaurant called Kandor Deep Dish, in Metropolis Illinois. The Superman Festival was two days away, and we were there making the final preparations for the wedding, and watching as the city set things up for the coming celebration. If you're going to be in Illinois, you really have to eat some deep dish, so when we saw Kandor's we all agreed to go in.

ADD INF: For the non-geeks, and those who are dead inside, Kandor is a Kryptonian city that was shrunken by Brainiac and put into a glass bottle. A Superman themed pizza place is about the coolest thing in existence.

Mary was very adamant the wedding also be a celebration of life, since she had once given up on the idea of living long enough to get married. She wanted to invite as many people, who had anything to do with bringing her and I together, to come celebrate with us if possible. I was quite amazed at the people who took time out of their lives to come get their geek on with us at the Superman Festival.

We would be reuniting with several people over the next few days, but that dinner is where things really started. Dr. Ormsby, who performed the bone marrow transplant on John and I was there, as was Dr. Hale, who was the lead doctor on Mary's cancer team.

Stephen Keatings, the blind man who cut off my hand, came along with his girlfriend Malory, who didn't miss a single opportunity to point out that Damon and Mary had been going out for less time than her and Stephen had, and were getting married. I was just glad to see Stephen seemed to be adjusting to his new ability of sight, and how he took Malory's ribbing with good humor.

Correction Officer Despain even showed up.

The person who blew my mind the most by showing up was Jennifer Summers. Mary and Naomi had spent a lot of time going through the Mormon Church volunteer center, and dozens of hospital staff requests, looking for her. Jennifer was the girl who called me and asked me to come to Utah and be a bone marrow donor. She was a bright young girl who took great joy in learning all of the intricacies that single call caused.

Mr. Ferninni was thrilled his new jawbreakers were selling so well, and he gave out bags, along with his business card, every chance he got. He's like a magician who has something in each bottomless pocket, but instead of cards or pigeons, Mr. Ferninni had candy.

Naomi, John, and I split a delicious pepperoni and pine nut deep dish, while agent Coulson, who insisted we call him 'Peter' for the duration of the trip, ordered a calzone that was easily as big as his head.

Kandor Deep Dish was no doubt hoping the festival would bring in tourists, and they were just putting the final touches on the decorations when our party came in. They had these amazing windows that somehow magnified the outside world, making it look enormous, and selling the bottled, shrunken city effect. There were other Kryptonian looking artifacts, like the candles on each table were under these tiny models of the Fortress of Solitude. Mary shook her head in embarrassment when Damon stuffed one of these into his backpack.

The waitress wore a red pleated skirt, along with red boots, and a red cape which couldn't have been easy to carry trays and pour drinks in. She also wore a very low cut, tight fitting Superman shirt that was difficult not to stare at.

None of us noticed Wendell's Nissan pull into the parking lot, or if we did, we thought nothing of it.

I ate enough cheese bread to stop the heart of a Tyrannosaurus, while waiting for the deep dish, triple meat pizza to come out of the oven. Naomi told me I probably shouldn't eat so much bread, because then I won't want any pizza. Silly girl. Damon and I alone could have probably shut the place down if we had been given the chance.

It was so great being there with those people who had been through all the crazy with me. We were a family in some strange sort of way. It was my hope we could stay connected and come to know each other much better. The pitchers were getting empty, so I took them up to the counter to get a refill before the real food got there. The hostess walks past me, with a new tray of cheese bread for our table, when her eyes meet mine there is that unmistaken look of recognition, and I prepare myself to sign something or possibly even perform a cure.

"Are you and your party here for the Superman convention?" She asks, as she gives the red and yellow shield on my shirt a good look.

"Is it that obvious?" I ask. She leans in close to me, like she's going to share the greatest secret ever told with me, but looks around tentatively to see if anyone is paying attention.

"How many people are in your group?"

"Thirteen," I say, remembering counting everyone right before we asked for a table.

"Come with me," she says, and we set down the pitchers and cheese bread on the table, before she takes me into a break room, just off of the main kitchen. I'm a little nervous, but her ample cleavage makes me willing to take the risk. I will do anything if there's the possibility I might touch a boob.

She opens a locker and produces a small pad of white paper and gives me about fifteen sheets or so.

"Look, nobody is supposed to know about this yet, and I'm not supposed to start giving these out until tomorrow, but since you and your group cared enough to show up early, I'm going to hook you up, ok?"

The papers she handed me are temporary tattoos with the Superman logo and the year stamped beneath it.

"Henry Cavill is going to be here, Sunday night, signing autographs and talking to a very limited number of people. You have to have the tattoo to get in and there's only fifty tattoos printed. These are almost impossible to get and there will be buttloads of Superman swag given away there."

Talk about being in the right place at the right time. I hadn't heard anything about Henry Cavill being here. I wonder if I might be able to talk him into signing a new cape for me to replace the defiled one. I thank the waitress profusely, and she gives me a wink and tells me I had better be leaving her a nice tip.

She is truly lovely and this is a very nice gift. I think I can do better than just a tip.

"Do you know who I am?" I ask.

"No. The bald head looks familiar though, but that could just be because I have a thing for smooth skin."

I pretend my ego isn't hurt, but there's a part of me that is also super glad there are still places I can go in this world and not be recognized.

"Since you don't know who I am, this might seem a little strange, but will you bear with me for a moment and answer some questions for me as honestly as you can?"

She looks me up and down, trying to see where the scam is going to come from, but then sees me for what I truly am, a bald geek who probably weighs a hundred and fifty pounds while carrying a fifty pound bag of rice, and soaking wet. We're both pretty sure that she could stomp the shit out of me in those red go-go boots if she wanted to, so she tells me 'why not'?

When I ask her if she, or anyone she loves, is suffering from any physical ailments, I can tell this is the last thing she thought I was going to ask her. She blushes a little at the thought, and I tell her if I thought there was any chance that she would say yes, that I would be asking her all kinds of naughty questions, but I'm serious about the health issue one. She thinks about it, as I wonder about what exactly might have happened if I *had* asked the naughty question. She finally tells me she's actually very healthy. The only thing that ever bothers her is she often suffers from these blinding migraines. She had been trying to cure it by controlling her water consumption and sleep habits, but about every month or so she gets one that just blocks the world out in blinding white.

I reach out and touch her head. I give the tiniest of pushes and assure her she will never have another migraine again.

"You're not an MDP are you?" She asks.

"An MDP?"

"Mentally Disturbed Person," She says, and gives me a great shot of side boob as she closes the locker door. She laughs and makes me promise to come back in for the Henry Cavill panel and we head back into the dining room.

On the way back to the table, I take a look into the kitchen to see if our pizza is ready yet. If I had looked to my left, where the parking lot was, instead of to my right where the kitchen was, I would have seen Wendell lying in the back of his truck bed with the tailgate down, setting up his rifle.

The pizza had hit the table and as delicious as it looked, Naomi was right, and I probably shouldn't have eaten so much cheese bread. I needed to give my stomach time to regroup for round two, so I decided to hand out the tattoos. I know the value I've been handed, and I also know some of us, like John and Damon, are prone to lose things, so I want to ensure we all have the tattoos. I decide that the safest thing to do would be to put the tattoos on everyone right now while we eat. Plus it will give me a chance to say hello to everyone. I take a bar towel and a glass of water and sit down next to John.

"Let me see your hand, buddy," I say.

"Why?"

"Free Superman tattoo." I hold up the white paper card with the S shield and he sticks out his chubby fist. I wipe his hand with the towel, marveling at his tiny sauce stained fingers. His feet kick from his booster seat as he takes another bite of pizza. I place the tattoo on the back of his hand, and while I hold it pressed against his skin, I kiss his fingers.

"I love you little man," I say.

"I love you Ben. You're my hero," he says, and my heart breaks open with joy.

"Oh please. I can't be your hero at the Superman convention. That's just wrong."

"Nope. It's you, Ben. You're the type of man I hope to grow into someday."

Naomi hears this and gives me the warmest smile I have ever seen. As I moisten the back of her hand with the bar towel, she asks me what I'm doing. I tell her I'm hooking us up with some awesome swag and steal a fast kiss before moving on. I continue around the table, explaining the tattoo, and thanking everyone for coming. Stephen tells me again how he's really sorry about my hand and would take it all back if he could. I tell him how I'm just glad he seems to have found some happiness and that things are looking better for him

When I took Mary's hand, and washed it with the bar towel, I remember being struck by just how beautiful she really is. The way her long, red hair falls into these almost perfect ringlets, and the way it brings out the green of her eyes, is truly stunning. She gave me a smile, and thanked me for all the help with arranging things for the wedding. I told her I wouldn't miss it for the world, and then I stood and kissed the top of her head, exactly .35

seconds after Wendell gave the trigger a final squeeze, and the top of Mary's head disintegrated before my eyes.

I tried to gasp, but I suddenly couldn't breathe, and there's was blood on the front of Mary's body that didn't look like it came from her head. Something slapped me on the back, like your mom used to do when you have a coughing fit as a child, and more blood splattered across Mary's torso.

Even though the top half of Mary's head was completely gone, her eyes remained locked on mine for such a long period of time, that I will never forget it, even though it was probably only a nanosecond in reality. Damon was the first of us to get moving. He grabbed Mary's body and let out a moan that had no place coming from human lips.

"You've got to save her Ben," he said, as the other people at the table began to scream and drop to the floor. As I turned back towards Naomi, I saw her throwing down John's booster chair, and forcing it under the table. I reached out to touch Mary, but my arms wouldn't work. I tried to lift them, tried to will them into moving, but it was no use. I felt my bladder let go and it was probably about then I noticed a large piece of my sternum was missing.

I never heard the shots.

I fell to the floor, and remember how cold the tile floor felt against my cheek.

"Help her Ben!" Damon screamed at me, but my arms still wouldn't move. It felt like I was trying to breathe under water, and I could feel a wetness inside my chest I had never felt before, as my blood began to fill my lungs. Something happened that I really can't explain, but I will try for the sake of the story: A glowing shape came out of Mary's eyes and floated above her for a moment. It looked like what you might imagine a lightsaber would look like if it were under water. The radiant purple light seemed to spark and smoke in the air and it made no sound. I don't know if it is what we call the soul I was seeing, I will let you interpret this as you see fit, but when I looked back into Mary's eyes it, was obvious she was gone.

Naomi was at my side, and when she saw my chest she placed her hand over the wound to stop the bleeding. I wish I didn't see just how far her hand sank into my chest at that moment, but I did, and I knew things were very bad. I took as deep of breath as my chest would allow, and tried to focus my mind on anything, but what was going on.

"In brightest day," I said, and Naomi bent closer to hear me. The waitress with the amazing rack yelled from her hiding place somewhere that the police and an ambulance were on the way.

I didn't get to have any pizza.

There was a light, like the one I saw in Mary forming in the periphery of my vision, but this one was a bright red.

"In blackest night," I said.

"I don't know what you're saying, baby," Naomi said, and began to cry. It blew my mind how she never once tried to protect herself, but only tried to help John and myself. That's why Naomi will always be made of awesome and will always be a better human being than I ever was. Agent Coulson had begun to return fire, but from his position, shooting through a window into a parking lot with his service weapon, he wasn't very effective.

"No evil shall escape my sight."

I remember wondering why the light I was now seeing in my vision coming out of me was red when Mary's was purple. In Star Wars, only the bad guys had the red lightsabers. Since the red light was coming from me, did that mean that I was a bad person, or did we just all shine in different colors when the moment comes for us?

Damon was frantically grabbing my amputated arm and touching the gray matter coming from the frighteningly large hole in the side of Mary's head.

"You have to save her Ben! Do something!" He yelled at me.

"I'm sorry. I can't. I'm so sorry," I said, as the red light blocked everything else out and then faded into blackness.

That was when I died.

TRAP OWT ENIN

THE START OF THE BREAKDOWN

> "The only way to discover the indestructible within you, is to constantly submit yourself to annihilation. Whatever remains is your true self."
> -The Book of Ben
> Inside beginning of large intestine

The police and paramedics were on the scene almost immediately, because they had been preparing for the huge influx of people the Superman convention brings to their town every year, and they quickly secured the area around the pizza restaurant.

The first paramedic on scene took one look at Mary, and then moved on to me despite Damon's protests. I don't know how I felt about my best friend asking for medical assistance to be given to his girlfriend, over his long time best friend. Logically this goes against the 'bro's before ho's' maxim, but I was dead, so these things seemed much less important at that moment.

One good thing about being shot, at a table half full of surgeons and doctors, is you get the best first aid available. Dr. Ormsby and Dr. Hale were on top of me doing CPR almost before I hit the ground. Naomi later told me, both doctors seemed reluctant to hand me over to the paramedics, but the first responders had the tools with them the doctors didn't, like AED machines and lactated ringers.

Everyone present did everything humanly possible for me, but sometimes people just die, and there's not a whole lot we can do about that, especially when bullets are involved. They hooked me up to the AED machine, and the Speak-&-Spell voice would periodically tell everyone to CLEAR, before pumping enough electricity through my body to make me look like Luke Skywalker when the Emperor was trying to kill him in *Jedi*. In between jolts, I was pumped with adrenaline, and just about everything else the paramedics had on the truck. Soon, the Speak-&-Spell voice began to say the battery was losing its charge, and another AED machine should be applied soon. They probably would have hit me with gamma rays, or thrown me into the sun, if they thought it would have helped.

    It didn't, and I died.

    Dr. Hale was the one to officially pronounce my time of death, but after he called it, John begged them to try one more time. Everyone knew it was pointless, but it's hard to argue with a broken hearted little boy, and besides, what would it hurt? I still had the AED pads stuck to me and all they had to do was turn it back on.

    "Please," John said, and when no one moved, he walked over and turned on the machine again.

    "Battery charge depleted," the Stephen Hawkings voice said, but then after a few seconds started talking again. "Checking for pulse…No pulse found…Shock recommended…Stand clear…Stand clear…Checking for pulse."

    Naomi tried to pick up John to comfort him, but as she wrapped her arms around his tiny body, he touched my cheek, and the machine fired its charge, knocking both of them across the room and even rendering Naomi unconscious for a moment or two.

    "Shock interference…please stand clear…checking for pulse…"

    A paramedic ran over to help Naomi and John, as Dr. Hale turned off the AED machine, and officially called my time of death.

    Then I farted.

Not a cute little toot, like when one accidentally slips out when you sneeze or anything like that, but more like the sound Peter Pan made when he would stick a knife into one of the pirate ships sails and tear it all the way down to the deck. Like a dog that farts himself awake, I sat up so fast, the Superboobs waitress screamed.

"I think I just shat myself," I said. Not the best first words for someone who has literally come back from the dead, but I didn't have time to prepare anything inspiring.

Dr. Hale later told me, I was officially dead for over nine minutes, and this was the longest period of time he had ever heard of. He also informed me I had probably suffered some brain damage. He gave me this news in the same way you or I might add a turnover to our happy meal order.

'Oh and btw, you've more than likely suffered severe brain damage. Who wants ice cream?'

♥

If you ever look at an anatomy chart of the human heart, you will see it's a little oblong shaped, which slants down on the left side of our chest cavity. Mine obviously slants down and to the right. This was the only thing that prevented Wendell's .30-06 round from shredding my heart like the pork at *Café-Rio*. The bullet hit the area of my chest over my heart, around the 4 o'clock mark, if you are looking at my body. This is where the bottom ventricles would be for a normal person. Mine happen to be at the 8 o'clock mark, so the bullet missed my heart by the smallest margin possible. It still managed to rip through the pericardium, and some of the cardiac muscle which required three surgeries to fix, so I will probably never run a marathon or win the Tour-de-France.

As far as the brain damage, you are probably a much better judge of that by now, than I am, but I will tell you, that ever since almost pooping on the floor that day, I smell burnt toast all the time. I don't know why, and no doctor has ever been able to explain it to me, but it's constantly there with me.

♥

I wasn't able to go to Mary's funeral, and of all the things which piss me off in this story, this is the cherry on the cake.

I was in, yet another hospital, having another surgery with tubes sticking out of places they have no right to, and with doctors conferring with each other ad-nausea.

Naomi and John went to the service though, and when she came to see me later after returning, Naomi told me how Damon was not doing well with the whole thing. I didn't really think he would be. I once saw him go ape-shit, because a Batman action figure didn't come with the Batarang it was holding in the picture on the back of the box.

I can't imagine what it must have been like for him, trying to simultaneously cancelling the wedding arrangements, dealing with all the police questions, and planning a funeral. I was supposed to be his best man. Shouldn't I be taking care of a lot of this stuff? I guess it's just one more way I failed my amigo in the long run.

It was just too late to cancel a lot of things for the wedding, so Mary ended up having the best catered funeral in human history. Naomi said, the irony of the wedding cake sitting next to funeral potatoes was one of the saddest things she had ever seen.

I have replayed those moments at Kandor's in my mind, more times than could be healthy, and a rather large part of me wished I had died that day, so I wouldn't have to live with the grief of Mary's death and Damon's suffering. I had some thoughts of suicide soon after. I'm not proud of it, but the fact is, two people had been killed directly because of me. Would there be more? If so, I knew I wouldn't be able to take it, so why just not end the whole thing now?

Naomi and John could tell I was in a funk, and did

their best to cheer me up, but it wasn't working. I was in a lot of physical pain, and frankly, I have been known to whine like a little girl when I have a cold, so you can probably imagine what I'm like in a hospital. I wish I could say I was a model patient, but I wasn't. I was mean to almost everyone around me and took out my frustrations on anyone I could. I snapped at the nurses and doctors who checked in on me. I bitched about the food, even if I requested a specific thing, and someone was kind enough to bring me. I told everyone how it just wasn't fair and how I never asked for any of this.

Then John told me to stop being such a wimp.

It's a very strange sensation to have a four-year-old call you a wimp. It's even worse when he's right.

He got right in my face and told me to stop being such a whiny bitch, because it was getting embarrassing. He told me I needed to cowboy up, because a lot of people were out there still counting on me. He scolded me, how there were others out there hurting worse than me, like my best friend, who had just lost his fiancé, so maybe I shouldn't be such a selfish asshole, and think about how others might be feeling, and maybe, just maybe be thankful I'm still alive.

Agent Coulson took the whole thing pretty hard as well. He stated he had become complacent in his position and that complacency jeopardized his reaction time. He had gone to his supervisors and explained this, but since he had complained about the assignment so badly when it was first given to him, the agency just thought he was angling for something new and denied his requests. Naomi told me, during the entire funeral, he glared like he wanted to shoot somebody.

If I had been there, I probably would have felt the same way.

When Damon came to see me, I couldn't even look him in the eye. He told me over and over he didn't blame me for what happened, but how could he possibly not? He brought me some comics, and I died a little bit inside when I saw one of them was from the Superman series he and Mary used to read together. I tell him how I don't think I will be able to read that one. If Mary can't read it, then why should I get to? He tells me we have to read it *because* Mary isn't able to. He said we owed it to her, and it was one of the few things we could do to keep her spirit alive.

I wanted to tell him how sorry I was, that I would take it all back, or trade places with her if I could. I wanted to tell him about the purple light and how her eyes met mine at the end. I wanted to say I'm sorry for not being able to heal her wounds and for not having the ability to take away the grief he was feeling. I wanted to apologize for not being a better best man and a better friend, and how I would never be able to think of Superman and not think of Mary at the same time.

Instead, I just cried.

In a very un-Damon-like gesture, he took my hand, and cried with me.

Then we realized how gay we looked and stopped.

♥

The first night after I'm released from the hospital, I had planned to catch up on some movies with John and Naomi. Just a very low key night, because I still wasn't supposed to be doing anything like Parkour or UFC fighting, yet. John had just made a hot bowl of popcorn and Naomi made these amazing peanut butter shakes that would probably stop the heart of a lesser man. I had on my Batman pajamas (with footies), and as I put my arm around my beautiful, smart, funny, and sexy girlfriend I was feeling things might be ok again for the first time since Metropolis.

As I pushed the button on the remote, the TV kicked on, and there's a picture of me, the one from the You Tube video where I'm placing my hand on the earth, because I'm about to throw up, but people think it's me stopping the earthquake, with the caption "Raised from the dead" underneath it.

I swear to god, half of the major events in my life I found out by watching *Entertainment Tonight*.

A reporter had gotten a hold of either the police report, or my medical records from the night of the shooting and discovered I had been clinically dead. We don't even talk about suing the media any more. If we sued everyone who printed, or televised, something untrue about me that's all our lives would be about. One of the Ten Commandments should have been about avoiding any litigation like the plague.

We also don't complain about confidential information being leaked to the media anymore. It's just part of life now, and I have learned money and celebrity have ways of opening doors that really should remain closed. Nothing is safe or sacred. Since the words were discovered, I've been trying to live my life as if everything I do is plastered across Facebook and I have seven billion friends who will see it. If it's embarrassing, I just don't do it, or make sure I won't be caught. My masturbation process looks like a scene out of *Mission Impossible*.

So, now the world thinks I've been resurrected. That's awesome…not.

I dip a kernel of popcorn into my shake and John cringes like I just farted in neon.

The news shows a video of Kandor's Pizza, where people are flocking to see the place where I died and then came back to life. Before we know it, we are all laughing, and I mean full on belly laughing, which actually hurts a little bit. This has to be the dumbest thing I've ever seen. People are touching the spot on the ground where I supposedly had died, Although Naomi and John both tell me I was actually shot on the other side of the restaurant, but I guess the real spot didn't provide an good enough view of the menu board, so my death site was conveniently moved. They touch the ground, and many of them cry.

The camera banks around to the reporter, and she is with a man wearing a Superman baseball cap, that is exactly like the one Mary was wearing when I first saw her. The sight of it fills me with an unexpected pang of regret. The man is Tommy Powell, who tells the camera how he is a homosexual who is suffering from full blown AIDS and was not expected to live for very much longer. Tommy tells us how he had come to the Superman festival in hopes of seeing me, because he was out of other options to try. After my shooting, Tommy went to the pizza shop and touched the ground (where nothing actually happened) and was cured from his AIDS. He claimed that, because he was cured, that meant I was not opposed to the homosexual lifestyle and loved the gays.

Now, it's true I do love the gays. I love pretty much everyone, but to claim this was proof of that, seemed a little bit ridiculous to me.

Immediately, we wrote Tommy off as a fraud, and I didn't think much about it. Then reports starting coming in about others who had visited the site and been cured from other kinds of ailments. I have no explanation for why this worked. There is no logical reason for this to be happening, but even today, there are records of people going to Kandor's Pizza and becoming healed after touching the tile floor, where absolutely nothing that has to do with me ever happened. Kandor's will even give you a free slice of Pepperoni if you tell them that's why you're there.

♥

The world did not take the news of my resurrection well.

The people who thought I was trying to be Jesus II went ape shit and the Pope (remember that cool guy who I sent the George Ramero movies to?) officially banned me from the Vatican, and the Catholic Church took an official stance against me. Hundreds of thousands of Catholics protested this decision and many actually left their faith over it, which just made the situation all the worse.

Others were turning on me as well.

People who were previously Pro-Ben now saw me as an abomination. Apparently, there is a line when it comes to performing miracles, and I had crossed it. There was fear about me now, and we could feel it almost constantly from that day until the end.

♥

Agent Coulson suggested, maybe I should lay low for a while, until things settled down. He assured me people would forget all about it as soon as the next celebrity scandal came along, so I did what I always do when it's time to hide…I made jelly beans.

I mentioned earlier how when I was in the hospital, I had some thoughts of suicide and I wish I could say they went away when I was released, but they didn't. I started playing the UNO game again, which was a lot more difficult to do with only one hand. It seemed to take forever to stick the pins through the cards, before slamming my palm down upon them feeling the release as the pain shot through me.

I remember one morning, when I was watching a vat of Berry Blue spin in the tumblers and I wondered what would happen to me if I just jumped in. All it would have taken was one little step and I could have melted away into a sea of blue confection. This was the closest I ever came to actually doing it. I never told anyone about how I was feeling and I probably should have. Mr. Ferninni stopped selling the gumballs and jawbreakers, which had to hit him a pretty hard financially. He also stopped giving tours of the factory, even though I never asked him to. I loved him for that.

As the sea of Berry Blue jelly beans spun in the buffer, I took a Banana yellow bean from a batch that was on the cooling racks and tossed it in with the blue. The felt inside the drum looked so soft, so warm, and I again found myself just wanting to climb in there to hide. Thousands of blue beans spun, and gently clicked together in the tumbler, and I would search for that lonely yellow bean I knew was in there. Did that bean know it was different from the others around it? Did it feel lost and alone or anxiety from being separated from the others that were like it? Could I find it again if I looked for it before I moved this batch onto the cooling racks?

Sometimes I would catch a bit of yellow, tumbling like a lifeboat on a rocky ocean of perfect blue.

I wanted it to be like that always. If I lived an entire life, looking for that single jelly bean, it would not be a wasted life. I wondered if Mr. Ferninni had ever experienced anything like this, and I was tempted to call him over, and just point into the blue and say "look", and he would look and he would understand. Then there would be two of us.

The Banana yellow bean surfaces for a moment, and then is devoured by thousands of blue teeth. As hard as I look for the yellow, I never see it again.

♥

After the judges sentenced me to death and they drug me through the streets, (I say 'they' as opposed to 'you' because I don't want you to feel like I hold you personally responsible, even if you did happen to be one of the seven million people who called or texted in your vote to have me killed) I remember experiencing true fear.

People threw rocks and screamed all kinds of obscenities at me. I'm amazed I even made it to the Golden Gate Bridge before they just swarmed and tore me apart. The I-beam was so heavy, and it seemed impossible to drag, but somehow I made it. Even after a thrown rock broke my cheek bone, and one shoulder had been pulled out of socket when they drug me through Union Square, behind a bus filled with the winners of the special crucifixion road trip contest, I drug that damn beam half way across the massive bridge.

I wasn't afraid of dying. Well…sure I was, who wouldn't be? But what I was really afraid of was, just how completely alone I felt in those moments. I knew Naomi and John were somewhere safe, probably watching this on live television like the rest of the planet, and I tried to connect to them somehow, tried to reach out and feel them with me, but I couldn't do it, and when I couldn't feel them anymore, that was when I really understood I was going to die.

♥

Naomi was great about giving me time to mourn and get my feet underneath myself again. She flew out and stayed with me, and I showed her the candy factory, and even taught her how to run some of the machinery. John absolutely loved the tumblers, and whenever I caught him staring into the colors, knowing he was processing major things in his mind, I wondered if we might not be the same soul that had been split into two different people.

"Why do you think Mr. Ferninni stopped selling the gumballs and the jawbreakers? He was making a fortune on those," Naomi asked me one morning, as I was trying to learn how to use a chocolate planer. It was important I learned the other machines and candy making techniques, now that I would be taking over the factory someday.

"This stupid resurrection thing the media is spinning has really freaked a lot of people out. There's been some negative publicity. I heard there were even some protesters outside the factory. Mr. Ferninni tried to keep it from me, but I heard some of the other employees talking about it in the break room. I think sales on the stuff, based off of me, completely tanked. I think he stopped selling them so I wouldn't see just how badly the sales have dropped off."

"He's a very sweet man," Naomi says.

"Yes, he is. I still can't believe he is leaving the factory to me."

"He told me you are the closest thing to a son he has," Naomi says, and I feel Adler's theory of inferiority kick in, and I regret I wasn't a better son figure to the man who had been so understanding of me, and had given me so much more than just a job.

John eats enough candy to make him sick but within a few days he's making jelly beans from start to finish. I used to joke how my job was so easy a child could do it, but seeing it actually happen is a little humbling. I know Naomi has been worried about the two of us a lot lately, and it's nice to see her smile and relax a bit.

It was getting time for us to make some serious decisions about our relationship, but neither of us wanted to push the other or to rush anything. We had enough crazy in our lives without adding to it. However, living in separate states was starting to take its toll. We got to see other often and whenever we weren't in the same state, we made use of Skype and the phone. In fact, I doubt we ever went more than an hour or so without reaching out in some way via texts or Facebook pokes or Instagrams. We did our best to make sure we stayed connected.

Still, we both felt this just might be the real thing and we wanted to see if we could take it to the next level. John hated to fly. It wasn't that he was afraid of it or anything, but without fail, the flight attendant would see this little boy and treat him like a child. John *is* a child, so how else should she treat him. He hated explaining himself and his vocabulary and mannerisms had a tendency to freak out most adults, at first.

The way we first broached the subject of living together happened at the airport. They had flown out to visit, and to help Damon do some things for the wedding, and it had been a really great trip. While they were waiting to go through security, John complained about how they had to do this again and how stupid the whole TSA process was.

"If you just lived out here we wouldn't have to do this anymore," I said, and suddenly it was out there. Naomi beamed, and her eyes got a bit watery, and I felt like I might throw up a little bit but in a good way. She kissed me and said we should definitely talk about it. After the tragedy, in Metropolis the conversation got placed on the back burner for a bit, but now it was time to move forward with the plan.

I had asked her during a phone call, how she would feel about moving back east with me. We both knew there wasn't really anything keeping her in Utah, and now, I had something of a future in the candy business. I think in some way, we were hoping we could be together and just have something of a normal life without words within my body, without healing people, without murders, just a simple boring life we could both grow old happily in.

The guy in me was a little worried about how John would react to it. I didn't want to change the dynamics or our relationship so drastically, and I didn't want him to think I was forcing myself upon him as a father figure. Naomi told me he probably desperately *needed* someone to force themselves upon him as a father figure, and I would be perfect for the job.

"We would have to get a bigger place though," She said. The apartment I lived in was slightly bigger than my body, and it's never fun to live in a place where past sexual relations have occurred. There is actually a little living space built onto the factory grounds we both felt would be ideal. Since it didn't look like a house, maybe the media wouldn't think we were living there, and would leave us alone. John loved the idea, and thought we could turn the factory into some type of spiritual Batcave. We would be like Willy Wonka, Bruce Wayne, and the Dali Lama rolled into one.

Naomi was also excited to learn about the factory and the history behind it. She would spend hours with Mr. Ferninni walking the factory floor, and asking him questions. She even thought we could possibly start giving public tours sometime, when things in the media calmed down a little bit.

It was the happiest I had ever been or would ever be.

♥

Agent Coulson (I made the mistake of calling him Peter once, and he handcuffed me to the toilet for an hour. Naomi could call him Peter, hell she could call him anything she wanted, but to the rest of us, his first name was AGENT) thought it would be a good idea if I learned to use a gun. I wasn't against the idea. Who doesn't want the chance to channel their inner Rambo? It made perfect sense but deep down, I knew if the time ever came I wouldn't be able to shoot someone. I just don't have that in me. Even shooting at the silhouette targets made me a little uncomfortable.

Coulson told me there are basically two rules to follow with firearms and if I followed them, things would be alright.

1. The gun is ALWAYS loaded.

2. Don't point the gun at anything you don't want to shoot.

Since I couldn't shoot with my right hand, I had to use my weak side. I had been getting a lot better using my left hand, just out of necessity, but my fine motor skills with that hand still left something to be desired. Since Coulson was right handed, he had a right handed pistol, I never even knew pistols were made right or left handed models, which meant all the things like the safety and the magazine release were meant to be used by the shooters right thumb. He told me that buying a left handed pistol shouldn't be too big of a problem, and modifications could be made to almost any firearm on the market.

Because of my limited experience, Agent Coulson suggested we start with a shotgun because since it has a wider spread, whatever that might be, meant my aiming didn't have to be so accurate. He pulls out this thing called a Moss-Burg that looks like it could probably kill you if you looked at it. The barrel looked so big that I swear you could drop a golf ball down it, and I wanted to look at it to be sure, so I did what felt natural and looked down the barrel pointing the gun directly at my face.

That was the first time 'Pete' hit me that day.

Remember rule number two, don't point the shotgun at your face, you big giant moron.

I was worried I wouldn't be able to cock the shotgun with one hand, but Coulson showed me this one handed technique I had seen Sarah Conner do in the second *Terminator* movie, but it still looked quite difficult and I wasn't sure I would be able to do it with my left hand.

"Don't worry. It's not as hard as it looks and besides…with all the times I've caught you jacking it lately, I really don't think it's going to be a problem," he says, and Naomi lets out a helpless little snicker. I make a mental note to put better locks on my doors and to clear my browser history as soon as possible.

Now it was time to shoot this bad boy.

I have to use a modified stance because of my handicap, which means I have to rest my right forearm over the top of the barrel, so that the recoil doesn't kick the barrel into my face. That's the theory anyway, but guns are heavy and more than a little frightening. Coulson pushes me up to the range line and stands directly behind me to help make sure my position is correct. My hearing protection isn't on my head quite right, so I nudge it with my stump, and the shotgun goes off, blowing a nice three inch hole in the ground about an inch and a half from the tip of my shoe.

That was the second and hardest time Agent Coulson hit me that day.

I try the Sarah Conner pump a few times, but it just isn't happening, and everyone there immediately realizes, putting a shotgun in my hand is the dumbest thing we have ever done. Naomi has no problem with it though, and she's a natural born killer. I try to tell myself that it's just because she has two hands, and I try not to notice how Agent Coulson stands behind her in this weird standing spooning fashion. He rests his hands on her hips, adjusting her position here and there, but the whole thing looks a little more intimate than I'm comfortable with.

I have a strong need to redeem myself and put a Band-Aid on my ego but I'm no better with the handgun. I can't work the slide, I can't aim for shit, and I it takes me forever to get a magazine seated. My silhouette has zero holes in it, but the white paper around it is covered in them, with no apparent pattern or grouping. Sadly, this all happens while shooting at a target that is close enough for me to piss on.

Coulson tries to show me again how it's done, and he puts five holes in the center of my target that could probably be covered by a dime.

It's times like these, where I wish I could simply slip on a mask or a cape and become someone else. Become someone else, so my inadequacies wouldn't hurt so much, or that I could believe in myself a little more. Sometimes being someone else is better.

Over the past few months, a lot of people have been telling me how great I am, and it's always something that goes down bitter. It seems like they are projecting an ideal of what they want me to be, rather than how I actually am. I try to be a good person, I really do, but on some cellular level, I know it's all an act, because what I feel most of the time isn't good and isn't nice.

I understand why Agent Coulson wanted me to learn how to shoot, but no amount of bullets could protect me from what was coming. Sometimes I look at the holes in my forearms, from where the bolt gun was fired through them, and try to remember what they looked like without the scars. It's funny. I have looked at my arms all of my life, but I can't remember what they were like before the stigmata.

The truly frightening thing about learning to shoot was, that even with my abysmally blatant lack of any type of skill, the great state of Utah saw fit to provide me with a concealed carry permit. The Utah permit is good in fourteen states, including mine, so I was officially covered. Naomi got hers as well, but neither of us ever carried a firearm with us. John was a little pissed he couldn't get one as well, but he had tried to fire Coulson's python revolver with even more disastrous results than I had. The python was almost as big as John was, and even with Coulson helping him, the recoil still knocked him flat on his ass.

Later in his life though, John would learn to master almost every weapon on the planet. He once wrote, how after I was crucified, he felt a little bit like how Plato must have, after watching Socrates die. I wish I could say John got over my death, but he never did. He became very bitter towards the world and developed anger management issues that make The Hulk look like a kitten. It's actually probably the saddest part of this whole story. Watching me die also killed something inside of John. The part of him that wanted to help people, to show them a possible way to become better human beings, to take away their suffering and heal their wounds…that part of him was also killed on that day. Now all that's left inside of him is hate. No one really thought about that when they were coming to get me.

No one really realized, that by killing me, they were making something worse than they could ever imagine.

♥

A huge part of me wanted to laugh at Agent Coulson's added security measures. I still have a hard time with the idea I could generate enough passion into someone that they would want hurt me. It's a really big world with lots of stuff going on in it, that's way more important than me, so why should I think I was actually meaningful enough to someone, they might try to take me out. It just seemed absurd. It was also incredibly naïve.

While Naomi and I were planning our future together, another group in the tiny rural town of Swainsboro, Georgia was deciding my fate.

At the Swainsboro Baptist Church, Reverend Hyrum Johnson was focusing his attention on me and people were starting to notice. I don't want to paint Hyrum as my nemesis, but it's a little hard not to. He was a lab experiment away from becoming a super villain. Think, Doctor Doom without the metal armor. If Hyrum had a superpower, it would be his charm and charisma. He is a very likeable guy and has a gift for the language. He has the ability to get inside your head, place thoughts there you might not have come to on your own, and even get you to act on those thoughts.

I can hear some of you out there saying 'not me'. You wouldn't let a snake oil salesman convince you to torture and slowly murder another human being…well, fuck you. Every one of you let it happen. Only one person snuck onto the bridge to pull my body off that I-beam and it wasn't you. I still get a little bitter when I think about how it all went down, and I really don't mean to take my frustrations out on you dear reader, but that shit hurt.

Like all great things, this one had a small beginning.

The good reverend began preaching about false prophets' months before he ever mentioned my name. He preached, there is a reason the first Commandment is: Thou shalt have no other gods before me. When you do things to determine your soul's salvation, you do the most important things first. That's why God put this one as his first Commandment, because it's more important than all the others. God needs to know he is paramount in your thoughts, because that's how he will get things done with you. In fact, the first four Commandments are about God claiming his status in your mind. All of this comes before lying, stealing, or even killing. God is supposed to come first in everything we do, period. If anyone or anything takes the focus off of him, he kind of becomes a diva about the whole thing.

Reverend Johnson preached about, our actions were the most important thing we could ever do, and how our thoughts counted amongst our actions. He said, our behavior revealed the ultimate truth about us in ways nothing else could. He preached about those, who would tell anyone who would listen, about how they wanted to lose weight, but then did no exercise and ate everything which didn't eat them first. About the people who claimed that they wanted to have successful relationships, but then slept with the worst people they could find. He moralized about those, who wanted to have God in their life, but then never invite him into their mind.

He encouraged everyone he came into contact with to take a step closer to their maker, and he was really good at it. He could do it in a way that made you feel like he genuinely cared about you and was trying to help, this is probably because Hyrum truly *does* care. He wants you to be happy and to be saved.

The best villains always think they are the good guy.

The Swainsboro Church began doing public demonstrations in a kind of neat way. They were worried about being associated with the Westboro Baptist Church, so when they would demonstrate, they did the exact opposite of what the Westboro people did. Instead of spewing hate and holding 'God hates fags' signs, the

Swainsboro Church would spread the message that God loves everyone and just wants to have a place in your life. Often times, they would line up opposite of the Westboro people, handing out materials teaching God's love for us. How God loved everyone, no questions asked, and just wanted to occupy a little bit of space in your heart and mind.

They set up a website recruiting volunteers to show up at the military funerals, where the Westboro people would be doing their protests, to hold up huge sheets of plywood to prevent the mourners from having to see the silliness and hatred. They would show up at the various Comic Cons, at the gun shows, at political protests, and basically anywhere people were gathering for a purpose.

The thing that really made the public love them, was that no matter where you saw them, they looked like they were genuinely having fun, and their message was one most everyone could agree with, or at least not think of as hostile or threatening. The Church did a lot of good that was in the public eye as well. They would show up for other groups' charity projects to help out, but more often than not, they would send so many volunteers, that it looked like the Swainsboro Church had organized the event instead of just showing up to assist.

They sold T-shirts that said, 'God Loves You', and these beautiful crosses that were made from mustard seeds which started showing up everywhere, like those yellow Livestrong bracelets before Lance Armstrong fell from grace. Even non-Christians wore these crosses, because they were so simple and cute. I have to admit that I even bought one for John, Naomi, and myself and was actually wearing mine when the torture began.

I honestly don't think the Swainsboro Church wanted to be the catalyst for my destruction. Things just snowballed so quickly, it was out of control before anything could be done to stop it.

One day, Reverend Johnson was on the *Ellen* show, talking about how people could get involved within their communities and help those who really needed it. Ellen made the comment that it was so great to see religion getting back to bringing people together and making people better, rather than driving them apart. She mentioned some of the spiritual things happening during our times and my name was mentioned. Hyrum gave a micro-expression of hatred, nobody noticed, and I may very well be projecting on to him.

"I would be hesitant to include what Ben is doing as something religious," Hyrum had said, and Ellen had asked him to explain.

"The validity of anything he has done has yet to be proven. Maybe there's something going on there and maybe not. It's possible these people he's claiming to heal aren't really healed at all, or maybe it's some type of placebo effect. Maybe it's all a fraud and they are paid actors, we just don't know. I've heard several people claim he might be the second coming of our Lord, Jesus Christ, and this is cause for great concern. Since through Christ we will be saved, anyone looking away from Christ runs the risk of becoming lost. Jesus is there for all of us, but we have to take that initial step towards him. We can't be moving towards the true Christ while we are worshiping or putting our faith into something that isn't him."

There were a lot of moans and even some 'boos' from the studio audience, but when someone showed me a video playback of the interview, I had to agree with everything he was saying, and was thrilled someone besides myself was saying I wasn't Christ.

Ellen's phone lines were immediately flooded with people I had cured or had been positively affected by me in some way. However, there were also a few calls with people agreeing with Hyrum, and saying some hostile things I blew off much too quickly. I'm pretty thick skinned when it comes to people, I don't know, passing judgment on me, I figure you don't know who I really am so who are you to judge me, and I don't really know you, so how can I understand where your opinions are coming from. That being said, if you start insulting my friends and loved ones, I'm going to have an issue with you.

Hyrum started to talk about Mr. Ferninni's candies and how they are an example of what is wrong in seeing me as the new prophet.

"While the fortune gumball is a cute idea, it's almost impossible to read the message contained within. The same thing can be said of basically all of 'The Book of Benjamin'. We get these fuzzy MRI images or electron microscope slides that are basically a Rorschach test for our current social mentality. From what I understand, these gumballs have generated hundreds of thousands of dollars in revenue. Revenue that is being used for nobody knows what. Plus, there is all the money from the Holy Jawbreakers and the millions of jelly beans that have supposedly been made by Ben himself."

I don't know what Mr. Ferninni has been doing with all the money and I really don't care. I can tell you for sure though, I never saw him driving around in Lamborghinis' full of prostitutes. I also think the money that Hyrum spoke of was greatly exaggerated. Besides, Mr. Ferninni is one of the kindest and most generous men I've ever met in my life. I can't even count how many times he has donated candy to fundraisers and school projects. Almost every child athletic league in our city gets a little candy sack for each child after every game, that Mr. Ferninni has never once has charged anyone for.

However, I'm not going to waste a lot of time defending Mr. Ferninni, because frankly, he doesn't need to be defended. I will point out that this is America and Mr. Ferninni's is a businessman. If he came up with a profitable idea and was able to run with it, isn't that the American dream? So Reverend Johnson, if you happen to be reading this, if you want to criticize someone and pass judgment, you had better stick to me, because the people around me are just out of your league.

"Like these miracle healings," he continued with Ellen. "Are we are just supposed to look at some fuzzy logic and believe what we are seeing is actually true. Has anybody really looked into who these people are and how they are benefiting by telling the world how much better their lives are now? What is their financial status after they came forward to the media? If I were looking at hundreds of thousands in medical bills, which I would probably be leaving to my family after I died, I might be willing to state I had been cured if it could take away some of that financial burden from my loved ones."

I was completely flabbergasted upon hearing this. Naomi told me later I shouldn't have been, and she was actually surprised this hadn't been brought up by someone before now. Other than John, most of the people who I had worked with had dropped back into anonymity. Most of those who contacted me and asked me to do something for them were never known to the general public. A rare few might have a blurb on their local news, and sometimes the media would run a story as a feel good fluff piece, but the data from studies on all those I've healed just hadn't been compiled yet, and it was just too soon for any data to tell us anything.

I will say this one time and one time only.

I never received payment of any kind for any healings I did.

I made money from some of my speaking engagements and talk show tours. Some labs paid me to run tests on my body or to run scans or to give samples.

Yes, I made money.

Not millions, but enough to live comfortably, but never from helping another person feel better.

I had to submit all my income records when I was incarcerated so you can research it for yourself. However, let's run a little tally of what all of this *cost* me shall we? Almost everything that came out of my body was deemed government property by the patriot act, that means poop, snot, blood, semen (Christ, you don't even want to know how many times I had to jack off into a test tube), hair, fingernails, you name it. I even had to take showers with these special loofas that would be collected after each use to test my dead skin samples. I lost my hand, I was wrongfully imprisoned, I was labeled a threat to national security, I was banned from Delta Airlines (admittedly that one was my fault), I had gasoline thrown into my face and then set on fire, which almost killed me. I was shot, and have had attempts on my life, and these are only the things that have happened to me directly.

None of these things even touch the brutality that was to come, so if I scored a little money here and there, I think I earned some compensation for my pain and suffering.

"I honestly didn't come on this show to discuss Ben and his work," Hyrum had said, "I'm sure his heart is in the right place, but I would caution people against putting faith in a man they can't absolutely trust." Hyrum wrapped up and then concluded his interview by showing a slide show of the various charity projects his church has been involved with or helped run. He gave Ellen and her studio audience a mustard seed cross before, Ellen showed the church's website and a link with how people at home could get involved.

Sales of his mustard seed cross skyrocketed after being on *The Ellen Show*.

♥

I never saw myself in competition with Hyrum because, honestly, what could we be competing for? The public didn't view it this way. The media created this rivalry between us that just never existed on my side of the fence. It seemed there was always someone sticking a microphone in my face, asking me what I thought of the allegations Hyrum had made about me.

The God Vision told me a lot of these things Hyrum never actually said, so I did my best never to take the bait and get involved in the mudslinging. I honestly don't think Hyrum or his church did anything to propagate this feud either in the beginning. I was too busy doing my own work to really get involved much in what he was doing, and I'm sure the same could be said for him. There were a few companies who were trying to market something based upon me to compete with the mustard seed crosses, but to me, that just seemed like throwing gasoline on the fire, and I had had enough experience with gasoline and fire to know to stay away from it.

Then, one day, I was walking across a college campus on my way to give a lecture, when I saw a line of students outside the building where I was supposed to be speaking. I said, hello, as I made my way past them, but many of them held their mustard cross out to me like I was some type of vampire.

I didn't really think much of it. I surely didn't see it as a threat. I thought maybe it was some new type of Christian high five or something, but I did not see it as hostile, why would I?

When I was introduced inside the auditorium, there were a few boos along with the applause. It wasn't much, but Naomi gave me a look that said 'What the hell was that?' My initial game plan was just to ignore it, but when it became apparent the heckling was going to continue throughout my presentation, I decided to address them head on, and in a diplomatic and civil fashion.

"What the fuck is your problem?" I said and tried not to notice Naomi's face palm from off stage. Several of the mustard seed crosses were pulled out and brandished towards the stage.

The mediator instantly tried to steer the conversation away from the protesters, but I was curious and wanted to know, so I said we might as well take some questions and find out what exactly was going on. There was a long pause and nobody in the audience made any movement towards the microphones.

"Come on, let's have it." It was very awkward in the auditorium. Awkward like 'somebody got a boner in gym class, awkward. Finally, a man who was wearing one of the crosses, but who wasn't clutching it to his chest like many of the others in the room, made his way down the aisle to the microphone.

"What would you say to those people who are claiming you are the second coming of Christ?"

Wow, this again. It's ok though I'm actually getting used to dealing with this.

"What's your name sir?" I ask

"What does my name have to do with anything?"

"Well…My name is Ben. I think everyone here knows that. I just what to know who I'm talking to," I say. He stands there giving me the stink eye, but makes no attempt to tell me his name.

"Very well…Sir…whatever your name is, I think those people who believe I might somehow be Jesus…shouldn't. If you had let me speak and give the talk I had prepared, I think everyone in this room would be put at ease about that. I hear a lot of people out there think this for some reason, but I would like to point out none of the people who have actually seen me speak or have done any type of work with me, make this claim. That's because, if you are one of the people who believe I'm the returned savior, and then once you get to know even a little bit about me, you are faced with two very easy choices; That I am not Jesus or I am Jesus and God has way lower standards that you probably believed."

"Why do you say that?" The man asks.

"Because, I once got lost on an escalator, what kind of leader could do that? They say power corrupts, and if people were to give me that type of power over them, I would surely use it for evil. God can do much better than me."

More people are now moving towards the microphones now.

"But, isn't claiming you're not a prophet exactly the kind of thing a false prophet would do?" A woman on the other aisle of the auditorium asks.

"The Oxford English Dictionary defines a prophet as: ...A divinely inspired interpreter, revealer, or teacher of the will or thought of God or of a god; a person who speaks, or is regarded as speaking, for or in the name...blah blah blah.

"I am none of these things. I am not divinely inspired (although I have met some amazing people who are, since this began) and I am definitely not teaching the thoughts of God."

"So you are not Jesus?" She asks.

"I am *not* Jesus."

Naomi smiles at me from off stage, but I can see the concern in her eyes. She hates it when the conversation turns to religion. Since the shooting in Metropolis, she looks at religious people like they all have the potential for violence lying just beneath their candy coating shell of righteousness.

A man in a pea coat steps up, with his hands stuffed deep into his pockets, and for the first time in my life, I'm worried he might have a gun. There is *no* security here to speak of and my fingers unconsciously touch the part of my chest where the bullet came out of me before taking Mary's head off.

"There was a report that was released by Brigham Young University last week, with their latest translations and interpretations of the words that are found within you. Are you familiar with this report?" He asks.

"I'm afraid I'm not, but this really isn't uncommon. Research scientists are discovering new things almost daily, and quite a lot of it never makes it back to me," I say.

"Is there a reason you're letting the Mormons conduct the majority of the research?"

I almost laugh out loud at the absurdity of this question. Almost. I'm amazed others in the room don't laugh, or possibly even mock him a little bit, but when I scan the audience, all I see are people stroking those stupid crosses. If I had been wearing mine that day, I would have pulled it out as a type of peace offering.

"From what I understand, scientists from all over the world are studying MRI scans, cellular structure, and about a thousand other aspects of my body I'm too stupid to explain. It was the Huntsman Cancer Institute that did the initial readings not Brigham Young."

"John Huntsman, who happens to be a Mormon," Pea coat says.

"I have no idea what his religious affiliation is, if any."

"He's a Mormon. His entire family are Mormons. Why did you give the initial research to a non-Christian organization?" He asks, and my mind is blown by a spattering of applause throughout the crowd.

"Everything I have ever heard about the LDS faith is that they are Christians, first and foremost, so I don't really understand what…"

"The Mormons believe there is more than one God, and we all have the power to become gods ourselves. This is an insult to the one true god. Furthermore…"

"Look. I am not here to debate the LDS religion. I am not Mormon, so anything I say about it would just be me talking out of my ass (much like you're doing right now). I will tell you, though there was never any discussion about which religious groups, if any, were given access to the research being done on my body. The LDS hospital was where the first doctors discovered there was something…unique about me, and with the amount of doctors who have been sticking their fingers up my ass since I was born, I think Dr. Ormsby and her team deserve some credit in this matter."

"The study out of Brigham Young University claims, a message found inside a polyp taken during a routine colonoscopy says, and I quote: "Religions of the world are dying and will soon be replaced by a greater human understanding." Are you saying religions are useless?" The pea coat man asks.

"I'm not familiar with this finding. For the record, if a polyp was taken from me, it was done so without anyone telling me about it. Also, whatever words, or symbols found within my body aren't *from* me. There have been languages found I don't speak, mathematical equations I don't understand, and symbols I don't have a meaning for. I can't control what the words say any more than I can will my fingernails to grow."

"But it's part of you. It came from you. You must agree with it on some level," a teen in the back shouts.

"That's like saying, if I have cancer I must agree with cancer or that everyone who is overweight is so, because they agree with being fat. Our bodies do things we can't control. Women…wouldn't it be nice if you could only have menstrual cycles when you're actively trying to get pregnant? What if nobody ever farted or had body odor? What if we didn't have to poop or pee?"

"So, you're comparing your message to a bowel movement?" A new face asks.

"No. I'm saying it's not *my* message. I don't know or understand where the words come from any more than any of you here in this room today. From what I understand, there had been nothing found that could be interpreted as hostile or negative in any way. Vaccinations have been made from formulas discovered within me. People are alive today who wouldn't be, because of the message. Unfortunately, there are also people dead today who shouldn't be because of…because of the message."

I look at Naomi and very strongly wish we were somewhere else.

There are more questions along these same lines that are so asinine, I will spare you from them, but I will share you some of the high points.

"If you don't agree with the message, what does that say for the message?"

"How can you not know what it all means?"

"If you're not using the power of God to heal people, than what power *are* you using?"

"How come your powers didn't help you save that boy in Massachusetts?"

"Why didn't I stop the earthquake before the tsunami?"

It went on, and got to the point where they weren't even letting me try to answer the question before launching into the next rant. Someone from the college administration, or possibly even a frightened person in the auditorium, must have seen where this was starting to go and called the police, because soon the campus security and local law enforcement were standing by the exits.

Then, when I couldn't take it anymore, my mouth got ahead of my brain and I said something without thinking. I lost my composure and blurted something out I would later regret. Tell me you've never done something similar in your life.

"Do you want to know the difference between Jesus and myself?" I said, and the verbal noise that had been filling the room dropped into complete silence.

"The difference between Jesus and me is that I'm here and he's not. Why don't you try to book him for a campus seminar and see what happens. Then you can ask him all these bullshit questions, and piss on him because he gave you the black IPhone when you wanted the white one. Fuck you people."

Someone threw a can of Diet Coke at me, and that seemed to be the turning point for the day. The boos and screams became deafening, and everywhere I looked I saw angry faces, that is all except for the one face who looked terrified...Naomi. A police officer was at my side, telling me it would be best if I came with him. I was about to tell him I wasn't going anywhere without Naomi, but then she was at my side with another police officer pushing us towards the doors and calling for backup.

That was my last public speaking event.

I would be dead less than a week later.

♥

What none of us knew, and what would become a moot point in the immediate future, was that the United States had begun displacement proceedings on me. I was being exiled from my own country. During a Senate hearing, the vote was passed with more than ninety eight percentile if favor of exile.

During this time, one of those government agencies that have three letters and drive around in the black SUVs had decided it was time for a military trained sniper to put a bullet in my head. Since I had survived being shot by Wendell's hunting rifle, I guess they decided to get serious and use a .50 caliber, with depleted uranium coated tip.

If I were to choose, I would have picked the sniper rifle over the I-beam any day of the week. Something quick and painless, where my grape would become pink mist before I knew what was happening.

For the first time in my life people, were afraid of me.

I didn't like it.

ADD INF: America wasn't the only country to

make the political decision to terminate my life. Several opposing nations thought I might be weaponized or I might be able to teach soldiers how to come back from the dead. One nation (does it really matter who?) built a tactical nuke to take me out.

NET
THE RAM

> "The living is soft. The dead are hard. Be flexible in all things, especially your thoughts and beliefs."
> -The Book of Benjamin
> Inside maxilla

Towards the beginning of this adventure, I was sent to the Aquinas Institute of Technology to have a discussion panel with several theology professors from around the globe. I wasn't informed the AIT was selling tickets to the student body for the event, and it was one of the first times I had ever spoken in front of a massively large group. It was also one of the first religious debates I had ever been to, and I felt very much out of my comfort zone. I had no knowledge to share, so I spent the majority of time on stage stroking my chin trying to look like I was in deep concentration and hoping not to pee.

The topic was Isaac and Abraham.

I knew nothing about them, or the story, and I very much regretted not reading the information the AIT had sent me about the debate. I'm trusting you already know more about Isaac and Abraham than I did, so I won't waste time here with it. Soren Kierkegaard wrote a great book about it called *Fear and Trembling*, which explains it on levels I would never even think of.

The whole point of the debate was, whether or not Abraham had made the right decisions in following God's commandments. It was fascinating, hearing these great minds toss the topic around, and it got even more enjoyable when they took questions from the student body.

I sat there, in a chair praying nobody would discover I had absolutely no reason to be on the stage whatsoever. I hadn't found my voice yet, and was still in a perpetual dazed state of mind about what was happening to me. If you happen to watch the You-tube video of it, you will probably laugh at my constant deer-in-the-headlights stare.

The debate basically split the panel and the student body into thirds.

The first third, felt Abraham had done exactly the right thing. Since he followed God's instructions to the letter, he proved his faith by doing something extremely painful and difficult for him. This group also made the claim, since the Bible is a story of God's plan, and since God's plan is perfect, then Isaac's choice must be the right one.

The second group believed Abraham should *not* have tried to sacrifice his son. Murder being wrong under any circumstance and being directly in conflict with the sixth commandment. Several from this group felt if Abraham had said no to God's strange command, he would have remained truer to God's actual wishes. Kind of like, how a father will tell his son for years he shouldn't drink alcohol, then one day the father offers his child a beer. If the kid had really been paying attention, he/she would turn down the alcohol even if the father had offered it.

The third group felt poor Abraham was in a no win situation and he was screwed no matter what he did.

All three sides made compelling arguments and I left with my head spinning. I was feeling like I was in completely over my head, and maybe if I just went back home, I could vanish into obscurity again. However, the question of Abraham's dilemma stayed with me for long after that panel, and I found myself thinking about the parable in the quiet moments of the night.

After all of this, I think I've gained some insight on this discussion, and I wish I had possessed it back then. I would have told the panel and the student body how they were missing the whole point of the story. It's not about

Abraham. It's not about his choices, nor is it about God's will. It's not even about doing the right thing. The one thing the story is truly about wasn't even mentioned at the panel.

The story is about the ram.

The poor ram, who woke up that day thinking it was going to be just another day like all the others. He didn't know God was about to throw him into the middle of some epic story. He didn't know he was going to be used and discarded like a Spork at KFC.

The Ram.

The only thing in the story to actually die and the thing nobody remembers.

♥

An autopsy showed Mary had been pregnant.

I found out through a Twitter feed, #Mary'schild. Many people started tweeting me, offering their condolences on the loss, while others seemed to blame me. I called Damon to see if he knew anything about this. He said he didn't, but when he turned on the television it was the lead story on Fox news.

Fuck you HIPPA laws.

Damon had no idea she was pregnant. I sat there, on the phone, listening to my best friend in the world try to hold his shit together as we processed this information. The loss was obviously salt in an already infected wound for him. We had cried so much lately, over the various horrors of our lives, that it didn't feel strange to us anymore.

I asked Damon to come over to the candy factory to get drunk, and talk about it with us, and because I wanted to get him out of the new home he had buried himself in debt over when he was making other plans for his future.

We sat around an old chocolate cooling table, drinking Jack, and eating jelly beans long into the night. Naomi drank coffee and kept the pot full in case we needed it later. At one point John went to the cupboard, and grabbed a shot glass for himself, none of us really questioned it. I poured him a about three or four drops.

"SHAZAM!" He said, and tossed back his glass. It was the first time I had ever seen him drink, but he seemed to be very comfortable with the idea.

After discussing it for a while, we came to the hypothesis Mary had not known she had been pregnant. Damon was so passionate about this, none of us even thought to object. He said there is no way Mary could have kept something like that secret, but later that night, while I was holding Naomi as tightly as I could, she mentioned how perfect it would have been for Mary to tell Damon about the pregnancy at the Superman Festival, maybe during the after party.

ADD INF: No one from the coroner's office, nor anyone from the various law enforcement agencies looking into the case, ever called to pass along the information the autopsy revealed. We tried, several times, to call, but was constantly put in a maze of red tape that led nowhere. I can tell you now Mary was, in fact, in the very early stages of pregnancy. She was unaware of this, which I am eternally thankful for. Her last thoughts were of Damon and she was very afraid of dying. These thoughts only lasted a nanosecond, but they were there all the same.

The whisky tasted like turpentine to me, but there was no way I was going to let my friend drink alone. Besides, we had a fresh batch of sour jelly beans that seemed to help wash away the taste of the booze, but was probably wreaking havoc on my stomach lining. Damon saw me eating the candy and dropped one of the sour green apple jelly beans, into his shot before pounding it back. The next round we all had to try it. Soon we were playing a game similar to quarters, but with jelly beans, and Damon became extremely good at bouncing a bean off the table and into the tiny class.

At one point I had to puke, and my vomit looked

like Hello Kitty jizz.

Naomi helped me put Damon on the couch (fine...Naomi put Damon on the couch because I was in the bathroom trying to push my shoes through my esophagus) and then she poured me a cup of strong black coffee and made me promise to drink some water and take some aspirin before I went to sleep.

As we sat at the cooling table, waiting for me to drink my fluids, the conversation turned to babies. I asked her if she ever thought about having another, and she flicked a sour blue raspberry bean towards my head, which I was far to intoxicated to dodge.

"I'm not against having kids. I just don't want to do it on my own again. It's not fair to the child, because as much as I want to be everything for John, the truth is he sometimes needs a dad. For so long, I couldn't imagine the possibility of a guy staying in for the long haul, so I kind of just turned that part of myself off."

"Well, what if you found a guy who wanted to stick around?" I asked, taking her hand from across the table.

"Are you offering?"

"Of course. I'm not going anywhere."

♥

There was this picture of Mary, the media would show every time they talked about her death and her pregnancy. It was one with her long, red hair, which made her look a little bit like Marcia Cross. Mary looks beautiful in this photograph and I think it's important we mention this for a second here.

The picture the media used had been photoshopped.

I know, because I was the one who took the picture, and frankly, I think Mary looks even more beautiful in the original.

The reason I'm telling you this, is because that photo is often what people think of when they visualize Mary. It's not the reality. It's just a simulacrum perpetuated upon you.

Mary didn't have the healthy tan she has in the photoshopped image. She had this gorgeous alabaster skin most natural redheads have. She had freckles. She had this tiny gap in her front teeth which she could whistle through.

None of these things are in the photo you've seen.

The image of Mary became a symbol for things that might have been. It was a hope for a better tomorrow all of us could identify with. It was a picture of a girl who was winning and that made us all happy.

It was also the image which probably caused my death.

America was angry those possibilities had been taken away from them, and the media fed this anger every chance they could. Someone had to be responsible for her death, and the death of her baby and since Wendell was already in custody, there wasn't a sacrificial ram to get stuck in the bushes.

A new hashtag surfaced on Twitter and became the most used hash-tag in Twitter history: #Ben'sepicfail.

It was the tsunami all over again. Why hadn't I saved her? How could I just stand by and let this happen? Mary's baby became a symbol for a possible future which would never be.

There were even rumors the baby had been mine and I had hired the assassin myself to cover the scandal. Fortunately, neither Damon nor Naomi ever acknowledged these rumors to be anything more than the tripe they were. Still, can you imagine what it must have been like for Damon to see Fox News play out these stories day after day?

People were starting to throw eggs at my apartment. One day, I came home to find someone had filled water balloons with red paint, and thrown them at my front door. When a mysterious fire started in the laundry room, my landlord asked me to move out.

The tires of Red 5 had been slashed so many times, a local tire shop started selling me retreads at a wholesale rate, but it wasn't until R2 himself was smashed in, that I started getting pissed off about it though. I had worked hard on him, and he was just a defenseless droid who had never hurt anyone. Damon took the car after I had gone and rebuilt it to its former glory. He even built a little eye piece, that would drop down from the celling at the press of a button, and tell you to 'stay on target'. Damon loved that car, and he even kept my Hermey key chain he spent so much time razzing me about.

When the media started talking about prosecuting me for Mary's death, I naively laughed, but Agent Coulson sat me down and told me it wasn't as farfetched as I was making it out to be. One night, over Chili-mac, he explained to us how, my being convicted of interfering with trade shipping routes by my omission of action in stopping the earthquake and tsunami had established precedence, and because of this, it would be much easier to try me again.

Several petitions had already been filed to congress asking for my prosecution or deportation. Facebook and Twitter cancelled my accounts without any explanation, and my name started showing up more and more frequently in the late night talk shows monologues.

Coulson had prepared a "package" for us that consisted of passports for the three of us, with new aliases, along with a list of countries which don't have extradition arrangements with the United States. This frightened Naomi, and I spent a long time reassuring her it was just paranoia and hype, and there was nothing for us to worry about, but as we climbed into bed and I stared at the ceiling, I thought about those countries on the list and wondered which one might be the best to visit soon.

♥

There is a comic convention in Atlanta, called

Dragon-Con, which is in direct competition with the San Diego Comic Con for being the biggest con in the world. While the San Diego con had gradually become more and more about the Hollywood propaganda machine over the past decade or so, Dragon-Con has become more and more a celebration of the love of the genre.

It's a gigantic, four day party, with parades, raves, concerts, and an awful lot of drinking. One of the funniest You-Tube videos I've seen is called, 'Sunday morning at Dragon-Con'. It starts out with a guy in a Stormtrooper costume, just sitting on a bench and staring at his shoes. The Stormtrooper sits motionless for a very long time and it makes the viewer wonder if it might be a statue or an empty costume or something. Then, in a blinding fast motion, the Stormtrooper takes off his helmet, and fortunately the camera cuts away before we see him vomit into it. The video shows drunken Supermen and Batmen with costumes in various states of disarray, and a few Wonder Women who look more like rape victims than cosplayers. It's a side of cosplay we rarely see, and it shows geeks take their partying as seriously as they do their comic books.

One of the highlights of the Con, is the Villains Ball that happens on Saturday night. It's a huge dance party, which almost always has a famous DJ hosting it. It's usually right after the costume contest and spirits are very high for the party.

I had bought tickets for all of us to go, months before the Superman Festival, and we had been putting costumes together. John had made his Dr. Octopus costume even better, and was positive he would win the costume contest. We had our hotel and plane reservations booked even before Damon had proposed to Mary. Then everything happened in Metropolis and our life changed. When the media started in about Mary's baby and how it might be my fault, our focus shifted on our personal safety, and thoughts of leaving the country. Dragon-Con just fell through the cracks.

I knew Dragon-Con had been pulled off the table, but I couldn't bring myself to cancel our reservations. I was hoping against hope, we would somehow be able to make it work and canceling would have been the final nail in the coffin for that dream.

I didn't cancel our reservations or tell anyone we weren't planning on going.

Of all the mistakes I made in my life, this is the biggest of them, and the one I regret the most.

A splinter group from the Swainsboro Baptist Church, calling themselves the Hands of God or the HOGs (I couldn't make this shit up if I tried) found out about my Dragon-Con itinerary, and decided to take matters into their own hands.

The HOGs showed up during the costume parade, with their hate spewing signs, telling us how we were all going to hell for being fags and dressing like queers. It was pretty easy for people to blow them off, because the geeks outnumbered the crazies, a hundred to one, but when the HOGs set off the paint can bombs during the costume contest, that was a little harder to ignore.

Members of HOG had infiltrated the sound and lighting crew, and placed the bombs inside speakers and behind the bar, to maximize the shrapnel they produced. Their claim was, the bombs weren't supposed to go off until later that night during the Villain's Ball, but crazy people aren't always the best with math and technology, so the bombs went off early. Later during the trials, one HOG member had mentioned this to the jury, saying they never intended the bombs to go off during the costume contest, because they knew there would be children there, and children were innocent in Jesus' eyes.

ADD INF: This isn't true. They intended the bombs to go off exactly during the kids costume contest, because they were planning on John and his Dr. Octopus costume being on the stage, and for Naomi and me to be there in one of the front rows cheering him on.

Four hundred and thirty-seven people died in the blasts.

Four hundred and thirty-seven people, who might be alive today, if I had simply cancelled a reservation or posted on my web-site we wouldn't be there. Seventeen of them were children under ten years old. Almost every newspaper the next day, ran the picture of six-year-old, Denise Worth, who had been on the stage wearing a ball gown that had been made to look like a Dalek from *Dr. Who*. Denise had been very shy when she had seen how many people were in the audience, but after only the tiniest of hesitation, she marched out on stage and pointed her plunger hand at the crowd saying, 'Exterminate', in such a way that the whole room would have laughed their asses off, if they hadn't been blown into kibbles first.

A second series of bombs went off fifteen minutes later, taking out forty-one first responders and another seventeen innocent bystanders.

That brings us to 495.

For you, it's just a number. However, I now know the story of every one of them, because of the God Vision. I know what happened to their families in the aftermath. I know the pain and fear they felt as they were dying. I know what every one of their last thoughts were, every single one. Four hundred and ninety-five additional ghosts to follow me around and ask me why. They will never just be a number to me, no matter how much I wish it were the case.

When the blast went off, I was with Naomi and John, watching a *My Little Pony* marathon (it was Naomi's night to pick), I think she was trying to take our minds off of missing the Con, but I can honestly say I hadn't been thinking about the convention much. While Denise Worth and her Dalek costume were being atomized by quarter inch hex bolts and framing nails, I was learning about Derp and Fluttershy.

John started feeling sick, and both Naomi and I just thought he had probably eaten too much popcorn and dark chocolate. I was also thinking it might be a ploy to watch *Cow and Chicken,* which was one of his favorites, but John wasn't really one to fake sickness just to get his way. We decided to pause the marathon between episodes and I got up to make John a grilled cheese sandwich and some chicken noodle soup. Naomi got John some ginger ale and while she tried to explain to us the intricacies of MLP, the Netflix app on the X-box timed out, and the television switched to normal broadcasting. I had just flipped John's sandwich over, and I remember being pleased because I had let it cook for the optimal amount of time, and the bread was a perfect golden brown. This almost never happens for me, and I usually have to flip the sandwich over and over a few times before I get it right.

"John, what's wrong?" I heard Naomi say, and turned to see John staring at the television, looking ghostly white. I know his hair had been disheveled from laying on the couch, but I swear to God in that moment, it looked like every single one of his hairs were standing straight on end.

Then we saw the television.

My first thought was, 'How could anyone possibly do something like this?'

My second thought was, '*Why* would anyone possibly do something like this?'

"My God, we could have been there." Naomi said.

And then I knew.

Back in 2012 when the Aurora, Colorado shootings happened at the midnight premier of *The Dark Knight Rises*, I took it personally, even though it really had nothing to do with me. I took it personally, because it was my people who had been victimized. I hadn't been in Aurora, but both Damon and I had been at a midnight showing that night, dressed up in capes, with a utility belt full of snacks, just like we had done for almost every other comic book movie released since the 1989 *Batman*. I couldn't even begin to tell you all of the midnight showings we have pre-bought tickets for, and showed up two hours early just to get a good seat. We even did it for the *Green Lantern* movie and we knew that was going to suck. We do it because that's who we are. It's one of the few times when we can truly let our geek flags fly and not have to justify it to anyone. I was absolutely heartbroken when I heard the news the next day. I couldn't even fathom a greater tragedy to hit the comic community.

    The bombing at Dragon-Con opened those scars and filleted my soul on a salmonella caked toilet seat.

    "With that single sentence, uttered by Naomi, all the why's and how's vanished and the pieces fell into a deformed jigsaw puzzle with my face on it.

    "We were supposed to be there," I said to myself, as I sat down on the couch in front of the television, completely forgetting John's sandwich on the burner. John sat down next to me and stuck his thumb into his mouth, which is something I hadn't seen him do since before our bone marrow surgery. The sandwich started to burn and Naomi took the skillet off the burner.

    "That was meant for us, wasn't it?" John whispered.

    "I think it was," I whispered back, and felt the tiny muscles in his body flex, before the thumb found its way back into his mouth.

    Naomi managed to salvage the soup and sandwich, and was bringing it over to John when the image of the Dragon-Con stage, all shattered with police and firefighters searching for bodies froze her in place.

    "Oh my God, we could have been there," she said again. She took another step towards the couch and then the pieces fell together in her mind too. She dropped the food tray and collapsed on the floor.

"My God. My God! We were *supposed* to be there. Oh my god all those people. This was us. This was because of us. This is our fault. This was our fault...our fault, our fault, oh god all those people...our fault...because of us."

I went to her, and as I helped her to the couch, I felt the cold thing inside my stomach begin to grow.

"I have to call Coulson," I said, and went to the phone.

I tried not to hear the personal motion alarms firefighters wear, so they can be located if they stop moving, going off from the television screen as I pushed the speed dial button.

"Little busy here, Ben. I'm going to have to call you …"

"Peter…It was us. We're the reason the bombs went off in Atlanta." There was a long pause on the other end of the line and I was beginning to think we had been cut off when he said three very forced and very clear words.

"Are you sure?"

"No. Not even a little bit. But we were supposed to be there and I thought you should know sooner rather than later."

"Hold on," he says, and I wait for him to do those things the government pays him for that I probably don't really want to know about. "Were you entered in the costume contest?" He asks.

"I wasn't, but John was."

There's a pause and then a sigh.

"I need you to be very clear about this. You're telling me that John was entered in the…" There's a rustling of paper. "Children's masquerade ball, novice division, ages five and younger?"

"That's exactly what I'm saying."

"Why weren't you there?" He asks.

"You know why. With Mary's assassination, and my hospitalization we just decided to lay low for a while.

We needed to get the earth back underneath our feet for a bit."

"Ok. Did you cancel your reservations?" He asks.

"No, we didn't."

There's a pause and more shuffling of papers as he writes things down.

"What about the masquerade ball? Did you cancel your place in that?"

"No. No, we didn't," I say.

"Why not?"

That was when the weight of the situation really came down on me. I hadn't thought we needed to cancel the costume contest. The thought never even entered my mind. Why *hadn't* I canceled? Maybe none of this would have happened. Or even if the bombings hadn't happen, I'm sure there is probably some kid out there with a really cool costume who didn't get into the contest simply because it filled up so quickly.

I am an ass hat.

I now live in a world where the things I don't do are just as important as the things that I do do.

Also…my brain just said 'do do'.

"I just never even thought about it," I say.

"Ok. I don't like the idea of you being alone. I'm sending some agents to get you and I will be there as soon as I can. How's Naomi handling this?"

How's Naomi handling this?

Why would he ask that? Why is he even asking about Naomi? Why did his mind automatically go there? Is there something going on between them? God, how did I not see this?

"She's ok. I'm ok too, by the way, thanks for asking. John's ok too, not that you asked or anything," I explode.

"Listen to me fuck-tard and listen to me really good. If what you're saying is true, then she just came very close to losing her son, because you are too busy trying to avoid being a grown man and want to play dress up. Now, what you're going to do, is reach down between your legs, grab whatever excuse you have for balls down there, and cowboy the fuck up. Because if you make this worse for them, or for me, by playing the 'poor me' card I'm going to harvest one of your organs with my thumbnail. You are going to be cooperative with the agency when they ask you questions. You are going to tell them everything you know about this and you are going to help us find whoever did this. No going off on your own. No sending a four-year-old to fight your battles."

"I never..." I begin.

"Shut your pretty little mouth while I'm talking here or I will ass rape you with the Thor's hammer you gave me last Christmas. Now...pack some bags...right now because if this is really happening, then you need to be in protective custody. DO YOU UNDERSTAND?!"

"Yes. I'm sorry. I will help in any way I can. However, I can't help but to notice you used two pretty homophobic slurs in that last threat. You told me I had a pretty mouth and that you would ass..."

The line goes dead and it comes to me that Agent Coulson is probably going to knee-cap me the next time he sees me. I'm not sure what exactly being knee-capped is, but it probably sucks more than the ending of *LOST*.

Let me tell you a little something about myself...when I get scared, when I feel overwhelmed by grief or horror, when I'm put into situations that make no sense to me, my instinct is to throw the maturity level of an eight-year-old at it, because that's all I really know how to do. It doesn't mean I don't feel the pain or the sorrow.

He didn't have to be so mean.

It doesn't take us long to pack. Hell, all my stuff in already in a suitcase upstairs in Naomi's room anyway. Damon fires me off a text, asking if I have heard, and if I'm ok. I'm sure he's put this whole thing together in his mind and I can almost see the rage and frustration between each letter of text. He texts that we should do something to help, and he texts about how he is setting up a donation fund and running an auction at the comic book store to help.

I haven't even finished packing my bag yet.

It's one way I wish I could be more like Damon. He thinks of others before he thinks of himself. A savior or messiah should be more like that, and a hell of a lot less like me.

As I come back downstairs with our bags, I look at the television for the millionth time since this happened, and see an image, which would stay with me for me remaining life.

There are cosplayers sifting through the rubble looking for survivors.

A man in a Superman costume is handing out water bottles to the first responders and the victims. A girl in a Black Widow costume is going through the triage area talking to the frightened children. Captain America is using his shield to keep sparks from flying into a man's face, as the rescue workers use a metal saw to cut him free from the collapsed rubble. A young boy, in a Batman costume that has built in foam chest and abdominal muscles, carries the debris particles he's strong enough to lift, to get them out of the way of the rescue workers.

It's amazing to see. What's even more amazing, is all the things that are happening like this, the world is not seeing simply because no one is there to hold a camera, because everyone is busy helping someone else.

ADD INF: The geeks respond in staggering fashion. Con attendance skyrockets over the next year. The next Dragon-Con sold out its 75,000 tickets in less than six minutes, shutting down web servers all over the world. Thousands more, who are unable to get tickets, simply show up and stand outside the host hotels, just to show support. Bruce Springsteen came out of retirement and played a free five-hour show for the people in the streets. The annual blood drive started turning people away after the first day of the convention. The costume contest was broadcast over national television, which was something even the San Diego Con hadn't achieved. It was never cooler to be a geek.

Time passed on, and like the rest of the nation, I was glued to the television after the explosions, watching as the details and reasons why slowly trickled in. Hyrum Johnson completely disavowed all members of the HOG organization, but all those who were found and brought into custody had been parishioners of the Swainsboro Baptist Church, and many said Hyrum himself had planned the attack. There was a shootout between the HOG and law enforcement officers at a compound outside of Swainsboro, where another six officers were killed before the compound could be seized. Inside, they found complete dossier files for me and all my friends. They even had one for Mr. Ferninni. All of them had home addresses, work schedules, places we frequented, travel arrangements, and kill orders. It was enough to convict all members of HOG.

♥

Things started happening with John around this time. They say everyone deals with stress in their own way, but John just didn't have the years, or the experience to deal with what was happening around him. The regression happened slowly, and I think there was a lot of denial surrounding it, between those who care about him. It started with the thumb sucking. I had never actually seen him do it before, but I just assumed it was something all kids go through at some point in their life. Something like a Freudian oral phase or boob fixation which most people naturally grow out of.

At first…other than that night on the couch when we heard about the bombings, we didn't really see him doing it. There would be times when one of us would check on him in the night or go to wake him up in the morning, and there the thumb would be, and his other hand would be tucked under his neck like he was trying to make a blanket out of his arms or something.

John would wake up, and the thumb would fall out of his mouth, never going back in until the next night and sometimes not even then.

Then there were the cartoons.

I know I'm probably going to sound like some elitist hypocrite when I try to explain this, and if you want to stick that label on me, I think I can deal with it. John had always liked his cartoons, and frankly, I like them too, so there would be times when we would just hang out together, watching them and talking. It was actually a bonding experience for us in a strange sort of way. We would watch the *Justice League* or *Samurai Jack* and John would tell me his thoughts on what the characters were doing, and we would try to decipher the life lessons the producers had embedded in each episode. John, often times, had views about how these shows could have been done better and he was probably right in these opinions, more often than not.

I used to love listening to how he would see Superman as a symbol for the republican agenda and the United States', feelings they have the right to be the world's police force. He made me see my favorite heroes in ways I never had before.

Before the bombings, he would pick apart anime plots and laugh at the subtle sexual overtones hidden in *Adventure Time*. Hell, once or twice, I had to ask him to explain something I had missed but he had picked up on. Naomi hated it when we would do this, but it was fun watching John's brain work, and see how he perceived the world around him.

Then, one day, after the bombings, he started

watching *Dora the Explorer* and *Blues Clues*.

Not that there's anything wrong with either of these shows. They are great and kids love them. However, they are geared for a little younger demographic than say, *Full Metal Alchemist*.

The same thing started to happen with his reading. John was a veracious reader and would usually ask us to take him to the library a couple of times per week. He loved fiction, and really liked the mind fuck a Phillip K. Dick story could put you through. He would also chew through a lot of Andrew Vachss. He really started reading those after what happened to the other John in Boston. He liked that Andrew Vachss, was a lawyer for children, and how all of his characters would do everything they could to protect and avenge the little people of the world.

John also had a love of Greek philosophy, particularly Marcus Aurelius and Aristotle. I asked him why, one day, and he said it was because they both believed we could learn how to, and then train to become better people than we currently were, that the trying to become more than you are today was really the only reason we are here at all.

He was fascinated with the story of the Spartans and the battle of Thermopylae. I think it was because he liked the idea of a few righteous men standing against insurmountable odds. If John could have it his way, he would be one of those 300 Spartans, clashing against the world at the Hot Gates.

Captain Marvel was always a favorite of his for obvious reasons. When young Billy Batson would say SHAZAM he changed from the small child who the world ignored, into something that could make a difference.

John wanted to be a hero.

He wanted to save you.

Remember that.

After the bombings, he stopped raiding the

philosophy section of the library, and even his selection in fiction seemed to shift to the saccharine tasting fluff rather than the writing you could sink your teeth in. Faulkner was replaced by Lemony Snicket, Dickens was replaced by Stephanie Meyer.

He was regressing in almost every way. It was like *Flowers for Algernon* in real life.

Naomi took him to doctors, especially after I was gone, but none of them could find anything wrong. All of them said it was just some psychosomatic reaction to what had happened. He bounced back soon after I was gone, but you know all about that already.

The thumb sucking was at its worst when Hyrum was on the run. Almost immediately after the HOG compound was shut down, an arrest warrant was placed on the good reverend. He ran and had a whole lot of people helping him out along the way. People were still passing around the picture of Mary, and talking about her baby, and how it was my fault. The media had picked up on the Dragon-Con connection, and now the picture of Denise Worth in her *Dr. Who* costume was being split screened with my picture whenever the media would talk about it.

Some of the people in the geek community began to turn on John as well. The footage of him and Damon beating up the man at the San Diego Con began making the rounds again. Memes of John in his Dr. Octopus costume began to surface, and one showed him standing there with Mary's body being held in one mechanical arm, and Denise Worth's body in another. The other two mechanical arms were raised over his head giving the Nixon 'V' sign. I had never seen Naomi so angry during this time.

It was especially painful, because it felt like our own people had now turned their backs on us. We were blacklisted from every convention in the nation. Even when we tried to help, by organizing fundraisers, our donations were returned with 'thanks, but no thanks' letters. Marvel comics sent us a cease and desist letter, forbidding John to ever wear the Dr. Octopus costume in public. Sales at Damon's comic book store dropped off to almost nothing, which made the other two comic book shops in my city extremely happy, because they were picking up all kinds of new costumers.

John told me he had never felt so alone. When I look back on it all, it's really not surprising he regressed a little bit.

I think he was just trying to be a kid again.

♥

There's a saying: where there's smoke, there's fire.

There's another that says: if it walks like a duck, and quacks like a duck, it's a duck.

When Agent Coulson arrived at Naomi's house after the Dragon-Con bombing, it wasn't to take us into protective custody, he took us into just plain old custody. Agents carrying shotguns kicked the door in, threw a bag over my head, and once again I found myself in the padded room wearing the straight jacket.

I don't know how long I was in there, because time gets strange when you're in solitary, but it seemed like days. I can usually tell by how often they come in and change the adult diapers they have to keep you in when you're wearing the jacket. I used to figure they would come change me at least twice a day, but I'm also pretty sure they put some type of drugs in my food so maybe I sleep a lot more than I think.

The water they give me tastes bitter.

I do what I always do when I'm in the room. I try to go inside my mind to the part with Naomi. Sometimes it will remember things we've done in the past, key moments in our life and our relationship. When my mind can't go to that place, sometimes it will make its own memories. If I focus really hard, I can make these memories feel almost as real as the ones that actually happened.

If I focus too hard, sometimes I can't tell them apart.

When they finally let me out of solitary, Agent Coulson puts me in a room with a big table and a lot of mirrors. I'm strapped down to the table, and for a moment I consider trying to pulling my stump out of the strap holding my right wrist. I don't though, because I really don't know what I would do with it once I got it out, and Agent Coulson is my friend, and friends don't hurt each other.

A woman sticks a needle into my arm and my mind goes fuzzy.

Coulson pushes a button on a video camera and a little red light starts blinking on top.

"Ben," he says real nice in my ear, "Please tell us everything you know. Don't make me do something we will both regret later. You've been doing so well lately. Why did you stop taking your meds again?"

They don't have to shave my temples, because none of my hair ever grew back after my head was burned. I try to find the place in my mind where Naomi lives, but there is a buzzing noise that hurts where her face should be. I try to focus, but I can't. When my mind gets like this and the pills don't work, I just say the only thing I can ever remember in these moments.

"In brightest day," I say, and I hear Coulson let out a sigh.

The earthquake was a natural disaster, and as far as I know, the technology doesn't exist to generate man made earthquakes.

The same woman who put the needle into my arm applies a gel to my temples with a Popsicle stick.

"In blackest night."

They ask me questions about the bombing. Questions I couldn't possibly know, because I was sitting on the couch in Naomi's house watching cartoons when the bombs went off.

I very badly want to someone to take me back to the game room to play X-box with John and Damon.

The woman puts the black rubber mouthpiece into my mouth and Agent Coulson pats my arm in the way you would pat a puppy's head.

"No evil shall escape my site, I say, but it comes out like, "O eril hal eskate eye syte."

The pads rest against my temples, and they don't move, even though I shake my head and bang it against the table.

The woman with the Popsicle sticks turns a knob.

The world goes white just like it did when I broke out of prison, and I feel my muscles flex harder than they ever have. Everything is tight, which is good, because if they weren't, I might just shit myself.

When the white goes away, the woman rests two fingers against the side of my neck and then sticks another needle into my arm before taking the black rubber from my mouth.

My fingers lightly touch the fabric of Coulson's white jacket and I can feel the starch that makes it a little firmer and less likely to wrinkle.

"Ben, please tell us you know," he says, and my mind finds Naomi's face, and I remember how her hair smells when we spoon in the morning.

"Let those who shine the bright green light," I say, and my muscles clench.

When the white comes again, my stump slides out from the leather strap, but nobody seems to mind. Coulson listens to my heart with his stethoscope and then tells the orderlies to take me back to my room.

They let me poop before putting the diaper and the jacket back on, and then I decide to take a nap. As I'm drifting off to sleep, the reality of the situation begins so settle in.

They just water-boarded me.

I was now officially a terrorist.

NEVELE
PONTIUS PILATE AND BARABBAS

> "The essential thing is not knowledge, but character. In both, utilization is everything."
> -The Book of Benjamin
> Inside the vitreous chamber of left eye

As I lay down in the corner of my room, I look up at the ceiling, think about Naomi, and listen to the sound of my own breathing. There's a small window in one of the upper corners, and sometimes if the wind blows just right, I can feel a slight breeze. The leaves of a tree sway into my vision through the window and then retreat leaving a field of blue in their place before they can regroup and attack again.

So many lawyers and doctors and law enforcement officers have been in to see me and question me lately, that I can't even tell them apart anymore. For some reason, every person who comes in has a clipboard. I don't know why they have clipboards, many of them never write anything down on them, but the clipboard is always there.

Agent Coulson would usually come in with whoever was holding the clipboard and then disappear through the door again, only to return when the interview was over. Sometimes he would pat me on the shoulder and ask me if I was doing ok. Sometimes he would leave a bag of gummi bears or peanut butter cups behind. Other times he would ignore me all together.

Then one day, a man came in and told me his name was Judge Herbert Rockwell.

Judge Rockwell stuck his left hand out to shake mine, knowing my right hand was gone, but still missing the point I was in a strait jacket, and couldn't shake his hand no matter how hard I tried. He smiled when he realized his mistake and laughed it off, which made me feel better, because I didn't want to appear rude.

ADD INF: Judge Herbert Rockwell was the great, great grandson of Porter Rockwell. Porter was the bodyguard to Joseph Smith and Brigham Young and was called "the destroying angel of Mormondom". Porter was rumored to have killed just as many men as Wyatt Earp and the Sundance Kid. It was said Joseph Smith gave Porter Rockwell a special blessing, saying as long as he held his faith in the Mormon Church, no bullet or knife would harm him. Porter Rockwell was the baddest of the bad in Mormon folklore, and Herbert tries his best to live up to the legend.

Judge Rockwell said he was there because he would be overseeing my case, and frankly, he needed to know if I was the real deal or simply full of shit. He talked to me at length about all kinds of things and I found him to be an enjoyable enough person, even if he didn't understand anything about who I was or the things I was trying to do.

The first day he came to see, me we just talked for a while, and he really didn't ask me a whole lot about my powers or about the words. He asked me how I felt about Naomi and what my intentions were towards her. We talked about John and he asked me if I saw myself as a father figure for the young boy.

The second time he came to see me, he brought in a several decks of cards. Some were just regular playing cards, others were tarot decks, and a few were from kids' sets like go fish and hearts. I laughed when I saw the hearts set, and when he asked why, I told him hearts seemed to be a recurring theme in my life, but I don't think he understood what I meant.

He would hold up random cards with their backs towards me, and then ask me to focus on the card, and try to tell him what the card was by only using my powers. I tried to explain to him my powers didn't really work this way, but he insisted so we spend a few awkward days playing this stupid game. There were a few times when I actually got the card right, just by sheer dumb luck, and whenever it would happen we would laugh, because it was so obvious 'my power' had nothing to do with me providing the right answer. He tried the experiment with a pack of Uno cards, and when we were done I asked him if I might keep the box. He asked me why and I explained my version of the Uno game, and the next day he brought in a box of shirt pins and had me show him how to play. I have to admit, I had really been missing playing the game and after he left, the throbbing in my left hand made me feel alive in a way that nothing else can.

I asked if they would leave the deck of cards and the shirt pins, but Agent Coulson said it wasn't a good idea.

Every time a doctor of lawyer would come and see me, I would ask if I could go home. I would also ask for information about what was going on with the Dragon-Con investigation because I'm not allowed to watch television or use the internet. Naomi would feed me details every now and then, but it seemed everyone was either hiding information from me or they genuinely just didn't know anything.

I'm water boarded a few more times, but I can't tell them what I don't know. I started to stash my pills because they make me feel foggy, and I want to be clear right now, but I think they caught on and have started putting the drugs in my food.

It seems like I'm sleeping a lot more than I should be.

Judge Rockwell finally stopped bringing in cards for me to try to guess and just asks me to explain how I'm able to do the things I can. He has a file with the various x-rays, MRI scans, and computer images of some of the parts of my body. He has a print of the famous HOPE photograph, from the Smithsonian, taken of my vertebral foramen which he stares at for a long time while we talk.

He asks me if I think I might be able to change what the words say by thinking about specific things, like how light will react as either a particle or a wave depending upon what the observer wishes to see. I explain how I thought some of the scientists at CERN did some tests along those lines, but I didn't really understand how they worked, or what exactly the results meant.

I apologized, because the drugs were making my brain foggy, and sometimes they made it hard to remember exactly how certain things happened. He asks about John, and the other people I have healed, and asks me to explain how I did it. When I tell him I don't actually understand how it all works, he asks me if I could possibly just show him instead.

He takes a pen knife from his pocket and puts a tiny scratch into the palm of his hand. The knife barely breaks the skin, and there's almost no blood at all, and the scratch is less than a quarter inch long. Agent Coulson takes the strait jacket off of me and tells me to just relax and show the Judge what I'm capable of.

I take the Judge's hand with my right, close my eyes and try to imagine the cut on his palm disappearing. It's hard to think clearly, because my brain is so cloudy from the water boarding, but I do my best. There's a pain behind my left eye I've never experienced before and it hurts to push. My left hand touches the burn scar on my temple and the pain behind my eye fades a little bit.

It's not working.

I can feel it's not working and I'm sure it has something to do with what they did to my head.

What if it's gone? What if I can't do it anymore?

I try to push a little harder, try to generate the heat from my hand, but nothing comes. After a little while, I let go of the Judges hand, and the cut stares at me. There is a little smear of blood from where our hands touched, and the smear looks exactly like the backwards 'S' that was in the word Simon, when the words were first discovered. I'm reminded of Bizarro's red backwards 'S'

The Judge smiles at me, but it's not the smile of something kind, it's the kind of smile of a predator when he knows his prey is cornered.

♥

Things were happening on the outside at an alarming pace. Americans aren't tolerant, when their children are killed by terrorist, so the demand for justice was pretty high. Every facet of the Patriot Act was used and abused, but people didn't seem to mind because it made them feel like things were being done.

A lot of anger was directed at me, and I took my share of abuse from the Patriot Act, but I didn't mind. I believed the sooner the government cleared me as a suspect, the sooner they would catch who was really responsible, which was something I wanted very much to see happen.

Every single one of those agencies who have three letters in their title, descended at some point on my home and the candy factory. They would show up at the door and show me papers, explaining their right to search the premises, but I didn't care. I never once read the papers they shoved at me. I have a tremendous respect for law enforcement officers, and if I could in some way help with their investigation, then I was going to do all I could.

Besides, they all had really big guns.

Barrels of corn syrup, fructose, food colorings, and every other ingredient you could think of were dumped on the floor to ensure explosives weren't hidden in the barrels and after they left, it took Mr. Ferninni days to clean up and get things working again. They took apart one of the tumblers to inspect it, and it never quite worked the same again. It would make this high pitch, whining noise every time it ran, and the jelly beans that came out of it were always cloudy and had a smoky taste to them, like the machine was crying out against its rape.

The comic book shop was searched, and Damon took a pretty big hit because the officers weren't exactly gentle with the comics, and after they left, it would have been difficult to find a single issue left in mint condition. Covers were wrinkled and torn, a lot suffered from foxing issues, and many just had to be thrown away because they were so badly handled, nobody would ever buy them. Even the issues that were bagged and boarded seemed to suffer.

The green LED light in the cardboard standee of Green Lantern's ring went out and never came back on again.

Naomi's home and our cars were searched. The doctors who had worked on me were questioned. I was asked ad nausea about the trips I had taken out of the country, and the people who I had come into contact with during those times. Fortunately, The Pope and The Dalai Lama aren't really high on the Most Wanted lists. This was how I found out Warren had been on one of the spiritual cruises John had spoken at.

Almost every person I had ever spoken to during the last five years of my life was questioned at some point. I got an irate email from the cape fucker, complaining about the harassment she was taking, which gave me a warm fuzzy deep inside my heart.

Of course all of this harassment turned up nothing.

The investigations into the Hands of God and the Swainsboro Church ended up being another story. I mentioned before, how the HOGs all claimed Hyrum Johnson was the brains behind the operation, what I didn't know at the time was, they had all offered him up as a plea bargain in their own prosecution trials. One HOG member, Jason Allen, who was the actual person to push the button that detonated the bombs at Dragon-Con, produced a kind of manifesto, written by the good Reverend, where he claimed it was our biblical duty to destroy false prophets who might lead people astray from finding spiritual salvation. It said, there were many false prophets out there who needed to be dealt with, but I was the only one that it mentioned by name.

All the evidence connecting the church to the bombing was there. Other evidence showed other attacks were planned, but hadn't been carried out either because of lack of preparation or the fear of failure. I found out, at one of my college speaking events, I had been sitting underneath a pressure cooker bomb that had simply failed to go off when it was supposed to.

The human mind is a strange thing. If I were to play the song *Boogie Wonderland* by *Earth, Wind & Fire* and then show you the clip from *Iron Man,* where Tony Stark is dramatically putting on the Iron Man suit, pretty soon our minds will begin to associate the two, even though there's no real connection.

I think this played a major part in what ended up happening to me.

The more they looked into the Swainsboro Church, the more evidence they found proving they had a major hate-on for me. Almost every time they were mentioned in the media, my name was mentioned too. Split screened pictures of Hyrum and I were flashed whenever the trial was mentioned, or whenever a new piece of evidence came to light.

We were linked.

This had started to happen, even before the Dragon-Con bombings. Remember how I told you Hyrum had talked about me on *Ellen*? How the paparazzi would ask me to respond to whatever allegations Hyrum had thrown at me? We were already linked in the minds of so many people, and they were being pressured to pick a side, long before Judge Rockwell set up the 1-800 numbers to cast your vote.

People started to question my actions just as much as they questioned those of the Swainsboro Church. Questions about Mary and John Peterson were asked all over again. People were starting to feel there had been a lot of tragedy in the world I had somehow been connected to. It was like how Taylor Swift would complain about all her boyfriends and write nasty songs telling how awful they were. Pretty soon, you had to wonder if maybe the problem was Taylor. After all, she was the common denominator in the whole thing.

Scuttlebutt was starting to spread about how all religious leaders were corrupt and none of them could be trusted. New laws were being passed almost every day stating just how much influence a religious organization could have over a community. The separation of Church and State hadn't seemed to matter this much since it was first put into the Constitution. There were bills debated on the Senate floor about the legality of performing miracles. It became possible for health care and insurance companies to sue me for lost revenue on the people I had helped. There were rumors the candy from Mr. Ferninni's factory contained hallucinatory agents that we used to help trick people into believing things that just weren't true.

People were hating me all over again.

♥

When things started looking bad, Hyrum ran.

I guess he figured he could start up a new church in Brazil, or he could become one of those television evangelist, and still broadcast into America and spread his message. What made this thought more appealing is, he had already established a huge following in America, so it wouldn't be difficult for him to get his followers to TIVO a weekly sermon or two. His new fame (it's true what they say about bad press) would probably give him even more fans, which meant more donations coming into some tax exempt PO Box outside the country.

An economics student once came to me, suggesting, I set up a web site which would enable me to try to heal people through some kind of Reiki, cyber bullshit, I could in no way actually do, but he told me the web site could also accept donations on my behalf. He had charts and graphs predicting what my monthly income could be from donations alone, and it was staggering. I'm sure Hyrum could have lived quite comfortably off his donations as well.

Something happened to Hyrum that was never released to the media, because frankly, I don't think anyone realized it happened…enter into our story Selena Aksenchuk. Selena was still in the womb when her family immigrated to America from Mother Russia after the fall of the iron curtain.

To say Selena is beautiful, would be the understatement of the millennium. She was one of those women who were so ungodly attractive you couldn't help but wonder if she was actually a human being, or some alien robot from the future sent back to kill us all with hotness. I could spend pages telling you what she looked like, but it would never do her justice, so just take your perfect fantasy women, and then times that by ten, and you will get what I mean.

Unfortunately, Selena learned at an early age she was exceptionally beautiful, and how her looks could have a certain affect over most men. Selena was one of those women who think just because they are attractive, they are naturally entitled to things the ugly people aren't. Men *should* by her drinks when she went out to the clubs. It was completely normal in her mind to have Facebook keep shutting down her page because her friend count was too high. She had finally decided to make a fan page instead of a normal profile, and her 'like' count was over a hundred thousand. She felt it was completely alright to let men buy her things in the hopes she might sleep with them, even though she had no intention of ever doing it. She was the girl who would let you buy her drinks all night long, and then leave with some other guy who happened to drive a better car than you.

One of the saddest parts about the world we now live in, is that you all know exactly the type of woman she is, and I'm positive you probably personally know someone just like her.

Selena could have you wrapped around her little finger almost faster than she could give you an erection.

Because men constantly threw themselves at Selena, she grew to hate men, which made it all the easier for her to use them like disposable silverware. Her father died when she was very young, which left her with all kinds of daddy and abandonment issues. Somewhere, so deep within her psyche she didn't even know it was there, Selena wanted a father figure and a man she could respect.

This was where the Reverend Hyrum Johnson came in.

Selena was 'escorting' a gentleman to a lecture Hyrum was giving, about how Jesus could help turn your idea into a Fortune 500 Empire. Before you laugh at this, it should be noted Hyrum actually had a pretty good success rate with this seminar. Not only did it make him a butt load of cash, but several of the companies he worked with went on to become household names.

The gentleman who was escorting Selena, and who eventually lost her to Hyrum, took his idea for a GPS statistics program, asked Jesus for help using Hyrum's plan, and now owns three overseas homes and a yacht. Although sometimes, in those quiet moments late at night or in the shower, he still thinks about Selena and the latex bra she was wearing under the black miniskirt when she ditched him for Hyrum.

It was after the seminar, the GPS guy decided he just had to meet Hyrum and possibly get a signature for his new book and tell Hyrum how much he enjoyed the seminar. Selena was a little pissed about having to wait, because she figured she could probably work the GPS guy for another grand before the night was over, but then she saw Hyrum.

She was immediately taken with Hyrum in his power suit and tie. It was an aphrodisiac to see the man up close who had just spent the last two hours playing this crowd like a fiddle. Whether his faith was bullshit, or something more, he seemed to have a connection to something that gave him the answers to some of the important questions. People could see that and they looked up to him for it. They wanted to have that too and were willing to pay an obscene amount of money if necessary to have it.

Selena wanted it, and although she didn't have the type of money flying around this convention center, she did have her set of perky, natural double D's, and a dress two sizes too small.

It wasn't her fault the GPS guy tried to show her off like she was his possession. Like somehow, if he could show Hyrum the type of arm candy he could buy, it made him a better man or something.

It ended up taking her less than forty minutes to get Hyrum to take her back to his room, and fuck her like an anger management doll. Selena was impressed she could bag a holy man in less than an hour, but then something happened she wasn't expecting…she felt a connection to Hyrum.

She had called other men 'daddy' before, but when she said it to Hyrum, it almost felt real on some level. He really did care about her soul and not just her body. He could talk about Jesus in a way that didn't make her feel like a bad person or a failure in God's eyes, just because she didn't have a connection to her maker. It made sense when Hyrum explained it all, and for the first time in

Selena's life, she felt like there just might be something more in life, and she had a good chance of reaching it. However, she couldn't do it in the same way she had been doing everything else in her life. She couldn't just get Jesus to want to fuck her and then have all kinds of happiness.

No, she would have to open herself up on a level she had never even conceived before and Hyrum had been there for her every step of the way. He was so supportive during the times when she got scared, and he never made her feel like a sinner for having sexual appetites. Hyrum said sexual intimacy was the Lord's greatest gift to us and Selena felt safe sharing it with him. After all, if he couldn't teach her how to use sex for something other than a manipulation tool, then who possibly could?

Selena had never officially become a member of the Swainsboro Church, because she didn't live in Georgia, and never bothered to join the churches online congregation. Hyrum liked to take her with him when he traveled, though. Every time he flew somewhere to give a sermon or raise funds, Selena would get an e-mail with her travel voucher, and Hyrum would put a generous amount of mad money into her account to buy lingerie and lubrications. It was the same routine when Hyrum decided to flee the country, except this time, Hyrum had transferred all of the money he had into her account, because he knew the government would freeze his assets once they placed the warrant out for his arrest. A little over eight million dollars went into Selena's account, and an envelope containing the keys and a deed to a house in Tahiti, Hyrum also put in her name to avoid losing it. Hyrum had set up an escape plan years ago in case the zombies came, or the bombs started to fly, and now it was working quite smoothly.

The plan was to meet at the Atlanta airport and then spend the rest of their lives in Bora Bora, soaking up the sun and living the good life. Selena got to the airport early, got her ticket, and then decided to go through security so she could grab a coffee and possibly an E.L. James novel before boarding the plane.

While looking at magazines in the airport terminal shop, Selena received a text message on her disposable phone telling her Hyrum was just entering the airport, so she decided to head back and meet him at security. She saw the men with guns and the TSA agents piling on top of a man on the other side of the gates, and the thought didn't even enter Selena's mind it could be Hyrum lying face down on the tile being handcuffed.

'Wow,' Selena thought to herself, 'they are really getting serious about those shampoo requirements.' Then she continued to scan the crowd for Hyrum. When the various security personnel picked the man up, Selena could see it was Hyrum, and suddenly everything made sense.

The money. The house. The bombing. Everything.

Her eyes met Hyrum's, and she could see the fear and pleading in them. He called out her name, and she quickly turned and began making her way back down the concourse. She looked back just once, and saw the agents taking Hyrum away. After walking to the end of the concourse, she sat down by Gate 22 and tried to figure out what to do. When it came time for her plane to board, she threw away the disposable phone, and handed the attendant her ticket. Waiting for takeoff was the longest thirty minutes of her life. She kept expecting men with guns and bullet proof vests, stopping the plane, and taking her into custody.

But they never came.

When the wheels lifted off, she stared at the 'please remain seated' light for what seemed to be an eternity. Every time the plane banked, she was sure it was turning around to land. Soon, the light went off, and the captain told everyone they were free to move around the cabin so Selena went into the bathroom and threw up.

Then she cried.

Then she remembered she had over eight million dollars in her account and a brand new home in her name waiting for her in a land without extradition laws.

She splashed some cold water on her face and returned to her seat. Soon she was over international waters.

The house in Bora Bora was more than she could have ever hoped for. Hyrum had planned to live the good life for whatever time remained of it.

The money was never traced to Selena and she lived a long, happy life in Bora Bora.

♥

Thirty-seven members of the Swainsboro Church congregation and all of the members of HOG offered up Hyrum in plea-bargaining deals. There was more than enough evidence to push for a conviction in the Atlanta bombing. However, Hyrum still had a lot of believers out there, and they weren't about to let their leader go down without a fight.

The argument was made again that the bombings had been my fault. One of those famous people on television who claims to be a doctor, but really isn't a doctor of any kind, said I was like a malignant cancer cell. That so many of the awful things which had been happening in the world could be connected to me. I was the patient zero in all of this. I was the cancer tumor that had to be removed to prevent the sickness from spreading throughout the body and killing the host. Somehow, he managed to shit a book almost overnight that debuted at number one on the *New York Times* Best Selling List, explaining in great detail how I had become the tipping point in our social decline. I was the outliner, the catalyst for the world's spiritual decline, but what more could you expect from a false prophet and the antichrist?

The book was EVERYWHERE.

Judge Rockwell read it while walking on the

elliptical machine in his den, even though he knew it violated his bias towards the case, and if people knew he was reading it, he might have to withdraw from representing me.

Judge Rockwell was also bucking for a Supreme Court Justice seat in the next few years, and he believed the right case could either make or break his chances.

I was going to be the case people remembered him by. I would be his O.J., his Anna Nicole, and his Charles Manson.

He needed my case to be something people could never forget. He wanted it to be one of those moments where people would know exactly where they were and what they were doing when the verdict came down.

It would have to be something bigger than had previously been done.

He petitioned to hear the Hyrum Johnson case, claiming both cases were so closely related, it just made sense to try them both at the same time. Little kids wearing cute costumes had been disintegrated, and the American people were hungry to see someone pay for it. We as a nation, had stopped looking for justice within the judicial system a long long time ago. Lawyers were a joke to the American people, and the approval rating for our government was at an all-time low. Judge Rockwell wanted to change this and he saw the Dragon-Con bombing as a way to do it.

However, things would have to be different. The trial couldn't be drug out through appeals for the next forty years. This wasn't going to be like 9/11, where we waited so long to punish anyone that people weren't sure it ever even happened at all. The American people had to see something happen soon. They had to feel like their voice still mattered. Like they had a part to play in how their country was run and how we punish those who would try to harm us.

This was how Judge Rockwell and the Supreme Court came up with the idea of letting the American people choose how justice would be carried out.

♥

It was actually a very simple plan, which had been brewing in the entertainment industry long before I came along. Reality shows became a huge success. Hell, I think at one time there was about five of them that had to do with cooking...*cooking*! Shows like *Cake Wars* and *Hell's Kitchen* were winning ratings wars. Again, let me point out these shows are about COOKING. How exciting can cooking possibly be? There were reality shows about rednecks, ice truckers, self-storage units, weight loss, singing, youth beauty pageants, UFC fighters, wedding brides, the Amish, cheating partners, bachelors, and bachelorettes. Then there were the reality shows about the people who were famous simply by being famous like the Kardashians, Paris Hilton, or Anna Nicole. To shed some perspective on this...Steven Seagal had a reality show and it was a success.

There was even a show called *Who's Your Daddy*.

Then there were the death and injury shows. Shows about car crashes, police shootouts, 911 calls, or just some idiot who breaks his leg on a skateboard while trying to skate off a roof top were on every other station at any time of day.

There were already plenty of reality shows about judicial trials and the prison system, so is it really hard to see how my trial was just the next logical step in the minds of television producers and the viewer at home?

There was also an unspoken race in the media world about who would be the first to broadcast an execution. Everyone knew it was going to happen eventually, the only real question would be, who would get to show it first?

♥

The stage set for the show looked more like a night

club than a courtroom. Laser lights flashed everywhere and people waved glow sticks all around. The live band played some edgy music and Judge Rockwell sat on his podium high above us all watching the whole thing.

An extremely edited video was played, showing me at my absolute worst. Quotes were taken completely out of context or just edited to say things I never once uttered, images of Mary, the little girl in the Dalek costume, and the boy being pulled out of the lobster trap were shown to the gasps of the studio audience. A death count from the Tsunami, along with the total dollar revenue I cause the nation's economy was shown, along with images of my previous incarceration, and the destruction caused by my escape.

There was no mention of the people I cured.

After introducing me like a prize fighter, they brought me onto the stage, wearing shackles and the orange Department of Corrections jumpsuit, that made me feel like a giant yam, and had me stand in a plastic phone booth looking thing, while two men wearing hoods and pointing assault rifles at me stood by.

I couldn't see into the audience, because the light flared off the plastic cage, but I could hear them out there and the sound made me want to hide. Why did they hate me so much? It's not like I'm a bad person or even an asshole. I think if any of them would just spend a little bit of time with me, they would see I'm not the image being presented to them.

I wanted to see Naomi.

I wanted to go back to my old life.

The charges against me were read, but do you know the part you've seen in a hundred movies where the judge asks the defendant how they plea? Yeah…that part never happened. It didn't matter anymore.

After being charged with the murders at Dragon-Con, the deaths in the Tsunami, the deaths of John from

Boston and Mary, I was also charged with fraud, which I found to be a little bit unnecessary after the murder charges, but it still hurt to hear. The supermodel host, with the silicon tits, cheek implants, and capped teeth stood there calling me a fake.

The video started to play again, showing many of the same things I was being accused of. Then after another fighter type introduction, they brought out Hyrum, shackled and in the same type of jumpsuit I was wearing, and he was placed into a plastic phone booth on the other side of the stage. Another two men in hoods and assault weapons stood by him.

The show was actually pretty long and tedious, so I won't bore you with the whole transcript, but the premise was simple enough. The supermodel host and the blockbuster movie star would present our case to the studio audience and the viewers at home, and when the show was over, people could call or text their vote as to which one of us would be found guilty. It only cost three dollars for the first vote and one dollar for each vote after that, with the proceeds going to the victims of the Dragon-Con bombing. Whoever was found guilty, guess who that ended up being, would be publicly executed on live television and the other would receive life imprisonment.

I'm surprised they didn't just make us fight to the death right there on stage.

When the show ended, I was placed in solitary confinement until the results could be totaled. I sat down on the concrete floor, hoping against hope they would pick Hyrum, but I knew that wasn't going to be the case. My previous experiences with the judicial system had taught me such, and I had little hope of seeing the end of the week.

They let me make one phone call, so I called Naomi.

She asked me if I was scared, and I so badly wanted

to be brave and tell her everything was going to be ok, and we were going to get through this, and have a long and happy life together, and how things hadn't gone too far…but I didn't. I told her I was terrified and asked her how I could get out of this.

The line was silent for a while and when she spoke, she told me the brutal truth.

"It's likely they are going to find you guilty and kill you tomorrow. I'm watching the numbers and it doesn't look good. I want to help you, but I don't know what to do. I have been on the phone with everyone I can think of, trying to stop this, but it's happening too fast. I don't know what to do, Ben. I don't know what to do."

The heartbreak and hopelessness in her voice made me want to wrap her in a blanket of my love and tell her everything is going to be ok, but we both knew it's wouldn't be.

"Do you want me to be there?" She asks.

"Absolutely not. John neither. I think you both should go very far away for a while. The bloodlust might spill over and I don't want you getting hurt. Plus, I'm probably going to break down, to beg for my life if I'm picked. I don't want you to see me like that," I say, and the silence between us is palpable.

"Oh my God! This might be the last time I get to speak to you," she says, and all the things I might not ever do again come flooding in. Little things you probably wouldn't think a person would think of at those moments. I will probably never talk on a phone again after this. I will probably never shave again, such a mundane thing, but it's there. How many times will I brush my teeth or poop again? Maybe one or two? Will this jumpsuit be the last thing that I ever wear?

I couldn't help myself from thinking about all the things that might happen to us when we die? What if this is really all there is and once we're gone, that's it? Just an endless abyss of nothingness. What if everything I am simply stopped existing? Would that hurt? Would I feel regret or shame? Would I feel anything at all? The thought, I might not feel anything at all because there would be nothing left to feel, caused my morale to swan dive into an oil slick of despair.

"I wish I could be there with you," she says.

"You are with me. You've been with me ever since I met you."

"I really don't like the idea of you being alone right now."

She's right. I do feel completely alone. I feel like the world I only wanted to make a little better is going to wipe me out like most of us smash a mosquito buzzing around our arm. They are going to murder me, and the universe won't even notice. But I can't tell Naomi that. I can't let our last conversation be me whining like the little bitch I am. I have to at least try to be a man.

"I'm not alone. You're with me," I say again and I can hear her start to cry. I can hear the agony in her voice, how she can't take a breath without it breaking apart in her throat, I can hear her slumped shoulders, I can hear her weak knees. Technology has brought us so close together while amplifying the distance between us.

I'm never going to touch her again.

I'm going to die alone and I'm never going to touch her again.

"Will you do something for me?" I ask.

"Anything. Just ask," she says.

There are so many things I want to say. I want to ask her not to be angry about what's going to happen, to not let it make her bitter. To not let John forget me, nor forget how much I love him. I want to ask her to be the person I know her to be. To be the person who made me the best man I have ever been. I want to ask her to never forget how much I'm in love with her, how everything I have done lately is because she made me want to be a better person. I want her to know how she made my universe a better place and how she showed me things I never even imagined could be possible. I want her to know, that for the first time in my life, I feel like I have a purpose, that I might just matter, and the only reason I could ever feel this way is because she loves me. I want to ask her to see herself through my eyes, because she will always be the image of perfection to me. I want to ask her to know how beautiful she is, in every way and how everything else pales in comparison. I want to ask her to get me out of this place and run away with me. I want to ask her to grow old with me and make all of this go away. I want to tell her, how tomorrow I'm going to try to die a noble death, to go out with meaning, and the only reason I might be able to pull it off is because she believes in me. I want to ask her to love me forever, or at least for what forever will be for me.

"Will you be happy?" I ask.

But before she can answer, the line goes dead, and a guard tells me our time is up.

♥

The cast of *Dancing with the Stars* performs a number, and Adele sings the national anthem, before Hyrum and I are brought back onto the stage. If this were a comic book, this is what would happen...Superman would be standing on the stage, waiting for judgment because Superman respects our legal system, and he will take our petty human shit because he's a nice guy, and as we all know, nice guys get shit upon a lot. He would try to explain how his actions are really for our greater benefit, even though we might not be able to see it for ourselves. He would explain how his world died and how he doesn't want to see that happen to us. He would sit there like the noble lion, while the jackals run around and nip at his heels. Superman would probably even let them slap the handcuffs on him, even though he knows he could snap them off if he were to hiccup hard, but he doesn't, he just sits there wearing them, listening, hoping we will see the reason, and make the right decision for ourselves.

But of course, we don't and we decide to punish the god, because we are actually so full of our own bullshit we think we can actually pull it off. We would pass our judgment, and then ever so slightly, Superman would lower his head in disappointment.

Then...Superman would calmly bend us over and do us.

Superman's pupils would turn blood red as his heat vision reminds us this man can kill us all, simply by looking at us, and we will know we've gone horribly wrong. But it will be too late by then. Superman would tear the building down around us all, but still manage not to let any of us die in the process, because he's not a murderer. Then we would realize we've made the God angry with our hubris and we would wish we could go back in time and take back all the bad decisions we made to bring us to this point.

Superman would punch the ground...cracking the very foundation of the Earth, and the ground we stand upon would shake and threaten to disappear from beneath us.

Superman would shout to the skies in a voice that shatters glass and makes our vertebra feel like they are going to fall out of our ass and if we were to look closely enough into his face...we might just see one steaming tear fall from his eye, because this isn't what he wanted, but he sees no other way.

Then at the very moment before our planet is turned into a black hole, Batman would show up. Batman, the man who is also hated by society, and who hates society right back, would show up and tell Clark to stop. He would tell Clark to stop because he knows Clark is getting dangerously close to crossing a line he won't be able to come back from. That once this line is crossed Clark will be something different, something more like Bruce, and more than anything else in the world, Bruce wishes no one would ever live the life he lives. Bruce would remind Clark why Superman isn't like Batman. Bruce would tell Clark, if he could make a pact with God he would trade places with Clark in a heartbeat, because Clark is a symbol of hope and hope is something that Bruce will never have.

Superman will tell Bruce how humanity will never change, that these men who tried to put the God in handcuffs are no different than the coward who shot Bruce's parents in the gutter, oh so long ago. He will tell the Batman that violence and power is the only language we will ever understand, and he will explain how he would rather destroy us all than watch us destroy ourselves.

Then Batman will say something super inspiring, like how it's not the superhero's job to carry man, but to simply catch them when they fall. To be something for them to stand upon as they reach for new heights. He would remind Clark of just how far we have come in such a short period of time and ask him to imagine what we might be able to achieve if we could only be led by the right kind of people and shown the way.

Superman would stop.

Disaster would be averted, and we would all be left with something to reflect upon, and there would be the hope we would become better people, and tomorrow would be different and we would find peace.

But this isn't a comic book, so none of those things happened.

Since I was being tried under the Patriot Act, the normal rules and laws of the judicial process didn't apply to me. I didn't have someone there to yell 'objection' for me or to plea my case. I didn't get to say anything in my defense, nor was I tried by a jury, just a phone vote which generated more votes than the last three presidential elections combined.

After the sit-com stars finished shooting their T-shirt cannons into the audience, and after two rap stars that had a long standing rivalry with one another stood on stage together, thanking the sponsors and showing we could all live together in harmony, Judge Rockwell took the bench.

A program that could have been about ninety seconds long was stretched out to two hours. There were presentations on the history of capital punishment and public executions to try to make people feel like this type of thing happens all the time. Before each commercial break, the announcer would promise they would be right back with the world's decision after a word from their sponsors, and then go into some more meaningless tripe when the show came back on air.

I sat there in my plastic cage and thought there was no way I could be picked. I hadn't been the one who actually planted the bombs that killed those kids. It hadn't even been my idea. My friends weren't the ones hording guns and killing federal agents when they showed up with questions. How could they possibly pick me? People are smart. They can see the things I'm being charges with are ridiculous. They will cast their vote and then I can start working on getting out of jail.

However, I also knew this wasn't true.

When Judge Rockwell announced I had won the votes, I really wasn't surprised. Part of me felt like this had been what my life had been about all along.

I was to be executed.

I just didn't expect it to be by crucifixion.

EVLEWT
TUGGING ON SUPERMAN'S CAPE

"Humans need to stop trying to fall in love, and simply become love itself"
-The Book of Benjamin
On the cardiac muscle inside the left atrium

ADD INF: This last chapter I'm going to narrate in the present tense because this is my story and this is the end of it. Besides, it's too painful not to.

The I-beam has been sitting in the summer sun all day and is hot to the touch. I can see little vapor trails rising off it, and drifting out over the bay before they cool and vanish. There are multitudes of faces along the bridge, voices screaming at me, hands throwing things at me as I try to make my legs move. There are so many people. I can see those who couldn't get onto the bridge, swarming into Golden Gate Park, watching this nightmare unfold on the big screen televisions and their cell phones. I can almost feel the others from around the world watching the live broadcast.

So many people around me and watching me, yet I've never felt so alone.

My psyche tears, as I long for Naomi to be here. For her to hold me and tell me everything is going to be ok. To make my fear go away like she always does, while never thinking less of me for being afraid. I want to pull the covers over us and spoon with her, until all of this madness stops. I want to see that look on her face again, when she realizes just how stupid I can actually be, and wonders how she ever got involved with me.

I want to tell her I love her more than I have ever loved another.

Why did I never share this with her?

The other part of my mind hopes she is as far away from this place as possible; that she's not watching this somewhere, not thinking about what's going to happen to me. I wonder if maybe it would have been better for her if I had never come to Utah. Maybe her life would have been more peaceful. Maybe John would have had a childhood.

The four hooded men on horseback crack their whips, and I feel the leather tear into my skin, as I try to drag the I-beam a few inches further. It seems so far I have to go, like the bridge will just go on forever. Why the horses can't drag the I-beam is beyond me, but I see the tools they are weighted down with and guess they have their own job to do.

The irony of the four horsemen isn't lost on me, and I wonder who these four men are and if they were chosen to do this or if they volunteered. Whatever the case might be, they seem to enjoy whipping me and kicking me to the ground, again and again.

If I had my other hand, this would be so much easier. I don't have any way to lift the beam or to get any leverage. If I could, maybe I would put one end on my shoulders or back and just let the other end drag, but I don't have any way to lift it, so I just drag the whole thing. Maybe if one of the thousands of people watching could step forward and help me like Simon did for Jesus, but none of them do. One of them throws something that hits me right in the balls, making my vision turn white with pain and causing me to lose my already shitty grip on this fucking beam.

The whip comes again and the leather hits my eye. There's this internal popping sound and I never see out of that eye again, although my life really didn't last long after that. Something slimy runs down my cheek, and I see a drop of yellowish goo drop to the pavement in front of me.

Vegas was taking bets on everything from whether I would actually be able to drag the beam to the center of the bridge, to how long I would last once they put me on it. There was even a bet paying a thousand to one odds that God would intervene and save me, but nobody was taking the action.

Colors flashed across my vision every time the whips would touch me, and I would try to imagine what flavor jelly bean those colors might be. I let my conscious vanish into the sound of the tumblers, and how the felt would touch my fingers as I took the beans out.

I wonder where Mr. Ferninni is now, and I really hope he understands why I won't be able to take over the candy factory for him.

ADD INF: A group of people decided to burn down the candy factory while I was on the bridge. They broke in, used paraffin and homemade napalm to start the blaze. Before they started the fire, they took sledge hammers to most of the machinery and walls, they smashed the tumblers where I spent some of the best moments of my life, and they annihilated the gumball and jawbreaker machines. A lot of Naomi's personal things she had moved in there were lost, although she never went back to the factory after I had died. The worst part of the fire was, Mr. Ferninni had been there and tried to stop the blaze with a garden hose, while waiting for a Fire Department who would never show up. He died from smoke inhalation on the factory floor. He was by far the kindest man I had ever known. All he ever tried to do was make the world a little bit sweeter and help people smile. You people killed him because some cancerous tumors, which happened to look like letters, formed inside my body and they frightened you. I hope it's hard for you to live with.

Damon was one of the people on the bridge, but I never saw him. He watched as I struggled with the beam and as they bolted me to it. He wanted to help me, to be a voice of reason, but he knew if he did, the crowd would tear him apart, and he would probably find himself strapped to an I-beam right next to me. I never once thought to blame Damon for not helping me, but I wish I had known just how close my friend was. Maybe I would have found some peace in his proximity.

The blisters that formed on my hand tore open and touching the beam sent jolts of hot pain through the exposed nerves. My hand was smooth where the skin had been rubbed away, and I wondered if this was how my hand first looked, before I ever made a fist with it and added the wrinkles and palm lines. Somehow, as I was able to move the beam a few inches, where it came to rest upon a rock and I could just squeeze my toes under it. This was enough to enable me to lift one end of the beam a few inches, and I thought I might be able to muscle it onto my shoulder, but then a boot from one of the horseman found my chin and I lost my hold.

The I-beam was so heavy.

If you ever want a good workout, I suggest you try to drag one across the Golden Gate Bridge. It's a killer.

The embarrassment over my naked body quickly faded, as the center of the bridge crept closer and closer. The pavement was hot, and more than once, I wondered if I could run to the side of the bridge, make it over the railing and jump before the four horsemen stopped me. Wouldn't that ruin all the fun you people had in store for me?

I asked one of the horsemen if he would just shoot me and get it over with, but he only pointed to the beam and kicked me to the ground again. His black hood showed only his eyes beneath it, and they had more hatred in them than I had ever seen, but there was something else even more frightening…there was euphoria. Whoever this person had been before he put the hood on, he was enjoying having this power and I wondered what his life would be when this was all over. Would he ever do anything which could compare to this again in his life? Would any of us for that matter? With every step I took, the world changed into something harder and harder to recover from.

It seemed to take days and I had never been so tired or broken in my life.

Out of the blue, I thought about the cape fucker. Where was she in all of this? Was she sitting on a couch somewhere, bragging to a group of people how she had once fucked me? I also wonder whatever happened to my Christopher Reeve Superman cape. Where was it right now? If they offer me a last request, I think I'm going to ask to have it back.

They didn't offer though.

I tried to count my distance by the people selling water out of picnic coolers. It seemed like there was one about every twenty-five feet or so along the bridge. All of them bragged their water was only a dollar, and we all would have to pay more at the center. It was hot outside and the humidity from the bay made everything sweat. I would have killed for a drink, even just a piece of dirty ice from one of their coolers. No one offered me any water though, so I kept going, hoping it would end soon.

There were vendors on the bridge, with their taco and hot dog carts, making a killing because nobody wanted to move and possibly give up their spot to get food, but everyone was hungry because the show was taking so long. Others sold t-shirts to commemorate the occasion, so they could wear it later, to let the world know they had really been here when it all went down. A girl ran out towards me with one of these shirts and a Sharpie to try to get me to autograph it for her, but the four horsemen shut her down quickly.

Swedish House Mafia played from the far end of the bridge and I could feel the bass pumping in my chest.

Some people reached out to me from behind the

barriers, hoping to get a handshake, or to be able to claim they touched me, maybe even get a video of it posted on YouTube. Most of them just shouted though, and threw things at me when they had the chance. Someone threw a soup can that hit my knee, and there was a loud cracking sound before I went down. The Campbell's can, lying on its side, staring at me like it was some strange Warhol interpretation. As I stand, my knee feels like there is sand and cement inside. It swells to a grotesque size and every time I put weight on it, or it happened to bang against the beam, the squishiness of it makes me want to pass out.

  I had no illusions I was about to die. I could see it on the faces of everyone around me. I wanted to just stop, to say I refuse to carry this hunk of metal an inch further, to tell them I wasn't going to die in the way they wanted me to. But I didn't. I wanted to live. I would have done anything if I had felt it might give me a few more seconds of life. I did not want to die and I was very much afraid to do so.

  The center of the bridge was getting closer, and more and more people crammed together to be as close to the action as they possibly could. Most of the voices were just noise and too difficult to understand, but sometimes words or phrases would make it through. Voices would tell me this was for Denise or John or the children of Dragon-Con.

  The giant cables on the top of the bridge slowly drop lower and with every step I take, closer to the middle of the bridge. I can see the giant sky lights, like the ones Batman uses for the Bat-signal, they have set up around the center of the bridge so people will still be able to see me once night falls. There is a part of me glad I'm getting to the center, because then I won't have to drag this impossibly heavy hunk of metal behind me anymore. The whips will probably stop then, too. My hand is so completely raw from the blisters and the hot metal I can't even feel it anymore. The whips and the curses and the thrown objects are coming faster now, because I'm getting so close to the end of my journey.

There's one of those giant crane trucks in the middle lanes they are probably going to use to lift the beam before they set in into the bridge. If they were planning on having a crane out here, then why the fuck did they make me drag the beam all this way?

The beam is laid down and the horsemen begin to set up a foundation platform to hold it in place.

If I were to jump, this would be the moment to do it. The horsemen are helping with the beam and no one is pointing a gun at me. It would be so easy. Two, maybe three, steps and then a drop into whatever comes next. The water in the bay looks almost inviting. It's truly a beautiful view. It's almost enough to make a person think things might be ok. Knowing how I die, you're probably asking yourself why I *didn't* jump when I had the chance. I'm sure many of you would have jumped, either to save yourself from the pain or to end your life on your own terms, but the truth is, I was just too afraid to do it. I wanted to live. The fear of taking that step into the sky was just insurmountable to me.

My breath comes in little shallow quips and I can feel my pulse pounding in my head.

My eyes meet some of those on the bridge with me, but theirs are always the first to look away.

"Please don't do this" I say and the cries stifle a little. Looking back, there are a million things I would have liked to have said. Things like, how every person there would feel the effects of what was to come for longer than any of them cared to. How my life had meaning and it was the only thing I truly did not want to be taken away from me. I wish I had said something inspiring, people could quote during moments of despair, or something courageous, causing people to believe in the human spirit.

Maybe even something ironic to put the thumb screws of guilt to the world after I had gone.

But I didn't say any of those things.

I didn't say anything at all.

I lay down on the hot pavement, more out of exhaustion than anything else, but I also try to make a smaller target for the people throwing things at me. There are a surprising amount of children present on the bridge. What kind of parent brings their kid to see something like this? Maybe they will leave before it gets ugly, but who knows.

So many cellphone cameras are recording this.

The four horsemen finish with the beam and one of them pulls some bars of rebar off the back of the crane. A group of men make their way through the crowd and there are a few cheers as they approach me. Two of the horsemen pull me to my feet and one of these men places his hand on my head and begins speaking in Arabic.

"Assalamu Aleikom Wa Rahmatoh Allah Wa Barakatoh," he says, and kisses me on both cheeks. He is an Imam and he's giving me last rights.

The other men come forward and bestow similar blessings on me from the various religions of the world. This act was the one and only act of compassion my race gave me at the end.

A priest offers me the Eucharist and I take it, because I know he will give me something to drink if I do.

"May God absolve you of your sins and welcome you into his kingdom," he says, and I chew my Jesus cookie.

Then came a Jew, a Buddhist, a Hindu, and a few other religions I couldn't identify. I guess they figured, since so many people had voted to have me killed, they had better cover their bases and absolve me of my sins in every religion known to man.

There are so many people on the bridge and down

in the park. I've never seen so many in one place, and the ridiculous part of my mind hopes the bridge will collapse, and then this crazy plan will be shot to hell and just maybe I can take some of these fuckers down with me.

But that doesn't happen.

The hooded men don't ask me to stand up or pull me to my feet; they just take a hold of my ankles and start dragging me towards the beam. The pavement is rough and rakes across my back as I try to kick myself free and find something to anchor myself to so they can't move me.

My body fat is around five percent and my limbs look like pipe cleaners, so it's not much of a fight.

The beam is hot, and as two of the horsemen hold my left hand against the metal, I feel something in my bladder let go. The stream of urine makes my shame sink to another level I didn't know I possessed. There is laughter from the crowd, but it quickly fades as one of the other horsemen holds the piece of rebar above his head.

Nobody thought to sharpen one end of the rebar for what was coming next. I guess they were all too busy deciding on what the t-shirt logo should look like or which mega-celebrity they could get to read a eulogy.

There's a pop and a whoosh, as the flame for the welder is lit. The blue-white flame kisses the end of the rebar, and after a few minutes it's glowing a dull orange.

An X is drawn on the inside of my forearm, and then the flat end of the scorching hot piece of reinforcement steel is placed against the soft flesh, where the x had been drawn. There is a hissing sound as the metal burns its way into the flesh and a smell that will stay with me forever. My arm spasms and tries to jerk free, but it's held too tightly, and there's nowhere for it to go. I didn't see the sledgehammer until it started its swing through the air, and by then, there was really no time to be afraid of it. The pain was like nothing I had ever experienced before. It was ten times worse than when Stephen cut off my hand or when my face was set on fire. There was a sickening CHUNK sound every time the sledgehammer falls. The hot rebar cauterizes the wound as it goes through my arm, but that sickening smell gets worse and worse. The crowd roars, but they still can't outdo the screaming inside my head. Once the rebar has pushed its way through my arm, the horsemen stick the bar through a hole drilled into the beam, and then lift my other arm above my head.

I didn't notice the welder heating up the second piece of rebar, because one of the horsemen was too busy playing John Henry with my body.

The Sharpie X is drawn on my other arm and I wonder just how sanitary the rebar is before it starts to burn its way into me.

The hammer falls again and again.

The third time the sledge falls, either deliberately, or on purpose, it misses the rebar post entirely and comes down on my elbow with explosive force. There's a crackling sound and my arm instantly has more joints in it than it should. Something warm and wet splashes against my face and I have no idea whether it's my blood or urine.

The horsemen flip the beam over so it's lying on top of me and the weight of it makes it almost impossible to breathe. My face is smashed between the pavement and the metal and when I open my eyes, I can see a black combat boot, inches away from my face. There are flecks of blood across the toe of the boot, and more spread out over the walking path. The hammer swings again as they bend the rebar so it won't fall out of my arms once they stand this thing up. Every time it makes contact, I feel like it's just going to pull its way out of my arm and royally screw up this insane plan.

An arc welder is lit again, and they begin to weld the rebar posts to the I-beam so they won't pull free. The cheers of the crowd are a dull roar inside of my head and I pass out for a moment from the pain and the difficulty I have breathing underneath the weight of the beam.

I wish I would have just died right then and there.

I wish I would have jumped off the bridge when I had the chance.

They flip the beam back over and then they weld another section of rebar by my feet.

A chain is hooked to the end of the I-beam, and as the crane stands it upright, I can see the smears of my bloody handprints all along the end I had been dragging. How the hell did I even move this thing, let alone drag it so far? The four horsemen hold the beam against the side of the walking path on the outside of the bridge. Sparks fly as two welders secure it in place. The crowd goes wild as the fire torch melts the metals together. Something hard thrown from the crowd grazes my ear and I look out over the San Francisco Bay.

There's a moment of vertigo as the crane moves the beam to the edge of the bridge and I understand why they put the section of bar at my feet. It's so I have something to stand on and support my weight a little.

When they did this to Jesus, didn't they put a spike through his feet?

I'm not on a cross either so I guess I'm really not the son of God.

As the weight of my scrawny body pulls down against the metal in my raised arms, it's almost impossible to breathe. I have to take these quick shallow breaths that just don't provide enough oxygen. My toes try to find stability on the bar at my feet, but it isn't thick enough or long enough for me to place both feet on it. Whenever a foot finds enough grip on the bar to lift my weight a little, it throws my center of gravity off, and my foot slides and I fall again.

They finish welding the base of the beam to the bridge and the four horsemen load their gear into the crane truck and ride home for meatloaf with their families.

I was alone with my public.

"How does that feel you piece of shit?"

"Fuck you, baby killer?"

"Let's see you cure yourself of that, Miracle-Boy."

There were a thousand of other insults thrown, but you get the picture. I felt so sad because none of them really knew the whole story. They had been spoon fed this propaganda by the media machine and now they were just riding out the high. If they only knew what type of person I am, I'm sure none of them would have any part of this and someone would step forward with a ladder and a hacksaw.

Forgive them Lord for they know not what they do.

I want my mom.

Tiny whitecaps dance across the bay in the cool ocean breeze.

Seeing a man pinned to a post isn't as exciting as you might think it would be, and the crowd quickly realizes there really isn't much more to see and the best part of the show is already over. Besides, everyone knows when I finally do kick the bucket, the media will broadcast it and it will be a bigger YouTube sensation than *What Does the Fox Say* within minutes. Slowly, very slowly, people start to leave the bridge and the park. Even *Swedish House Mafia* starts to run out of ways to remix tracks, and after a few hours the music stops.

There is the tiniest amount of give from the rebar in my right arm, and once I discover it's there, it's all I can think of. The bars stick out far enough I would never be able to slide my arm out over them, but the play in the bar is irresistible to pull against, like how a canker sore won't heal because you keep tonguing it.

I keep tugging at the bar in my arm, because there's nothing else to do, and it takes my mind off how hard it is to breathe and how hot the San Francisco sun is. A trickle of blood drips from the hole in my forearm, and I swear there is a millimeter more of play in the bar. It's almost enough to make me forget how badly it hurts every time I move in any way, but the looseness of the hole around the bar gives me hope for some reason. At least it gives me something to focus on as I wait for the end.

"Shazam," I say, but the lightning doesn't come to change me into somebody else.

I say the Green Lantern oath, but nothing happens.

I even try praying, but I get the same result.

As the sun begins to drop into the western horizon, the realization hits me, I probably won't be here when it comes up again in the east. How much longer could I possibly have? How long have I been here already? The crowd has thinned out a bit, but there are still quite a few die-hard lookiloos hoping to get lucky and see me perish before their boredom forces them to leave.

My toes dance along the piece of rebar at my feet, searching for something to stand on and take the weight off my arms a little bit. Just in case you don't know…when you're crucified, it's suffocation that kills you, not the exposure, or from the injuries of being stapled to something. Every breath is a force of willpower. Sometimes my toes will grab a little bit of traction and I can lift my body enough so my lungs will have a little more room to expand. It's like I'm drowning and I feebly flail about hoping my head will rise above the water level just one more time.

Every time my toes slip off the metal, the pain in my arms awakens anew.

I sound like Darth Vader having an asthma attack.

My skin if slowly turning a disgusting shade of blue.

How long I have been hanging here, I honestly can't say. Whatever God it is who is supposed to pull the sun across the sky in a chariot is on the job though, because my shadow had moved a few feet across the pavement. I wonder if someone could tell what time of day it is by looking at the shadow I make on the bridge. I wonder what they will do with the beam once I die. Will they leave here like some kind of monument, or so it will be ready for the next guy who tries to help someone feel better? Will they take it down and cover up all evidence of its existence so people can forget they took part in this? I wonder if the people who called in to vote for me will now get all kinds of SPAM mail asking them to vote on other death penalties and murder contests. I hope so. It would serve them right.

The movement around the hole in my arm increases every time my foot slips off the rebar. The blood trickling down my arm increases, and if I listen closely enough, I can hear it as it drips onto the hot pavement below.

If I spit hard enough, I can clear the pedestrian path, but it passes from my view almost immediately after it clears the rail of the bridge. I try to listen to hear it hit the water, even though it's impossible. It gives my mind something to do until my short attention span loses interest. I'm thankful for the distraction though, and wish more would come to me.

I wonder where Naomi is at this moment. I hope she can feel me thinking of her and that she's thinking of me. Those brain waves entangling with one another are the only connection I will ever have to her again.

As the sun sets, the police start to clear everyone from the bridge. I'm not exactly sure why. I interpret it as the end is near, though. Maybe they are worried people will steal parts of my body as souvenirs. They probably want to make sure my body is intact so they can dissect me to see if there's a key to the words somewhere. They also might be worried about the words they haven't discovered yet. What if there's something dangerous they don't want the public to know about?

Maybe they will even pull me off the beam after all the people have been cleared away to see if I will be able to heal myself from this.

Maybe this is all some kind of test.

Maybe one of them will just put a bullet through my skull to put me out of my misery.

There are protests as the police start moving people from the bridge. I see an officer on horseback and I wonder if he may have been one of the horsemen who whipped me and pounded the rebar through my arms. I try to get a better look at him, but my arms and shoulders block most of my vision.

I do have an amazing view of the bay though.

I actually have a blessing here. We all want to have our deaths mean something. To be able to choose how we check out. We hope we will say something inspiring, or at least not have our last words be something stupid like 'hey watch this' or 'hold my beer'. A veteran who I helped cure from Parkinson's disease once told me, when it's your time to die, you had better make sure the bullet holes are in the front. People are going to remember how I die. The least I can do is try to die with a little bit of dignity.

ADD INF: I know dignity was something I had long since given up on. I think that ship sailed when I pissed myself, as the horseman started swinging the sledge hammer like a bad Thor imitation, but the thought of honor was all I had, and ask yourself honestly, would you have done any better?

There was nothing noble left to say and nobody around to hear me say it if I did. A Buddhist once told me, the mind has a really hard time being in despair if your face is smiling. It has to do with our mind/body connection being out of sync with each other. Maybe if I could act like I was happy and not suffering, my mind would believe it just a little.

The only thing happy I could think of to do was whistle.

It helped. I found the whistling helped my labored breathing and gave my mind something to do. I whistled every song I could think of. Lady Gaga to Liberace. Metallica to Mozart. I whistled until I couldn't whistle anymore and my throat felt worse than my arms. I whistled until I was basically just puffing air with rhythm, and then something really strange began to happen...I started to feel happy.

Maybe it was my body going into shock, endorphins being released, a mental breakdown...I didn't care. I was glad it was there.

The police had cleared the bridge and the sun was starting to set. I could still see the people in the park though, and the party didn't look like it would be ending anytime soon.

I had to pee again so I let it fly. As the stream fell onto the walkway, I decided to try to spell my name one last time. Moving my hips caused my toes to slip off the bar and the urine splashed against my leg and the I-beam. I heard something tear and the trickle of blood running from my arm became a steady stream.

However, three bold letters were on the walkway and the sight of them filled my heart with joy.

BEN

I had to poop too, but I figured I would wait and let that happen when my bowels relaxed.

I started to get cold as the evening breeze touched my body. I couldn't see the sun anymore, but my shadow was long and had moved a good three or four feet from when they stood me upright.

Panic came back with a vengeance, and like an animal that will chew off its own foot when caught in a trap, I decided I was going to be free no matter the cost. I began to thrash as hard as I could, pain be damned. I pressed my feet against the beam trying to force my body away from it. I would jump as high as possible, pushing my toes off the bar and then letting the weight of my body rip against the bars in my arms. The gap between the rebar and the flesh of my arm became all that mattered to me. If only I wasn't an Ichabod Crane looking skinny bastard, maybe the weight of my body could pull me free. Maybe if I had any measurable upper body strength, I wouldn't die like one of those bugs you see pinned to a piece of cork board for some kid's science project.

This was just like the Uno game.

If I wasn't fully committed, it would never work.

In my mind I shuffled the deck and drew a card off the top.

Blue 7.

Seven times, I pulled with everything I had against the metal that tried to encage me. Seven times, I imagined my arm pulling itself free and coming down on the shirt pins, bringing me the tiniest amount of peace.

I shuffled the deck in my mind again and took the top card.

Red 5. I missed my car.

Five times, with all the might I possessed I pull.

Again and again, I yank my arm down, using all the weight I can muster to make the blows count. I stopped feeling anything in my arms a while ago, and there is a sick smell coming from the wound. I think my arm is dying. The phantom limb tries to flex its fingers and fails, but the wound seems to give a little more each time. There's a clicking sound in my arm as the rebar bangs against one of the bones in my forearm, and the hole in my arm looks big enough to maybe push a golf ball through, which lets my bend a little bit more.

Every time exhaustion would set in, or after I would black out for a moment, I would shuffle the Uno cards and pick the top card.

I will be free from this beam or I will die in the attempt.

I will not just sit here and wait to die at their leisure.

I don't know how long I thrash against the post, but when my arm finally comes free, it's dark, and I can see the first stars of the evening reflect across the bay. My right forearm is now a giant V, but it's free. The skin and muscle finally gave away, and I was able to pull the rebar through the stump. My arm hangs down across my body, and the blood on the walking path has obscured my name, which makes me sad.

I don't know what I was planning to do once my arm was free. It seems rather futile and stupid right now because I'm still trapped.

The truly stupid thing is, now it's even more difficult to breathe. The post at my feet is slick with blood and I think at some point my bowels gave away, even though I was trying to hold out. It's almost impossible to stand, but that's what I make myself do, simply because it's hard and if it's hard that means I'm not dead yet.

I'm so cold, but I don't think it has anything to do with the winds coming off the ocean. Now it's a race to see what will actually kill me, the blood loss or the lack of oxygen. Don't they say that if you fall off a skyscraper, you will pass out or die before you hit the ground? Something about the mind protecting itself? If that's true, why haven't I passed out yet? Where is my psychological comfort to shield me from being able to see the scratches the rebar has left in the bones of my forearm?

Fuck, please just let me die.

I try to whistle again, but it's just too difficult. When my feet slip from the bar, it's almost impossible to breathe and it takes everything to get my feet underneath me again. I don't even know why I try, but something inside of me ignores my pleas to die and makes me stand on the stub of metal long enough to take another breath. I don't know where this part of me is coming from, but it's not ready to die just yet, even though the rest of me had long since given up.

"Just what makes that little ant..." A voice comes from my throat, I fail to recognize whispers.

"Think he can move a rubber tree plant?" The voice is so soft I can barely make out what it's saying, but it's definitely real, and it's definitely mine, not just some projection from my dying mind.

It's so cold. I don't remember ever being this cold.

"Cuz everyone knows an ant, can't, move a rubber tree plant."

I pass out, and when I come to the eastern horizon is glowing in anticipation of the morning sun. Maybe I will be warmer when the sun comes up, but somehow I doubt it.

I take another breath and it's the hardest one I have ever taken in my life. It feels like I'm breathing through a coffee stirrer, and no matter how hard I inhale, I can't take in enough air. I'm pretty sure I can count how many breaths I have left on my fingers. Blackness starts to form at the edge of my vision and my skin has gone from having a slight tinged blue, to looking like the kid who ate the blueberries in *Willy Wonka*. Then...at the time when I absolutely need it the most, my best friend places his hand upon my shoulder.

"Jesus, Ben...what have you done to yourself this time?" Damon asks, more to himself than to me. Without thinking about it, I hold up my newly split arm in an, 'oh hi' motion, and a new level of pain shoots through my chest. It's frightening to me how little I'm bleeding. Doesn't that mean something? Is that why I'm so cold? How many more beats does my backwards heart have left in it?

"Stay here," Damon says, which I think is funny because where else would I go.

"Please hurry," I say, and he is gone again and I'm alone again.

More than anything, I do not want to be alone right

now. I'm so afraid, and I want someone to hold my hand, and tell me everything is going to be ok. Orson Wells once said, we are born alone, we live alone, and we die alone. I've heard of dogs and elephants who, when sensing their deaths approaching, they will leave or hide so they can be alone. I don't understand this at all, because I really think I'm going to die here, and all I want is to be with someone.

"Hold still," Damon says from behind me, and then there is the unmistakable sound of a hacksaw on metal.

"No, Damon. Please stop for a second," I say, and the saw stops. "I can't breathe. Need you to lift me," I say, and Damon understands. He lifts my mutilated arm over his shoulder and my legs try to straighten. With his help I take a breath.

I feel like a cancer victim who has had his lung tumors removed. I can hear the air filling my lungs and it's the most beautiful sound I've ever heard, not including Naomi's laughter. My skin starts to look less like a bruise, but I'm still so damned cold.

"We've got to get you down. Can you stand?" Damon asks, and now that I've had some air, it's easier for my feet to find traction on the rebar. The hacksaw sound starts again and I get a good look at the gun Damon has in his waistband.

"Where did you get a gun?" I ask, but he doesn't answer me. Suddenly, I ask myself how Damon got onto the bridge and how he can possibly be here with me right now. "Oh God, Damon! You didn't hurt anyone did you?" I don't remember hearing any gunshots, but my mental process hasn't exactly been clear lately. The gun looks a lot like the one I took into the Boston Bar to commit murder with.

"No Ben. I haven't hurt anyone," he says, and the saw continues to sing its song to the San Francisco Bay.

It's dark now, but the light from the spotlights still blinds me.

Where are the police? I'm sure there are cameras recording this, so where are all the people coming to stop Damon from cutting me down?

The rebar bends as the saw passes the halfway point through the bar and the shift in my weight causes me to scream.

"Sorry," Damon says, but doesn't stop sawing.

The hacksaw finally cuts through and I fall a good ten feet onto the pedestrian walkway. I land flat on my back and the impact knocks the wind out of me. Breathing troubles seem to be the theme for today. The rebar is still stuck through my arm and the weight of it makes it hard to move it around. There is a sucking sound and then a pop as Damon pulls the carbon steel from my body. I lift my arm and stare at Damon through the charred hole in my forearm.

"Peek-a-boo," I say, but Damon doesn't get it.

I sit up and rest my back against the I-beam, the side facing the inside of the bridge where there's no poop and blood. The beam is cold, but I almost can't feel it.

"I'm so cold," I say.

"I've got something that might help," Damon says.

The package he sets at my feet is wrapped in bright blue paper with a red ribbon. I look at the present and for a moment I have no idea whether it's my birthday or Christmas or exactly when it is.

"But I didn't get you anything," I say, and Damon smiles and sits down on the pavement with me.

"I was going to give this to you at the wedding, but…" He says.

"I'm so sorry Damon. I never meant for any of this to happen."

"I know that Ben. You don't have a mean bone in your body, but you've got to understand this can't continue. Something's got to change," he says.

The package is pliable in my hand. It's the type of

present that made you sad when you were a child, shaking it under the Christmas tree, because you knew it was clothes.

"You got me a shirt?" I say.

"Just open it dickhead," he says, and takes a cigarette from his coat. I haven't seen him smoke for a while, and Damon only smokes when something's bothering him or he has something he doesn't want to do, like when he told me he had slept with my girlfriend.

It's hard to open the present with one hand. My fingers and dexterity aren't exactly at one hundred percent right now and tearing the paper hurts. However, it's good things hurt. If things hurt, it means I'm not dead yet, so I keep tugging on the blue paper, making things hurt even more.

The familiar yellow and black symbol swimming in a sea of red almost stops my heart. There is a black mark on the red, and as I hold up to my face, I see the signature.

'Christopher Reeve'.

"Aren't you going to put it on?" He asks.

"Is this real?" I ask, already knowing the answer. The material has an energy to it that could never be faked.

"It's the real deal."

My mind is spinning so hard I forget my shredded arms and naked body.

"How did you do this? This should be impossible," I ask.

He takes another long drag off the cigarette before looking at his shoes.

"You're not the only one who can perform miracles. Now put it on," he says.

There's no way I can put it on. This needs to be encased in vacuum sealed plastic for the world to look at. I'm already freaking out I might have smudged or stained it. This piece of cloth is worth more than anything to me.

"Put it on," he says again.

"Hell no! It will get ruined." I protest.

"I don't think any of that really matters anymore, do you?"

Damon drapes the silky material over my shoulders and I feel it happening. Something happens when you put on a cape. It's impossible to feel bad. You feel a little taller, like your moral standing just took a triple shot of espresso. Inside of yourself, you become the person you've always wanted to be. When it's a Superman cape, that experience multiplies. It's the great thing about Superman. The cape and the tights are who he truly is. It's the glasses, the normality, the mundane, and the everyday humdrum we all think of as our lives, *that's* the disguise.

Superman reminds us we are more than we think we are.

I pull the red around me and feel warmer. Damon puts an arm around me and I sink into the embrace, resting my head on his shoulder.

"Where do you think Christopher Reeve is right now?" I ask. This is the first time in all the years we have known each other we have talked about what we think happens to us when we leave this place.

"He's got to be in a better place than this," Damon says.

"Do you think he can fly where he is now?"

Damon takes another drag, but his lip quivers ever so slightly before he looks away.

"I doubt he even needs the cape to do it," he says, and the thought makes me smile. I want to look at the signature again, but it's on my back and I don't want to take it off. Besides, it's so hard to move.

The sun feels good on my shoulders and it makes the shadow of Damon and me sitting by the I-beam look like a big penis.

"Look at our shadow. We're the *Two Broke Girls*." This is what Damon and I call my testicles, because one is blond and the other brunette. He laughs and tells me he gets to be the brunette with the big tits. I guess that makes me the blonde with the quirky personality.

The bridge is so big and empty. Where did all the people go? I look at the park and it's empty too, except for a man throwing a Frisbee to a Black Labrador, who catches the plastic disc before it hits the ground every time.

The Frisbee is the exact same color as my cape.

"I think I'm ready now," I say.

"Are you sure?" Damon says, and flicks his cigarette over the edge of the bridge.

Everything hurts. It feels like my entire body has fallen asleep. The pins and needles sensation fires every time I shift or speak.

"Yeah. I'm ready. Will you…?"

"You know I will, buddy," Damon says, and kisses the top of my head.

"Thank you. I'm sorry," I say.

The bullet enters my brain and all my pain vanishes.

EUGOLIPE

"⌐║║║¯//"
-The Book of Bubbles
From inside blowhole

    Jessica Park was a twenty-year-old college student, who died instantly when an aneurism burst during her biology lab around the same time I was dragging the I-beam across the Golden Gate Bridge. Jessica was a marathon runner and an organ donor. When her heart was removed for transfer, the surgeon happened to notice some strange scarring to the inside of the aorta. The surgeon adjusted the lights above the operating table and drug his latex coated index finger over the scarring. The word 'BELIEVE' could be read clear as day on the inside part of the tissue. The surgeon took a photograph, and then the heart was placed in a forty-five year old man who lived a long and happy life after the transplant. Jessica's other organs were not examined, but the words were present throughout her entire body.

    Seven years before my execution, Rhonda Bastine, an elderly woman living out her retirement in Glasgow, died from natural causes. She was cremated as per her family's request and no autopsy was performed. Rhonda was the first person in history to have the words written within her body. No one ever knew they were there.

♥

    Bubbles the dolphin was a favorite at the San Diego Sea World and had been part of the regular show for more than a decade. During a routine physical, several symbols were discovered within her blowhole that looked something like this:

When bubbles died of old age an autopsy was performed, and these symbol ran through the inside portions of all her bones and arteries. Images of these symbols have been sent to top linguistics experts, military code crackers, and everyone else that might have aided in their interpretations. To this date, no meaning has been found, but every expert agrees that they are not random and possess all the structure of language.

♥

Kuparr of the Ngiyampaa Aboriginal Tribe died at the age of 56 after an infection in his leg became gangrenous. The words were present in his body and the world never knew.

♥

Forty-seven days after my death three boys found an abandoned wasp's nest in the Montana outback. One of the boys thought it was cool and took it home with him. He decided to cut the nest in half, because he thought he would be able to see the tunnels the wasps used to navigate the hive like those glass ant farms he had seen at school. When he looked into the hive, there were no tunnels, only letters.

♥

During the century after my execution, there would be over three hundred documented discoveries of the words. There were over seventy thousand undiscovered incidents.

Acknowledgements

No book is ever written alone. There are so many people I would like to thank for making this book possible. My first readers who encouraged me to share and who also helped with the editing process; Cami Krueger, Amanda Bailey, John Baker, Heather Karrington Stratton, Micky Carlson, and of course my Mom. Jamie C. Winters for his amazing cover and work ethic. I would also like to thank those who read my first book and made me feel like I might be able to do it again.

This book has not been approved, licensed or sponsored by any entity or person involved in creating or producing The Daily Show, DC or Marvel comic, film or television series. Or by those involved with any other product named.

For further information on Darren Lamb, his books or his teachings please go to
www.theworstbuddhist.com
https://www.facebook.com/theworstbuddhist

ISBN for paperback 978-1-50275-823-3

Made in the USA
Columbia, SC
25 May 2021